Painting THE MOON

◆— A CHILTON CROSSE NOVEL —◆

TRACI BORUM

Unlocking New Worlds

Painting The Moon
Copyright © 2014 by Traci Borum. All rights reserved.
First Print Edition: June 2014

ISBN 13: 978-1-940215-32-7
ISBN 10: 1-940215-32-3

Red Adept Publishing, LLC
104 Bugenfield Court
Garner, NC 27529
http://RedAdeptPublishing.com/

Cover and Formatting: Streetlight Graphics

This is a work of fiction. Names, characters, places, and incidents either are the product of the author's imagination or are used fictitiously, and any resemblance to locales, events, business establishments, or actual persons—living or dead—is entirely coincidental.

For Daddy, with love.
I miss you every day.

Art is magic. Take an empty canvas, blank and shapeless, and inject it with depth, colour, and purpose. Artists are creators. We create energy where there's dullness and produce life where there is nothing.

-Joy Valentine

Chapter One

THE MOMENT SHE SAW THE letter, she knew. The London postmark gave it away.

Noelle set down her keys and coffee, deciding to abandon the rest of her Saturday errands. She needed to take this letter to the ocean. She couldn't read it here, standing over junk mail and bills.

She kicked off her sandals and walked down the steps of her beach house, grateful for San Diego's mild weather even in mid-October. And grateful she wouldn't have to walk far, with the ocean practically at her doorstep.

When she picked her usual spot at the water's edge and sat down, the foamy water crept toward her toes like long, greedy fingers then slinked back again. Noelle always sought the ocean during troubling moments—craved the sea air on her face, the tinge of salt on her tongue, the comforting swoosh of powerful waves. But sometimes, even the sea couldn't keep her from feeling hollow. Stranded and alone.

She'd already torn the envelope's seal on her way down the steps. Opening the letter, she noticed the date, wondering why the news had taken two whole weeks to reach her.

Dear Ms. Cooke,

We regret to inform you of the unfortunate passing of Ms. Joy Valentine.

Great Aunt Joy had died alone in that cottage.

Noelle stared deep into the ocean as tears stung her eyes. Everything had gone quiet: the crash of waves, even the faint tapping of a neighbor's roof being re-shingled two doors down. All silent.

In the dull gray sky above the ocean, Noelle could see almost slideshow-like, vivid images of her great aunt. Her thin-lipped, lopsided smile; wiry, gray hair secured by a pencil into a makeshift bun; deep wrinkles around her mouth and eyes from decades of smoking. And next, flashes of summers spent in England with her and Gram—white-haired and soft-spoken, the opposite of her sister. Those women had taught Noelle to paint, to enjoy literature, to savor life. Her surrogate mothers, she always called them. Now both gone, the end of an era.

Noelle shivered and wished she'd brought a sweater. It always seemed colder at the water's edge. Brushing away a tear, she returned to the letter, skimming for more detail. She stopped at this:

> *As Ms. Valentine's only living relative, you have hereby been named executor and sole heir of the estate. Please contact our office for further details.*

Sole heir. Noelle considered what that might entail. Her aunt's modest cottage nestled in a village in the Cotswolds, Chilton Crosse. And the art gallery! Noelle hadn't stepped inside in fourteen years, since she was seventeen. If she concentrated, she could still smell the pungent turpentine and old, musty wood that greeted her when she opened the door. The back room had served as a working gallery, where artists set up and painted while visitors wandered quietly, gazing at masterpieces-in-progress. Occasionally, Aunt Joy even participated. But that was before her sudden retreat into obscurity. Noelle recalled the scandal of that winter, a decade ago, with perfect clarity. Online articles screamed out the embarrassing headlines: *Famous Cotswold Artist Has Monster Meltdown; Storms out of Art Show.*

No one ever knew what happened, never discovered the trigger that had caused Aunt Joy's breakdown and subsequent retreat into reclusiveness. Noelle had tried to call her, write her, but the dozens of letters went unanswered. She didn't know whether her aunt had even received them, or whether Joy had tired of all the probing questions: "Are you okay? I'm worried… why won't you return my calls?" Joy finally sent one brief letter to Noelle, assuring her she was fine, but that she wanted—needed—to be left alone. She asked that Noelle respect her wishes and her privacy. And so she had.

Restless, Noelle rose and brushed the sand off her jeans. She needed to go inside, make a cup of tea, and banish the chill.

She headed back to the house with the letter, thinking about Joy's funeral, wondering if it had been a media circus, with paparazzi descending on the unimposing village to fill the inches in their columns the next day. Or perhaps the church was almost empty, her aunt a forgotten figure even in her own community. In either case, Noelle wished she'd been there. And more than that, she wished she'd made contact with her aunt before she died. Just one more time.

She maneuvered her way toward the kitchen through the maze of stacked-up boxes—surely, her roommate, Casey, would retrieve them next week after the honeymoon. But something caught Noelle's eye. The painting above the mantel, one that had been there for years, one she'd strolled past a thousand times.

Now, though, she couldn't look at anything else. She drew closer and clicked on a nearby light to study the painting's detail. One of Aunt Joy's creations, given to Noelle on her fourteenth birthday—a seaside painting of England's Cornwall coast. She touched the edge of the frame and peered at the canvas. A white-blond little girl stood at the cliffs, staring into the ocean and holding a broad-brimmed hat, its ribbon floating in the wind. Noelle could almost hear the bluish-gray water crash against the rocks as she looked beyond the little girl, into the endless sea.

Joy explained it that day, as a teenaged Noelle tore the gold wrapping paper. "The little girl in the painting, that's you on your very first visit to us. I think you were five. I knew how frightened you were, being in England with virtual strangers. But the moment we took you to the sea, to Cornwall, you responded. You seemed calm, at home. And I wanted to paint you that way. To freeze you in time."

9

Noelle took a few steps back to sit on the couch, to wish herself into the painting. To those summers spent in England, where everything remained safe, intact.

Not that she didn't appreciate her life now. But lately, she'd become... stilted. Uneasy. An unfulfilling job, a stagnant social life, where she only played a role of herself, a pretend version. But those precious English summers centered her, brought out her genuine self. And she craved that again more than ever.

On Monday morning, Noelle brushed out her honey-blond bangs and gave them a spray, planning what to say to the lawyer, Mr. Lester. She needed to phone his office before work, over a quick breakfast. Last night before bed, she'd done the math in her head, taking time zones into account. 8:00 a.m. San Diego equaled 4:00 p.m. London.

She stood in the kitchen with her back against the countertop and slathered cream cheese onto a bagel. Knowing that Casey was married, truly gone, gave the house a specific emptiness. Especially since Noelle hadn't found a roommate to replace her yet.

She took a bite and dialed the number of the London firm. She thought she'd have to wait a few rings, but on the very first one, a thin male voice answered, "Hello?"

Nearly choking on the bagel scraping down her throat, she swallowed and tried to respond. "I'd like to speak with Mr. Lester."

"This is he."

She took a fast sip of orange juice, cleared her throat, and said, "I'm Noelle Cooke. I received a letter from your firm on Saturday. About my aunt passing away. Joy Valentine?"

"Oh, yes. Noelle." He stretched out all the vowels. Everything sounded better wrapped in a British accent. "Thank you for responding so promptly."

He issued condolences and apologized for not contacting Noelle sooner, explaining his first notification went to an old address, then they got down to business.

"As you're aware, your aunt has left you her entire estate. This includes the properties of Primrose Cottage as well as the Artist's Gallery."

"I'm still in a bit of shock over all this."

"Yes, quite. There are decisions to be made. The gallery is... how do I put this delicately? Financially unstable."

"Oh. I had no idea."

"Miss Cooke, these matters would actually be best discussed in person. I know it's asking much, but might you be able to travel to England? My office is in London, but I have an early business meeting in Bath, near Chilton Crosse, day after tomorrow. You could stay at your aunt's—or rather, *your* cottage. The curator could also meet with you to discuss the gallery."

The idea of seeing the cottage and gallery was thrilling. She assumed no one but Joy had stepped inside those cottage doors in the past decade. Perhaps its contents might offer hints about her aunt's reclusive period.

"I could meet with you there on my way back to London," Mr. Lester continued. "There are many papers to sign and—"

"And decisions to be made."

"Indeed. Urgently, in fact."

In this Age of Technology, they could still handle the details if she stayed in California. Email, phone, FedEx, fax—back and forth, back and forth. But doing so might stretch things out to weeks, and Mr. Lester indicated they didn't have weeks. The debt collectors might pounce soon. If she did travel to England, they could manage things in a few days. Plus, she could use that time to sort through the contents of the cottage—old family heirlooms, dishware, or valuables she wanted to keep.

Dan, her boss, would balk about her leaving with such short notice, but too bad. She would remind him that she had vacation time and sick leave, lots of it. Surely, she deserved time for a personal emergency. Noelle could work the rest of the day then leave for England late tonight, with Desha covering her workload and meetings until Thursday. Dan couldn't say no.

"Yes. I can do that," she told Mr. Lester decisively. "Let me make some arrangements and get back to you."

"Excellent."

"Oh, one more thing. The letter never mentioned. How did my aunt pass away?"

"It was a stroke that took her. Instantly, from what I heard."

She hadn't suffered.

The moment she hung up with Mr. Lester, Noelle remembered she would have to postpone the interview tomorrow with John Hill Advertising. She had worked so hard the last two months, polishing her resume, searching online listings for new job openings, scheduling secret interviews during lunch hours or after work. Nothing had panned out yet, but she had been particularly hopeful about tomorrow, a second interview with the senior manager. John Hill represented salvation, her escape from a job and a company she had once loved. But everything had soured drastically when Dan took over last year. The office politics, the backbiting, the pointless meetings and toxic environment. Enough was enough.

She took another bite and peered out the window. She loved it here—seagulls, beaches, the steady shush of the ocean. But the house, even the gorgeous beach view, had lately become redundant.

Can a "seven-year itch" apply to someone's whole life?

The last time Noelle had been at the airport waiting for a plane, she'd been seventeen—impatient to board and glad her mother had dropped her off at the front rather than sitting there with her, flipping through a magazine, smacking gum, and checking her watch until time to wave her daughter off and get a pedicure.

Noelle sat back in the metal seat punched with little round holes and stared at her reflection in the giant airport windows. Maybe because of the pitch darkness outside, or even the bleak midnight hour, she started to think about death—how it had managed again to carve out an unwelcome place in her life. It visited, oddly, in five-year intervals. First, her mother ten years ago, then Gram five years later, and now, Aunt Joy.

But Joy's death had forced an uneasy truth: Noelle stood alone in the world. Left behind, stripped of security, like the last person on a desert island with only herself to rely on.

She couldn't count on her father. She hadn't spoken to him in eight months. His second family—a socialite wife and two teenagers, a daughter and a son—kept him too busy. No room for Noelle. Besides, he could never manufacture the closeness she shared with Gram and Joy. Even if he actually cared to try.

On the plane an hour later, Noelle buckled her seatbelt and watched the commotion around her. People stuffed too-large bags into overhead compartments, tapped on iPhones, and asked the stewardess questions about the flight. They all looked so blasé, so relaxed. But she wondered if they secretly feared flying, as she did. If any of their stomachs churned and gurgled at the thought of liftoff, of a plane thrusting into the air, rushing them thousands of feet above the safety of earth.

It didn't help that Noelle's too-narrow seat, flanked by an overweight man and a snoring elderly woman, made her claustrophobic. She remembered Aunt Joy's advice when Noelle had once voiced her flying fears as a teenager: "Close your eyes and think of something safe. Picture something instantly relaxing. Visualize it. Take yourself there."

Instantly relaxing. England.

In a matter of hours, she would be on British soil again. Closing her eyes, she smiled, picturing "her" England. The fields and sheep, the cobblestone roads and antique buildings, the cool summer breezes, the sweet smell of honeysuckle. As a teenager, she spent hours purposely breathing deep, saturating her lungs with the fresh air of the Bath countryside. If she concentrated hard enough, she could be there again.

Noelle ignored the captain's "fasten seatbelt" warning and the piercing roar of engines, forcing her thoughts back to those summers in specific detail—Gram's enormous estate, with Aunt Joy on the porch painting canvases, her flowing nightgown rippling in the breeze, and Gram offering an endless supply of tea and scones.

And in that world, in that place, Noelle recognized someone else. Adam. There he stood, smiling at her, refusing to be ignored. All those years, she had meticulously tucked him away in her mind, locked his memory inside a box. Because the danger in opening it was that she might not be able to close it again.

The mere thought of him sent that familiar shot of teenage angst and adrenaline through her body. Adam, her best friend. Her first love.

The plane bumped along the runway, and she braced herself for the gentle pushing down of gravity as the plane lifted.

Take yourself there.

Noelle squeezed her eyelids tight and pictured Adam again, her best distraction. She remembered their first introduction at fourteen. Gram had invited the "boy next door" over to keep Noelle company. He wore faded jeans and an England World Cup T-shirt. Noelle thought he was gawky, and she didn't know what to make of all that wild, curly hair. But those eyes. Dark and mysterious and deep-set, as though holding back a secret he was still deciding whether or not to reveal.

Theirs had been a relationship of the most complicated sort. The fragile, imbalanced kind, teetering delicately between friendship and the potential for "something more." At least, that had been Noelle's way of seeing things. For all she knew, Adam never saw her as anything more than a sister. Odd, some might say, to consider someone a first love who she'd never even kissed. Well, there *was* that almost-kiss, in the river that day...

But somehow, friendship seemed even more meaningful than romance. Deeper, more intimate. During those four English summers together, Adam confided in her about things he wouldn't discuss with anyone else—his parents' constant fighting, the loss of his little sister at age five, even his secret sketches of buildings and houses. The two of them sat under the big oak tree on Gram's estate for hours, picking at blades of grass, flecking off splinters of bark from the trunk while spilling secrets, or teasing, or saying nothing at all. And then, as unexpectedly as their friendship began, it came to an abrupt end. She wondered whatever happened to him, whether he was still in England. And whether he ever looked back on those summers with the same nostalgia she did.

The plane leveled off, and the anxiety drained out of Noelle's body as the Fasten Seatbelt sign dinged off. She reached for her Kindle and forced herself not to think about Adam, to stuff his memory back inside that box, right where it belonged.

Stepping through the sliding doors to exit Gatwick Airport, Noelle experienced the rush she'd been waiting for. Sure, the exhausted part of her, the one that had endured the hours-long flight and the line at customs, anticipated slumping in the backseat of a cab and shutting her eyes. But as she walked outside, her senses snapped awake. She inhaled the damp odor of fresh rain, scanned the low clouds hanging from a gray English sky, and smiled.

Telling Dan about England hadn't been as difficult as she'd dreaded. As soon as he'd heard the words, "My aunt died," his face dropped and his voice eased into that hushed, awkward tone people suddenly adopted when they heard tragic news.

But Dan being Dan, his clipped boss-voice returned, grumbling about meetings and workloads to cover. Only when Noelle reassured him she'd taken care of everything—mentioned Desha by name, showed him their back-and-forth texts—did he finally agree. He gave Noelle three days. Exactly three days, no more.

Noelle rolled her suitcase toward the long cab queue, her spirits sinking. But an eager cabbie a few cars down, stout and middle-aged, motioned her toward his car with an inviting smile then offered to lift her heavy bags into his trunk. Although Primrose Cottage stood nearly ninety miles west from the outskirts of London, Noelle had decided against a rental car. Driving on the wrong side of the road was fine when she had experimented as a teenager on empty country roads. But after a tiring plane ride and years without practice, a cab would be wiser, the expense be damned.

She scooted to the middle of the brown leather backseat and told the driver, "I'm headed to Chilton Crosse, in the Cotswolds." He hesitated, and she added, "I know it's a long drive. Too far?"

He pushed the button for his fare. "No trouble at all."

The trip would take up half his afternoon, but at least it gave him a sure fare. And she would tip him generously. She settled back, relieved to let someone else deal with the rush-hour traffic. That would be worth the cab fare alone.

The moment they departed the London congestion, something in the air changed. Noelle lowered her window to breathe it in. That *something*. That crisp, delicious, heady fragrance only the English country air could offer. Strong enough to clear her senses of the stale cigar odor that permeated the cab.

The sun winked at her through dark clouds, filtering shadow and light onto the ground. She took in everything: the clusters of sheep grazing the manicured, patchwork fields; the uneven, stocky stone walls that divided properties; the occasional abandoned cottages, hundreds of years old. Remnants of another time. All as picture-perfect as she recalled.

"Looks like we're here," the driver announced.

Noelle had dozed off somewhere along the way, so that the ninety-minute drive seemed more like ten. During her English summers, Noelle had only visited the village of Chilton Crosse a few times, when she and Gram came to pick up Aunt Joy in May and drop her back off in late August. She spent the bulk of summers, though, at Gram's Windermere Estate in Bath, twenty miles west of the village. Gram prepared one of the many guest rooms, one for Noelle and another for Aunt Joy, and during those months, the three of them became an unlikely little family.

The cabbie slowed the car to allow Noelle a lingering look at the village, nestled in a lush valley of trees. As the cab drew closer, she recognized the edge of the main street, Storey Road, which ran through the heart of the town. A creek bubbled underneath a bridge as the cab crossed over. Little shops flanked both sides of the street: a busy pub, a post office, a bakery. Each one dressed in the same traditional beige-colored limestone found in any Cotswold village. Everything appeared uniform and tidy, with sloped tiled roofs and diamond-shaped windowpanes.

As leisurely as the cab travelled, Noelle half-expected curious townspeople to peer out windows or pause their sweeping and chatting to stare back at her. But they were used to tourists gawking and slowing down to ogle at them, zoo animals in their habitats. They seemed oblivious to the stranger in their midst.

"Primrose Cottage?" the driver asked.

"Yes, it's past the end of the street, up here. That road." She leaned forward and pointed. The driver turned onto an isolated road that took a couple of bends and turns before a cottage appeared at the top of a hill. A broad, thatched roof covered the two-story cottage, enclosed by a surrounding stone wall with a wide, hinged gate.

"That's it!" Noelle said with more enthusiasm than she'd intended.

The driver slowed to a stop then opened her door. She walked toward the gate, spotting tangled vines of ivy crawling up the cottage's exterior.

"Miss…"

Noelle paused. "Oh! I completely forgot. My bags."

"Be happy to carry them in for you."

She opened the gate and let him go first. The slender stone pathway led directly to something that reminded Noelle of a castle door, made of dark knotty wood, rounded at the top, with iron hinges and an iron latch at the doorknob.

"The key," she mumbled. "Mr. Lester mentioned where to find it." She squatted and reached to the right of the two stone steps to find a plastic rock. She flipped it over then slid open the flap to produce a small key. Inside, the cabbie set the luggage down, and she thanked him for the long journey, asking his fee and giving him an extra thirty pounds on top.

"Thank you, miss!" He tipped his tweed cap and headed back to the idling cab as Noelle shut the door.

Flipping on lights, she shook off the eerie sensation of being an intruder in her aunt's house, wandering in unannounced. But she owned the cottage, as Mr. Lester had repeatedly pointed out. Well, at least until it sold. Noelle knew the moment she'd read the letter that selling was the only option. She couldn't afford to keep the cottage, and she certainly couldn't move here and abandon her life in California. The beach house, her friends, a steady job with the possibility of a better one. Still, a shame not to keep the cottage in the family.

Things looked exactly the same as she recalled—the staircase to her right, leading to the bedrooms above; the kitchen straight ahead at the end of a long hall; the main sitting room branching off to her left. The wooden floors click-clacked beneath her flats as she stepped down into the sitting room. She remembered the off-white walls and chocolate-brown beams spaced evenly apart on the low ceiling. The petite cast-iron stove that stood in the center of the far wall. The window seat that overlooked the gardens. She remembered the couches, too, with their flowered patterns and puffy cushions in the quintessential English style. Noelle had somehow imagined that during Aunt Joy's self-imposed exile from the world, she had let the place go, lived in a dingy, dusty, dark space, hardly ever opening a curtain to let the light inside. But the sitting room looked surprisingly normal and airy. Beautiful.

She stepped past the back garden window to a second door and entered the kitchen, a warm delight of butter-colored walls, tiled floors, and a wood dining set that matched the cupboards almost exactly. A microwave, a dishwasher, even a fairly modern oven, or "Aga" as she remembered the Brits calling it. Walking through, she figured out why cottages had a reputation for being so cozy and petite. Low ceilings, low kitchen cabinets, even a smaller refrigerator and dishwasher. Perfect for Noelle. She was petite, too—or "doll-sized," as Aunt Joy used to say—at only four-foot-eleven.

Noelle abandoned her luggage and trekked upstairs for the second half of her tour. She didn't recall visiting this floor of the cottage. She'd only ever taken tea in Aunt Joy's kitchen or sat on Aunt Joy's sofa. She'd never had a reason to visit the upstairs before. The guest room and master were both, as she imagined they would be, simply but smartly decorated with delicate lace curtains, floral bedspreads, and wooden writing desks in each.

She noticed a third door, opposite the master. She drew closer and jiggled the brass knob, but it wouldn't budge. Locked up tight. Frowning, she tried again. Maybe the doorjamb was sticky or stubborn. She spotted an old-fashioned keyhole below the knob. Standing on her tiptoes, she reached to the top of the doorframe, sliding her fingertips across in hopes of finding a key. No luck.

"What's behind Door Number Three?" she whispered and bent down to peek through the keyhole, hoping for a clue. Nothing but darkness.

Hunger pangs gnawed at her. She'd eaten nothing all day but a mediocre roast beef sandwich on the flight over. Travel-weary and out of sorts, especially with the time change, Noelle decided food should be priority.

The mystery door would have to wait.

Chapter Two

*If you paint from memory, trust yourself. Don't pause and fidget
and wonder whether your perception is accurate enough. If it comes
from a true place inside you, it will be all the accuracy you need.*

A U-SHAPED MAHOGANY BAR, A GLOWING fireplace flanked by comfy high-backed chairs, pictures of red-jacketed hunters on a tartan wall, and a steaming shepherd's pie in front of her. Noelle's idea of Pub Heaven.

Joe's Pub sat in the most prominent spot on Storey Road, directly in front of the centerpiece of the village—a stocky stone gazebo with a cone-shaped tile roof, planted right in the middle of the road. Minutes ago, as Noelle had walked to the pub, she pondered the history of the gazebo, of its original function. But tonight it served as a dance floor for an elderly couple in the hazy dusk of evening.

When Noelle edged up to the pub's bar, a burly man in his forties with squinty brown eyes and thick hair approached her. He didn't see her at first and scratched something on a notepad while humming a tune.

"Excuse me." Noelle tried to ignore her eager stomach, which had started growling audibly when the wafting scent of rich pub food, spices like garlic and rosemary mingling with the zesty gravy of what smelled like a pot roast, hit her senses.

"Oh. Sorry. What can I get for you?" He slid the notepad across the bar with him, pencil poised to take her order.

"Do you have shepherd's pie?"

"We do!"

"I'll have one of those, with a beer. Err... lager? Please." She only ever drank alcohol at parties or weddings, and even then, she limited herself to half a glass. *But when in an English pub...*

The man tilted a glass to the tap, and the foam built up. He lifted the glass and set it on the bar, pointing his pencil toward her with a half grin. "You're from the States."

"How'd you guess?" She took a sip and tried not to wince in front of him. The lager tasted rich, bitter.

"Oh, now, that's an easy one. Beautiful blond hair and perfect teeth—dead giveaway." He winked.

Noelle smiled, wondering if her cheeks had flushed pink. "I'm from San Diego."

"California girl, eh? Well, welcome to our fair village." As another customer approached, he told Noelle, "I'll bring your order out when it's ready. Better grab that fireside table fast. Best seat in the house."

She edged toward it, careful not to spill her lager. Easy to see why the table was so popular. The blaze's heat instantly comforted her while she settled in to wait for her pie and to people-watch. To her left, a table of tourists discussed their next stop. Behind them, a lively group of teenage boys in grass-stained rugby uniforms animatedly discussed the game they'd just played. At a booth near the doorway, a gathering of old men chatted, puffing on cigars and lighting pipes. She imagined them assembling at the exact same time every night, to smoke and talk the evening away.

The bartender appeared with her meal, setting the steaming plate before her. "You're a lone traveler, eh? A tourist?"

Though completely ravenous, she had to be polite. "Sort of. I'll be sticking around for a couple of days, at least. It's a beautiful place." For now, she preferred to keep her situation private, uncertain how the villagers might react to her presence here, being Joy's niece.

"You'll get no argument here. Nicest village in all the Cotswolds, if you ask me."

Noelle lifted the fork as a subtle signal, which he seemed to understand. "Well, I'm Joe. I'll be at the bar if you need anything else."

She thanked him and pushed her fork into the crusty mashed-potato-and-beef feast, watching the steam rise. The meal could've been horrible and she wouldn't have cared, but it tasted creamy and scrumptious, and she ate every last bite within fifteen minutes.

By the time she left at half past eight o'clock, the whole of the village, except for the pub, had turned dark. Shops had long since closed, and only a couple of teenagers roamed about on the otherwise empty street. She'd had every intention of slowly browsing the shops, but tonight wasn't the night. Still, one stop just couldn't wait. The art gallery.

She approached the building across the street, observing the "Closed" sign hanging on the front door. The glow of a nearby street lamp illuminated two paintings displayed in the window, and Noelle leaned in for a closer look. One, a country scene of two children, playing in an open field. The other, a watery image of London, of Big Ben and Parliament. She didn't recognize them as her aunt's work. Perhaps other local artists had painted them.

She wanted so badly to turn the knob and walk in, browse the other paintings inside, see if the gallery looked the same as she remembered. The rare times she'd visited, her aunt had set up an easel in the back room, and Noelle would sit quietly and watch. She could still smell the turpentine, hear the swish of her brush.

She would have to make a quick decision about the gallery, to sell it or keep it, perhaps even as early as tomorrow, with Mr. Lester. Part of her couldn't bear the thought of it belonging to someone else. But that was for tomorrow. The long travel day had caught up with her, and she wasn't sure she had the energy to make it back to the cottage, up the hill, up those stairs, into the soft bed. It all seemed so far away.

She woke up early the next morning to a memory. Something to do with Adam. Being in England again had filled her to the brim with old memories, moments she hadn't retrieved in ages. And they seemed as vivid as the day she lived them.

The clock read 6:00 a.m., she noticed with a deep sigh. She flipped to her other side and hugged the pillow, shutting her eyes tight and wandering back into the memory. There they sat, she and Adam, under that huge oak tree at Gram's estate on a warm summer evening, both of them gloriously sixteen years old. Cicadas chirped their noisy songs, and tiny black ants minded their own business as they marched up the tree trunk. She remembered Adam reading *A Twist in the Tale* by Jeffrey Archer—a collection of short stories, each with surprise endings. Noelle sat cross-legged beside him, sketching a ladybug in the notebook she always brought with her. Every so often, he took in a sharp breath or chuckled as he turned a page. Sometimes, knowing he wasn't looking, she peeked at him, focusing on his dark eyelashes, his perfect mouth, his freshly cut brown hair. Then she quickly looked down again at her notebook.

Finally, he couldn't resist. "Okay, okay." He waved at her. "You've got to hear this one."

"Adam, I can't sketch and listen at the same time."

"Well, try. This one's brilliant. You'll love it, I promise." He licked his lips, cleared his throat, and began. She never minded his reading aloud to her. His boundless enthusiasm and dreamy British accent made a lethal combination.

He started to read while she flipped over a new page, bored of ladybugs, to try something new. Adam used different voices for all the characters and gestured dramatically as she fixated on his sneaker. She'd never sketched a sneaker before, never realized how challenging and intricate it could be getting the right form down, detailing the textures of the stripes, the sole, the laces.

"Are you listening?" he asked occasionally.

She mumbled, "Mmm," and he continued.

When he reached the end, he slammed the book shut in triumph, as though he had written the clever story himself. "So? Did you guess the ending?"

Noelle finished filling in the little round hole at the base of the lace and looked up. "Hmm? Oh, right. The ending. Yeah. Great, I never would've guessed."

Adam smirked. "You didn't hear a bloody word, did you?"

"I told you I can't sketch and listen at the same time."

Adam yanked the notebook from her hands, out of reach.

"Hey! Give me that! I'm not finished!" She tried to look angry but couldn't stop a smile from growing.

With one hand, Adam staved her off as she lunged and grabbed for it, and with the other, he held the notebook high, observing her work. "A sneaker? An old, worn-out sneaker is more important than a piece of lit-tra-chure?"

When he brought the notebook in range of her hand, she snatched it from him. "Well, I didn't know you'd be giving a quiz afterward. I've never done a sneaker before. I needed a challenge."

"Actually, it's pretty damn good. So, is that my birthday present?"

Noelle took up her pencil again. "Yes, I think it will be. That's all I can afford, anyway." She wrote "Adam's Sneaker" in bold letters across the top, placed her initials in the right bottom corner, and tore it out of the notebook with flair.

"I'll cherish it forever." He folded the paper neatly and stuffed it into his jeans pocket.

"Wanker," she teased.

"Complete and utter non-listener."

"Ooh. Is that supposed to be an insult? Because it sounded kind of lame."

Smiling into her pillow, Noelle watched him in the glow of a lazy setting sun, grabbing her in a playful headlock before piggybacking her all the way to the manor.

The memory turned stale as Noelle opened her eyes again. What she wouldn't give to reach back in time and plead with her sixteen-year-old self that day: *Tell him. Just tell him how you feel. Because very soon, it will be too late. Soon, that door will close forever. Now or never. What do you have to lose?*

But that was the point. If she *had* told him, and Adam hadn't reciprocated, she would've been humiliated. And worse, she might've lost him. As a friend, or as anything else. And at sixteen, she hadn't wanted to take that risk.

The memory frustrated her, that maddening rhetorical question of "what might have been." She could lie there for hours, wrestle with sleep, and try to push away those old summers. But it would accomplish nothing.

Time to get busy, do something, force away the questions. Jet lag had made her tired and energetic at the same time, and she could use that energy to make progress cleaning and sorting. First, though, she needed a plan.

She tossed aside the sheets and quilt, planning to brew some coffee downstairs and create a "to-do" list of things she could control.

After two cups of coffee, a thorough list, a shower, and a quick assessment of nearly every room in the cottage, Noelle finally took a few minutes to explore the garden—an acre in total, with a manicured lawn, multi-colored flowers, and durable shrubs. Pristine and beautiful. And private. Not a single building as far as the eye could see, only a countryside landscape divided by short stone walls. She pictured Aunt Joy on the porch with her morning tea, her senses soothed by the garden's beauty.

Next, Noelle called Mrs. Henderson, a Cotswold realtor. They agreed to put the cottage on the market the following week, once Noelle had returned to San Diego. Noelle would prepare the house as much as possible before Mrs. Henderson stopped by for a viewing.

In an hour, Mr. Lester would arrive at the cottage to go over the paperwork. Barely enough time for her to find the market and purchase some essentials. Noelle had braced for soppy weather the entire time, remembering how it loved to rain in England, but a rare burst of sunlight and a cloudless blue sky greeted her as she opened the front door. Even with the sunshine, today was still October-cold, so she bundled up the collar of her thick blue coat and headed out with her list.

An elderly man sat in a chair in front of one of the nearby shops, a bakery next door to Joe's. He wore a dark fedora and olive-colored jacket and waved gregariously to passers-by with a withered hand. She pulled out her cell phone, knowing how tourist-y this would look but not caring. She inched closer, snapping the old man's picture. He held a plate with some food samples, their toothpicks sticking up like long cactus needles.

"Good morning, young lady. Care for a bite of scone?"

"Don't mind if I do." She reached for a toothpick. "Mmm. Wonderful."

"My daughter Julia's recipe. It's won first prize in the village fair, five years running."

"Is this her bakery?"

"It is now. I passed it down to her when I got too old to manage things. I'm almost ninety years old, you know. The bakery has been in my family for three generations."

"That's impressive."

"Mr. Bentley!" Another elderly man hobbled over.

Noelle tried to sneak away to let the two men have their conversation, but Mr. Bentley leaned forward and said, "Come back for more samples anytime. I'm here every day," then refocused his attention to his friend.

Adorable. The village greeter.

Walking on, Noelle snapped a few more quick pictures of the limestone storefronts, of children playing jacks on the sidewalk, of an aloof gray cat strolling carelessly along, of the dark storm clouds starting to form at the far end of the horizon. They might be coming her way.

Searching for the grocer's, she made note of the other shops around her. An Indian restaurant stood beside a beauty shop called "Snippity-Doo-Dah." Across the street, an antiques shop and a dainty women's boutique flanked a specialty tobacco shop. Beside those, a toy store sat next to a clock shop. A traditional English church occupied the end of the street. Its steeple rose high above its elongated stone building, likely hundreds of years old, with tombstones jutting up inside a compact graveyard. As though paying tribute to Noelle, its newest admirer, the church bells chimed the eleven o'clock hour.

Noelle put away her phone and returned to her mission, spotting the grocer's store at the end of the street. She pulled open the door and triggered a tinkling bell. From behind the counter, an older woman with ash-blond hair and too-red lipstick looked up from her copy of the *Daily Mirror* with a loud, "Good *mor*-ning!!"

"Hello," Noelle responded cheerily. She tried to remove a stubborn basket from the stack beside the door, finally shaking it free and placing the metal handles over her arm.

"If I can assist you, let me know!" the woman called out.

Compared to San Diego, where gourmet markets and health food stores abounded, the selection was incredibly scarce. Still, she found the necessities quickly: eggs, bread, tea bags, a tin of biscuits, milk, fruit, coffee, and an already-cooked roasted chicken she would have for tonight's meal. Stepping up to the counter, Noelle placed her items on the countertop in generous handfuls, hoping to speed the process along.

"I'm Mrs. Pickering. Haven't seen you around here before." The woman tapped prices into her register slowly. Too slowly. "New to Chilton Crosse, are you?"

"I've been here a few times. Years ago." Noelle considered how much detail she wanted to give. "I'm… visiting."

"Are you staying at Primrose Cottage? Joy's place?"

"How did you—?"

"Well. Martha Malone went on her evening walk along the creek last night and saw a cab taking a young blond woman up the road to the cottage. Now, I'm the last one to be in *any*one's personal business, but Martha came into the store and volunteered the information to me. Anyway, seeing you walk in, I assumed…"

Noelle sighed under her breath. "Yes. That's me. I'm Joy's niece. Well, great-niece."

"Joy used to be such a friendly, active member of the community. Until the 'incident' several years ago, of course…" Her voice lowered into a hush. "Such a shame." She even added a "tsk" at the end.

As tempted as Noelle was to find out exactly what happened all those years ago, she didn't want to participate in the tarnishing of her late aunt's name. Probably all gossip, anyway. The Mrs. Pickerings of the world usually held fewer aces in their deck than they led people to believe.

As she put away her groceries, Noelle opened a cabinet and an odd thought struck her. Her aunt's dishes and saucers sat there, completely unaware anything had changed. Noelle tried to imagine the last time Joy had eaten from them. *Was she happy? Was she lonely? Did she know it would* be *her last time?*

Someone had already cleared out the pantry shelves, but one empty container with "Biscuits" written in gold print still remained. Things had been so hectic yesterday, then today, that the weight of everything hadn't quite hit Noelle yet. The nuances and details of someone leaving this earth, leaving behind things like a cottage and dishes and a biscuit tin for someone else to find.

Fighting the desire to sit indoors all day and let melancholy hover like a cloud, she prepared a cup of tea while she waited for Mr. Lester. She needed to stay sharp for the meeting, which would presumably be full of financial figures and confusing legalese. She could spend time later, contemplating the sadness between the lines.

The moment she put the kettle on, the doorbell chimed. A thin, wiry man stood on the other side of the door. He was dressed in a navy jacket and slacks, pressed to perfection. Though his hairline receded slightly, his close-set hazel eyes emitted a youthful spark that made Noelle assume he was closer to her age. She had expected the lawyer to be much older.

"Mr. Lester?" She opened the door wider.

"Err... no. I'm Frank. Frank O'Neill." The man pointed to himself. "The curator. Of your aunt's gallery."

"Oh! Yes, of course." She motioned him inside. "Please come in, Mr. O'Neill."

"Call me Frank." He walked past her then followed her into the sitting room. "And you're Noelle?"

"Yes. I'm making tea. May I get you some?"

"That would be lovely, thank you."

Within minutes, they sat across from each other beside the cast-iron stove, politely sipping tea. Frank finally cleared his throat and said, "I'm terribly sorry about your aunt."

"Thank you. I wish I had attended the funeral. But I didn't know about it—her passing—until a few days ago."

"Such a beautiful service. Most of the village turned out for it."

Noelle didn't know if it was out of respect or curiosity.

"So, tell me about you. What do you do in California?" He talked with his free hand, his gestures slightly effeminate.

"I'm in Human Resources. At an insurance agency." She didn't know Frank well enough to tell him HR wasn't exactly her dream job. That she fell into it right out of college—starting out as a secretary and training to become a human resources assistant. She always envied those people who seemed organically connected to their work. Who had passion for it, obtained purpose from it. Who always knew what they wanted to be when they grew up. "How long have you been the gallery's curator?"

"Two-and-a-half years. Might I be blunt?" He set his tea on the table and folded his fingers together in his lap. "I'm not sure how much you've been told about the gallery."

"Mr. Lester said there were financial difficulties."

"A kind understatement." He shook his head. "Well. You'll know soon enough, so I might as well be the one. We're headed for bankruptcy. Unless we can make the balloon payment by the end of next month."

"Oh. I had no idea things had become that dire."

"I'm afraid so. 30,000 pounds worth of dire."

"You're kidding. That's about 50,000 U.S. dollars?"

"Yes. And I wish I *were* kidding. I suppose it's a blessing that your aunt never knew."

She blinked her confusion, so Frank explained further. "That was my decision, wanting to protect her from things. She didn't have a strong hand in the gallery, preferred to stay out of the financial aspects completely. The curator before me was to blame. When I came along after he quit, I found the financial records in shambles. Receipts missing, bills unpaid, money unaccounted for. A nightmare. I did the best I could, and for a while, we stayed afloat. But the damage was done. Now I'm afraid it's either go bankrupt or sell."

"Is there a potential buyer?"

Frank chortled. "It's worse than bankruptcy, trust me. Some big shot from Dublin wants to turn your aunt's gallery into a tourist trap." He nearly choked back the words. "One of those horrid, tacky shops that sell magnets and coasters with Chilton Crosse emblazoned on everything. Revolting."

Noelle tried to process the severity of it, her aunt's gallery in real trouble. Heartbreaking and impossible. She didn't know why she cared so much when she wouldn't even be there past Thursday. The practical side of her urged, *Sell. It's the wisest thing to do. Who cares what the new buyer turns it into? You'll be long gone by then...*

"The villagers are quite affected," Frank confided. "They despise the idea of selling. Especially to someone like the Dubliner. There was even discussion about throwing a fund-raiser."

"Really?"

He grinned. "Barmy, isn't it? Considering the enormous amount of money it would take. The village council actually met last week, about the possibility. But they decided it would be futile. Plus, we shouldn't compete with the raising of funds for the school. It's in terrible disrepair. And because it's a three-hundred-year-old building, there are historic standards to adhere to. And that takes money. The council has even made some calls to architects who might consider waiving their fees. Sort of a pro bono project. It's especially appealing to architects whose specialty is to preserve English history." He paused, chuckled. "I'm sorry. I do have a tendency to ramble on. We were talking about the gallery, weren't we?"

Noelle nodded, steering the conversation back to the fundraiser, back to the idea that, futile or not, people had actually considered banding together on behalf of her deceased aunt. "I think it's amazing that people cared so much about Aunt Joy. To consider a fundraiser."

"Yes. I thought so, too."

"May I ask you something about my aunt?"

"Anything,"

"Well... I'd been out of contact with her for years. Not for lack of trying," Even after receiving Joy's letter asking her to stop making any contact, Noelle almost hopped a plane to England in spite of her wishes, but she couldn't afford it. At some point, years later, Noelle finally stopped taking Joy's silence as a personal rejection. But even after her death, when it no longer mattered, Noelle's curiosity about those reclusive years remained strong. "I have some questions about her, and I'm not sure who to ask. Or really, how to ask."

"I'll do my best," he offered.

"I assume she sort of locked herself away, here in the cottage, after that evening years ago."

"The art exhibit, yes."

"And I never knew why." She wanted to be bold, stop beating around bushes. "Do you know why? Does anyone know what happened that evening, to make her hide away?"

"There's speculation, of course. But no. Nobody knows the reason. And I doubt you'll find many villagers willing to theorize, even to her niece. I think they're a bit... protective of her. We all are. Let's be honest—she put this wee village of ours on the map, and so there's a sense of duty, of protecting that memory. She's one of us. Even if, after that night, she decided not to be one of us anymore."

Frank hadn't given her a single substantive answer, nothing to chew on, but the one he had given was satisfying.

A knock on the door shifted her attention. "Oh. That will be Mr. Lester."

Frank stood. "I must be going anyway. I'm sorry to be the bearer of such bad news. About the gallery."

"No, no, it's fine. I appreciate your visit."

As they reached the front door, he pulled a business card from his jacket pocket. "Please call if you have any questions. Maybe there's still a way to save the gallery."

Noelle opened the door, and Frank offered his hand to Mr. Lester, a stocky, balding man with a moustache. Nothing like she'd pictured over the phone, for some reason. His thin voice didn't match his stout stature. Cordial nods exchanged, Frank passed between them to leave.

"Please come in," Noelle told Mr. Lester, suggesting tea as they walked to the sitting room. He declined and sat on the sofa, snapping open his briefcase.

"I apologize for being late," he said. "And for not being able to stay longer than a few moments. I have an unexpected London meeting."

"It's fine." She sat beside him as he sorted through a thick stack of important-looking documents. She watched, glad for his no-nonsense approach. After that surprisingly personal conversation with Frank, she wanted a good old-fashioned, get-down-to-business meeting.

As he drew out the papers, Noelle said, "There's something I'd forgotten to ask about over the phone. At one time, my aunt and grandmother owned a small seaside cottage in Cornwall. I remember going there a couple of times as a little girl."

"Yes. That's still part of your aunt's estate. She's been leasing it for years, even though I recommended she sell. But it always seems to have a tenant, so it pays for itself. In fact, I believe the current tenants have a lease through the middle of summer. Are you thinking of selling?"

"No." Noelle wanted to hang onto every little bit of her heritage she possibly could.

In a matter of minutes, she had signed every paper, understanding only a fraction of the jargon he spouted as he handed her one document after another. Release forms, tax forms, and financial forms. Everything a blur.

"Mr. Lester," she said as he put the signed papers back into his briefcase. "Frank O'Neill told me more about the gallery. The balloon payment."

"Oh, yes. Shame. The estate managed to take care of the funeral bills, but there's not much left over, certainly not enough to help the gallery. Your aunt was quite wealthy a couple of decades ago, but since her painting stopped, so did her income. You'll sell, won't you? There's an attractive offer on the table."

"Well, I'm not sure. There's still a bit of time left."

"Not enough, I fear. My best advice is to sell. The smartest option, probably the only one. But of course, the gallery is yours. Entirely your decision. Ring me when you're ready, and I can handle things for you."

She had hoped for a more definitive answer, some real guidance in one direction or another. Mr. Lester had been Aunt Joy's trusted lawyer for years, and she didn't feel capable of making an enormous decision on her own in a short amount of time. "I will. Thank you."

She escorted him back to the door, and just as she opened it for him, he stopped short. "I nearly forgot. Another important document." He reached inside his blazer.

"Do I need a pen?"

"This requires no signature. I think, out of all the documents, you'll find it the most compelling." He handed her a light-green envelope and left. Thunder rumbled as she closed the door and turned the envelope over in her hands. "For Noelle," scrawled in shaky handwriting. Aunt Joy's.

Noelle needed something solid beneath her. Back in the sitting room, she sank into the sofa and rotated the envelope in her hands. She recognized the stationery. Last night, crawling into bed and reaching for the lamp, she'd noticed the stack of pale green stationery still left out on the writing desk in the corner.

Breaking the seal with careful fingers, she drew out the letter and unfolded it. Aunt Joy had dated it three days before she passed away.

Dearest Noelle,

I've thought about writing this letter so many times, but the words always sound rubbish. I'm trying again, and I'll see it through.

I regret losing touch with you for all these years, not responding to your warm letters, your phone calls in the beginning. Especially when you needed me the most. I'll never forgive myself. The distance between us is entirely my fault. I have no doubt you've turned into a kind, beautiful human being, and it's my loss, not watching you grow into your adult self.

I'm a silly old woman who's only thought about myself the last decade. I've hidden away in this cottage like a frightened child, slapping away the hand of any who tried to help or become a friend. And I'm coming to the end. Call it a hunch, or even a premonition, but I realise my time is short. I can feel it, sense it. So, I'm rushing to make some things right, tie up loose ends.

As I'm sure you know by now, I've given you my cottage and the gallery. I've made you my executor because I trust you. When you come to Chilton Crosse, you'll find a few surprises lurking about. Know this—what's mine is entirely yours. Do whatever you see fit. I trust you to handle things with dignity and honour.

I know you don't understand all this yet, but you will. What you'll discover is the heart of me. Some people have secrets they want kept hidden, even after they die. But I'm tired of hiding. Every flaw, every detail, every treasure—I'm giving you permission to share them, if that's what you decide.

All my love,
Joy

Noelle let her eyes go blurry, pondering the weight of the words. Aunt Joy had appreciated her letters. More than that, she'd held herself accountable for her own exile. It was important to Noelle that her aunt regretted a bit of that reclusiveness, because that kept her from enjoying any contact, from getting to know her grandniece over the past decade.

And because Noelle's mother had passed away only two months before Aunt Joy hid away in Primrose Cottage, she'd been doubly abandoned that year. Of course, her aunt was grieving too, which Noelle had assumed played a small part in her meltdown at the gallery show that night. Still, Noelle had needed a mother figure in her life, and Aunt Joy couldn't be that. Wouldn't even try.

But as she read the letter once more, her aunt's words healed little parts of her. Because of the apology, the acknowledgment of regret. That was enough. Noelle clutched the paper to her chest and leaned back on the sofa cushion. Aunt Joy could've bequeathed her only a precious letter, and Noelle would've been content.

Even so, it referenced surprises, secrets, and treasures. She couldn't imagine what Joy was talking about. But she was eager to find out.

Chapter Three

The canvas holds equal amounts of fear and self-doubt. "What if you can't get it right?" it asks as you apply the brush. "What if you're not good enough?" Brace yourself, shake off the doubts, and paint anyway.

NOELLE HAD BEEN GATHERING CLEANING supplies from the upstairs closet for the past few minutes, whistling a Beyoncé song stuck in her head, when she'd heard something. A faint but rapid tapping on glass, maybe the window. It didn't sound like a front door kind of knock.

Curious, she padded downstairs and followed the sound toward the kitchen. The knock had come from the back door, the one that led to the garden. She made out a figure through the door's paned windows, an older man with snow-white hair, dressed in a khaki windbreaker and jeans. He didn't look dangerous. Still, he hadn't knocked at the front door like a normal person. She moved forward and spoke through the closed door. "May I help you?"

The stranger mumbled, but she couldn't make out the words. Hesitant, she unlocked the door and cracked it open, questioning the wisdom of giving a stranger any kind of access.

"Pardon, miss. I didn't mean to frighten ye. I'm the gardener, Mac MacDonald." Even with the door open, she still couldn't interpret his thick Scottish accent very well.

"Oh. Aunt Joy's gardener?"

"Aye."

"Nice to meet you. I'm Noelle, her niece." She remembered Mr. Lester mentioning something about a gardener. Noelle opened the door wider for him. "Please, come in." She let him pass through then led him to the sitting room.

Mac held his cap and threaded the brim through his fingers over and over in a circle, then took a seat beside the stove when she motioned toward it. Her third visitor in a few hours' time. Ironic, for a cottage well known for its hermitic tendencies. She offered some tea.

"No thank ye, lass. I won't be stayin' long." His dark gray eyes held a sadness, and he kept them mostly downward, toward the cap he'd placed on his knees. "I can't tell ye how sorry I am about your aunt. She was a good woman."

"Thank you. That's very kind."

"Oh, no kindness about it. 'Tis the truth. Best person I ever knew." His gravelly voice trembled, and Noelle thought he might be fighting tears. He cleared his throat and looked up at her. "She gave you the cottage, eh?"

"Yes. I'm still pretty shocked. We lost touch for several years, so I never expected..."

"Joy talked about ye. All the time."

"She did?"

Mac nodded. "She looked forward to your letters. I think she kept them together in a box somewhere, read them more than once. You were the only one of her family who bothered to keep in touch."

Noelle didn't know what to say. Joy had not only read her letters, but they had held such value that even Aunt Joy's gardener knew of them. Uncomfortable with her own emotions bubbling up, she needed to steer things in another direction. "You were her gardener for how many years?"

"Oh, 'round about fifteen. Been keeping up the gardens in the last two weeks, too, ever since she... well, nobody asked, but I thought I should stay on, keep the grounds presentable."

"Yes, that was a wonderful idea. In fact, do you mind staying a bit longer? I'll be putting the cottage up for sale, and I want it to look its best. Do you know anyone around the village who might do some minor repairs?"

"I can do anything ye need. I'm a handyman as well as a gardener. Be pleased to help. I can start tomorrow."

"That would be a great relief. I'm sort of overwhelmed at the moment. Oh, I did have a question. Do you know anything about a room upstairs that's locked? I can't find a key anywhere. Maybe it's just a fluke, an accident, that it's locked, but it sort of has me intrigued."

"Ah, the Mystery Room." Mac nodded. "It's the only one in the cottage I wasn't allowed to touch. Your aunt kept that room locked up tight." He shrugged. "She never said why, and I never asked. 'Twasn't my business to know."

Noelle wondered if he secretly knew the contents but didn't want to tell her. Even in these few minutes, Noelle could tell he was intensely private. And people who wanted privacy often respected other people's.

"I wonder if we should pry it open at some point," Noelle pondered. "In order to sell the cottage, I mean."

"Aye."

"Aunt Joy also left me the gallery. But that situation's a little more complicated. I would love to keep it. To hold her legacy in the family. I've got some big decisions ahead of me."

"You'll make the right ones, lass. I have no doubt of it."

"Thank you, Mac."

For the first time, they genuinely locked eyes, and she caught a hint of a smile. The deep creases around his eyes bore witness to years devoted to outdoor laboring. She guessed his age as early seventies, easily a decade younger than her aunt had been, but perhaps his weathered face and light beard only made him look older. She liked him. His sweet sincerity made her trust him.

"May I ask you a question?" she said. "It's a little... delicate."

"Aye, lass."

"Well, I know that my aunt died of a stroke, but I don't know any details. Was she alone that day?"

"Nay, I was here. In the garden, watering some new flowers. I heard a crash inside the kitchen. I called the doctor, but when they arrived, 'twas too late. She died in my arms."

"Oh. I'm sorry. That must've been horrible for you."

Mac nodded, tears threatening again.

"I'm glad she wasn't alone," Noelle whispered.

He stood with some effort. "I'd best be going." He put on his cap and walked toward the back door.

She followed him and said good-bye, fascinated to meet probably the only person who saw her aunt during her reclusive period. She speculated about the sorts of things Mac might have been witness to all those years, what he might have seen or known that the rest of the world, and even her own niece, never knew. Still, he seemed the type to protect her eccentricities from the rest of the village. At least her aunt had been able to trust one person.

Later that afternoon, Noelle had kicked into gear again. She revisited her extensive list and wondered how she would possibly squeeze everything in between today and tomorrow. Sure, she'd mostly worked out the tedious details and phone calls. But she still had to deal with the cottage itself. With the enormous job of combing through every room, every drawer, every corner—clearing out, throwing away, tidying up, to get each room pristine and show-ready for the realtor.

To that end, she spent the next two hours tackling the guest room, which Aunt Joy had used as more of a storage space. Noelle unpacked six boxes containing all sorts of items: old art magazines, many featuring Joy's Cotswold paintings; vintage clothing; even an old, tattered doll from her aunt's childhood. None of these items seemed particularly secretive or mysterious as Joy's letter indicated.

One more box to go. She lugged it, thankfully small and light, onto the twin bed. The pads of her fingers were raw and sore from ripping tape off boxes, and she groaned a little as she pulled off the stubborn tape and mashed it into a sticky ball.

She peered inside. An old shawl, a needlepoint pillow, a vinyl LP of Ella Fitzgerald. Digging deeper, she found a stack of photos, all taken at Gram's Bath estate, all at different time periods. Black-and-white photos mixed in with colored ones. Noelle sat on the edge of the bed, entranced, slowly flipping through the gold mine of memories. The estate itself, imposing and beautiful; a rare picture of her grandfather looking serious and handsome in his tall hunter's boots and Windsor cap; some shots of the gardens, enormous and immaculate, with a grand fountain and even the shrub maze that she and her best friend, Jillian, raced through as little girls. And one photo of her mother.

Noelle lifted the picture closer, recognized her mother as a teenager, arms up, dancing, head tossed back with a generous smile. Aunt Joy once described her mother at that age as "impetuous" and "glamorous." The only old stories Noelle knew of her mother involved a bevy of suitors and enormous parties that Gram allowed her to throw, likely in order to encourage a search for a suitable English husband. Instead, she stumbled across a handsome young American hitchhiking through Europe, and that was that. "Impetuous" eventually turned to "irresponsible," as she married him after only six weeks' time, moved to the States, and had a baby she wasn't ready for.

Noelle could never quite shake the idea she'd been more of a burden to her mother than blessing. Even now, whenever her mother crossed her mind, she knew the unease of disappointment. Of things her mother did or didn't do. Things that could never be enough, that told Noelle she wasn't important enough. She recalled the first memorable letdown, the summer she turned fourteen.

Her mother had dropped her off at the airport for a summer in England. Noelle was thrilled to visit Gram and Joy again, especially since three years had passed since her last one. But by the end of that summer, during what Noelle assumed was a fun trip to see her grandmother and aunt, she realized it had all been a ruse. Her mother had shuffled her off to another country for a specific purpose, to get her out of the way so she could quietly divorce her father. Even Gram and Joy weren't aware of the visit's purpose, she discovered later. Her mother had tricked them, too.

Noelle had departed from San Diego that May thinking her parents' marriage remained flawed but fine and returned in August to her mother's grim face. "Honey, we need to talk." Noelle's father had removed all traces of himself from their house that summer—his clothes, his shaving kit, even his beloved golf clubs—after discovering his wife's affair. The divorce was final before Noelle even stepped off the plane. As many times as she'd tried since her mother's passing, Noelle had never fully forgiven her mother for that. For changing her entire world without even bothering to let her know.

Uncomfortable with how one picture could set off an avalanche of memories, Noelle moved her mother's teenage smile to the back of the stack, ready to abandon the pictures altogether, when other memories, blissful ones, made her reconsider. The next picture, and the next, and the next, a whole host of images from Noelle's lovely teenage summers all spent at the estate. Gram and Joy in mid-conversation, laughing at something the other had said; Aunt Joy, brush raised to a canvas, her face full of artistic intensity; Noelle, legs curled up, reading a book, oblivious to the intrusive lens.

She flipped to the last photo and stared hard. A seventeen-year-old Noelle, fresh-faced, slightly tanned, flanked by two much taller people. Jillian, her best friend, on one side and on the other side, Adam, his arm draped around Noelle, his dark curls touching the top of her head as he leaned in, smiling his crooked smile. They had taken the picture in Gram's garden during that final summer, right before their lives pulled them in separate directions and forced the three friends into adulthood.

"Look at us. We were so young," she whispered.

Until her current visit to England, she had no reason to look back, to recall the best summers of her life. They had slipped into the oblivion of the past, never to be repeated or duplicated. But here lay a slice of it, urging her to return. Looking at the three of them, smiling together, she realized no friends since Adam and Jill compared. Back then, she naively assumed all future relationships would be that effortless, that real and intense. But as she discovered after college, adults didn't form friendships by the same code as young people. Games were played and walls were constructed, carefully and deliberately, to keep people from coming too close. The mask she wore as an adult wasn't even in existence back then.

In the picture, she wore a teardrop pendant, given to her by Adam only moments before the camera had frozen them in time. "I remember this..." He'd handed her a gold package, proud of himself for wrapping it. A birthday present during the summer she turned seventeen.

Last she'd heard of Jillian, she had dropped out of a community college and flown off to Italy to make a living as a glamorous model.

And Adam had gone away to Oxford and who knew where after that. Surely married today, with three lovely children and a fancy house by the coast.

Frustrated at the reminder of a past to which she couldn't return, Noelle memorized the photo then placed it with the others inside an empty shoebox she'd pulled from the closet earlier. Those pictures were too precious to do anything but keep for herself. A slice of history she couldn't let go of.

Not yet, at least.

Noelle stared at the clock and counted backward. Midnight her time, 4:00 p.m. Dan's time. After sorting the guest room boxes, she'd turned all her focus on the rest of the cottage. Dusting, cleaning, moving, rearranging, and discarding. All requiring heavy labor of one sort or another. Room to room, up and down stairs. Exhausting.

She examined her efforts hours later—twelve bags of trash, seven boxes of items to give away or sell, and four boxes she wanted to take home to the States. Progress, but still so much to do. She hadn't started the kitchen yet. All those drawers and cabinets. Or even the little nook under the stairs, filled to the brim with odds and ends. And she hadn't even had time to visit the gallery!

Finally sitting down to rest her weary feet and aching lower back, she'd realized she hadn't made airline reservations for tomorrow. That had been her deal with Dan, three days. Impossible. She simply needed more time, and Dan would have to understand. She made a quick call to Desha to make more arrangements then phoned Dan, clicking her foot against the writing desk in the master bedroom as she waited. When he answered, she cleared her throat and braced herself.

"Dan, it's Noelle. I can't be home in time for Friday." She winced, and when he said nothing, she continued. "This is taking longer than I thought—lots of details to sort out. It's really complicated—"

"Noelle, that's not acceptable. You can't leave me hanging."

"But I'm not. Really. Desha can cover for me tomorrow and Friday, no problem. You don't have to lift a finger. Everything's taken care of."

Silence. She tapped her foot harder, waiting.

"I'm not thrilled."

"I remember our deal. But this isn't my fault. It's beyond my control. Monday morning. I'll be there."

"Bright and early. Or else the consequences will have to be strong."

Not knowing if "consequences" meant "firing," Noelle said, "As early as you need. Thank you." She hung up, relieved, and shifted her attention to all the other remaining challenges ahead. The gallery decision, more cleaning up, and that locked door.

Chapter Four

Look at your canvas the way you should be looking at people,
at the world. From different angles. Examine it from far away
and squint your eyes. Then, come up close and see how the
textures change—the light, shadow, depth. It's the same painting,
but it changes depending on where you're standing.

W HY DOES *ENGLISH RAIN SEEM* so different from California rain? Noelle pondered the question as she stepped over puddles on her way down the hill. It didn't look or sound any different, didn't create special pitter-patter sounds hitting her umbrella or fall with a particular kind of slant unique to England. She might have to be content never knowing why.

Aunt Joy owned a plethora of umbrellas in almost every color. Noelle appreciated this particular eccentricity when she'd grabbed a blue one and headed to the gallery.

Mac had arrived at the cottage early in the morning, working on the outside of the cottage and garden before Noelle even awoke. Seeing the top of his silver head through the kitchen window had startled her as she reached for the kettle, groggy and yawning. She'd offered Mac some tea, and they sat for a few minutes, listing minor repairs to make over the next few days. Other than some nods and grunts, he simply listened, drank his tea, and stepped back outside to continue his work. A man of few words.

Frank O'Neill, on the other hand? A man of too many words. The moment Noelle had closed her blue umbrella and opened the door, itching to step inside the gallery for the first time since her arrival, he approached her, hands poised and ready for conversation. He threw out a barrage of questions about the meeting with Mr. Lester, the duration of her stay in Chilton Crosse, what her decision about the gallery would be.

She wouldn't be able to browse the gallery in peace until she answered his questions, so she tried to tackle them all at once. "I meant to call you last night, but there was so much to do. No news on the gallery. I'm still mulling over all the possibilities, with Mr. Lester's help. I'll be leaving Sunday night because of the work still to do, getting the cottage in order."

"I fully understand." He raised his hands suddenly. "Oh! Have you met Mac MacDonald yet? He can be a great help to you."

"Yes! In fact, he's at the cottage right now with a long list of things."

A muffled chime floated into the gallery. She tilted her head, hearing another, and another, trying to figure out their source. *The back wall?*

Frank explained, "That's the clock shop. Next door." He rolled his eyes. "Dozens of them, lining the walls. Enormous antique grandfather clocks. Old Mr. Rothschild insists on having them chime simultaneously."

"Every hour?" Ten o'clock. Still four to go.

"On the hour," Frank said with another eye roll and lowered his voice. "I once tried to approach the village council with a complaint, hoping to get a petition going to stop the noise. But apparently, since only the two shops on either side can hear the chimes, we were outnumbered. Mr. Rothschild was within his rights to set the clocks however he pleased." Frank shrugged. "Truthfully, I barely hear them anymore. And some people have actually called them charming."

"Probably the ones who aren't on either side of the shop."

"Precisely."

"Frank?" a female voice called from a back room.

"That's Holly, my assistant. Let me see what she needs, and I'll return in a bit."

Noelle had waited for this moment since she'd first peered inside the dark windows two nights ago. Waited to walk the long gallery hall, smell the pungent "gallery" smells of paint and turpentine, view the larger space in the back where Aunt Joy used to perch her easel. Funny, though, how time changed the details of memory. She recalled the walls of the hall being a paler shade of blue, not this current dark navy color. Perhaps Frank had painted them. Or perhaps her memory had played tricks on her. She also didn't remember the two benches in the middle of the room being quite that small.

As she walked toward the paintings, about ten lining each side of the rectangular room, one made her pause. She peered down at the corner signature, "NC." Her own painting, completed at seventeen, during her last summer in England. She never knew what happened to it.

She remembered that day well, trudging up the hill of her grandmother's estate with her easel and paint box, finding a stunning patch of countryside as her inspiration. She'd spent hours trying to capture on canvas the sunbeams filtering shadows through the tree branches. A card, "For Display Only," rested on the painting's nameplate. She loved the idea that her aunt had been proud enough to display her work but sentimental enough not to sell it.

She moved to the next one. Clearly a Joy painting, a rich sunset with stunning colors over a rolling Cotswold hillside. Joy had even created a subtle pink reflection on the tree trunks below. Noelle recalled the sensation of being drawn to a painting so vividly that her senses were almost tricked into believing it was real. *Is this why Joy painted, why she loved it so much?* It allowed her to be somewhere else, of her own creation, for a sliver of time.

How heartbreaking it must've been for her aunt to stop painting. To deprive herself of the escape that art provided, especially during a time when she needed that escape the most.

A pair of giggles behind Noelle broke her focus. Two little girls, about eleven years old, had come in with their mothers. One of the girls sprinted toward Noelle to escape the other one. "I'm sorry!" she whispered, nearly bumping into Noelle.

"It's all right. Do you like the paintings?"

"They're lovely," the little girl said in her posh British accent then went straight back to giggling and skipping around the gallery with her friend.

Noelle envied them. She remembered how easy things seemed at that age. The world felt warmer, safer—her parents still married, her father still a strong-ish figure in her life. And as the little girls settled into a corner together, playing a clap-rhyming game, Noelle realized she'd been around their age when she met Jillian at Windermere one summer.

Gram had called her downstairs and introduced her to the family who had recently moved in to the neighboring estate, Willowbrook. A skinny girl with sparkling eyes and strawberry ringlets had stood before her. "Meet Jillian Bartleby. She's going to keep you company this summer," Gram had said. Generally shy about meeting new friends, Noelle had taken a step backward, but Gram had gently nudged her forward again, whispering, "Say hello. She's our guest."

By that afternoon, the two little girls had become easy friends, playing hide-and-seek in the garden's maze, pushing each other back-and-forth across the length of the library on the tall, wheeled ladder, and sitting cross-legged under the dining table, talking about the "ick factor" of boys. Both the girls were hungry for playmates—Noelle because her shyness often kept her from making friends at school, and Jillian because she had already been to three different boarding schools in the last five years. Summer became her only true stability, the only time she lived with her parents in a real home.

Jillian told Noelle the most amazing tales about boarding school—ghosts in the halls of the living quarters and stern teachers with permanent scowls who threatened lashings for misbehavior. She always laced the stories with extravagant details, greatly embellished, no doubt, and Noelle would listen, holding her breath until the end.

Jillian was everything Noelle would never be. Tall and wispy, utterly comfortable in her own skin, full of life, confident she was good enough and worthy enough to match wits with absolutely anyone. Noelle wished sometimes she could switch places with Jillian and see what it felt like to be that unafraid.

As the little girls grew tired of their clapping game and wandered away to find something else for amusement, Noelle wondered how long it would take before they lost touch, as she and Jillian eventually did. And what hollow excuses they might offer themselves for allowing it to happen.

After leaving the gallery to run a few necessary errands then working to clear out another section of the cottage, Noelle realized she'd missed teatime. Only a couple of days in England, and already teatime at precisely four o'clock had become a tradition. Probably because of all those summers of strict ritual. Gram had insisted the entire household come to a halt when the four o'clock chimes rang deeply from the hall clock. No matter if Noelle had been in the middle of a swim or on the last page of a novel, she would be summoned to the Great Hall to sit with Gram and Aunt Joy for strong Yorkshire tea, shortbread biscuits, almond tea cakes, and an assortment of scones and jams.

Secretly, Noelle always looked forward to that particular hour of the day. She became a grown-up, all proper and sophisticated. Though Gram didn't require her to wear formal clothing, Noelle was required to display her best manners. No crumbs dropping onto the floor, no jam on her face after a bite of a scone, no slouching and talking about "frivolous" subjects. At least once a week, Gram invited company over during that time, a neighborhood friend or one of her bridge club ladies, which gave Noelle even more incentive to be proper.

As she drank her tea in Joy's cottage, she broke the drop-everything rule to go on an online mission. Something had nagged at her since the gallery. Those girls playing together had reminded her, once again, of her youth. She had lost those years in between her teens and adulthood too fast, in a blink.

It only took a few fast clicks to find Jill again. Her modeling career had been brief, but she'd developed quite an online footprint. Noelle sifted through biographies and forums to find a site with an actual phone number. Probably the wrong one, but it wouldn't hurt to try. She took a final sip of tea and dialed.

"Hello?"

"Hi. I'm looking for Jillian Bartleby." No, that wasn't right. The webpage said she was married now. "Sorry." Noelle squinted at the screen. "Holbrook. It's Jill Holbrook."

"That's me."

"Well, I'm not sure you'll remember me. My name is Noelle Cooke. Years ago, we were friends—"

"In Bath. At Windermere. For heaven's sake, yes. I remember you!" Jill's shriek of excitement calmed Noelle instantly, lowered the formal wall between them. "How on earth did you find me?"

"Well, you're a star model over here, apparently. It wasn't too hard."

"Over here? Are you in the UK?"

"I am. Unfortunate circumstances. Remember my Aunt Joy?"

"Famous painter? Smoky voice, serious eyes. They could stare right through you. Scared the life out of me more than once. I could never tell if she was being serious or dripping with sarcasm."

"That's the one. Well, she passed away a couple of weeks ago."

"I recall reading about that. I was sorry to hear it."

"Thank you. I inherited her cottage and the gallery, too. I flew here from California on Tuesday to sign legal papers, sort through the cottage."

"Joy—wasn't she your mother's aunt? You must've been surprised she didn't leave a portion to your mum."

Noelle's long pause probably told Jill everything. "My mother actually passed away. Ten years ago."

"I'm so sorry. How awful. An illness?"

"A car accident." She struggled to get back on track, sound upbeat. "So, that's why Aunt Joy left me everything."

"Well, I think that's lovely. Does this mean you're sticking around?"

"No, in fact, I leave in a couple of days. I'm putting the cottage up for sale, getting it ready. It's quite a chore. But I wanted to look you up before I had to go back to the States."

"I'm thrilled you did. So, how the devil are you? Spill! I want to know absolutely everything!"

Noelle told her about California, about the beach house and her strong desire to change jobs. Then her unexpected jaunt to Chilton Crosse and what a whirlwind it had all been.

"The Cotswolds. You're a stone's throw from us!" said Jill. "I'm in London, married to a gorgeous Welshman—a surgeon. He puts up with all of my little vices."

Noelle suppressed a chuckle. So Jill-like.

"And how about you?" Jill asked. "Married as well?"

Always the awkward part, matching lives with someone else and seeing who came up short. "Actually, no." Noelle rotated her empty mug, preparing all the right clichés.

But this was Jill. Not a stranger. Not someone she had to work hard to impress. In spite of the years that had turned them into sensible, respectable, socially aware adults, Noelle took a chance to turn back the clock a bit. To remember sitting on the floor under the dining room table in Gram's estate, talking about boys or plotting ways to steal more gingerbread from under the cook's watchful gaze.

"Okay. Here's the truth. The only two serious relationships I've ever had were complete disasters. First Greg, right out of college. Older than me, professional, motivated, but distant. He lost all interest in me, and I tried everything to keep him but couldn't. And then Steve, two years ago. Even worse. Classic bastard. He cheated on me, borrowed money from me and never gave it back, lied to me."

"Oh, I've dated a Steve or two in my time. Maybe they were brothers."

Noelle chuckled. "You know, I might just be one of those girls, destined to be alone." She hadn't planned to let one of her greatest insecurities tumble out so easily. "I can't seem to get it right."

"I highly doubt you'll end up alone," Jill reassured. "But even if you are, there's nothing in the world wrong with that. I loved my single days. They were terribly empowering."

"I do enjoy the freedom. But it sounds like you and your husband are a good fit?"

"We are. But I've never had to compromise so much in my life! It's been a struggle sometimes, putting his needs before mine. I can be a selfish bitch, but he knew that when he married me."

"Oh, Jill," Noelle snickered. "I've missed us. And all those summers. Do you ever go back there sometimes, to those days?"

"Sure, sometimes. Do you know the first memory I had when I heard your voice again? You'd think it would be sappy or sentimental, but it was completely silly. The time we went into that insanely posh jewelry store in Bath. I bet you ten pounds that you couldn't walk up to the snotty salesman behind the counter and ask to look at three pieces of jewelry whilst using that fake cockney accent of yours. And twenty pounds if you didn't crack a smile. You were brilliant! I had to feign allergies and hold a kerchief up to my face to keep from laughing!"

"I remember that! I pulled it off, didn't I?"

"The most entertaining twenty pounds I ever spent."

Noelle remembered the look on that poor salesman's face. "Now, be honest, didn't my accent sound too Dick-Van-Dyke-in-Mary-Poppins?"

Jillian cackled through the receiver, barely able to speak. "No, no. It was perfection. The right mixture of nasal and twang!"

"I thought he'd throw us out! Thank goodness he was a typical Brit, too polite to be brutally honest in public."

"Lucky you. And wasn't Adam with us, too?"

"Yep," Noelle said, seeing his lanky frame.

"Adam Spencer. 'Scrumptious Adam.' I called him that during my crush phase."

"I remember." Noelle had been crushed herself, when she found out Jill liked Adam romantically. And relieved when it hadn't worked out.

"I can't believe I asked him out. We were all sorts of wrong for each other. I should've known. Never date a friend. Do you know I actually saw him recently?"

"You did?"

"Well," she clarified, "if two years ago constitutes 'recent.' Bumped right into him in the West End. We had tea, chatted for a bit, and I haven't seen him since."

"He lives in London, too?"

"Well, he did then. I assume he still does. He's an architect—quite successful, with his own firm and scads of employees."

"Married, I assume?"

"No. Well, not at the time, at least."

"Really? That's odd. I thought... well, never mind."

"Of course, a lot can happen in a few years."

"Tell me about it."

"We should call him."

"Call him?" Noelle swallowed hard.

"Call him. As in pick up phone, dial digits, talk into receiver. It would be a grand reunion. Three Musketeers and all that rubbish."

"He's probably not even in London anymore. And I'm sure he's too busy, anyway. Or he's forgotten about us. Plus, I'm leaving in two days."

"Hmm. Protesting a little too much?"

"What do you mean?" Noelle never knew if Jill realized the intensity of her feelings for Adam. But that didn't mean Jill didn't have her suspicions.

"I don't mean anything if you don't mean anything. Now, tell me. Can you squeeze in a visit to see your old friend before you leave? Say, tomorrow evening? Gareth would love to meet you. He's a fab cook. We could have dinner here, at the house, then maybe take in a show at the West End?"

Noelle hadn't expected this. She had no business driving all the way to London for an entire night out, with still so much work to do before boarding the plane on Sunday. But she couldn't possibly leave England without seeing Jill. "Yes. Absolutely, I'll come."

"Perfection. I'm so looking forward to it. We'll have loads of time to catch up then. I can email you with directions."

They exchanged contact information, then Noelle heard Jillian air-kiss the phone. She added a cheery, "See you then!"

Noelle clicked off and stared at Jill's email address. Talking to Jill had taken her back in time the way no memory could do. For a moment, Noelle was her old self again, that youthful self. And she sometimes longed for those parts lost to adulthood. She missed them achingly so, perhaps because they *were* irretrievable.

Returning to her laptop, Noelle couldn't help herself. She typed in his name, plus "London," plus "architect," and waited for the result. And there it was—"Spencer-Murdoch Architecture." Breathing faster, Noelle clicked on the sparse menu, hoping to see Adam's picture, to confirm the "Spencer" was really him, but nothing came up. "Under Construction," each page told Noelle as she clicked in vain. Another quick Internet search yielded nothing, either. The first three Adam Spencers lived in Scotland, Cornwall, and New York, none with accompanying pictures. At this rate, it would take her a week to find him. His name was much too common.

What does it matter, anyway, finding him or not finding him? She would be back in the States by Monday, back to her regularly scheduled life.

Chapter Five

*Art isn't perfect. It shouldn't be. Much like life, it should
contain ragged lines or unusual colours. Unexpected shadows
and darkness you didn't see coming. Let the painting be
what it is—gloriously imperfect, sublimely real.*

A NERVOUS, EXCITED FLUTTER OCCUPIED NOELLE'S stomach
all morning. Thankful that her mother, ages ago, had taught
her to pack an outfit for every occasion, no matter where she
traveled, Noelle pulled out and ironed the only dress she'd brought,
chocolate-colored silk with a light vanilla sash. Perfect for the theater
and for tonight's dinner with Jillian. Her friend would be stylish, would
wear something perfect and gorgeous, and she wanted to be able at least
to stand in the same room with her and not be embarrassed.

On her way to London, questions swirled. *How different does Jill
look now? Will I even recognize her? And how different will I look to her?
Will we still have an easy connection in person, the same one we had on
the phone?*

Jillian's townhouse hadn't been difficult to find, though maneuvering
around the streets of London in rush hour traffic had been another
story. Mac had insisted on loaning his car to her for the journey, a
durable, compact Subaru. After some polite protests, she gave in. A taxi
seemed exorbitant and unnecessary, so she'd spent an hour this morning
practicing on the back roads of the village to get her bearings, driving
on the wrong side of the road. Thank goodness, Jill's place was on the

outskirts of London, so she hadn't been required to face traffic in the heart of the city.

Exiting the Subaru, Noelle looked at the row of pristine townhouses. A million-dollar neighborhood with million-dollar people. She wrapped her brown wool coat tighter and found the correct address then walked up four steps to the door. She pressed the bell, brushed away a stray hair, and breathed, impossibly nervous at meeting the adult version of her childhood friend. Before she could blink, the door opened wide and there stood Jillian. Familiar eyes, familiar smile, beaming with excitement.

Jill reached down, embracing Noelle, squeezing her almost to the point of discomfort. They overlapped excited greetings—"I can't believe you're here…" "You look amazing…" "It's been *so* long!"

Jill's hair had turned, or maybe had been colored, a darker shade of red than Noelle remembered, her freckles well hidden with flawless makeup. Her green eyes dazzled in the leftover evening sun, with only a few tiny crow's feet giving away her real age. She wore a stunning emerald-green sleeveless dress that gathered at her slim waist.

Jill ushered her friend inside the immaculate foyer and took her coat. The home contained all the elegance Noelle expected—marble floors, chandelier overhead, crown molding throughout. A tall, lean man probably ten years Jillian's senior, with thinning hair and a warm smile, walked in from another room. He extended his hand, and in his distinctly Welsh accent said, "I'm Gareth. Lovely to meet you."

"You as well!" Noelle replied.

Jill took Noelle's hand and guided her into the sitting room, neutral-colored and formally decorated. As a timer dinged in the kitchen, she told Noelle, "Why don't you and I have a chat while Gareth finishes up the food?"

"Drinks?" Gareth asked.

"White wine for me, darling."

"I'll have the same." Noelle followed Jillian to the generous taupe sofa. How silly to have felt so nervous about seeing her friend again.

As they sat, Jillian told Noelle about her plans for creating a high-end maternity clothing line. The year after she met Gareth, Jillian had stopped modeling and opened an exclusive clothing boutique in a ritzy part of London.

"Speaking of maternity, are you guys ever planning to..." Noelle hoped she wasn't overstepping.

"Oh, heavens, no."

Gareth chose this moment, intentionally or not, to step back into the room, quiet as a phantom, to hand the ladies their drinks then pop back into the kitchen.

Jill continued. "We quite love our freedom. We can travel, not be tied down. We're one of those odd couples content with only each other. That's enough for us. Plus, I'm not the mother type. I've always known it." Jill leaned in, her voice softer. "Though, truth be told, I think Gareth wants a little one, but he says 'no' on my behalf. To make me happy. He would make the most incredible father." She shrugged. "All right. Your turn. I want to hear more about that adorable village. What's it called, again?"

"Chilton Crosse. It really is charming."

"Is it too 'country'? I mean, is there anything to do there?"

"Well, it's a far cry from London, but it has a grocer's, some quirky shops, and a pub, and even this fancy restaurant called Chatsworth Manor on the outskirts. Really, the village is like something out of a movie. And the people are friendly. I especially like Mac, Aunt Joy's gardener. It's nice to have someone around who remembers her."

"I wish you could stay. Is it even an option, keeping the cottage?"

"Not at this point in my life. I just don't see how I could--"

A bell rang. *Another of Gareth's timers going off?* But when Jill sprang to her feet and headed toward the front entrance, Noelle realized it was the doorbell, instead.

"I'm sorry," Jill called. "Let me get this..."

Noelle set her glass back on the table as voices drifted from the front hall. A cordial exchange, perhaps someone Jill knew. A friendly postman or maybe a neighbor.

The door closed, and when Jill returned, she wasn't alone. She clung to a man's arm. He wore a dark suit with a cream-colored shirt underneath, his hair thick and wavy. He chatted with Jill as if he'd known her for years.

He stepped into the living room then glanced over at Noelle and stopped. When she recognized those dark eyes, she knew.

"Adam."

Adrenaline pulsed through her body. Even as he resumed his pace, Jill still on his arm, Noelle wasn't entirely sure he wasn't an apparition. Utterly unprepared, she willed her jelly legs to cooperate and stood to meet him.

"I can't believe it. Noelle." His smile stretched wide as he said her name. They continued to stare, the lost years hanging between them, reconciling past with present, adolescent with adult. Noelle imagined him comparing her face with the face he knew years ago, as she was doing with his now. Any trace of his gawky boyishness had disappeared.

Her words came out in a bumbling mess: "I just... you're... I mean... I can't..."

"It's unreal, isn't it?" He grinned his lopsided grin and leaned in to kiss her cheek. Then he wrapped her in a full embrace, warm and strong.

When they backed away, Jill stood next to them, smug and proud. "Do you like my little surprise? The three of us together again? After all these years gone by. I think we look fab. Not a single day older."

"Yeah. You look exactly the same." Adam stared at Noelle. "How can that be?"

Jill cleared her throat melodramatically.

"Oh, you too, Jill," he added. "Of course."

Gareth entered the room, and Jill made the introductions. The men shook hands, but Noelle couldn't pry her gaze away from Adam. Jill muttered to her husband, "Come along, Gareth. I think we should check on the food."

Alone with Adam, Noelle had no idea where to begin. She felt the need to reintroduce herself. Strange, knowing the depths of someone's soul for a brief sliver of time then being presented with this. An older version of that same soul, one she didn't recognize anymore. Even the most mundane details of his adult life were lost on her—the car he drove, the house he lived in, even his favorite music. The distance of time and age had created virtual strangers.

"So," Adam said. "How can it be thirteen years? Impossible."

Noelle followed his lead to sit on the couch, remaining a reasonable distance away as she sat down and crossed her legs. "Longer than that— fourteen? It's unbelievable."

He unbuttoned his jacket, shifting to face her. *How can he be so calm?* She was much too distracted by her own shallow breathing and the thumping in her ears. Maybe he just knew how to cover it well.

"I'm sorry to hear about your aunt passing. I read about it in the papers. So, that's what brought you here? Well, not *here,* here—to the middle of Jillian's living room—but England-here?"

Noelle nodded. "I only got word of it a few days ago. I still can't believe she's gone."

"It must be surreal, being back in England. How long are you staying?"

"I leave on Sunday. I'm trying to get her cottage ready to sell."

"It's in one of those little villages in the Cotswolds, eh?"

Noelle loved the way his accent divided up the word "little." "Yes. Chilton Crosse." She tucked a stray hair behind her ear and made herself look at him. She couldn't get over how familiar but foreign his eyes were. Same deep-set chocolate richness surrounded by new tiny wrinkles of maturity. The years had added changes she hadn't been able to witness as they appeared. She had missed out on his skinny, awkward hands transforming into the strong, defined hands of a man. Or the wild curls of hair relaxing themselves into waves. She even caught sight of a tuft of dark hair at the base of his neck that hadn't been there as a teenager.

"Chilton Crosse?" Adam said, snapping Noelle out of her daydream. "I didn't realize that's where Joy lived. It's not far from Bath, where my parents are."

Noelle remembered it well—his parents' Bath estate stood in close proximity to Gram's. "That's right," she confirmed. "Bath is about twenty miles away."

"Matter of fact, our firm just got a call this week about a possible project there."

"In Chilton Crosse?"

"Yeah, some school project. A renovation. Mother knows someone on the school board and probably gave them my name." He leaned in to add, "Truth be told, it's just her way of forcing me to visit her more often."

"Are you going to do it? The renovation, I mean." Her heart lifted at the thought.

"Not sure yet. Still need to check schedules, make some calls. But it's under serious consideration. The firm likes to do a pro bono project every year. My partner and I finished one recently, so we're on the lookout for a new one. Although this school might be quite the undertaking. From what I know, the building is a couple hundred years old. It would require mounds of research. The idea does intrigue me, though."

She recognized that gleam in his eye when it came to architecture. Even as a teenager, he loved reading books about the history of buildings. He used to say old buildings had old souls.

"So," said Adam, shifting gears. "Catch me up on things. You live in the States, yeah?"

She focused all her energies on actually making conversation with Adam—apparently *not* a figment of her imagination. "Yes. San Diego. I work in Human Resources. Nothing special."

"Married? Kids?" He asked casually, as though it didn't matter to him either way.

Noelle smoothed out her dress, buying a couple of seconds to figure out how much she wanted to tell him. She hadn't been prepared to talk about her dating history tonight, especially not with Adam Spencer. "No kids, never married. There were a couple of 'maybe' guys along the way. But they ended up being frogs instead of princes. Especially the last one. But, you know, live and learn… onward and upward."

"Hmm… clichés and platitudes. I get it. You hate that question, don't you? People poking around about your love life? Bloody rude of me."

When she started to explain, he waved her off and shook his head. "No, no, I understand. No reason to confide in me. Only one of your oldest and dearest friends sitting here. Nobody special at all."

Giggling, Noelle clasped his waving hand then released it. "Stop it. Okay. I'll tell you more." She took in a breath and tried to let down her guard. At least a few inches. "So, the last guy—Steve. A non-commitment type. 'Someday' was his favorite word. Leaving him was the smartest decision I've probably ever made."

Adam's smile disappeared. "Sorry about that. I'm a wanker for pressing you to talk."

"No, it's fine. It was a couple of years ago. I'm over it." She shrugged and looked at her lap.

"He sounds like a real bastard."

Surprised, she said, "Yes, actually. He was. He... well, he cheated on me. More than once, I found out later."

"I'll never understand men like that." Adam clenched his jaw. "No woman deserves that treatment. Especially you."

The frustration in his eyes on her behalf made the last of her jitters scurry away. She remembered this Adam so clearly, still insightful, protective, and easy to talk to. "So," she said, re-crossing her legs, "how did Jill twist your arm into coming tonight?"

He rubbed at his jaw with his hand, something he did when he sorted through details of a story, deciding which ones might be important enough to tell. "She rang me late last night, out of the blue, told me about some extra theater ticket she had and wouldn't even think about taking no for an answer. Said she had a surprise. But I never imagined it would be you."

"Good surprise?"

He tilted his head. "You already know the answer to that." His tone directed a hint of boyish charm her way. Her pulse beat faster.

"Two minutes!" Jillian called from the kitchen.

"Two minutes, eh? Right. Time for the speed round." Adam rubbed his hands together in preparation.

"My turn for questions," Noelle insisted. "So, tell me about your firm. It's in London?"

Adam ran his hand through his hair, smoothing out the waves. "Yeah. Built my own firm with a partner. Met at Oxford. We opened a year after graduation, and it's taken off. Just got a big contract on an apartment building in Chelsea. Might be hiring another couple of people next year for that."

"I'm impressed. And jealous. You've always known what you wanted to do. I remember all those sketches you made, books and books of them."

"What about you? Those sessions you had with Aunt Joy. Did you keep it up? The painting?"

"Naw. I knew oils would never pay the rent. So I went for something practical instead."

"HR sounds interesting enough."

"No, not really. I—"

"It's tiiiime." Jillian peeked around the doorframe then walked into the room with hands clasped together like a teacher about to address a class of unruly second-graders.

Adam whispered to Noelle, "Two minutes, on the dot. She's a drill sergeant." He offered a hand to help Noelle up and followed her toward the dining room, but with the buzz of his cell phone—"Sorry, I should get it"—he pivoted back to the living room.

Noelle's Adam radar had returned full force, after years gone by. During those youthful summers, she had developed an internal tracking system that pricked up, alerting her to Adam's presence anywhere in her vicinity. She knew exactly where he was without having to look directly at him. It didn't matter if he stood several feet behind her or talked to someone clear across the room. All her senses piqued, heightened, aware of him somewhere nearby. And for the first time in years, her radar clicked on again. He mumbled something into his phone, ended the call, and followed her again in time to pull out her chair at the table.

Gareth had lined the table beautifully with white bowls of vegetables—baby carrots, crisp green beans, roasted potatoes. Each of their plates already held its own guinea hen, petite and garnished with parsley.

"I can't believe it." Noelle reached for her napkin. "This was too much trouble!"

"Nonsense." Gareth shook his head modestly.

"He spoils me constantly," Jill admitted. "If he wasn't a surgeon, he would be a gourmet chef. I have a feeling he secretly wishes he had his own restaurant."

"Someday, darling. Someday." Gareth winked.

"Let's dig in!" Jill took the basket of bread from the end of the table.

They filled their plates, an occasional "Mmm" or "Wonderful," rising up as they ate, every bite as delicious as the last.

Jillian switched back into hostess mode, keeping the conversation flowing between bites. Chitchat about the boutique, Gareth's research article being published, followed by questions to Noelle about Aunt

Joy's gallery, and to Adam about his architecture firm. Nothing too heavy, nothing too personal, which helped Noelle to relax.

When everyone finished, Gareth and Adam cleared the table and brought out the coffee cups and chocolate pie. "My, we certainly have them trained," Jillian said.

"You know these modern men, Jill. Unafraid to show their feminine sides," Noelle teased.

"Just as long as you don't tell anyone," whispered Adam, handing Noelle her coffee cup.

After they'd pushed forks into the smooth pie and enjoyed a couple of bites, Jillian broke the silence. "All right, Adam Spencer. I've been good enough, but I can't stand it anymore. I'm absolutely dying of curiosity. Here you are, all evening long, and you've been utterly mum about a significant other. Girlfriend? Wife?"

As much as Jillian's bluntness jolted her, Noelle hung on Adam's pause as he formed his answer.

He wiped the corner of his mouth with his napkin and cleared his throat, looking around the table. "Well, yes. There is someone, actually. Her name is Laurel. She's the daughter of a client. We've known each other almost three years, and things have... progressed. We're engaged, in fact. As of last week."

Noelle's heart caught in her chest. Engaged.

Stillness lingered before the wave of congratulations. Gareth shook Adam's hand across the table while Jillian rushed over to hug his neck. "Oh darling, that's wonderful. I'm pleased for you." To Noelle's relief, Jill didn't beg every last detail of the proposal. "Oh, blast! Look at the time. I'm afraid we should be going. We want to be in our seats before the curtain rises. And we have to put away all that glorious food."

Noelle had forgotten all about the theater. Adam's abrupt announcement had caused a dramatic crack in her comfort level, and she struggled to maintain her composure as she helped Jill stack and gather plates. At least it gave her something to do. When she and Jill stood alone at the sink, Jill said, "Engaged? Can you believe it?"

"Quite a surprise."

"Are you all right?"

Noelle studied her face then offered her best attempt at a convincing smile. "It's been an eventful evening."

"Are you furious with me for my little surprise? Bringing Adam here without telling you? I thought it would be a harmless bit of fun."

"No. No, I'm not mad." She didn't know what she was at the moment.

Jillian wrapped her arm around Noelle's waist in a side hug. Noelle reciprocated then found the bathroom to freshen up before the show. And to summon the strength to push through the next leg of the evening.

Chapter Six

The canvas is forgiving. If you make a mistake, if you regret a colour choice or texture, erase it with your rag and start again. If you still can't get it right, leave it alone and work around it. Use it. Make it into something it wasn't supposed to be.

D URING THE BRIEF DRIVE TO the West End, Gareth and Jillian sat up front, with Adam and Noelle in the backseat. Jillian made small talk, something about the state of London theater, while Noelle peered out the window at the dark sky, wishing she could step out of the car at the next stoplight and go home. Last night, she hadn't known what accepting Jillian's invitation would entail— an unexpected reunion, followed by a crushing bit of news, all in less than two hours' time. Emotional whiplash.

When they arrived at the theater, the bustle of finding parking, producing tickets, wading through the crowd, and looking for seats all happened in a thirty-minute rush. They were seeing *The Phantom of the Opera*. On any other occasion, Noelle would have been ecstatic. She'd never seen *Phantom* before. But tonight, it only meant she'd have to live publicly with her discomfort for another three hours.

With only five minutes to spare, Gareth led them to their velvety crimson movie-theater-style chairs, only four rows from the stage. Noelle, flipping through the program, sat between Jillian and Adam. Ten pages of colorful ads shouted at her in bold print to "Visit Chez Gerard for a fine dining experience" and to let her know that "the Funky

Buddha is *the* place to be." Finding the program notes, Noelle pretended the lengthy cast list fascinated her as she secretly begged for the curtain to hurry up and rise.

Adam produced a new pack of gum from his pocket, opened it, and offered it to Noelle.

"Thanks." She didn't really like gum, and she'd have to chew it all night or find a discreet place to spit it out later. Still, she wanted to be polite. So she took it.

Finally, the orchestra played the introductory notes. She watched the actors on stage in their elaborate costumes, singing about the dark side of love, and wished they would feed her some answers along with their lines. She wanted to stand up and ask the cast, *Why is our timing so horrible? Why was I brought here to see Adam in the first place? To sit next to him, knowing again that we have no chance anyway?*

Maybe it would have stung less if Adam had told her right away. If only he had looked her straight in the eye that very first moment, shaken her hand, and immediately said, "Hi, Noelle, nice to see you again, I'm happily engaged." Maybe if he'd done that, she wouldn't have spent the next hour falling for him again, allowing the old feelings to resurface so effortlessly, forgetting completely that she was leaving the country in two days anyway. But she *had* fallen, and because of that, she had to spend the next few hours doing damage control on her emotions.

Gradually, note by note, the characters and story entranced her, and she escaped into the aching beauty of the music and the longing of the Phantom. She related to it, wanting so desperately someone you would never have. Could never have.

As tears rolled down during the final song, Noelle sensed the weight of Adam's stare. He touched her arm, and in the soft glow of the stage lights, his eyes squinted with concern. He gave a hint of a comforting smile then offered his handkerchief. Noelle took it with a thankful smile and dabbed her tears away.

Everyone buzzed about the *Phantom* during the brief ride back to Jillian's. Overlapping comments about the play, promises to meet up again, thanks to Jillian for the invitation and to Gareth for the elaborate meal. As the car pulled into a spot in front of their townhouse, Noelle folded Adam's handkerchief and passed it over to him.

"Keep it," he whispered. He shifted toward her in his seat, not concerned that Jill and Gareth were already exiting the car. "Are you okay?"

"Yeah. I guess the music really got to me."

"It's a powerful story. One of those that can circle in your head for days afterward."

"I agree."

As they got out, Jillian begged Noelle to stay overnight, not drive back to the village at such a late hour. She kindly refused with the very legitimate excuse of having a thousand things still to do before her flight. She didn't tell Jill how exhausted the evening had rendered her. And how desperately she needed to be alone with her scattered thoughts.

Taking her cue, Adam said a polite "no" to a nightcap. He needed to get back home. Noelle assumed "home" meant "Laurel."

Adam walked Noelle to her car and opened the door. "It was incredible, seeing you again." As he reached down for a hug, Noelle had to stand on tiptoes to reciprocate. She smelled the new leather of his jacket as she backed away. "I wish you didn't have to get back to the States yet. I wanted more time to catch up."

"Me too," she lied. Catching up only would have made things more painful. Leaving soon was best.

Adam leaned against the doorframe. "Is someone watching for you?"

"No, but I'll call Jillian when I get there. And I've got a cell phone. I'll be fine."

"Okay. So. Take care of yourself."

Noelle wondered what they would've done with this final moment if he hadn't been engaged. Exchanged cell numbers and email addresses, kept in touch an ocean away with the ease of a few clicks. But in the end, a few text messages wouldn't amount to anything substantive. They lived separate lives in separate places.

Noelle stepped inside the car, careful to tuck in her long coat before Adam closed the door. She started the car and waved good-bye. Turning the corner, she drove with one hand, clutched the handkerchief with the other, and dealt with the mess going on inside. Let all the questions have their way.

What if Mr. Lester's letter had reached me two weeks ago? What if Adam and I had reunited before *he got engaged? Would it have mattered?*

She traveled further back. *What if that horseback ride to the river during our final summer had ended differently? What if that one missed opportunity had determined every other moment after that?*

"Damn," she whispered through a sob.

When Noelle reached the edge of London and the traffic had cleared, with nothing but an open country road toward the Cotswolds, she put her mind on autopilot and revisited that day at the river. She remembered the unusually sweltering August sun and how she'd taken advantage of the rare English rays to do some tanning. Half-asleep on a blanket with the sun beating down, she laid in her pink bikini near the fountain in Gram's garden.

"You need a good dunk in the river."

Noelle twitched, hearing Adam's voice, and she shielded her eyes to see him standing in front of her, hands rubbing together in preparation. He only wore swim trunks and sandals. His chest had filled out that summer with some definition, some muscle. She'd been staring too long and looked away. "Now?"

"Yeah—C'mon. Gorgeous day for a ride and a swim."

The thought of a sparkling body of water sounded more appealing than broiling under a hot sun, so she got up and slipped into her jean shorts.

The Avon River ran through Bath. The year before, Adam and Noelle had found a perfect, tranquil spot in a bend of it, enormous trees with rustling leaves and plenty of room at the water's edge to have an elaborate picnic or a long nap after a swim. Tourists sometimes took specified trails along the river but only occasionally veered from it to interfere with Adam and Noelle's "place." Most of the time, they could swim uninterrupted.

Saddling up Ginger and Spice, the only two horses in Gram's stables, they galloped the two miles to the river bend and tied the horses to a tree. Noelle adored riding, ever since Adam had taught her two years before. It took him a month to convince her she would be safe with him and with the horse. But once he coaxed her along and rode behind her in the saddle, once he taught her how to hold the reins and connect with the horse, she fell in love with riding, with the freedom of the powerful hooves beating underneath, taking her away.

The river sparkled and winked in the sun and invited them to come in. Removing her shorts again, Noelle waded in, skimming the top of the tepid water with her fingertips. Adam splashed past her with a dramatic dive.

"Show off!" she yelled, splashing him back. They spent the next hour drifting lazily, talking and soaking up a beautiful day. "So, are you ready for Oxford? Or, I guess the better question—is Oxford ready for you?" Noelle had asked with a grin, letting the water lap up to her neck as she paddled beside him. As they drifted toward the river's edge, her toes could almost touch the bottom.

Despite being the same age, newly seventeen, Noelle would be starting her senior year of high school in the fall, while Adam would start college. Adam had once teased her that because British students sometimes graduated earlier, they were smarter than American students were.

"Yeah. I think so. I'm checking out the housing next week. Move-in is the week after."

"I want to go to college. I hate high school," she pouted.

"You can hold out one more year. Did you get the Oxford applications yet?"

"Yeah—yesterday. I'll fill them out on the plane. It'll give me something to do. I can't wait to get out and live on my own." She thought ahead to what the following year at home would hold for her, and whether her mother's recent marriage to "Tom" would even last the summer. Likely not.

She shifted to float on her back, using Adam's shoulder to steady herself. But he tensed up and gasped loudly, pointing beside her in the river. "Snake!"

Noelle screamed a raw, high-pitched screech, her body jerking and splashing to an upright position as she jumped into Adam's arms for safety. "Where? *Where?*" She scanned the water for an enormous, slithering reptile swimming toward them, jaws open.

Adam's chest rose and fell in quick pants, and he suppressed a smile. Noelle shoved him away in the water. "You wanker! You scared me to death!"

His laughter echoed throughout the riverbed nearly as loudly as her scream had. Her senses still overly acute from the empty threat of a snake, she lunged at Adam playfully, pushing him down into the water. His dark curls disappeared then bobbed up again as he emerged, still laughing, to wipe his dripping face with both hands. He returned the favor. Expecting it, she shut her eyes just in time and came up smiling too, rubbing her eyes clear of water.

When she opened her eyes, Adam placed his hands around her waist, drawing her in close to him. They floated, face-to-face, breathing heavily, water dripping from their eyelashes down their cheeks. He'd stopped laughing. She had never seen that expression on his face. Serious, focused, with no hint of sarcasm or playfulness. His gaze drifted down to her lips then back to her eyes. Noelle swallowed and blinked, unsure of what to do. Or what he would do. She didn't try to wriggle out of his grasp, but part of her wanted to. The look in his eyes made her almost as nervous as the idea of an approaching snake.

It happened in slow motion. His lips parted, and he leaned in, closed his eyes. His lips brushed hers, but a shrill whinny from one of the horses startled her. She flinched in Adam's arms and looked toward the shoreline. A group of riders had pulled up beside the tree where Ginger and Spice were tied.

"'Scuse me," one of them yelled in a Texas accent. "Mind if we park awhile?"

Adam released Noelle gently and yelled back, "No, go ahead," then drifted away from her.

They waded back to shore in silence, Noelle slogging her hands and feet as though weights had been attached. She wanted to go back, replay the moment without the riders, and find out what would've happened without their horribly timed interruption. She would never know if Adam would have backed away at the last moment, joking around. Or if they would have gone through with the kiss she'd dreamed about so many times. It might have changed everything.

The moment they reached the estate to return the horses to their stalls, Adam hopped into his car with a hasty good-bye. Surely, an actual kiss would have been less damaging to their friendship than an almost-kiss, than never knowing. That night, Noelle cried into her pillow, analyzing the afternoon in her head, wondering if they would ever get a second opportunity at a kiss or if they had just spent their one and only chance.

Two weeks later, ending her final summer in England, Noelle boarded a plane for the States, leaving part of her broken heart in England. She never did make it to Oxford, never resolved her questions.

Staring through her headlights at the road, Noelle wanted to know if Adam remembered that day at the river, whether he recalled it with the same clarity or perspective. Even so, it didn't matter anymore. Adam was engaged. Spoken for. Tonight, for a few glorious moments, just as in that river, a potential moment, an almost "something," had been interrupted. But more heartbreaking than the first time.

Chapter Seven

Painting is an act of discovery. Let the brush take you where it leads. Don't be afraid to lose control a little, to see what's around the corner. You might end up someplace magical, a place you never would have dreamt of on your own.

FINISHED. NOTHING ELSE TO DO.

Saturday evening and Noelle had just taken a long, careful tour through the cottage, viewing every detail through a realtor's eyes, preparing it to be show-ready. Mac had seamlessly patched and painted a few of the cracked ceiling spots upstairs, along with stopping a leaky faucet, re-grouting the entire kitchen back splash, and cleaning out the cast iron stove. Noelle had dusted every inch of the cottage, sorted through boxes and bookshelves, and given or thrown away anything she couldn't use. All the furniture would stay with the house, and Mac would give several items to people in the village who needed them. She'd have her own boxes shipped to the States next week.

With all the sorting and cleaning she'd done, Noelle had expected to find some secrets along the way, but nothing appeared out of the ordinary. She entered the kitchen and smiled, seeing everything polished and gleaming. The countertops, the Aga, the cupboards, all ready for their close-up. She'd tried to clear out any clutter or unnecessary items from the surfaces, but in the corner near the toaster, she spotted a ceramic dish she'd meant to put away. Heart-shaped and topped with a lid Aunt Joy had probably painted. The two dancing marigolds held

Joy's characteristic offbeat perspective. Whimsical but earnest. Too tired to make yet another trip upstairs to put the heart into her suitcase along with a few other items she couldn't bear to part with, Noelle made a mental note to retrieve the dish tomorrow.

Tomorrow. She couldn't believe she would say good-bye to England so soon. Her San Diego life seemed so far away, and not just physically. In five short days, England became a second home. Seeing Jill again, especially, had thrust her back to the past, but even more so, seeing Adam. Her insane schedule today, though, had forced his image away. She buried herself in all the too-much-to-do and let yesterday be yesterday. She would leave on a plane tomorrow, leave Adam behind. Best to put an ocean between them again. As it should be.

Also in these brief days, Noelle had immersed herself in the village, in Aunt Joy's cottage. She knew every crack, every corner. Well, except for that locked room. All her cleaning and moving, and still no luck finding the blasted key. She hated the idea of ruining a perfectly good door unless she absolutely had to. But as a last resort, she would have Mac bust the lock tomorrow morning before her flight. Surely, with his handyman skills, he would find a way to replace it artfully.

Rain tapped against the window. Noelle took her jacket from the chair and wandered toward the back door, suddenly desperate for the solace of nature. Too much time indoors had made her forget a world existed outside, a world she craved as she took her first step out into the twilight. The rain had coated the entire garden in a beautiful, glossy sheen and filled it with color. Even the bark of the trees had darkened, their trunks more vivid and defined with the rain dripping down them. Several leaves on two trees had already changed a stunning shade of autumn yellow. Noelle breathed in the garden's dewy, sweet smell. An inexplicable sadness hovered as she thought about leaving this part of England behind. Of not being able to stay, to watch all the trees eventually turn, one by one.

A soft meow rose up from a nearby fern, and Noelle squinted at a ball of fur hunched to escape the rain. She parted the fronds, barely able to keep her head covered by the awning of the porch. The drenched cat blinked its glowing green eyes and meowed at her again.

"C'mere, Kitty. Don't be afraid."

The cat had no intention of biting her, but it wouldn't come out by itself. She thrust her hands deeper and picked it up underneath its limp, bony shoulders. Water doused the top of Noelle's head, but she didn't care as she cradled the frightened cat and stroked its wet fur. The dark gray coat reminded her of a cat she had as a child, Chester. He slept at the end of her bed every night.

"I've seen you around the village."

The cat trembled in her arms.

"It's all right. You're safe."

"Looks like you've made a new friend." Mac approached from the other side of the porch, wearing a hooded jacket, slick with rain.

"Hi, I didn't see you there. Yes, he's a timid little thing."

Mac rubbed under the cat's chin. "A stray. I've seen him at Mr. Bentley's, begging for samples. But he seems to have found a home here."

"I wish I could take him back to San Diego."

"So it's tomorrow, then?"

"Tomorrow it is."

"I'm finished with the shed. Everything else is in order. Unless you can think of something we've missed?"

"I can't think of anything. Oh, except for the room upstairs. I still can't find the stupid key. I'm too tired to mess with it tonight. Would you mind dropping by tomorrow morning to figure out a way to open it?"

"Aye, lass. No trouble."

"Maybe you could bust the lock. I think we'll have just enough time to assess the room and clear out whatever's there before my flight leaves. I'm sure it's just an old storage room. If we're lucky, maybe it's even empty."

The cat trembled again.

"Thank you, Mac—for all your help. I couldn't have done any of this without you."

"'Twas nothing, lass. I wanted to do it."

"Why don't you come in for a minute? I'll make you some tea. Let's get out of this cold rain."

"Aye, that would be grand."

Inside, Noelle wrapped the cat in a flowered tea towel she'd planned to pack, handing the bundle gingerly over to Mac as though offering him a newborn. She'd kept the essentials for tea still handy, knowing she'd have at least a cup tonight and one in the morning, and drew out two cups and saucers then filled the small kettle.

"Have you considered staying?" Mac shifted the sleeping animal in his arms. The cat meowed his protest and closed his eyes again. "You do have a cottage. In pristine shape."

"I can't deny I've let the idea flit through my mind once or twice. I love it here." She leaned against the counter. "But I just can't. Not in reality. I mean, my life is in California. I have a job, and friends, a house. And nothing to keep me here. I'd be crazy to consider staying. Or barmy, as you might say."

"A lot of good decisions seem barmy on the surface. Sometimes, those are the best decisions."

The kettle whistled behind her, and she took it off the burner. She poured two mugs of tea and brought them to the table, removing the cat from Mac's arms so he could have a free hand to drink. The cat purred from deep within the towel as she sat down.

"Mac, do you have any regrets?"

"What sort?"

She stroked the cat's nose. "I don't know. In life, in your past..."

"Aye."

She immediately wanted to know what they were, but Mac probably wasn't going to be specific.

"'Tis human," he continued, "to have regrets. And people who tell you otherwise are lying to themselves."

"You're a very wise man, Mac MacDonald."

He gave as close to a half-grin as she'd ever seen and shook his head. "Nay, lass. I've lived a long, long time. Any wisdom comes with experience." He finished off his tea then pushed back his chair. "Thanks for this. Nice to have a bit of a chat now and again. What are you planning to do with him?" Mac pointed toward the tea towel.

"Not sure. I'll keep him here tonight, out of the rain. Maybe I can find a willing prospect tomorrow. Would you mind putting the word out for me, see if anyone might take him?"

"Aye. I might know a couple o' folk who would consider it. See you early tomorrow." He let himself out the back door, and Noelle looked down at the sleeping cat purring in her arms. His eyes opened to green slits.

"Well, I can't just hold you all night, can I?" She balanced him in her lap to rub his fur dry. He swatted at her hand with his free paw.

She placed him gently on the tiled floor, and he wandered around his surroundings, rubbing against the table leg then her leg.

"Now. What shall we have for dinner?"

Noelle, padding down the hallway in her bare feet, had to make one quick stop before bed—turn off the table lamp in the hall outside the bedroom. She had just changed into her new lilac flannel pajamas, the ones she'd bought yesterday at Mrs. Bennett's boutique.

She curled her hand under the lampshade to click off the light and paused. A few feet away in angular shadows stood the door—that enigmatic, imposing, frustratingly locked door. Even with the craziness of the past few days, she'd had time to wonder what her aunt had hidden, what dark, foreboding secret she had locked away.

Staring ahead, nearly boring a hole in the door, Noelle remembered something. She'd read her aunt's final letter more than once since Mr. Lester had given it to her, and something always nagged at her. Aunt Joy was trying to prompt her, nudge her in a certain direction. Give her clues to "surprises lurking about" and permission to reveal her "secrets" to the world. Joy *wanted* Noelle to find her secrets, to look inside that room. Wanted her to make an effort to open that door.

On a whim, Noelle marched downstairs. Her new friend meowed at her from behind. He refused to follow and sat on his haunches at the top step, waiting.

Noelle experienced an odd premonition of sorts, a strong urge to move, go downstairs, and let her body lead her in the right direction. Something was taking her to a specific place. To the kitchen. That heart-shaped box.

The heart of me. That's what the letter had said. She breathed faster as she approached the counter and reached for the ceramic box. She cupped her hand over the painted lid to lift it and peek inside.

A petite silver key, tarnished with age. Noelle gasped. It couldn't be so easy. Under her nose the whole time. Surely, the key fit some random closet or maybe the shed. But not that upstairs room.

Still, she walked back up with the key to where the cat sat, meowing, staring toward the locked door as though he sensed something, too.

Noelle tiptoed along the hall like a character in a Hitchcock film, alone, late at night, half-expecting to find something gruesome. She almost heard creepy music as she swallowed her nerves and tried the key. She inserted it into the keyhole and rotated it with an easy click.

She cracked open the door and groped for a light switch on the wall. Finding it, she took the first step inside and breathed in something pungent, something familiar. Noelle's eyes confirmed her suspicions as they roamed the entire space.

Paintings. Dozens upon dozens of them leaning haphazardly against every wall, everywhere she turned. Among them, jumbles of brushes and rags. Her aunt's own personal artistic paradise. The pulse of the room thumped in her ears as she walked into the middle of it, open-mouthed. For years, everyone had assumed that just because her aunt had hidden away, her talent had been stagnant. That she had stopped painting. But this room proved otherwise.

Noelle had never seen any of these paintings before. They seemed clustered together into specific themes—darker paintings, modern paintings, nature paintings, even portraits. All of them stunning. All of them brilliant. Rich, vibrant colors, bold textures, dark themes. Aunt Joy hadn't lost her touch, hadn't given up her craft. If anything, she had honed her talent into something indescribably beautiful and thoughtful. Joy had wanted the world to see her progress, post mortem. Her best work.

Viewing the rest of the room, Noelle noticed the only piece of furniture, an old rocking chair with an easel standing near the window, presumably to catch the incoming sunlight. A half-finished painting perched on the easel, waiting for its owner to return.

Noelle moved closer and stared at the incomplete canvas, a landscape, and tears stung her eyes. She wondered if Aunt Joy knew she would never complete it. Standing in the middle of what art critics with dollar signs dancing in their eyes would surely deem a treasure trove, Noelle looked at the canvas and only saw her aunt. The woman who had taught her to paint, who had given her advice about life, shown her more interest during those English summers than even her own mother. In the past week, Noelle hadn't taken a true opportunity to mourn, to say good-bye to Aunt Joy. The weight of her own grief pressed down on her shoulders as she scanned the canvas, pictured her aunt's final brushstrokes.

Blinking away tears, she noticed a cluster of sheep in the bottom corner of the canvas. It sparked a memory. When she was fourteen, Noelle had begged and begged her aunt to teach her how to paint. Joy's answer for days had been, "I'll consider it." And just when Noelle had nearly given up begging, Aunt Joy presented her with her very own set of oils. Noelle could see every detail now, the caramel-colored wooden box with a bright golden clasp, the crinkled covers of the metal paint tubes inside. Aunt Joy asked Noelle what she most wanted to paint, and she'd answered without hesitation, "Sheep." She'd been obsessed with them that year—their soft wool, their noisy bleats—and even wanted to take one back to the States with her as a pet.

"Sheep it is!" her aunt had responded with a cigarette-coated laugh.

That afternoon, Aunt Joy and Noelle had worked for hours without stopping, until the light grew too poor to continue. And by the end of the day, Noelle had painted in the dead center of an overly bright green pasture a single sheep, enormous in scale, with an awkward boxy build and offset eyes. But her aunt had proclaimed it the most beautiful sheep she had ever seen, and Noelle had believed her. They painted every summer after that. Noelle still heard the swishy brushstrokes, saw the easels side-by-side in the garden, smelled the blueberry scones Gram baked almost every day to set silently on a tray between them.

And during those lessons, Joy issued wise nuggets of advice, honed by years and years of artistic experience. Wisdom about technique, perspective, and texture—and life. Noelle always heard the message between the lines, even at a young age, and knew Joy was talking about more than just a paintbrush or canvas. Noelle always thought Joy should write down her bits of artistic wisdom and maybe publish them someday.

After those summers, Noelle had stopped painting. She wasn't sure why. Perhaps life got in the way, and more important things like college, friends, and jobs trumped it. Or perhaps the absence of England, the absence of Joy, her mentor, made her feel too insecure to pursue it. But standing here in Joy's secret room, Noelle's senses filling with the beauty of art, she longed for it again.

She stroked the edge of the unfinished painting, tears splashing down both cheeks as she smiled through them. "Thank you, Aunt Joy," she whispered to the canvas. "For trusting me with your secret. And for all those summers. I wish I could've had more of them with you."

A sudden clatter yanked her attention to the other side of the room. The blur of a gray tail scampered away from a knocked-over can.

"Silly cat." She wiped tears away with her pajama sleeve. "There aren't any ghosts in here. Nothing to be afraid of."

She looked around at the paintings, realizing the massive job in front of her. She needed to do some sort of inventory but didn't know where to start. The darker paintings drew her eye first, being so unusual. She'd only known Aunt Joy to paint peaceful Cotswold landscapes, with perhaps a cottage or church in the background. Their serenity had made her famous in the first place.

In fact, the Duchess of York spotted one of Aunt Joy's landscapes in a gallery on a trip to Bath many years ago and had fallen in love with it, purchasing it along with two others. She'd hung one at Buckingham Palace and the two others at her private residence. Her husband had even commissioned one of Joy's paintings for the Duchess's birthday the following month. When the press got wind of it, they proclaimed Aunt Joy a "fresh, new talent, worthy of the royal seal of approval." From that moment on, prestigious art magazines heralded her as *the* Cotswold artist in residence, and the cost of her paintings skyrocketed tenfold.

Kneeling on the dusty floor, Noelle studied one of the dark paintings, a storm with a stranded boat in the middle of a vast ocean, and noticed the rich textures of the black skies. Sure, the colors made the painting dark. But so did the stark tone. The forlorn sensation of being lost and alone on a wide body of water with no help, no hope in sight. Had Aunt Joy not locked the painting up in her cottage, Noelle might not have been convinced she was the artist. But Noelle looked at the right-hand corner to find the proof—*JV*.

Noelle pictured the lawyers, the gallery owners, the art critics, all of them salivating to get their hands on these new treasures. But her aunt had given Noelle permission to do as she wished. Even one of the paintings sold would surely save the gallery. She debated whether she should sell all the rest or save a couple of the paintings as her own. Maybe even hang one in the Chilton Crosse gallery. Part of her didn't want to touch anything. She wanted to preserve the room, remember Aunt Joy in her element, and keep a sort of museum dedicated to the creative process. The thought of someone turning the space into a boring guest room with stiff-backed chairs and a floral comforter made her cringe.

Tonight, she needed to catalog the paintings on her own. Others would do that more formally, more officially. But taking her own informal inventory was her way of maintaining some sort of control before the madness began.

She scurried to the master bedroom, where the cat had stretched out on her bed.

Trying not to startle him, she found her cell phone for taking pictures then a note pad and pen from the desk drawer, and walked back to the art room, eager to start. It promised to be a very long night. She couldn't even think about what this would mean for her plane trip tomorrow, how she could possibly still make it in time. But she would figure it out somehow. The paintings took priority.

Something rubbed at her cheek over and over and over, something warm, wet, and scratchy. Noelle opened her eyes to see a gray blob hovering over her face. Flinching, she realized it was the cat, licking her awake.

She scratched behind its ears and rose onto her elbows. The hard floor had created a crick in her neck. So it hadn't been a dream. The paintings surrounded her in better order than before, thanks to hours of hard work. But they still looked a bit lost, waiting to find a home on some important person's wall.

The cat sauntered in a broad circle around her, his shoulder blades rising and falling in perfect fluidity. "What time is it?" she asked and sprang to her feet, the crick reminding her to slow down. A faint knock came from downstairs, and she remembered Mac had promised to help her with the now unlocked door.

"C'mon, Kitty. We've got something to show him!" She scooped him up, still in her flannel pajamas, and headed downstairs as if it was Christmas morning.

She didn't tell Mac about the discovery, only that she'd found the key last night and had unlocked the Mystery Door. A couple of minutes later, she and Mac stood together in the center of the room, motionless, silent, absorbing everything. She watched his stoic expression, wanting so badly to read his thoughts.

"Incredible," he finally offered.

"Did you have any clue?" she asked him. "That Aunt Joy was still painting?"

"Nay. I knew she spent a good bit o' time upstairs, doing something. But I never imagined this." His work boots clunked on the floorboards as he walked in a slow circle to stare at certain paintings, pausing every so often and scratching at his stubbly chin. "Incredible," he said again and met her back in the center of the room. "Now what?"

"Well, I've made a list of all the paintings, tried to put them in some sort of order. I suppose the lawyer and probably Frank will want to see them next, do their own cataloging."

"This saves the gallery, aye?"

"Yes! Even one of them would bring in probably 30,000 pounds. Or more, considering the circumstances. But I'm certainly no art dealer. We can bring Frank in for that. He can tell us more."

"He'll be gobsmacked for sure."

Noelle pictured Frank's face, astonished, and she smiled. "Yep, 'gobsmacked' is exactly what he'll be."

When Frank did arrive, she didn't tell him what to expect and let him enter the room ahead of her. When he stopped short in the doorway, Noelle nearly bumped into him. She nudged him forward, and his lead feet obeyed. She recognized all the signs of gobsmacked-ness right away.

"I can't believe it," he whispered, his mouth agape as he swiveled to look all around the room.

"I know." Noelle clasped her hands behind her back, loving his reaction already.

He reached out to touch one and snapped his hand back as though the painting had bitten him. "No, really. I can't *believe* it."

"I know."

He sidestepped along the room, squatting and pausing in front of every grouping to look more closely. Then he returned to the center of the room and wrapped his long arms around her. "Do you realize what this means? We're saved!"

"It appears so," she said, her words muffled into his shirt.

"Sorry." He backed away and threaded his fingers together. "Do you know what else this means?"

"What?"

"You, my dear, are a very wealthy woman. In fact, the wealthiest woman in the village. Maybe even the whole of the Cotswolds!"

"I wouldn't go that far," she said, already uncomfortable with the idea of great wealth. She still couldn't wrap her brain around any of it.

Frank gasped. "Look at that! I missed this one!" He walked to the easel in the corner. "Amazing. Her final painting. The most valuable of all, even unfinished."

"That one's not for sale," Noelle said. "I'm keeping it."

Frank nodded. "As well you should." He pointed at the stormy pictures. "I still can't believe how dark these are. They don't look anything like her other work."

"I agree. I wonder why."

"I'm not sure. Artists often go through dark periods that reflect in their work. But I never thought of your aunt as dark. Quirky and eccentric, absolutely. But dark? I wonder what happened to make her paint these." He looked at Noelle squarely. "What a gift she's given you, beyond the grave. I still can't believe it."

"I know. Neither can I."

Chapter Eight

Be bold in your paintings—with colours, with technique. Take risks.
Because when you take the easy path, the expected one, your art
suffers. And your work will always be mediocre and uninspired.

CALLING MR. LESTER HAD BEEN the easy part. He'd been as unemotional as she'd expected about the paintings, his voice holding almost no surprise. *How can that be?* She'd heard of stiff upper lips, but Mr. Lester was ridiculous.

Still, he'd been terribly helpful. He'd given her tips about the first steps to take, as well as some valuable advice to chew on. He told her Sotheby's in London would be the best venue for a high-profile auction of all the paintings. Also, he told her to be cautious about spreading the word too early, lest the media get hold of the information and stalk her at the cottage. Plus, she had to consider security issues, with all that valuable artwork stored inside the upper room. Before saying good-bye, Mr. Lester promised to stop by the cottage tomorrow on his way to Bath, with "new decisions" to be made and more paperwork to sign.

Calling Dan had been the not-so-easy part. She translated the time zone in her head—8:00 p.m. in England meant noon, San Diego time. She had already missed her flight because of the paintings. Dan would not be happy.

"Hello?" His voice sounded flat, rather than his normal level of perturbed. Maybe a good sign.

"Hi, it's Noelle."

"You're back?"

"Err... no, I'm still in England."

Silence.

"Let me explain, Dan. There's been a new development. An amazing one. I'm actually not supposed to tell anyone, but you need to know. My aunt—she was this famous artist in England—well, last night I discovered these paintings she did. Stacks and stacks of them. She painted them during her reclusive period, so nobody even knew they existed. I found them late last night in the cottage. Can you believe it?"

More silence.

"Dan, I need a couple more days at the very least. There are important legal issues that have to be sorted out. It's beyond my control, really. But I can still get Desha to cover—"

"No."

"What do you mean?"

"No, you can't have a couple more days. Impossible. I need you here. Tomorrow."

Noelle's skin flushed hot. She didn't like constantly having to beg. It had become humiliating. Still, she stayed calm, rational, took a couple of measured breaths. "Dan, I don't think you understand. These paintings are valuable. They're worth thousands, maybe even hundreds of thousands. This changes everything. Don't you see that?"

"All I see is that I ended up giving you nearly a week at the drop of a hat to deal with the loss in your family. That's more than most people get. And yours was a distant relative you hadn't seen in over a decade, not even a parent or a sibling."

Noelle's mouth dropped open at his callousness. She knew exactly where the conversation was headed.

"Bottom line, Noelle, how important is your job to you? Paintings or no paintings, you have a choice to make. If you're not at the office first thing tomorrow morning—"

"Then what?"

"Don't come back at all."

An odd calm descended. "All right," she said. "Then I won't."

She clicked off her cell and tossed it onto the sofa. Proud, surprised. She had imagined that moment a few dozen times in her mind, but it had always been just a fantasy, hanging up on Dan, cutting ties with him once and for all. She never actually thought she'd have the guts to quit on a whim. She thought of him now, stunned by her call, scrambling to cover her appointments, her meetings, her deadlines. Served him right.

The weight of the snap decision hit her all at once, and the calmness dissipated. She'd been part of that company her entire adult life. At the very least, that job had given her a sense of constancy and security for the past ten years. She'd made friendships there, had business connections. In fact, still had employees who depended on her. *Am I insane? Or have I finally come to my senses?*

It took several minutes of pacing, of fidgeting, of going over the conversation again and again before she finally digested everything. But once she accepted Dan would not be calling back, begging her to return, she realized the freedom she'd been given. Freedom not only from Dan but also from the incessant workload, from employees, from paperwork, from everything.

Her future rolled out in front of her, entirely blank. No agenda, no schedule. No phone calls to return or deadlines to meet. No interviews with potential employees droning on about irrelevant details: how many dogs they had or how their daughter had just gotten divorced. No mandatory meetings with bad coffee. And no more Dan. Suddenly, the time on her hands belonged solely to her. Time to think about her life, figure things out. Time to explore more of England, stay as long as she liked.

Those paintings *had* changed everything. They'd given her sudden freedom. Freedom she didn't even realize she had been craving.

Later that evening, filled to the brim with tea and scones from the bakery, she pushed her feet beneath the soft sheets and reached for her dog-eared copy of *Pride and Prejudice*. A flash of gray from the floor to the bed startled her.

"Don't *do* that!" she told the cat. But he rubbed against her arm, demanding her attention and making her chuckle. "I'm sorry. C'mere, little man."

As he curled up and laid his back against her, she knew he belonged with her. Especially considering that Mac still hadn't found anyone to take him off her hands, and that, at least for the foreseeable future, the cottage would be her home, she decided to keep him.

She played with his swishy tail. "Is this your new home?" she asked, and he meowed. Glancing at her Jane Austen novel, she told him, "I should call you Mr. Darcy. What do you think?"

He licked his front paw, absorbed in his own activity, completely ignoring her. A snobby, aloof, temperamental English cat. Mr. Darcy it was.

Three days after finding the paintings, Noelle sat with Frank and celebrated over a pint. Joe had managed to save the fireside table for them at peak lunch hour and even offered to bring them complimentary chocolate cakes. By now, the entire village knew about Noelle's "find," though she'd tried to keep it a secret. But once Mrs. Pickering found out, all was lost. Noelle pictured her going door-to-door, hunched shoulders, smarmy grin, cupping her hand to her mouth and whispering into each ear, "Did you hear the news?"

However the news broke in the village, Noelle couldn't be angry, because everything that needed to take place already had, like a rapid but controlled blaze—phone calls made, papers signed, brainstorming done. Noelle had lost track of all the emails, calls, and faxes she'd exchanged with lawyers, art dealers, and the bigwigs at Sotheby's since Sunday. Ironically, it had taken up more time than a full-time job.

Immediately after quitting her job, Noelle had scrutinized each painting with Frank, making important decisions before others tried to make them on their behalf. Of the fifty-three paintings, all grouped into particular sets, Noelle would keep six of them. Three of Frank's choosing would hang permanently in the village gallery. They would loan eight to various museums on a rotating basis. Two were set aside for immediate sale, hopefully bringing in more than enough money to save the art gallery and ensure its future solvency. Two Sotheby's vans had carried off the rest of the paintings to London in the middle of the night. Mr. Lester had arranged that with one phone call. The Sotheby's people had absolutely salivated at a special auction of Joy Valentine's secret paintings. The date was already set. Valentine's Day.

"I can't wait anymore." Frank set down his lager and rubbed the tips of his fingers on a napkin.

"More news? Okay, what have you not been telling me?" Noelle asked, unprepared for more surprises. Their meeting was only supposed to be for a celebratory drink, not business. In fact, she'd rather hoped not to discuss paintings, auctions, or sales figures for at least the next half hour.

"Well, remember Mr. Durante? From the gallery in London?"

"I think so. We've talked about so many curators, I think I've lost track."

"He was my first choice, remember? The one who acted the least interested, but I knew he was faking?"

Frank had called all his art-world contacts for his own little bidding war, offering them a chance to purchase the two paintings he'd hoped would save the gallery. Noelle knew how good he was at drawing interest, at creating enthusiasm just by being enthusiastic. She'd been happy to let him handle things, eager to know the results. She hadn't imagined the results would be quite so soon.

Noelle nodded. "Durante. Yes, I remember now."

"Well..." Frank leaned in, lowering his voice to an exaggerated whisper. "How does 78,000 pounds sound to you?"

Noelle's eyes widened. "Are you joking?" His unchanged expression told her he wasn't. "So, he ended up buying both? That's a stroke of luck!"

"No. I don't think you understand." He grinned wider. "78,000 pounds. Each."

"You mean..."

Frank leaned back, letting it soak in.

"That's..." She did the math in her head. "Over a quarter million U.S. dollars? Isn't it?"

"It is."

"Oh my. That's insane, Frank. I mean, I love my aunt's work, but a quarter million for some brushstrokes on a canvas? It's... surreal, the price some people are willing to pay. I almost feel guilty."

"Well, don't. Trust me, Mr. Durante and his clients have more than enough to spare. That's chump change to some of them. And just think what Sotheby's will bring, if this is any indication. When the word gets out, collectors are going to swarm the auction. Whatever will you do with all that money?"

"I can't even go there yet." She shook her head. "I'm still not quite sure it's even real."

"Oh, it's very real. Real enough for you to buy yourself a mansion, anywhere you please. A London penthouse, maybe?"

Noelle smiled. "If I do anything, it'll likely be with the gallery. Renovate, maybe add a second story. Would you be opposed?"

"Opposed? I would welcome it. What a fabulous idea. That building needs a complete makeover. But what about your penthouse?"

"You know that's not me. Besides, I could never be happy in London." *Too close to Adam,* she wanted to add but didn't. "Chilton Crosse is more my style. I think this place suits me."

"So, does that mean you're staying? You've decided?"

She knew deep down, the minute she hung up with Dan. She would stay. The next day, she had even called the realtor to halt placing the cottage on the market. But a firm decision to uproot herself, move to another country, couldn't be made on a whim. She would still give herself time to make sure. So she said as honestly as she could, "It's a strong possibility."

"Well, I'm pleased. You've brought your American enthusiasm to this place and livened up a stuffy old village. Plus, you've given us all something to talk about."

Noelle leaned forward a little, wanting direct eye contact, wanting to make sure he heard. "Frank, thank you. You're the one who pulled it all together, made everything happen. I couldn't have done any of it without you."

"Aww." He waved away her flattery.

"No, it's true. And it's not just your expertise. You've made me feel welcome in the village. Not the total outsider American I expected I'd be."

"Well, you're welcome. And I should be thanking you. Just think of the commission I'll get on even one of those paintings!"

"You're incorrigible." Noelle smirked.

"I can't help it. Cheers to us!"

As they clinked glasses, Noelle's thoughts went fuzzy, from either the ale or the news; she couldn't tell which.

"I have your cake," the waitress, Lizzie, said, appearing with one plate and one box. Frank had asked for his to go; he was on his way to Bath for some gallery business. Lizzie, the antiques shopkeeper's daughter, was new at the pub. A twenty-nine-year-old beauty with natural ringlets and sparkling green eyes, she had recently caught the eye of Joe.

"Thanks. It smells delicious," Noelle said.

"Can I get you two anything else?"

"I think we have everything we need."

"And *then* some," Frank muttered, drawing his mug to his lips.

"See? Incorrigible!"

Frank snickered and rose up, clutching his cake. "I'd better get going. Call me if you hear anything more from Sotheby's."

"You know I will."

Alone with the fire and the chocolate, Noelle revisited the crazy notion of packing up her San Diego life and moving here. To a beautiful but obscure Cotswold village.

But why crazy? People did it every day—took risks, moved on, started fresh. She thought about what moving might mean. In actual, everyday terms. Leaving the States behind permanently. No Thanksgiving or Fourth of July. No hot dogs or baseball. Not that she even enjoyed baseball. Or hot dogs. But they represented something all-American. Her heritage. Of course, her heritage included England, too. Her mother had been raised in England until she'd "betrayed" that heritage at nineteen by running off with "that American," as Noelle had once overheard Gram mutter.

Besides, due to Noelle's pending financial windfall, she'd be able to visit America anytime she pleased, at the drop of a hat. She could even buy a house there someday. Become bi-coastal. Money wasn't about fancy cars or penthouses. It was about having choices.

She finished her cake and left a hefty tip for Lizzie then zipped up her coat. The days were becoming drastically colder.

When she stepped outside, someone called her name. Adam, a few feet away, was walking briskly toward her. He wore a dark suit and tan trench coat, with a slim leather case slung over his shoulder. He smiled and waved when they made eye contact. "You're here!" he said.

She had assumed he would halt in front of her, but instead, he took one more unexpected step and leaned down for a fast, tight hug. Before she could ask what on earth he was doing there, he released her and said, "I thought you were back in the States by now. Were there hang-ups with the cottage or the will?" His light brown eyes looked almost golden in the sunlight.

Tourists dodged them on the street, so Adam led her nearer the pub's wall, out of the way. Suddenly out of breath, out of sorts, Noelle tried to get her bearings. "It wasn't the cottage, but... well, I guess you haven't heard. About Joy's paintings."

His crinkled brow confirmed it. "What paintings?"

"The night after Jill's dinner, I opened up this locked room upstairs in Joy's cottage and found them. Row after row of never-seen paintings. She must've done them during all those reclusive years."

"That's unbelievable. I'm sure you were stunned. What happens next? Will they be in museums, galleries?"

Noelle told him about Sotheby's and the auction, how the paintings would be distributed, and that she kept a few for herself. She liked the easy small talk. It allowed part of her brain to process the jarring fact that Adam was here in the village.

"The paintings you kept—are they at the cottage?"

"Frank suggested storing them in the gallery for a bit. Safety concerns. He has a top-of-the-line security system."

"Smart thinking." Adam nodded. "Could I see them? I mean, do you have time?"

"All the time in the world, now. I quit my job. I'll be staying put. At least for a while, until I figure out what to do with the rest of my life."

She couldn't read his expression, but his smile widened by a millimeter or two. "It's interesting," he mused. "Joy sort of... brings you here, with the cottage. And then she helps you stay, with the paintings. It's like she wants you here."

"That's what I was thinking, too. That she had a hand in it or something. Like she's orchestrating things from beyond." Knowing how New Agey that sounded, she added, "Well, something like that. So, you know why I'm here, but you didn't tell me why you're here."

"After we talked at Jill's about the renovation project, I couldn't get it off my mind. Stayed up hours that night, doing online research about the historical period, the level of renovations required. Even emailed a few contacts to see if they might be interested. They were, and so, here I am. I've got my first meeting with the vicar and the council in"—he checked his watch—"twenty minutes. I came early. In fact, I was headed to the pub to kill some time."

"Well, then, kill some time with me instead. The gallery's across the street."

"Exquisite." Adam stepped back to take in the whole painting. He crossed his arms, tilted his head. "I wouldn't have recognized this as your aunt's work. It's too…"

"Dark?"

"Yes. Almost bleak."

They stared at the ship lost in a storm. In the end, after all the inventory had been completed, Noelle had kept two contrasting series for herself—three landscapes, vivid and peaceful, and three storms, grim and somber.

"I think this one reflected whatever was going on inside her all those years," she said. Noelle swapped the first storm painting for the next, dark clouds filtering through a bare winter tree, white branches spiking up like thin, crooked fingers. She was using an old easel of Frank's in the back room to show Adam the paintings. She wore gloves as the man from Sotheby's had taught her.

"What made your aunt hide away in the first place?" Adam asked. "Did you ever know?"

"All I know is, during one of her showings at a gallery, a decade ago, she had some sort of… episode. A meltdown or breakdown. She stormed out of the gallery, and all the papers covered it the next day with various theories. None of them probably right. That's the last the art world ever saw of her."

"Curiouser and curiouser." He shifted his focus to the third painting, which Noelle was placing onto the easel.

"I think this one's my favorite." Noelle scanned it up close, remembering how it stood out from the rest when she first discovered the contents of the locked room. The end of a storm, the remains of a black sky off in the distance. And in the corner of the painting, the subtle beginnings of a colorful rainbow. Something beneath the rainbow caught Noelle's attention, something she hadn't noticed the first time. A brush stroke out of place. That was unusual for her meticulous aunt. Noelle squinted further but couldn't make it out.

"What is it?" Adam asked.

She reached into a nearby drawer for Frank's monocular, a magnifier specifically designed for close analysis of paintings. "Not sure yet…"

And there it was. Three dark gray brushstrokes, clean but hidden in the shadows of the corner. It looked like a letter. Or a symbol.

"You found something."

She handed him the magnifier. "There," she pointed. "It looks like a signature. A letter, maybe? *W*?"

He hunched forward and examined the corner for several seconds then nodded. "That's what it looks like. Although the middle stroke is too high. Maybe it's something else."

"I wonder if it's in the other paintings."

Adam helped Noelle gingerly swap paintings on the easel.

It took several seconds, but she found it again. The same symbol, this time located in the opposite corner. "Ha!"

"Let me see." The excitement in Adam's voice matched hers. He looked through the monocular and confirmed it. "You're right! She's embedded this… thing… on purpose. I'd bet she put them inside all the paintings you found."

Exhilarated, Noelle smiled. "I'll check the rest of these, too. Mr. Lester needs to be told. If Sotheby's hasn't already discovered them. But I think all they've done so far is catalogue the paintings. The experts won't examine them until next month."

"The mystery symbol will jack up the price, too, for the auction."

"I hadn't considered that."

"If it's a *W*, could it have been her middle initial or something?"

Noelle paused at the easel. "Her middle name was Lillian. And I can't think of anyone with a *W* initial in the family. I'll have to do some research."

"It could be someone important to her. A relative? Ooh! Or a secret lover?" He raised one eyebrow for effect.

"A lover?" Noelle grinned at the idea of her reclusive, elderly aunt having a secret lover. "I think you're getting carried away."

Adam, undeterred, said, "It almost looks Celtic. Maybe it's a Gaelic letter? Or even—" The chimes from the Timekeepers shop interrupted him. "Oh, bollocks."

"What?" Noelle faced him.

"I'm late. Bloody hell."

"Run! You can still make it."

He grabbed his briefcase and saw Noelle's phone on the table. He took it and tapped something on the screen. "Here's my number. Text me. I want to know more about this... whatever it is you've found in your aunt's paintings." He handed her the phone and leaned in for a friendly kiss on the cheek. "Incredible to see you again."

Noelle didn't know which prospect delighted her more—the thought of a secret symbol embedded in her aunt's paintings, or that a surprise visit from Adam had ended with getting his contact information.

Chapter Nine

Embed a sense of history inside each painting.
That will add context, resonance.
Let it be known that this place, this vision, existed
long before your brush chose to capture it.

FINDING THE ONLY PARKING SPOT left in front of the manor, Noelle steered her car between the lines. Yesterday, after finding the symbol inside the paintings and after contacting Mr. Lester about it, she made a decision. She wanted to revisit her roots in Bath, particularly Gram's estate. Perhaps it would jog some long-buried memories or lead her to clues about the symbol. Plus, visiting the estate was something she'd longed to do ever since she stepped on British soil ten days ago. Afterward, she could do some shopping, buy a new wardrobe, make a whole day of it.

Rather than borrow Mac's car again, Noelle sought Joe's guidance this morning. He put her in contact with an old farmer in the village, Mr. Elton, ready to sell his used car. Not wanting to commit yet to purchasing a car but knowing she might in the near future, she asked if she could test drive it to Bath. Mr. Elton heartily agreed.

She stared through her windshield at Windermere looming up toward the sky, an elegant, imposing manor. She hadn't been back since that last day of summer, just before her senior year of high school. As familiar as the structure looked, it still held a specific unfamiliarity. It didn't "belong" to her anymore. It belonged to the State.

As indicated in her will, Gram had donated Windermere to the British National Trust upon her death five years ago. Joy would certainly never have taken it, and Gram didn't wish to burden anyone with the estate's outrageous costs. By the end of her life, Gram barely possessed the funds to keep it up and running and decided to open up half of the building to the public to offset the massive upkeep costs. When she died, the Trust opened the entire house to tourists.

After parking, Noelle moved toward the striped Tudor exterior, where perfectly manicured shrubs still lined the entrance. She waited in line behind a woman and her son then stepped up to pay the admission fee of nine pounds. She walked toward the main hall, which led to the grand staircase she remembered so well. As a little girl, she'd nearly broken her wrist trying to slide down the banister. She followed the other tourists through roped hallways into the Great Room, listening to guides reveal the layers of history.

Windermere had been Gram and Joy's—and her own mother's—childhood home. Noelle could've easily given this tour, herself. Could've easily told the guests about the formal landscaped gardens on three hundred acres of land. Or about the manor's expensive paintings, the Elizabethan furniture, the tall gilded ceilings.

Instead, she obediently followed the guide, spouting his obviously memorized script as he moved them room to room. But when he pointed something out, Noelle always saw different details. The crackling fireplace beside which Gram had taught her to needlepoint, the slender library ladder she had climbed up as a child to select a stack of books for the summer, and the wall where she'd hung the poster of Nirvana that Gram had allowed her to have in her upstairs bedroom. And there, at the end of the hall, had been Aunt Joy's summer bedroom.

Eager tourists shuffled behind and in front of her, oblivious to her history there. Noelle wanted to interrupt the guide, tell him that without Gram and Joy here, bickering and chattering, the tour was incomplete. That Gram and Joy remained as essential to the manor as the "Seventeenth-century, handcrafted Grandfather clock" the guide had just pointed out to them.

Outside, finally free from the rigidity of tour guides, Noelle wrapped her scarf about her neck and thrust her hands deep in her pockets, preparing to wander the grounds. Down the back steps, she paused to take in the gardens, breathtaking as ever and showing off their magnificent floral fanfare. A fountain marked the center, with a cherub at its top holding a vase pouring out an endless stream of clear water. Noelle wondered how many pence coins of hers still lay at the bottom.

Past the gardens, the countryside looked exactly as she remembered except for the transforming of summer grass into autumn straw. Down a hill on the east side of the estate stood an outdoor tennis court. Noelle walked onto the green cement in her black flats and imagined the hollow bounce of a tennis ball smacking back and forth between imaginary players. Tennis had been the only sport she ever enjoyed. She won tournaments at home during the school year and kept up her practice at the estate's court in summertime, mostly with the ball machine Gram had purchased for her as a birthday gift. Noelle didn't have a real partner until fourteen-year-old Adam came along. She taught him how to play that summer and beat him every time after that. Once he had gained the skill to become a formidable challenger, she sometimes thought he'd let her win.

A particular afternoon came to mind, a week in August, when they were sixteen. Balmy, with a slight breeze, and clouds to shelter Noelle and Adam from the overbearing sun. They had played two sets, gearing up for a tiebreaker on their third. Right before tossing the ball into the air to serve, Adam had yelled across the court, "The loser pays for an evening out!"

"What do you mean?"

"Fancy dinner at a classy restaurant."

"You are *on!*" Noelle yelled back, eager to win.

That set ended up being their closest ever. Adam's serves and returns remained accurate and strong, and Noelle struggled to pace herself, though she would never have admitted it.

It all came down to the last two points, and Noelle won them more easily than she'd expected. Adam hit an easy shot into the net, and his next ball flew out of bounds on her side. She never did find out if he had choked at the end or, playing the gentleman, thrown the match completely.

That evening, after a refreshing shower, Noelle curled her hair into ringlets and put on more makeup than usual—in summer, she rarely wore more than some powder and lip-gloss—then stepped into a black mini-dress, fully prepared for one of Adam's wisecracks about the light dusting of freckles all over her arms. But he didn't tease her. When he arrived in his father's silver Bentley and saw Noelle, he stared at her up and down, giving a sharp whistle. He called her "fancy" then drove her to a restaurant in Bath called The Boatman. As they sat down and the waiter placed a starched white napkin in her lap, Noelle shrugged off the notion that it might be a date, though it certainly had all the makings of one. But she couldn't get her hopes up. She wanted to enjoy the evening for whatever it was.

Over a dinner of shrimp and steak, they acted like the sixteen-year-olds they were, talking about music and giggling over some obnoxious, tipsy man at the next table. After a rich dessert of sticky toffee pudding, Adam paid, tipping well, and they drove back to the estate.

Adam had shut off the engine and run around to her door, opening it with a melodramatic bow at the waist. "Me-lady…"

He offered his hand to help her out, still in bowing position, and she accepted in her best fake accent. "Thank you, kind sir."

At the front door, Adam paused, and Noelle asked him to come inside to say goodnight to Gram. He balked and clawed at his necktie for the tenth time, saying he couldn't wait to get home and change. But she wanted him to stay that way for a while longer—his hair less unruly than usual, his shoulders broad and strong in a crisp, tailored suit. For a moment, they stood in silence, holding hands and swaying them back and forth. She thanked him for the steak, and he told her, "A bet's a bet. You won the match."

She wouldn't see him again until the following summer. His family was going on vacation to Italy the next day. "Have a great time in Rome," she told him. "Send me some postcards. Make me jealous of all the great places you'll visit."

Adam flashed his boyish smile and pulled her in close for a hug. But just as their bodies met, he backed away. "Hang on a minute," he said and sank to his knees.

"What on earth are you doing?"

"Getting down to your level, Shortie." They were practically eye-to-eye.

"You're insane," she said as he drew her in for a firm hug. "You'll ruin your suit."

"What do I care?"

They lingered there, Noelle's fingers brushing his collar. When he backed away, something pensive remained in his expression. She thought he might say something, but instead, he kissed her cheek. His lips were warm and soft, and she imagined what they might feel like on her own.

"See you next summer," he whispered. He stood up tall again with a grunt and walked back toward the Bentley with a pretend limp. She didn't know it then, but one more summer was all they would ever have together.

"Pardon me. Miss?"

Startled, Noelle turned to see a man, standing with her on the tennis court, hand extended in polite gesture.

"I'm sorry, but the estate closes in ten minutes."

"Oh! I didn't realize the time." Noelle stole another glance behind her at the court, the pounding of tennis balls fading, and followed the man back up the hill.

After a quick supper at the Jane Austen teahouse and a bit of shopping in Bath, Noelle walked into her cottage, planning to make a fire and banish the chill inside.

Her cottage. She didn't realize it until this moment, but visiting Windermere had solidified everything. She had to stay in England, her home. *Why not make it official?* She postponed making the fire and called Desha, calculating the time difference as the phone rang. Noon, California time.

"Hello!" Desha yelled into the phone, people chatting in the background. "Wait! I can't hear you."

Noelle pictured her friend at a busy restaurant, dashing to a less noisy spot, perhaps the ladies room. Finally, she returned.

"Desha? It's Noelle. I've made a decision." Thankfully, she didn't have to go into too much detail. Desha would want to get back to her lunch. She already knew about Dan, about Noelle quitting her job, even about the paintings discovered upstairs. But she hadn't known about Noelle wanting to move to England for good.

"I can't believe you're really doing it! Good for you."

"I want you and Pam to have my house. To rent it. Or even buy it. If you want it?" Desha's sister, Pam, had just gone through a divorce. The sisters were looking for a place to rent together. Noelle hoped this would be their solution and hers as well.

"Of course we do. I love your house!" Noelle knew the exact expression Desha wore without even being there. Her friend's infectious smile had just widened.

They agreed to talk again later to hammer out the details. After hanging up, Noelle brainstormed the possibilities. Desha and Pam could keep all the furniture, since Noelle didn't need any. In exchange, Desha could pack up Noelle's essentials—clothing, books, wall hangings, kitchen utensils—and ship them to England.

Noelle carried her package to the sitting room and propped it against the sofa. Aside from eight new outfits, she'd bought the loveliest Monet print, the one called *The Garden at Argenteuil*, and she knew just where she would hang it—upstairs in her bedroom, so she would see it every night before falling asleep.

The temperature had fallen briskly inside the cottage since she'd been gone. She made her apologies to Mr. Darcy, whose tail formed a question mark as he crossed her path. She added two logs to the cast iron stove in the sitting room and created a blazing fire then made a cup of tea to cap off her eventful day.

Chapter Ten

*Insert your secrets into the painting. No one else needs to know about
them. Something important, something symbolic. Something that
only you would understand. It will make the painting truly yours.*

"OH, YOU GOT IT!" NOELLE clapped her hands and did a
little hop as she walked toward Mac. She'd been making
toast and eggs when she heard hammering, so she peeked
outside to find the source—Mac, setting up a three-tiered fountain in
the middle of her garden.

"Aye, lass. It came faster than expected."

Last week, after Noelle found the paintings, Mac had offered a sort
of cottage-warming present. He showed her a gardening catalogue and
told her to pick out anything she liked. At first, she protested, saying her
stay might not be permanent. But Mac convinced her that, even if she
ended up selling, a new garden fixture would help with the resale value.
That day, flipping through the catalogue, a fountain caught her eye.
It reminded her of Gram's at Windermere. But this model was simple,
not too fancy and not too gargantuan. It even had a cherub on top, like
Gram's, pouring water out of a clay pot.

Mac squatted in the twiggy grass on his hands and knees, trying to
fit the pump into the base.

"Can I help?"

"No, lass. I've got it." He squinted as he reached for the socket. "There!" He rocked back on his heels and placed his hands on his knees to assess his handiwork.

"Perfect. Thank you, Mac. Ooh! The toast!" She darted back inside and pulled out the toast a second before it burned. She put the whole breakfast together within minutes and slipped her coat on, insisting that Mac have breakfast with her in the "new" garden.

As she set the wrought iron table with paper napkins, jams, and utensils, Mac tested the fountain. Soon, they ate breakfast to the sound of a bubbling stream. Mr. Darcy lurched back, unsure about this foreign contraption. But when he realized it wasn't the enemy, he leaped up onto the rim and sauntered around the fountain as if he owned it.

"You knew, didn't you? That I'd be staying here?" she asked as she dabbed globs of strawberry jam onto her toast.

"Aye, I had a notion."

"I made all the arrangements," she confided. "It's done." Immediately after hanging up with Desha yesterday, Noelle imagined receiving her things from the beach house. She imagined specific places in the cottage she would put each of them. Especially her favorite treasure, Joy's painting of Noelle at the Cornwall seaside. It belonged in the cottage now.

"I'm glad, lass." Mac reached for the salt.

"I wanted to ask you something. About Aunt Joy's paintings."

He balanced fluffy eggs on his fork and took a bite, listening intently. She told him about the embedded symbol, the discovery she made with Adam a few days ago. "Can you think of anything special to my aunt that starts with the letter *W*? Or even a symbol that looks like a *W* that might've been meaningful to her?"

Mac searched his plate as he continued to chew. Then he shrugged. "Nay, not that I know of."

"Okay. Worth a shot, anyway."

They ate the rest of the meal in silence, and Noelle thought about the symbol. She crunched a bite of toast and mused how a person could take secrets straight to the grave, leaving those behind to wonder, struggle to make guesses. She pondered the end of her own life, what secrets she might leave behind, or what private feelings she might take with her to the unknown.

Mac, a swift eater, wiped his beard with his napkin and said his good-byes. He needed to fiddle with Mrs. Cartwright's broken Aga.

Noelle lingered at the table, amazed at how the garden brimmed with life even in autumn. The hearty foliage and shrubs contained vibrant splashes of color. And beyond the garden, gray ridges of clouds striped the sky. Her favorite kind, bands of dark and light. If she squinted at just the right angle, the ridges almost looked like mountains. Most people chose the enormous, puffy, pure white summer clouds as their favorite. The ones you could mold into shapes, dinosaurs and dogs and bears. But Noelle always preferred these subtle, muted, melancholy clouds. The kind that didn't change form the moment you turned away.

Lugging Joy's clunky ancient vacuum from the upstairs closet, Noelle made a mental note to buy a new one soon. She needed something powerful enough to suck up those millions of cat hairs that kept showing up on her lovely wood floors. And on the carpets. And the bed, the couches, the chairs.

Mr. Darcy, terrified of the evil contraption, had darted downstairs the moment she'd opened the closet. It roared to life, reminding her of the scene in *Mr. Mom*—the scary vacuum monster that ate baby blankets while Michael Keaton wrestled it to the ground.

She started in her master, pushing and pulling the vacuum across the wooden floor with great effort, already knowing her back muscles would not be happy with her tomorrow. Bumping across the Oriental rug beneath the bed, she moved on to the other corner of the room. The cord yanked behind her, so she freed it from the tangle caught around the foot of the bed. When it came loose, she pushed the vacuum forward and hit something. Hard. The solid leg of that beautiful, antique writing table. She clicked off the vacuum and looked closer at a small dent on the left edge of the desk. And a slivered crack right behind.

"Oh, damn." She pushed the vacuum away to give herself more room. Noelle knelt down and grazed her fingers across the crack.

There appeared to be a compartment of some sort inside the thick leg, which extended to the back of the desk. It had cracked open from the weight of her mishap with the evil vacuum. Gingerly, she put her fingers inside the crack and pulled forward. With a bit of effort, she opened up a narrow door about eighteen inches tall and three inches wide.

Her heart beat faster, similar to the night she'd found the paintings in the locked room. And the day she'd discovered the symbols with Adam. *Surprises lurking about*, Aunt Joy's letter had said. Noelle pried the door wider and peered in. Seeing a book wedged inside, she reached in and wriggled it out carefully. A brown leather-bound journal, fairly thick, no title or name on the front. She touched the wrinkled edges.

Sitting on the floor, legs crossed, Noelle opened the cover, breathless. Its thickness came not from the book, but from Polaroids paper-clipped to the pages inside. Snapshots of Joy's paintings, the same paintings Noelle found inside the locked room. She flipped through them one by one, noting the Polaroids were grouped in clusters, the same way the paintings had been grouped on the floor of the locked room. A cataloguing, of sorts. Without disturbing the pictures, she skimmed the entries. She'd expected artist's notes, maybe brainstorming about color choices or brush techniques or ideas for new paintings.

But instead, this seemed to be a diary. The pages held pain, loss, and sadness. A brief history of a decade's worth of life lived in seclusion.

The first page had been mostly ripped out, with only a fragment of crossed-out text remaining at the top. Her aunt's handwriting, certainly. And the date, scribbled in the corner, a few days after her mother's accident.

Noelle squinted to interpret the crossed-out text. *It's unbearable, the grief in my sister's eyes. It haunts me when I try to sleep. And the guilt over what might have been makes this—*

That was all she could read. She was almost glad for the loss of the text. She didn't know if she wanted to relive those days again— her mother's funeral and the last time Noelle saw Gram and Aunt Joy together, bonded in their grief. A surreal and painful day.

Forcing her attention back to the journal, Noelle moved to the next entry, dated the month of Joy's art show meltdown. In order to read the entry, she removed the photos, recalling each painting in living color when she'd discovered them locked away. The series held three paintings, perhaps Aunt Joy's darkest of all. The black inside of what looked like a cave; a deep forest with glowing eyes peeking out behind foliage; and two ghostly images with spiteful faces, on the verge of choking each other. Noelle still had difficulty reconciling this Joy with the peaceful countryside landscapes for which she'd become famous.

She set the pictures aside and returned to the book in her lap, the entry entitled, "Betrayal."

I didn't think she would ever find out. That she ever could find out. What does it matter now, anyway, some might say? Over forty years later. But that's the trouble. It does matter, more than anything else ever did.

Damn that letter for ever being discovered. For peeking out of some dusty old box for my sister to find. And damn the car that agreed to bring her there last night, to my most important night-of-nights, my biggest art show yet. I'll never forget the image of her, shaking that fragile, yellowed letter in my face. One that held secrets she was never meant to know.

Thank goodness, she had the courtesy to drag me into the bathroom to do it—to yell at me through angry sobs, shout at me all the names I deserved. Thank goodness that all the critics and guests ever heard were muffles and raised voices.

But that didn't stop me from making a fool of myself. From chasing after her into the main gallery, begging her not to go and grabbing the edge of her coat, pleading for forgiveness. When I dropped to my knees and looked up, she shrieked through quivering lips: "How could you have done this? Betray your own sister? I never want to see your face again!"

She slammed the door, and the look on the curator's face told me everything. It said that I had humiliated myself in front of very important people. And that they would never look at me, or my art, the same way again. It was over.

Sisters. Betrayal. Aunt Joy and Gram. That incident had caused Joy's sudden and very public retreat into seclusion. The incident was to blame for the darkness inside the paintings.

Did they ever speak again afterward? What had Gram discovered that made her so livid? Noelle turned the pages of the other journal entries, leaving the Polaroids intact to return to and savor the pages later, slowly. Skimming them quickly, though, she didn't see another reference to the rift.

It broke Noelle's heart, picturing them so fractured. She loved them equally, Gram and Joy. *Am I supposed to pick sides? Even having no idea what the betrayal entailed?* Betrayal to one person could mean an entirely different thing to another. Perhaps it wasn't "so" bad—perhaps Gram had overreacted to something. But then, it wouldn't have mattered so much, forty years later.

Joy had written the journal, hidden it inside that secret space for a reason, maybe for Noelle to find someday. So that Noelle would know her flaws, see the imperfections of her relationships, and see her for who she was. Human.

All those summers ago, Joy had always been the "fun" sister, sneaking Noelle a cigarette when Gram wasn't watching, convincing Gram to extend Noelle's curfew just "one more hour." But today, Noelle saw that fun side a little differently. Perhaps as rebellion beneath the surface. A mischievous desire to push boundaries. *Was Joy jealous of Gram? That Gram's husband didn't die in a car accident like her own husband did? Or jealous that Gram was able to have a child, a grandchild, while Joy never had children of her own?*

The painting of the two ghostly figures—Joy and Gram at odds. Raw figures, dark and beautiful, because Joy had painted truth. Not just sheep in a field or an orange sun in the sky. She'd painted reality in all its ugliness.

How often do you get a chance to see into someone's soul? And how many people would be that brave to let you see it in the first place?

A loud banging from downstairs made her gasp. The front door. She'd lost all track of time and space with her new discovery, and the knocks thrust her back into the present.

She hadn't expected the children quite so early. She still needed to tear open the candy and spill it into bowls. She imagined a goblin at her door, or perhaps a munchkin-sized Spiderman or Harry Potter, complete with a painted-on lightning bolt scar.

She scooped up the three pictures and tucked them back inside the journal then placed the book inside the desk's main top drawer, where she also kept a brainstorming list of possibilities for that embedded symbol. So far, nothing added up. Not even Frank or Mr. Lester was able to help, though they made a couple of wild suggestions of their own. Even if one of their guesses about the symbol was correct, they couldn't verify it. Only Aunt Joy knew the answer. Perhaps they would never find out.

Hours later, when the last of the little tykes had gone, Noelle returned to the journal upstairs. Her first instinct was to flip through it quickly, but something even more pressing awaited her. She needed to tell someone. She remembered Adam's "Text me!" command, and this was the perfect opportunity.

She sat cross-legged on the bed and typed out a message. She read it over, changed a few words, read it again. Then she sent it. *No news about symbol. But found a new Joy surprise. In a secret compartment.*

That first text to someone was always the hardest, wondering whether you were bugging them, whether they would even answer back. And what that might or might not mean. But about thirty seconds later, a text from Adam appeared with a "ding." *I want deets. Spill!*

Noelle smiled and responded, *An old journal. With photos.*

Ding. *Have meeting on Thurs afternoon in CC. Would love to see it!*

She hadn't thought this far ahead. The idea of him in her cottage only increased her nerves. She was only used to seeing him in public. Still, it made the most sense. She wanted to keep this journal private, not flaunt it around the village.

Sure. Come to cottage.

Shooing away the butterflies at the thought of seeing him again, Noelle set her phone aside and retrieved the journal. Back in bed, she settled under the covers and shifted her pillows around, hoping no Halloween mischief would disrupt her evening. Yesterday, Joe had warned her that teenagers sometimes egged houses or played pranks in the village. Hopefully, they'd leave the "new girl" alone.

Mr. Darcy had finally come out of hiding and sat at the end of her bed, licking his front paw with his eyes closed. Eager to revisit the journal, Noelle could easily stay up all night long, race through it in one sitting. But something told her to slow down and enjoy the journal, entry by entry. Allow some time to digest these special pages. She should treat it like the treasure it was, rather than some fast novel she could devour in two days.

So, in the calm of late evening, without the demanding knocks of children at her door, Noelle opened up to the beginning and re-read the first entry. Her quiet time with Aunt Joy.

Chapter Eleven

As much as you enjoy the rush of accomplishment, equally welcome the sting of frustration. Accept it as part of the process—that brush effect you can't get "just right" or the failure to mix the colours the way your mind's eye sees them. Without the frustration, we can't fully enjoy the beauty of success.

NOELLE HADN'T EXPECTED HIM SO early in the afternoon. She assumed Adam would visit the cottage after his meeting, not before. But there was his text: *Five minutes away!* She had exactly enough time to clear the remains of this morning's breakfast and dab on some lip gloss, fluff up her hair.

By the time she'd finished primping upstairs and retrieved the journal from her nightstand, a knock tapped at the front door. Mr. Darcy meowed, and Noelle clutched the journal as she took the first step down. She made herself breathe before she opened the door.

"Hey," she said. She gave him a bright smile, still amazed at how handsome a man he had grown into. The strong jaw, the confident posture, the broad shoulders...

"Hey, yourself." He walked past her as she let him through. "So, this is 'the cottage.' Charming."

"Thanks. I love it. Already feels like home."

"Who's this?" Adam looked down at the cat circling his ankles to sniff them.

"Mr. Darcy." He purred and rubbed against Adam's shins. "And apparently, your new best friend."

Adam set down his leather case and scratched Mr. Darcy's ears. "You're a cute little chap, aren't you?"

"When's your meeting?" she asked.

"I've got about twenty minutes."

"How's everything going? With the project?"

"So far, so good. It can move like a snail sometimes, a renovation like this. And we're just in the prep phase. I'll probably have some key meetings with the vicar and the counsel this month here at the village, then things might slow down for a bit. But I'll still be busy— researching, contacting people and getting them on board, then drawing up the plans. I'll be mostly in London for that."

"Sounds exhausting. When would the renovations actually begin?"

"We're eyeing February, depending on the weather. And the entire project will take several months to finish up, maybe even a year. Hey, is that it? The journal?" He spotted it in Noelle's hand.

"This is it. You wanna go in here for a bit?" She tilted her head toward the living room, and they walked inside together, Mr. Darcy following along.

"I like what you've done with this."

"It's all Aunt Joy. I was amazed, how tidy and well-kept everything was."

"Yeah, you always think that people who are recluses would live like hoarders or something. Just stacks of newspapers in every corner. But I guess your aunt was productive. I mean, the paintings prove that. She didn't stop living. Just stopped... seeing people."

"Exactly."

They sat together on the sofa, and Noelle handed him the journal. She wasn't sure yet whom else she might tell about it. She hadn't told Frank, Mac, or Mr. Lester and didn't know if she ever would. Unlike the paintings, the journal felt so intimate. A peek into Aunt Joy's soul that colors on a canvas didn't reveal.

Adam delicately turned the pages, touched the paper clips, and paused to glance at the photos. "Amazing."

"It's such a treasure. But it also feels like I'm invading her privacy somehow, reading it."

"I think she wanted you to have it, though. I mean, she gave you the cottage. Surely she knew you'd stumble on this someday, and the paintings, too. I think she trusted you."

Noelle remembered the end of Joy's letter. Adam was right. *Tired of hiding. Permission to share... every detail, every treasure.* It felt appropriate, sharing it with Adam. But for now, only Adam.

"Where was the secret compartment?" he asked.

She told him about the vacuum mishap that led her to the journal. "I've only read the first entry. I thought I'd take my time with them," she explained. "The first entry talks about the rift with her sister, my grandmother. It seems to be what triggered her becoming a recluse. But she doesn't give any real details. It's still a mystery, what happened between them."

"Have you told your mum about this? Maybe she could shed some light on what happened that night?"

Noelle always hated this part. Not for herself but for the other person. Breaking the news about her mom always made the other party feel awkward. "She actually passed away. About ten years ago. In a car accident. I didn't have a chance to tell you yet."

"Oh. Blimey. I had no idea. I'm so sorry."

"Thanks. And I don't think Mom ever knew anything about a secret or trouble brewing between Joy and Gram. The rift didn't seem to happen until the art show, which was a couple of months after my mom's death."

Adam nodded. "You said the first entry gives at least a little detail, though?"

"Read it for yourself."

"Are you sure?"

"Positive. Plus, I'd like another person's perspective. And Aunt Joy wouldn't mind."

"How do you know?"

"You were like family to us back then, all those summers. She adored you."

He winced. "I always felt a little afraid of her. She was a tough broad."

"She could be. But she had a heart of gold."

Adam sorted through the first batch of Polaroids then flipped to the first page and read slowly, his expression solemn. "It's so... raw. I'm glad you trusted me with this." He handed back the journal.

She had been right to share it. And more than that, whatever awkwardness still lingered between them as adults, her friendship with Adam had stayed firmly intact. The foundation of respect remained at the core. She could trust him.

Is it possible? Keeping him in my life this way, as just a friend? Unthinkable a couple of weeks ago, at Jill's. But lately, with him popping up unexpectedly, she'd let down her guard a little, welcomed that easy chemistry they shared as teenagers. In the end, she'd rather have him in her life, in any capacity, than not at all.

"Do you have time for a cup of tea?" Noelle asked.

"A quick one, sure."

She had brewed a fresh pot of Earl Grey just before Adam's arrival, so the tea was ready in a snap. She handed his to him then blew on the surface of her cup. She didn't know where it came from, but before she could stop herself, she asked, "So, what does Laurel think of all this?"

"All this?"

"You know, the new project. The school..."

"Oh, she's fine with everything. I mean, she doesn't know much about the project, the details. I think it bores her. She only knows that it's taking up a lot more of my spare time."

"Yeah, I guess that would be tough on a relationship." She'd just circled the elephant in the room but didn't really care.

"It can be," he agreed. "I suppose we're rather used to that, living separate lives. Our work has always kept us busy, apart. Just more so these days. She does a lot of traveling with her job. And now I guess I do, as well."

His businesslike tone about his fiancée made Noelle even more curious. She pressed a little further. "Tell me about her. I mean, what brought the two of you together? You said she was your client's daughter?" Perhaps subconsciously her ability, or inability, to hear about his fiancée without becoming anxious would test her previous theory, that she was capable of being "just friends" with Adam.

"Yeah, he brought her to the office one day on their way to lunch, and we hit it off, I guess. She asked me questions about architecture, said she'd studied it in college, so we had that in common back then."

"Back then?"

"You know how it is when you've been with someone for a while. Time goes by, and those early things in common sort of get pushed back. You forget them sometimes. You know, that stupid cliché about people growing and changing. It has to happen, I guess."

"Mmm." Her discomfort rose, and she almost wished she hadn't brought up Laurel at all. Besides, other people's relationships always seemed oddly sacred, like a pool into which an outsider shouldn't be wading too deeply. Just as Adam had handed back Joy's journal, not wanting to pry too far, perhaps Noelle should hand the subject of Laurel back to him.

But before she could attempt to change the subject, Adam's phone rang. "Sure... Uh-huh... Yep, brought those with me... Will do." He clicked off and said, "It's the vicar, Michael. Needs to speak with me before the meeting starts. Guess I should get going." He rose from the couch and nearly stepped on Mr. Darcy, who'd made a pillow of Adam's shoe. "Thanks for the tea. And for sharing the journal."

Noelle set down her cup and followed him to the door. "Have a good meeting."

"Will do." He paused as if he forgot something then offered a quick peck on Noelle's cheek. As his cheek scratched lightly at her skin, she reminded herself, *This is the British way, a typical courtesy. Their version of shaking hands. Nothing personal. Just friends.*

And then he was gone.

Noelle pushed the bell again, wondering if she'd gotten the time wrong. She stood on Jill's doorstep, Joe's scrumptious carrot cake in hand, and waited. She and Jill hadn't seen each other since their big dinner party with Adam nearly three weeks ago, but they'd kept in steady touch with texts and calls. Jill knew all about the secret paintings, the symbol, the big Dan call, and moving permanently to Chilton Crosse, but not about the journal.

Jill had invited her here again for dinner, this time just the girls, with Gareth on call this evening. Noelle had recently purchased that used car from Mr. Elton, to his great delight. She didn't need anything fancy or expensive, especially since her driving skills on the wrong side of the road remained shaky. It would take months before she could gain the sort of confidence she needed in order to buy a new car.

After a third doorbell ring, Noelle fished out her cell phone. Maybe Jill would answer a text. As she fumbled to tap out the first word with the cake gently balanced in her other hand, the door flew open. Jill clutched a tissue, and her eyes were pink and puffy.

"What's the matter?" Noelle walked in past Jill, who closed the door, shutting out the cold air behind them. "Is it Gareth?"

Jill shook her head then blew her nose.

Noelle set down the cake and put her hand on Jill's arm. "It's okay. You can tell me."

"I'm... I'm pregnant. I just took the test. Three times. It's pink."

Relieved, Noelle had to suppress a grin as well as the urge to issue a hearty, "Congratulations." Clearly, this was not the time. "Come here," she said and leaned in for a tight hug.

When they backed away, Jill pointed to the living room, and they moved to the couch together. "I know this is supposed to be like a sappy commercial." Jill folded her tissue with a huge sigh. "I'm supposed to be jumping up and down, thrilled, and you're supposed to be the girlfriend who's congratulating me."

"But this was a surprise..."

"A damned inconvenient one! My boutiques are doing well, and I'm incredibly busy with my new line. A maternity line. Ha! The irony."

"Jill." Noelle tried to lighten her tone, prayed for the right words. "I know you can't see it now, but there is good in this. I mean, you and Gareth are a strong, happy couple."

"True. But right now, I guess I'm in shock or something. This was not in the plan. I only missed that one pill, and now I'm going to be fat for the first time in my life."

"You won't be fat. You'll be 'with child.'"

"And my boobs will droop and get all misshapen!"

Noelle worked hard to hide a laugh.

But Jill looked down, her lip quivering. "I'm really afraid, Noelle. I'm too selfish to raise a child. I won't make a good mother."

"I don't believe that for a second." Noelle held her friend's hand, wishing she could do more. "I know you, Jill. You are a loving, giving person. You will be an excellent mother. You are good at everything you do. This will be one of them."

Jill squeezed her hand without looking up.

"Does Gareth know?"

"Not yet." Jill's eyes brimmed over again. "That's the thing. I don't want my negative feelings to spill onto him. Because I think he'll be ecstatic. And I don't want to ruin this big moment for him."

"You want my opinion?"

Jill reached for a fresh tissue on the table and nodded.

"You're the one who said it best. You're in shock. But you'll have, what, about seven or so months to get used to the idea? It's not like the baby will be here tomorrow. Maybe, over time, the idea will grow on you?"

"Maybe." Jill shrugged.

"Gareth loves you. I've only met him once, but it's written all over his face. And you told me before, he would make a wonderful father."

"True. But I feel like... this awful person. I mean, what woman isn't happy with the news she's having a baby? Especially if she's in a good relationship? Aren't I 'supposed' to be happy? What's wrong with me?"

"Nothing! I just happen to think certain things are meant to be. And this feels like one of those things. You just don't know it yet."

For the first time since Noelle had arrived, Jill smiled. Just the shadow of one, but it gave some hope. Jill was going to be okay.

To dispel the gloom, Jill popped up, wiped the last of her tears, and suggested they eat. Not that she felt much like it—she'd been ill with morning sickness all day. Noelle followed her to the kitchen, where Gareth had kept their meal to warm. As Jill prepared the food, she also changed the subject. She asked Noelle all about the village, the cottage, and prodded about Adam and his new renovation job. "So how much have you seen of him?"

"Quite a lot, actually. In little spurts. He's had to attend a couple of meetings to get things started."

"Sounds like you'll be seeing a lot more of him."

"Probably." Noelle tried to sound casual as she helped Jill uncover the vegetables. "So. Guess what I'm thinking of doing? Signing up for art classes, here in London. Just for fun, flexing those muscles again."

Jill wasn't the only one who could deftly change the subject when she didn't want to talk about something.

Noelle didn't realize it until she stared at the calendar and counted out the Thursdays. Tomorrow was Thanksgiving. Not that it meant anything in the UK. And anyway, her Thanksgiving back home would have been sharing an overpriced, catered turkey with Pam and Desha then mapping out the sales they'd hit the next day, all the while knowing everyone else in the country had loads of family around. Still, she couldn't help picturing sweet potatoes with crusty marshmallows, thin slices of smoked turkey, mounds of dressing and mashed potatoes, maybe a Thanksgiving parade on TV, and feeling homesick. Restless.

The weeks since she'd discovered the paintings had rushed by in a flash, mostly because of her busy days at the gallery. Noelle helped Frank whenever she could, now that the gallery buzzed with hordes of tourists—more than ever, since news of Joy's discovered paintings had hit the media. Sometimes, the line to get inside spilled out the door, and the phone never stopped ringing.

Tonight, Noelle wanted to escape the chaos and put her busy days on pause, if she could. She didn't care if the light of dusk was dimming quickly. She craved a little countryside peace and quiet and knew precisely where to get it. Sitting on the new wrought-iron bench Mac had recently placed in the garden, looking out onto beautiful hills and fields.

Mr. Darcy stalked a beetle in the shrubs while Noelle buried her hands inside her warm jacket pockets and gazed across the patchwork countryside. The winding down of a day, the shadow of a dark sky blanketing everything with a hush. Her most favorite time of day, as it had been in California. Sometimes she still missed specific elements of her other life. The sea air kissing her senses, the seagulls hovering, the sandy beaches stretching out for eternity. She missed the sound of waves, the powerful rushing *swoosh* through cracked windows at night. But she never had *this* in San Diego, wide-open countryside, rolling hills, soft coos of a lonely dove. A quiet, a stillness here, that the ocean masked.

Soon, the chill became too much. Noelle headed back to the cottage feeling restored, guided by yellow squares through her windows, beacons to light the way. She fed Mr. Darcy and made some fresh hot tea, craving one of the blueberry scones she'd picked up at the bakery the day before. Giving it a few seconds' nuke in the microwave, she sat down to check all her devices.

Jill had sent a reassuring text: *Gareth putting crib together tonight. Premature, I think. But it makes him happy.* Jill had told him the news of the baby the same night she'd told Noelle. He'd been as thrilled as expected, which seemed to comfort Jill, make things easier to handle.

Noelle checked her laptop and found two new emails from Adam. Though he hadn't been to the village since visiting her cottage to get a peek at the journal, he'd been emailing her frequently. At first, they talked only about the school project or Joy's journal or the paintings. But lately, they had broadened out to other topics, joking around or talking about pop culture, world events, reminding her of the letters they used to write as teenagers across the ocean during school semesters. Pen pals.

She clicked on his first message and smiled at the nickname. He'd bestowed it on her during a particularly dreary, rainy day during that final summer at Gram's, when he had touched her blond hair and said, "See? We still have a little sunshine. Even in the gloom." She thought he'd forgotten.

Hey Sunshine—

Next CC meeting scheduled in a couple of weeks. Maybe we could catch lunch or something?

Adam

Noelle opened a second email from him to find only *P.S.—In My Place. Coldplay.* Adam had created the game years ago as they endured the rainy days inside at Gram's estate. They'd sat on the floor of the library, Noelle doodling on a sketchpad and Adam filling out a crossword. One of them offered up the title of a song, and the other one had to match at least one word in the title by using a new title. On and on, back and forth, with no end. Adam had started it up again two emails ago.

She hit "Reply" and typed, *Lunch is fine. Just tell me when. P.S.—too easy—Another **Place** to Fall. KT Tunstall. Your turn.* :-P

Chapter Twelve

Be prepared to change your perspective. Always stay open-minded
to a new one, until you've painted that very last stroke. Give
the painting a chance to become what it wants to become.

"FINE, MR. WINDHAM. I LOOK forward to it. See you on the 11th, then." Frank hung up and added Mr. Windham's name to his notepad. "That's one more," he said as Noelle returned to her paperwork. She'd set up a work area at Frank's table in the back room of the gallery.

"How many is that, in total?"

He poured a cup of tea, which he handed over to Noelle. "Ten." He poured himself a cup, too, then sat and crossed his leg over one knee. "Unless Mrs. Peterson decides to ring back. She's checking on something first."

Frank had been returning calls all morning from new artists who wanted to display their work at the gallery. The recent attention surrounding Joy's paintings provided a perfect opportunity to stock the gallery with a variety of local artists.

Holly, Frank's assistant, rounded the corner. "Do you need anything from the Emporium? We're running out of some supplies, so I thought I'd make a quick run."

"No, I can't think of anything."

Holly disappeared back around the corner, and Noelle stood to stretch her legs. She'd been sitting for hours, sorting through paperwork and helping Frank make calls.

"You've worked hard today," Frank said. "Why don't you get out of here? I can handle the rest of those." He took the papers before she had a chance to protest.

"Thank you, Frank." Noelle reached for her coat. "Oh, I've been meaning to ask—any more thoughts on the symbol Joy embedded in the paintings? I talked to Mr. Lester yesterday, and he said they're deep in the examination process at Sotheby's. And if there's any way we can solidify what the symbol means before the February auction, it would be helpful."

Frank shook his head. "I'm afraid not. Though I admit, it's kept me up nights. I've researched, brainstormed, and revisited the rare, brief conversations I had with your aunt. I even contacted a couple of her former art colleagues. Nothing came up. I could take a thousand guesses, but none of them would be right."

"Well, thanks. I've come up empty, too." She snapped the buttons on her coat. "Still, having a 'mystery symbol' will probably make her paintings even more intriguing to buyers come Valentine's Day."

"Indeed."

They said their good-byes, and Noelle opened the front door to find the perfection of a cold, clear, early-December afternoon. Cloudless turquoise sky, hint of a crisp breeze.

She waved hello to old Mr. Bentley handing out his bakery samples across the street. Excited children played games on the sidewalk while their mothers chatted or window-shopped. A gathering of seniors had clustered underneath the stone gazebo in the center of town, snapping pictures.

Watching them all, Noelle knew they no longer considered her a tourist. She was a villager now.

That evening, Noelle skimmed her phone for texts. Nothing. She hadn't heard from Adam for a few days in a row. Unusual, but he was probably swamped with work. He virtually had two jobs these days: his firm and the school renovations. Still, the disappointment grew, not hearing from him. A distraction was in order. She climbed into bed and pulled out another entry from Joy's journal. She'd only read three entries so far; she loved the idea of going slowly instead of rushing through. Typically, after reading even just a page, the words circled in her head for days afterward.

As always, Noelle expected the paper clip to contain Polaroids of paintings. But this entry only held a single photograph. An aging, yellowed, black-and-white photograph with a half-inch tear at the side. She released it from its silver clasp and stared at the four people staring back at her. She recognized two of them instantly—Aunt Joy and Gram, young, dressed in their 1950s wear: patterned dresses that fell below the knee; pillbox hats atop precise, curled-under hair; and white gloves, properly clasped in front. They smiled slightly and squinted into the sun.

The other two were Uncle John and Grandfather, neither of whom Noelle had ever known. Uncle John died in a tragic car accident about a decade later, a devastating blow to Aunt Joy. She never remarried. And Grandfather lived about twenty years after that, dying of a heart attack the very year Noelle was born.

Aunt Joy had shown her this photo during one of those teenage summers. Noelle had walked into the library one afternoon to see Joy crouched onto the rich Oriental carpet, sorting pictures from a box—lifting them out one by one, remembering, moving to the next one. Noelle tried to back out of the room, leaving Joy undisturbed, but her heel caught the edge of the carpet and she tripped, drawing Joy's attention.

"Sorry," Noelle had said.

Instead of being irritated, Joy had waved her in, patted the carpet, and invited her to stay. They spent the afternoon browsing the pictures together, including this one. In fact, Joy had lingered on it the longest. "Very handsome," Noelle had offered.

Joy wrapped an arm around Noelle's shoulder, still looking at the picture, and said, "Enjoy your youth, Noelle. They're simpler days." Her voice cracked with emotion. "This was taken before the accident changed everything. Before it altered my future. We were so happy here.

Not knowing what was ahead. Part of me wants to step back inside this picture, just remain there. When life wasn't nearly so... complicated." Noelle had wondered then what that meant and still did. If it had anything to do with the letter Gram had waved in Aunt Joy's face at the gallery.

Noelle turned her attention to the next journal entry, entitled "Memories."

It's impossible to capture a memory on canvas. Too many factors and perspectives involved. Too much room for error, room to get the memory wrong. So I shan't even try. I found this picture inside an old box of things while cleaning out a closet. And I stared for over an hour, letting it take me back there. A place I rarely go. Because it's too difficult to nudge myself back to the present afterward.

Those Glory Days were fine days. Laughter and art and music and smoking and drinking. And love. Always love.

Looking at us this morning, the four of us, made me wonder—how accurate is a photograph? How much can you truly depend on it? The crispness of the edges fades over time, just as the memories do. You adapt them to fit your version of the past, what you wish had taken place instead of what actually did.

A friend snapped the photo, just before we took off to the horse races. A very good day. A breezy, sunny, glorious day. The four of us laughed and even sang songs on the way to the track. I wish we had been frozen in time the way this photo has frozen us. Because the complications and heartaches that would follow... well, none of us had any idea. How could we know! There we stood, smiling—so innocent, so dashing.

I came close to tearing up the photo tonight but decided against it. No, let these young people stay innocent. Let them enjoy each other and not have any idea what's ahead. That's the least I can do for them.

Noelle found a table in the back corner and took the seat facing the door so she could see Adam when he arrived. She had suggested the bakery for today's lunch, since she thought he might be tired of the pub.

Minutes ago, she ordered the items he'd texted her from the meeting—ham sandwich, potato soup, coffee, plus the same for her. She hoped he would turn up before everything got cold.

When she looked up from her coffee, Adam approached the table. "Hey," he said, shrugging out of his coat before sitting down. "That old man out there"—he pointed backward toward the door. "What a hoot. He must be a hundred years old."

"Ninety, I think. Mr. Bentley. He's amazing."

"You won't see anything like that in London!"

"Are you being a London snob?"

"Quite the opposite. I love how quaint this place is. It's refreshing."

She spread her napkin out on her lap. "How much time do you have?"

"Not very long. Need to head back to London soon. Thanks for ordering. What do I owe you?"

She waved him away. "It's on me, no worries."

"I'll get yours next time, then." He blew on his first spoonful of soup. He looked more tired than usual. Dark circles rested under his brown eyes.

"How's the project going? Are things coming along as planned?"

"So far. In fact, the first draft was finished last night. Still have lots of changes ahead before we can finalize them. But at least we've got the core idea down on paper. I've got the plans in the car, if you want to take a look."

"I'd love to."

He told her about the progress, all the people volunteering their time to work on it with him spearheading everything. And as he talked, it occurred to her *this* Adam seemed oddly disconnected from his teenage self. Each time they'd met lately, she leaned less on the memories of their teenage years and more on the man he'd become, special on his own. If she'd met him today for the first time, she wouldn't need to rely on old teenage memories to feel something for him. To fall for him now.

Damn. There she went again.

"Well," he muttered between bites. "I've completely hogged the conversation. Sorry. Tell me more about how things are. Are you settling into the village well? Is it starting to feel like home yet?"

She told him about working with Frank more often and getting to know Holly. Then about Mac, how protective he was of the cottage, which made her feel safe. And how she had learned nearly every person's name in the village, along with how they were connected to each other—friends, sisters, husbands, wives. "I think they've finally quit seeing me as that strange American who's invaded their village, taken over Joy's cottage. I wouldn't call myself one of their own yet, but maybe someday."

They finished the meal and made the short trek to Adam's car, still parked at the church at the end of the street. "This is pure hindsight," Adam said, "But I suppose before I accepted this project, I should've asked how you felt about it. Me, being here in 'your' village."

"You mean, like, getting my blessing?" It sounded so old-fashioned when she said it that way.

"In a sense, yeah."

"It's incredible, what you're doing. Why wouldn't I approve? You've got it. My blessing, my help, my anything you need. I'll even make calls for you, get my hard hat on—"

"You have a hard hat?" He raised an eyebrow.

"You know what I mean."

He squinted sideways at her. "A hard hat might suit you, though. Of course, you'd need a blue one to match your eyes. I wonder if they make them in blue. I should check into that."

He pressed his key to unlock the door with a chirp then offered a ride to her cottage, which she accepted. The cold air was starting to seep into her bones.

At the cottage, he kept the engine running but got out to find the plans in the backseat. She walked around to his side of the car. When he unfolded the papers, they revealed squares and rectangles with numbers of dimensions and abbreviations. Obviously, she didn't view or interpret them from Adam's detailed perspective, but she could see how much work he'd put into them. On his own time, with his own money.

"These are great," she said, wishing she had a better word than "great."

"Thanks. I'm happy with them." He folded the plans again. "So, I don't have any more meetings planned before the holidays. Sort of a lull while I play catch-up at the firm. Guess I won't see you until after Christmas?"

"Yeah, guess not." She didn't want to ask where or how he would be spending his holiday. Surely with his future wife and his future in-laws. The thought made her too-full stomach turn.

"Guess I should go." Before she knew it, Adam had caught her up in an embrace. Her cheek lay against his warm chest. The hug only lasted a couple of seconds, but it was long enough. It was everything.

He whispered "Happy Christmas" before letting her go then kissed the top of her head and backed away to open his door.

Stay, please stay, she begged him in her mind. Instead, the words came out, "Drive careful. Be safe."

She watched him pull away, knowing that was the same warning she should be giving herself when it came to Adam.

Chapter Thirteen

A painting offers immortality. When we put our colours onto the canvas, we put ourselves there. And as long as that painting stands, even a hundred years from now—whether in a stranger's parlor, a loved one's home, or even a museum—we exist.

HOLDING THE ORNAMENT BY THE top of its thin gold twine, Noelle watched the pair of miniature ice skaters twirl. For the last hour, she'd trimmed the Christmas tree near the sitting room window. Mr. Darcy pawed playfully at a ball Noelle had given him earlier to distract him.

She hung the skaters onto an empty tree branch with haste. "I'd better go," she told Mr. Darcy. Even though Joe had told her the pub party was a "come-and-go" affair, she didn't want to be too late.

It took her a few minutes to dress in dark slacks and a festive gold sweater, brush and spray her newly trimmed hair, and freshen her lipstick. Normally, she didn't need to dress up in the village. But tonight was Christmas Eve, a reason to get a little fancy. She wrapped up in a long wool coat, wiggled her hands into her leather gloves, and told Mr. Darcy goodnight. She could brave the weather for the block-and-a-half walk. Taking her car would be silly.

That little-kid fascination with Christmas snow never really went away, Noelle noted as she shut the front door and lacy flakes drifted down. She walked down the snowy path then pivoted to see her snow-capped cottage with Christmas tree lights winking through the window. It all reminded her of an enchanting snow globe.

A couple of minutes later, Noelle carefully stepped down the last part of the slick incline at the bottom of her street where Mistletoe Cottage stood. Mary Cartwright, the postman's wife, decorated their cottage to the hilt each year—lights on all the windows, on the shrubs, with a stocky Christmas tree prominently displayed in the front window—all presumably living up to the cottage's Christmasy name. As Noelle walked further on, she paused at the art gallery's window currently displaying a copy of her aunt's *Christmas Village* painting. One of her very first, actually. Children skating on a frozen pond, two cottages in the distance, a snowman in the corner. Frank had told Noelle that displaying the painting for the whole of each December had become a tradition. He had asked Noelle to be the one to hang it in the window three weeks before, a ceremonial passing of the torch.

Opening the pub door, Noelle stepped into a boisterous, cheery atmosphere, immediately glad she came. Wall-to-wall people sitting at tables, standing at the bar, or throwing darts at the corner board, laughing, chatting, eating. And drinking. The tinge of alcohol punctuated the air, and Joe, the Master of Ceremonies, offered up pints of lager to the masses. He caught her eye in the chaos and waved her over. Noelle weaved her way through the crowd toward the bar and squeezed into a spot just vacated by a man attempting to walk five topped-off mugs back to his table. Mr. Bentley, a few spots over at the bar, told some elaborate story to a small crowd of people. Odd, not seeing him at his post with his plate of food samples.

"Glad to see you," said Joe, his smile genuine and cheerful.

"I wouldn't miss it! I think the entire village is here," Noelle shouted over the crowd noise and struggled out of her coat, careful not to elbow anyone.

"Yes. Even our good vicar." Joe nodded to his right. The handsome collared vicar stood with his young wife, holding a pint and laughing with everyone else.

Nat King Cole sang about chestnuts and Jack Frost, and Noelle said wistfully, "Mmm… I love that song. Reminds me of home."

"Nothing like Mr. Cole to set a holiday mood."

"Do you do this every year?" she asked. "Throw a party?"

"Every year for the last ten. Lots of folk are alone on Christmas—widowers, couples with older kids who live far away. I wanted to have a place people could go. No reason to spend a holiday alone and depressed."

"Amen to that!"

"Can I get you a plate of our Christmas Eve special? Roasted turkey, stuffing, cranberry sauce, and plum pudding to top it off."

"Sold."

A few minutes later, Joe appeared with a plate and a pint. Noelle climbed up on the tall stool and decided to stay at the bar for now. She wouldn't dare try to make her way with a plateful of food through the crowd. Plus, she doubted any tables were open.

A few delicious bites into her meal, she glanced up and noticed Joe at the other end of the bar, whispering something into his new girlfriend's ear. He and Lizzie, the waitress, had recently become inseparable, and everyone in the village had observed it. Noelle started to return to her plate, not wanting to stare, but Lizzie's stunned expression forced her gaze to stay.

The shock on Lizzie's face quickly became a joyful smile as she nodded "Yes" to Joe. He pulled something from his pocket and placed it on Lizzie's finger as tears streamed down her cheeks. Joe scooped his new fiancée up in his big, burly arms and twirled her around. Most people had been too busy drinking or singing Christmas songs or throwing darts to notice the intimate moment, so Noelle felt particularly honored she had. What better time for an engagement than a season devoted to love? She thought of Adam, about how he was celebrating his Christmas Eve. And what his proposal to Laurel might have looked like.

Joe took Lizzie by the hand while he grabbed the microphone usually used for Quiz Nite. He switched off Bing Crosby and tapped the mic before he said, "Attention, everyone!" He kissed Lizzie while the crowd settled down. "Please," he said louder, "Everyone—I have something to announce." All at once, the crowd's buzzing faded to a soft hush. Joe swallowed hard then smiled and said with great pride: "Lizzie Gallagher has just agreed to be my wife."

Raucous cheers broke out, with applause and whistles from all corners, as Joe gave his new fiancée a passionate kiss.

"A toast!" someone shouted from the back of the pub. Others joined in the chant, and soon the whole pub pulsated with it, "Toast! Toast! Toast!" Everyone who held a glass raised it high. "To Joe and Lizzie!" someone said.

"To Joe and Lizzie!" the crowd chimed in unison. Noelle's eyes glistened with tears as the happy couple beamed.

As people swarmed the bar to give individual congratulations to the couple, Noelle scrunched her shoulders to make room. Knowing she could congratulate them later, privately, she decided to leave the rest of her meal and return to a quiet cottage. She'd had enough bustle and noise for one evening. Gathering her coat around her shoulders, she stepped awkwardly off the tall stool but paused when she heard her name called.

"Leaving already?"

"Oh. Hi, Frank. I didn't see you. Yeah, it's getting a bit crowded."

He leaned in for a quick double-cheek kiss. "Well, Happy Christmas!" he said. He had draped his coat over his arm but kept his scarf on. He looked particularly fashionable this evening. "Oh, and have a cracker."

He held one end of a shiny paper tube. Noelle had seen them in a catalog before—Christmas crackers, an English tradition. Pull both ends, and the tube snapped apart with a *pop*! Out would pour a tiny trinket, some candy, a corny joke written on a square of paper, and a colored paper crown. Many partygoers wore them already, an entire room full of faux-royalty.

Noelle grabbed her end of the cracker and waited for Frank to latch onto his end before she started to pull. She winced in anticipation of the inevitable *pop*, and the tube ripped raggedly in half. Normally, the person ending up with the bigger half kept the cracker's contents. But Frank, holding the bigger end, exclaimed, "It's yours!" and pushed the items from the cracker toward her.

"Thanks. I'll see you next week. Merry Christmas!" She gathered the trinkets and put them into her pocket, planning to sort them out at home.

Approaching the door, she recognized a figure in the corner, hunched slightly and holding a mug, clearly not his first. Noelle released the handle and meandered her way toward him. "Hi, Mac. Can I sit?"

Glassy-eyed, Mac took a second to recognize her then nodded. "How are ye, lass? 'Tis a fine party." He extended his hand in a sweeping wave.

"Yes. It is. I didn't know you'd be coming."

"Aye. Join me in a pint?" His head bobbed slightly when he spoke, his eyes half-closed. "No, I don't think so. I'm about to head home."

"Oh, to that lovely wee cottage."

Noelle leaned in. "Mac, are you all right?"

"I'm fine enough. Don't ye worry about old Mac. He'll take care of himself. Been doing it all his life..." He polished off his mug in one swig and wiped his mouth with the back of his hand.

When he raised his finger toward the bar to order another, Noelle said, "I have an idea. I wanted to have some coffee at home, get away from all this noise. How about you join me in a cup? I could use the company. And Mr. Darcy would love to see you."

She was prepared to have to persuade him into it, but Mac zipped up his coat, reached for his cap, and stood, weaving slightly. "Lead the way, lassie."

Thank goodness, he wasn't so drunk that he had to lean heavily on Noelle up the hill, but she did support his arm most of the way. The snow didn't help, and a couple of times, when they slipped, she thought they were doomed to fall and break an arm or leg.

Inside, she sat him down by the fire, and Mr. Darcy snuck out of hiding to see him. Mac let out a chuckle and bent over with great effort to rub his ears.

"I'll be right back." Noelle hurried to make a pot of coffee before he changed his mind. She returned with two steaming mugs to find Mac half-asleep, petting the purring fur ball on his lap.

Suddenly, he looked up and pointed at the air behind her with his free hand. "That's where *she* always put it, too."

Noelle turned around to see what he meant. "Oh, the tree? I guess a part of Aunt Joy is still in this place."

"Aye. 'Tis." Mac took his coffee and stared down at the mug, his mouth forming a sort of pout.

"You miss her, don't you?" Noelle sometimes forgot that Joy had left behind a friend when she died. A friend who still mourned her, especially during a holiday.

"Aye. She was a fine woman, that one." He took a long sip then let out a wide yawn and scratched at his beard. For a moment, seeing Mac in this sad, drunken state, missing Joy, the thought flittered through Noelle's head that Mac might have had deeper feelings for her aunt than he let on. That he knew more about her aunt's secrets than he let on. But he already claimed not to know anything about the locked room, the embedded symbol. No reason to doubt him.

"Mac, why don't you finish your coffee and lie down? I'll be just a minute." She left to find an extra pillow and blanket from the closet under the stairs. When she returned, she took his mug and helped him get up from the chair, sending Mr. Darcy sprinting for another place to sleep. Mac spread his long legs on the couch, murmured something indiscernible into the pillow, and let out a sigh while Noelle covered him with the blanket. He started snoring by the time she finished poking at the glowing embers of the fire.

Not exactly how she had pictured her Christmas Eve, but she liked having someone here.

The next morning, Noelle awoke to find no trace of Mac, except for the blanket he had neatly folded and placed atop the pillow. She hoped his quick exit hadn't been a sign of embarrassment.

Noelle cleared away the blanket and pillow then fed Mr. Darcy, secretly wishing Mac had stayed at least to share breakfast. Her first Christmas alone. All during her twenties, Noelle had either shared the holiday with a boyfriend or with her single girlfriends and occasionally with her mother. Once, she spent it with her father and his family in San Francisco, but the awkward meal, filled with stilted conversation, told Noelle he knew nothing about her life. She ended up creating a lie about work to wriggle out of dessert.

As for Jill and Gareth, they had spent the Christmas holidays in Italy, visiting old friends. And she didn't dare let herself think about Adam. Not where he slept last night, or what he put under the tree for Laurel, or even whether they pulled a Christmas cracker together. Not today.

Her stomach growled, prompting her to make breakfast. Yesterday, she had purchased all the makings for French toast, a dish her mother made every Christmas morning for Noelle as a child. She gathered the bread loaf, the eggs, the powdered sugar and cinnamon, turned on the range, and found the right-sized pan. In a matter of minutes, she sat at the table, eating forkfuls of sticky sweet bread. As good as she remembered.

On her last bite, she reached out for the cluster of trinkets at the other end of the table. She'd been too distracted by Mac last night to sift through her cracker treasures, but today she sorted through them one at a time. A tiny set of jacks, a paper crown, a joke. She unfolded the blue crown and balanced it on her head then read the joke aloud to Mr. Darcy, who twitched his tail during the punch line. "How do rabbits travel? By hareplane. Get it? *Hare*plane." Noelle tossed the lame joke aside, crumpled up her paper crown, and told Mr. Darcy, "We are officially pathetic."

In order to feel less pathetic, she decided to open the gifts—five in all, from Frank, Mac, Jill, Desha, and her father. She hadn't expected anything from Adam, but a Christmas card might have been nice. Not that she'd sent him one, either. She considered it then re-considered, wondering if Laurel might not approve. Kneeling by the Christmas tree, Noelle reached for the first present and pondered why it had taken her so long to spend a Christmas in England. All those years when Gram and Joy were alive, not once did Noelle come to visit for a holiday. Gram had issued a standing invitation early on, but Noelle had never taken her up on it. She'd always been too busy with school or work.

Taking her time, she unwrapped the gorgeous Lladró figurine from Desha, the lavender scarf from Jill, a set of paintbrushes from Frank ("Hint, hint!" read the card), the silver flower charm for her bracelet from Mac, and a touristy *Famous Pubs in England* from her father. He knew all about her move across the pond and the inheritance of the cottage but nothing about the paintings. He wouldn't have cared, anyway.

As she gathered the paper to toss away, she imagined Gram and Joy, spending their Christmases, before the rift, alone in that enormous estate, drinking their tea and eating plum puddings together at the elongated dining table. Noelle heard Joy's raspy laugh as Gram read out the corny joke or made her balance the crown on her sister's head. Noelle would have given anything to have them with her this morning.

After placing the last of the custard tarts inside, Noelle secured the medium-sized box with green and gold ribbon. Two days after Christmas, the Brits celebrated Boxing Day, a custom where they took boxes of food and clothing to charities and churches, or goodies and treats to local tradesmen.

Noelle made several delivery stops that afternoon—a box for Joe and Lizzie, one for the postman, Mr. Cartwright, one for Mrs. Pickering, a box of clothing to donate at the vicar's, and finally, a special box for Mac. After his Christmas Eve intoxication, she'd been reluctant to seek him out. He probably didn't want to be found. Still, she took a chance and walked to his cottage about a half-mile north of the village up a sloped hill. His front garden was immaculate, as expected. Trimmed rose bushes, manicured lawn, pristinely cut shrubs.

A series of unanswered knocks told her Mac wasn't home, so she placed the box on his doorstep and closed the top securely so the night critters wouldn't get the goodies before he did. She had left a card inside saying simply, *Thanks for all you do. Noelle.*

Mid-afternoon on New Year's Eve, Noelle awoke on the couch. The last time she slept in the afternoon had been in college.

Yawning, she remembered she'd been watching TV and petting Mr. Darcy before dozing off. The past week had been an exhausting blur of holiday activity, so a little daytime snooze had apparently been in order. She muted the television and perked up her ears to a sound outside. A scraping noise, distinctly rhythmical. *Swish, (pause) thud. Swish, (pause) thud.* Unable to identify it, she let her curiosity take her to the front door to find the source.

Mac. Well, the back of him, at least, shoveling snow from the narrow path. Noelle shut the door again softly and made a fast pot of coffee. For some reason, she wanted to have something in her hand, an excuse to talk to him, a coward's way to start a conversation. She walked out into the bright sunlight with the piping mug, one hand shadowing her eyes to see him more clearly. "Mac?"

Having just flung out the last patch of snow, he turned and placed the shovel down, leaning on the handle.

"I brought you some coffee."

"Thank ye, lass." Mac took the mug from her, his gray-blue eyes squinting in the sun.

"Did you have a nice week?" she asked, unsure of how far she wanted to pry. Or how far he would let her pry. The cold January air stung her cheeks.

"Aye. 'Twas all right. Went to see my daughter over in Cardiff."

"Oh, that's nice."

"I received your box. The lemon squares were my favorite. And the new scarf." He was wearing it now. "Thank ye for it."

"You're welcome." Noelle blew out a sigh. "Look, Mac—"

"Lass, I—"

They chuckled together, breaking the tension.

"Let me start. Please." Mac stared at his coffee as he spoke. "I didn't expect you to find me that way... inebriated... on Christmas Eve. I don't hold my liquor well, and that evening, I was... a wee bit sad."

"Mac, don't worry. I was sad, too. My very first Christmas alone. In fact, I wish you had stayed over through Christmas morning. We could've been two sad, lonely people together."

"Aye, but I wouldn't have been much company. 'Twas quite the hangover I had." He shook his head.

Noelle mirrored his smile, relieved they were as back to normal as they could be.

After a light lunch of chicken salad and fruit, Noelle spent the afternoon unpacking. When Desha had mailed the San Diego boxes before Christmas, Noelle had removed the essentials and promptly hung the Cornwall painting right where it belonged, prominently in the sitting room, then Mac helped her move the rest of the boxes to the upstairs guest room until she could sort them properly. She'd meant to clear them away much sooner, but other things kept getting in the way.

She needed to keep busy, today of all days. Jill, back from her Italy trip, had called to invite Noelle to an impromptu New Year's Eve party. If she could be certain Jill hadn't invited Adam and Laurel, she might have actually said "Yes." But even then, she would be taking her single self to a house full of couples and finding the nearest bathroom at midnight to avoid the awkward kissing part. So, instead, she'd faked a headache and politely turned Jill down.

It didn't take her long to empty the six boxes from California—books, some kitchenware, various knickknacks. When she finished, she swept the floor in broad strokes, maneuvering dust and dirt into one growing pile in the center of the room. She crouched to sweep underneath the bed, and a hard object the broom had caught clinked against the wood. She swept the object closer, and it came to rest at her feet. Noelle picked up a purple object and dusted it off with her fingertip, the adjoining chain dangling over the top of her hand. The purple pendant. The birthday present Adam had given her during their final summer as teenagers. Perhaps it had fallen out of one of Joy's boxes, the ones Noelle had cleared out weeks ago while getting the cottage ready for the realtor.

She recalled the very last time she'd seen the pendant, the night before she left the estate that final summer. How upset she'd been with Adam, how she tore the necklace off in her bedroom. When she departed for the States, the pendant stayed behind. She couldn't bear the reminder of it. Joy must have known its importance, saved it for her, packed it away for safekeeping. No other explanation.

As the pendant dangled from the chain, Noelle remembered the day Adam had given it to her. She'd clicked open the tiny box and watched the sunlight reflect through it, turning the dark amethyst into something transparent, ethereal, as she lifted it out.

She and Adam had played checkers in the grand parlor of Gram's estate on a rainy day, where Adam surprised her with the small package. They weren't supposed to celebrate their birthdays until tomorrow.

"It's gorgeous," she'd told Adam.

"Your favorite color." He had looked so proud, as though he deserved an award for remembering.

"I know." She pushed down the urge to be sarcastic. But looking closer, noticing the shape, she frowned.

"What's the matter?" he'd asked, worried.

"Nothing. It's silly. But... a teardrop shape. It's a sad shape."

Adam grinned and rolled his eyes. "That's not a teardrop."

"It's not?"

"No." He took it from her then stepped behind her to place the chain around her neck. His fingers grazed her skin, gave her chill bumps. "This is a splash of purple paint. It's supposed to remind you of who you are. An artist."

"A paint drop. Not a teardrop?" She touched her neck and swiveled to face him.

"Exactly."

"I love it."

Time had dulled the paint drop's surface. Noelle walked into her bathroom and gave it a quick rub with a damp washcloth, watching the shine return. She reached back under her hair, secured the chain around her neck, and looked in the mirror. The pendant sat at the perfect height, just above her V-neck sweater. But instead of making her smile, it made her frown. She had the pendant. But not Adam.

This, on top of the bleak midwinter weather and enduring another lonely holiday, made Noelle want to escape. If she looked back, she realized something had been nagging at her for days. She had to shake it, push it away. An idea formed. She knew how she could escape, knew the one thing that might lift her into a place where she could lose perspective of time, of memory.

She had to paint. Or at least, she had to try.

Sensing a change in the air, Mr. Darcy followed her across the hall to the art room, where she had first discovered the paintings. All these weeks, she had left it alone. Left the half-finished painting where she'd found it on the easel, the art supplies in a neat pile in a corner. She recalled seeing a couple of completely blank canvases, presumably saved for the next of Aunt Joy's unfinished series. They leaned against the wall, waiting for Noelle. Almost as if Joy knew she needed them.

She gathered supplies then planted herself on the floor squarely in front of the blank rectangle leaning against the wall, having no idea what she would attempt. She rotated the canvas back and forth, squinted, imagining the possibilities. Then she picked up the brush and created the first stroke, hearing the luscious *pshhh* of the bristles. Within minutes, she'd covered the area almost completely with a simple off-white wash. She would figure out later what to create on top of it. This was the easy part. A child could do it. But even as she made the wide, deliberate strokes across the canvas, she let the insecurities take over. She hadn't picked up a brush in well over a decade. And sitting in the room of an artistic genius, the intimidation became too strong.

Exasperated, Noelle dropped the brush into the nearby can of turpentine and left the room, closing the door behind her. She would paint again. Just not today.

She removed the pendant then walked into the bedroom and opened up the desk drawer. She didn't want the reminder of Adam around her neck, the emotional weight of it. Inside the drawer, she found that picture, the one with Adam and Jill as teenagers on either side of her. She lowered the pendant on top of it, watching the gold chain descend in a delicate spiral on top of itself, on top of them, and shut the drawer tight.

Chapter Fourteen

Don't be too selfish with your art. Share it. In fact, paint something strictly for someone else, to go on someone else's wall. Don't always paint for your own pleasure. It's good to practice a little selflessness.

S ENDING YOU A PHOTO. JILL never texted photos, didn't even know how, as far as Noelle knew. So when Noelle received the text from her friend, her curiosity grew as she waited. And waited. She pictured Jill fumbling with her phone, clicking buttons, getting aggravated, cussing under her breath, maybe even begging Gareth for help.

Finally, Noelle's phone dinged again. She looked down to view the picture, a black-and-white image that quickly came into clear view. A button nose, eyes, fingers, and toes.

Her phone rang before she could dial Jill's number. "Did you get it?" Jill asked.

"It's a baby!"

"Of course it is, Silly."

"No, I mean, it's not just some abstract blob. It's clear. Like 3-D or something."

"Isn't it fab? Technology these days. Gareth wants to frame it, put it on the dresser."

"I'm so happy for you guys. How are you doing with all this?"

"Better every day. You were right. It just took me some extra time. When I saw that little face on the monitor this afternoon, I melted. She's mine. And she's beautiful. I'm not having an ugly baby."

Noelle snickered. "She? You're having a girl!" Noelle's turn to melt. Jill would be a fun mom to a little girl, playing dress-up, having tea parties.

"I think this sonogram made it real for me. I needed to see her, to hear that heartbeat, to know she was a real little person. She even waved at me, I swear it. I can't wait to meet her."

"Me, too. I couldn't be happier for you guys. So, the due date?"

"End of May. It'll be here before we know it!"

Jill shifted topics, brought up last week's New Year's Eve party, confirming that Adam had come with Laurel. Noelle couldn't help herself. She had to know. "What is she like? Laurel? Spill everything."

"Hmm. Laurel is... not what I expected."

"How do you mean?"

"Well, she's very tall, nearly as tall as I am. And brunette. Not being mean, but she's sort of... plain-looking in the face. That does sound horrid of me, doesn't it?"

"What's her personality?"

"Nice enough, I guess. We didn't have much time to talk, things were so loud and hectic, but the couple of times I looked over, she was texting. Adam stayed with her most of the time, but I never saw them talking. He talked to other people. Frankly, she looked quite bored. She's just—"

"What?"

"Not what I pictured Adam would choose for himself."

"What did you picture?"

Without a beat, she said, "Petite, California blonde. With light-blue eyes and a sweet spirit. Living in the Cotswolds, just about to become a millionaire from paintings discovered in her aunt's upstairs secret room."

"Stop it, Jill." Her friend was teasing, but it stung—the acknowledgement that even Jill knew Adam and Noelle should be something more.

"Seriously. Are you sure you're okay with this? I know we've never talked about Adam that way before. But I sensed something between you two, way back when I first had you both to dinner before Christmas. I mean, that instant connection, even Gareth commented on it afterward. The banter, the laughter, the easy conversation. Like you hadn't been apart a single day."

Noelle wanted to break down and tell her. Finally say it aloud to someone, that Adam's engagement had devastated her, especially the timing. That it still did. And that she realized along the way she'd never stopped loving him. Not for a single minute. Ever since their reunion at Jill's house, Noelle had talked herself into believing they were just friends. That she was being noble, respectful of Laurel. When all along she knew differently. She was a complete coward, afraid to tell anyone her true feelings. Even to Jill. Even to herself.

Knowing Jill, though, she would get involved on her friend's behalf, maybe even try to break up Laurel and Adam just to help out. The very last thing Noelle needed. No, best to keep it hush-hush and maintain some level of control, some level of dignity in a messy situation. Keep calm and carry on.

Noelle said dismissively, "Maybe I'm not okay with it. But what does it matter, anyway? He's going to marry her. In fact, I'm sure there's already a wedding date set."

"They haven't set a date yet. But they're looking at early fall—maybe September or October."

Just as seeing the sonogram finally made the baby real for Jill, picturing Adam's potential wedding month on a calendar did the same for Noelle. All this time, the engagement had been some vague image in some abstract place and time in the faraway future. But not anymore. Still, Noelle had to pretend. "See? A few short months away, and he'll be a married man. He's already made his choice."

"But that was *before* you moved here. Before he saw you again."

Noelle wished she had never started this snowball of a conversation in the first place. Her own fault for bringing it up. "Can we drop it? Please?" she begged. "I'm happy for him. I only want him to be happy."

"If you say so. Consider it dropped."

"Thank you. Let's talk about something else. Something good. Baby names!"

"Notice the contrast in hues around her eyes." The professor pointed with his laser light to an area on the screen then clicked his remote for the next slide, a black-and-white image of a dog baring its teeth.

Noelle tried to stare at the slide, but her attention drifted back to the professor, a younger version of Viggo Mortensen, that *Lord of the Rings* actor—longish-brown hair, chiseled jaw, pensive, soft-spoken. He made it difficult to concentrate. Last week, when she attended her first art class at the community college in London, the professor suggested she move to an advanced course, taught by a Mr. Evans. She'd only missed one class and wouldn't have far to catch up.

Viggo's twin, Mr. Evans, folded his arms and asked for questions. Noelle looked around the room at the other students. All different ages, the youngest in his twenties, the oldest possibly in her eighties.

Hearing no questions, Mr. Evans clicked off his projector and gave the homework assignment for next week. "Paint something. Anything. I don't care if it's still life or active, animal or object. The only requirement is to inject yourself into it, something personal. Snap a photo of it, email it to me before class, and we'll analyze them on screen next week."

Noelle panicked at the thought of being forced to paint, much less showing her work in public to perfect strangers on an enormous screen. But she had originally sought out these classes to flex that artistic muscle again. To chase after her youthful passion, now that she had time. And so she would. Noelle closed her spiral notebook and followed the mass exodus of students out the door.

Later that night in her art room, a hot cup of tea on one side and Mr. Darcy on the other, classical music playing from her iPod, she sat cross-legged in front of the same canvas she had whitewashed several days ago. The one she'd given up on without even trying. She had no idea what to paint. None.

And then she thought of her first painting, that awful, boxy sheep. Surely, she could attempt it now. And if she hated it, she could start all over again.

Noelle smoothed the crease with her finger then tore off a piece of tape and carefully secured the thick silver wrapping paper. Mr. Darcy, who had leaped up onto the chair to watch her at the breakfast table, pawed at the tape dispenser every time Noelle reached for it. She had tried luring him away from his new game with treats and toys, but to no avail, so she'd given up altogether.

Inside the nearly wrapped box lay the Waterford crystal wedding announcement frame she would give at tomorrow's shower for Joe and Lizzie. She could hardly believe their wedding was a week away. When people asked Lizzie why they were getting married so quickly, only a month after Joe proposed, she always responded, "I found my soul mate. Why should we wait?"

Noelle's cell buzzed on the table, a text from Adam. Only the second communication since they last hugged good-bye before Christmas. The first, a brief email exchange last week, started when he asked how her holidays went. Harmless chitchat. And now, the text that said simply, *Seeing light at end of work tunnel. Will make trip to CC soon.*

She didn't know what "soon" meant, but before she could tap out her question, a knock on the back door made her pause. The familiar tan of Mac's jacket appeared through the window, and she called, "Come in!"

He removed his tweed cap and chuckled at Mr. Darcy, who was twitching and dancing around to remove sticky tape from his paw. Noelle remembered the date. "Oh. Yes. Let me find your check." She rummaged through a nearby drawer and found an envelope with Mac's name on it. "Here you go."

"Sorry to intrude. You look occupied."

"Oh, you're not intruding. This is for Lizzie and Joe. Their shower is tomorrow."

"Aye."

"Did you ever do it? Get married, I mean." She returned to her ribbon and looked up. "I know we don't talk about that sort of stuff, so tell me to take a hike."

"I'm a widower. Over two decades." His lips pursed together as though he felt the sting of the loss, even now.

"Oh. I'm sorry."

"Don't be, lass. We packed a lot into those years provided to us. And had our daughter. And two grandchildren."

"That's wonderful." She struggled to picture Mac as a married man. He seemed the eternal bachelor type.

Mac replaced his cap and thanked her for the check then left as unobtrusively as he'd come. As he shut the door behind him, Noelle's cell rang. She'd thought it might be Adam, following up on his previous text, but it was Desha.

"Hey!" Noelle had left her a birthday voicemail earlier that morning. They hadn't talked in weeks, and as much as Noelle adored her new British life, she loved hearing an American accent.

"Thanks for the bag! How did you know I wanted one?"

"You told me last month." Noelle smiled into the phone.

"Oh, right!"

Noelle put the cell on speaker and set it down to continue with the ribbon.

"How are things in the Cotswolds?" Desha asked.

Noelle caught her up on the normal surface-level things: her art class, the big auction next month. She still hadn't told Desha about Adam and probably never would. She wouldn't even know where to start.

"There's something I have to tell you," Desha said in that hushed-tone thing she did whenever she had something scandalous to talk about. "Brace yourself. It's about Steve."

"Steve?" Noelle evened out the ribbon's ends. She hadn't heard that name in ages. Her last boyfriend, the Cheater.

"I'm not sure how to say this."

"Just spit it out. I can handle it. I promise."

"He's getting married next weekend."

Steve, the bastard who said he'd rather be murdered than ever get married. "How did you find out?"

"Well. Becky bumped into Avery at a club last night, and he told her the news."

"Do I know her? The fiancée?" Not that it mattered.

"No. Some girl from Santa Fe."

Noelle set down the scissors harder than she'd intended, scaring Mr. Darcy, who darted off the chair to escape. "Well, *good for him.*"

"Are you okay?"

After a beat, shaking off the idea that Desha felt sorry for her, Noelle said, "I'm great! Listen, there's someone here, and I need to go." Close enough to the truth. Mr. Darcy was still in the doorway, waiting until the scary scissors stopped being a threat. "I'm sorry. Have a terrific birthday—eat some cake for me!"

"Okay, bye! And thanks again for the bag!"

Noelle clicked off the phone. She stared at the gift for several seconds, the painful irony of weddings all around her, then signed the card. *Joe and Lizzie—Best wishes on your marriage. Love, Noelle.*

She sat down with her to-do list for the day. But the page contained only Steve's image, marrying some girl from Santa Fe. Moving forward with his life. It didn't help that Valentine's Day was coming up, stubbornly reminding her she had no valentine of her own.

Noelle steadied her hand to dot the blue jay's eye with a tiny prick of black paint. She wiped off the brush with a rag and stretched her back muscles.

Frank had been over at the corner desk most of the morning, making calls. Yesterday, he had phoned Noelle with an idea to turn the gallery back into a "working" gallery, as Aunt Joy had done in the early years. He begged Noelle to be the first artist. Her immediate response was, "Oh, no. Absolutely not. Emphatically no." But later that evening, in her second art class, she found a new excitement, a new confidence. Mr. Evans had spent the most time on her sheep, pointing out to the class its textures and the particular shade of ivory she'd used for the wool. He'd even asked her how she mixed the colors to capture it. Inspired, she started a new painting. This time, a blue jay. And then she called Frank back with a "Yes."

This morning, when she set up the barely started canvas on the back room easel, the familiar wave of insecurity hit her, and she almost backed out. A crazy idea, painting in public. The pressures, the judgment, the lack of artistic solitude. But the serendipitous timing of everything gave her courage to try.

She had started out slowly, mixing colors, dabbing the paints, stepping back from it, messing up, and trying again. And minute by minute, stroke by stroke, her fingers remembered Aunt Joy's artistic advice from all those years ago: *Trust yourself. Lose control. Take risks. Accept frustration and imperfection. Share your art with others.*

Three hours later, she'd finished almost a third of her painting. She rubbed her back again and watched Frank pour a cup of strong tea, which he handed over to her.

"Can I see?" Holly peeked her head from around the canvas.

"Sure."

"Oh, beautiful," she whispered, stepping around. "It looks like one of your aunt's, I think."

"Thank you. That's high praise."

In the last half hour, regular villagers such as the postman's wife, Mary Cartwright, and the local schoolteacher, Mrs. Farraday, and even the vicar and his wife visited the gallery to see Noelle's painting. Frank had likely advertised her very first in-gallery painting session somewhere in the village. Or perhaps had told Mrs. Pickering, which amounted to the same. The villagers' curiosity got the better of them, wondering whether Noelle had inherited any of her aunt's artistic talents.

The front door bell rang, and Holly disappeared around the corner to return to her post. Noelle stood to rinse out her teacup after finishing it off. "I think that's all I can do today. My eyes are getting tired." She reached for the canvas to return it to the storage room, but Frank waved her away.

"No, no. I'll get that in a sec."

"Are you sure?"

"Yes, Boss, I'm sure. You've worked hard today." He stepped back to see the painting. His opinion meant more than curious villagers, wandering tourists, or even Holly.

"Beautiful. The deep blue, the depth perception here." He pointed under the bird's wing. "It's going to be absolutely gorgeous. We'll hang it in the front window when it's finished."

Noelle's worries melted away. "Thanks, Frank."

He helped with her coat. "Any glitches with the auction? Has Sotheby's told you anything?"

"Things seem to be good. I got an email last week from the manager. Everything's on track."

"I wanted to ask you something. If Holly held the fort here, would it be possible for me to… tag along with you? To the auction?"

"If I go, I would love to have you there with me. I certainly don't want to go alone."

"If?" His face filled with horror, as though she was insane to consider for a single moment not going.

The nearer the auction came, the more hesitant Noelle became. She wasn't sure about attending. Not because she would anxiously wonder how much a piece would or wouldn't get, but because her aunt's paintings would walk out the door forever, belonging to perfect strangers who'd never even met Aunt Joy. The finality of it made her wistful. She could never make Frank understand, so she said, "It's just a bit overwhelming, the closer it gets."

He nodded. "It's still surreal, isn't it?"

"I'm not sure it will ever stop being surreal."

Chapter Fifteen

You are the only one who can make the decisions—where to cast the shadow, where to add a more vibrant colour. No one else can decide it for you, so lean on your own judgment. Be comfortable with it.

THE CHURCH HALL HUMMED WITH pre-wedding activity, and Noelle sat in the middle of it, patiently sprinkling birdseed onto a wafer-thin mesh square in the palm of her hand. Practically all the ladies in the village had gathered to help prepare for Joe and Lizzie's wedding and reception tomorrow.

Twisting the mesh to form a bag, Noelle fashioned a pink ribbon to secure the bundle and thought about the unity of the village. The flowers, cakes, dresses, all made by local townspeople. She had never experienced this sort of town-kinship before. Certainly not in a city the size of San Diego.

Noelle's cell rang. Seeing Adam's name, she abandoned her birdseed bag and walked toward the door. The echoing of laughter and noise in the church hall made it impossible to hear anything.

"Hello?" She found a secluded bench outside and sat down.

"Hey, it's Adam. Sounds like a party there."

"We're getting ready for a wedding. Lizzie and Joe, the pub owner."

"Oh, yeah. The vicar told me something about a quick engagement for those two. I didn't know the wedding would be *that* quick."

"They're a sweet couple. I think they're just eager to be together and didn't see the point in waiting. Are you in London?"

"I'm in my car, headed your way. I'm about ten minutes from Chilton Crosse, in fact."

Noelle performed a lightning-fast mental assessment of how she looked. Windblown hair, hardly any makeup, faded jeans. *Ten minutes?*

"I know it's short notice," he explained, "but I'm meeting my parents for lunch. Since they live in Bath, I figured you might want to join me? I could pick you up and drop you back off afterward. They'd love seeing you after all these years."

As tempting as the invitation was, Noelle couldn't just up and leave the church hall, abandon the women who had so much work ahead, even for a long lunch. Plus, seeing Adam's mother, a well-kempt, perfectly-coiffed socialite who would examine her head-to-toe at first glance, required much more preparation than only ten minutes.

"That's a sweet offer, but I can't leave. I'm helping out for this huge reception. So much to do. I'm sorry."

"Okay, no big deal. Just thought I would ask."

"Maybe another time, though?"

"Of course."

Noelle lifted a piece of birdseed stuck to her jeans and mashed it between her thumb and finger. "How are your parents? Are they doing well?"

"They're good. Active, busy. Though Father did have a mild heart attack last year. Gave us a scare. But he's fine now. Recovered quickly from it."

"I'm glad. Sounds frightening."

"Oh bugger," Adam said. "I think my phone is breaking up. Can only hear every other word now. Guess I should let you get back to your function."

"Okay. Have fun with your folks. I'll take a rain check."

"Great. Talk to you la—"

She hadn't gotten a chance to ask when his next meeting in the village was. Surely, he needed to return to the project soon after his lengthy hiatus.

Noelle's Adam Radar strengthened as she imagined him driving along the outskirts of the village, blaring his music, donning his sunglasses, and driving too fast.

Noelle shuffled the Polaroids like a deck of cards, skimmed the adjoining journal entry. There should be four paintings in the set, but she only counted three. She hadn't memorized every single painting she'd found in that locked room months ago, but the idea that a Polaroid was missing from the block of this entry's "Water" artwork nagged at her. She had to be sure.

When Noelle had discovered the journal in the desk's secret compartment on Halloween, she had been so absorbed that she didn't thoroughly check the space for possible fallen Polaroids. Perhaps not all of them had been so tightly paper clipped as the others. She pushed back the sheets and stuffed her cold feet into her warm slippers. Mr. Darcy stared at her from the foot of the bed through slitted eyes, watched her crouch at the writing desk and tap open the wooden door with great care. She pushed her hand inside the dark space, as deep as her arm was long. Something sharp pricked her finger—the Polaroid, wedged into the wood's seam. Then her pinkie touched something soft, velvety. She abandoned the Polaroid and drew out the new object.

A pink ring box. She cracked it open to reveal an unusual gold ring with some sort of symbol.

She twisted the ring out of the snug pillow and held it between her thumb and index finger, tilting it back and forth to see the symbol up close. The very symbol she and Adam saw with the magnifier inside Joy's paintings. The embedded *W*.

She reached inside the compartment again, not wanting to forget her purpose for being there, the Polaroid, then clicked the secret door shut, pushed off the floor, and brought the ring with her back to her bed. She studied it closely, observed the miniscule dent at the back, the dull, well-worn surface. She couldn't stop staring, wondering who might've given this gift to Aunt Joy in the first place.

Chapter Sixteen

How do you paint an emotion? Something abstract and impossible to grasp? Think of something that represents that emotion: a man at a gravesite, a newborn baby, a bride holding her bouquet. When we see these things, we recognise them instantly: sorrow, hope, love.

OPENING HER FRONT DOOR, NOELLE spotted the looming rain clouds, far enough away that she decided against an umbrella. Surely, she could walk the short distance to the church without being caught in a downpour. Under her long coat, she wore a dress with black lace overlaying a forest-green lining, her favorite dress she'd ever owned, bought in a small Bath boutique a couple of weeks ago. There, she'd also found the vintage black-pearl barrette that she wore in her hair, braided loosely and clasped at the nape of her neck.

Walking briskly, she reached the market center and noticed Joe, head-down in the middle of the street, fidgeting with the wardrobe bag in his hands. She called out his name.

Looking up, he smiled then whistled a catcall.

"Oh, stop. You're getting married today." She tapped his arm with her purse.

"That doesn't mean I can't tell a fellow villager how gorgeous she looks."

"Why, thank you." Eyeing his plain T-shirt, which held what appeared to be a jam stain near the collar, she replied, "And you look... not quite ready yet. But soon-to-be gorgeous."

"I'm getting dressed at the church. There's not much time left."

"I need to hurry, too. I'm supposed to meet Mrs. Pickering and help her with something before the ceremony." A familiar car pulled up behind them and stopped a few feet away. Adam, grinning inside his black convertible, top down.

"What are you doing here?" Noelle called out, taking the few steps to the driver's side.

"I stayed overnight at my parents' in Bath. Thought I'd surprise you."

"Mission accomplished."

"Wow. Look at you." He stared at her hair then looked her up and down with a smile. "Nice dress. So, today's the wedding?"

By now, Joe had stepped closer to greet him. "Adam, mate! Haven't seen you 'round here in ages."

"I had to take some time off from the project, catch up on work. Plus, the holidays and such."

"Well, you're just in time for a wedding. Join us," Joe insisted. "Starts in half an hour!"

"I wouldn't want to intrude."

"Nonsense. You're part of the village now."

Adam's attention shifted back to Noelle. "Well, I do have a suit with me. The folks still make me dress up for dinners." He smirked. "As long as you're okay with it."

"Of course I am!" *But will Laurel be?*

"Sorry to run, but I'm going to be late for my own wedding." Joe took off for the church.

"So, I guess this means you'll need some place to change," Noelle told Adam. "The cottage?"

"Hop in."

She eased into the black leather passenger seat. Adam followed the road, parking behind Noelle's car outside the cottage. The moment he shifted into park, the skies opened, releasing coin-sized drops of rain.

Noelle shrieked and scrambled to get out of the car, hunching into her coat, raising the collar above her head as far as it would go. "My hair!"

"You go—I'll put the top up!" Adam yelled as she rushed through the gate and up to the cottage.

Inside, she peered into the hallway mirror. The rain hadn't completely ruined her hair. It would only need a quick touch-up. She had kept the front door open for Adam and watched through a sheet of rain as the top of his car clicked shut. Adam darted inside, his wardrobe bag draped over his arm.

For some reason, the sight of Adam utterly soaked and out of breath, his dark wet curls sticking to his face, struck her as hilarious. She tried to cover her mouth, turn her head away, but she couldn't stop herself. "You're a drowned rat," she said.

"Thanks a lot! I'm a freezing drowned rat." He started to unbutton his shirt. "Can you do something with this? It's soaked. I've got an extra shirt in my wardrobe bag I can put on for the wedding."

"Sure. I'll stick this one in the dryer." He peeled off the shirt, revealing wet chest hair. A flash of Colin Firth as Mr. Darcy in *Pride and Prejudice* invaded her thoughts. She blinked to remove the image. She didn't have time to daydream. They could not be late for the wedding.

She took the sopping-wet shirt, careful not to hold it too close to her dress, and tossed it into the dryer. She grabbed a fluffy clean towel from a basket and returned to Adam. "Come with me. I have a plan."

He rubbed at his hair with the towel and carried his bag up the staircase. Mr. Darcy padded up after them.

Noelle pointed to the guest room. "You have ten minutes. There's a hair dryer in that bathroom. Do you have everything else you need?"

"My jacket might be a bit wrinkled."

"Here. Let me have it." He unzipped the bag and pulled out the jacket. "You go dry your hair and get warm. I'll iron this. And hurry up! We cannot be late!"

"Yes ma'am!" He closed the door behind him.

In her bedroom, Noelle plugged in the iron and set up the board, laying the jacket across it. While she waited for the iron to warm up, she hurried to check her hair in the mirror, finger-combing stray strands. She added more gloss to her lips and a quick dab of powder to her nose. Through the wall, Adam's blow dryer hummed.

Five minutes later, she finished ironing the jacket sleeve and saw Adam standing in the doorway. With his hair still curled slightly from the moisture, and at that distance, he looked seventeen all over again.

He reached up to fasten the top button of his shirt, and she noticed it again. That tuft of chest hair peeking out at her.

"Noelle?"

"Huh?"

He nodded toward the iron.

"Oh!" She'd held it in place too long. Steam rose when she lifted it up, but she'd done no damage. She held up the jacket for his inspection.

"Brilliant."

She turned off the iron and grabbed her coat again. "C'mon. We're barely going to make it!"

They took Noelle's car, since Adam's interior was still damp with rain. At the church, she pulled into the last spot with four minutes to spare, the rain having slowed to a puny drizzle.

Noelle hadn't stepped inside the church since yesterday, and she marveled at the lovely job Mrs. Wickham had done with the flowers. Red roses adorned the front of the church, with tall, white candles lit throughout. Beautiful.

Noelle and Adam found two of the last seats at the back of the church, on Joe's side, and settled into the pew. A minute later, the organ music began and three bridesmaids in Wedgewood-blue dresses floated down the aisle. Lizzie appeared next, wearing an angelic white lace dress and holding white roses. Of the fifteen or so weddings Noelle had attended in her lifetime—cousins, college friends, co-workers, even her own parents as they married other people—Joe's seemed the most genuine. Maybe because of the candlelight or the gleam of tears in Lizzie's eyes, but something made the atmosphere in the church tangibly romantic. The lightheaded, contagious zing of excitement that emanated from two people deeply in love.

During the vows, a bizarre, out-of-place sensation struck Noelle. Less than four months ago, she hadn't even known where Adam lived or what he had done with his life. He really only existed deep in her memory. But today, he sat beside her, inches away. The faint rhythm of his breath, the tapping of his leg beside hers, clearly not a figment of her imagination.

After a musical rendition of "The Lord's Prayer" by the vicar's wife, Rachel, the vicar introduced for the first time, "Mr. and Mrs. Joe and

Lizzie Tupman!" The couple kissed amidst boisterous cheers and strolled down the aisle arm-in-arm.

After the ceremony, the crowd sifted through the back door to move, en masse, out of the church and toward the pub for the reception. During the procession, no less than four women had stopped Noelle, asking her to introduce her "handsome date." Each time, she responded, "This is Adam Spencer. An old friend of mine. And the architect for the school renovations." Each time, the inquirer pursed her lips and said, "Ooh, nice to meeeet you," as she shook his hand and looked him up and down. His half-smile told Noelle all the attention amused him.

The moment they entered the pub, Mrs. Pickering whisked Noelle away from Adam and assigned her cake-cutting duties at a table in the back corner. She could hardly say no to Mrs. Pickering, especially since she'd been a no-show right before the wedding, and hoped Adam could fend for himself. Occasionally, between dispensing slices of white cake, Noelle caught Adam across the bar laughing or nodding along with someone. He spent most of his time with the vicar, likely catching up about the project. They even took off for a while, still chatting away, probably going on-site to discuss the plans.

"Lass, you look lovely." Mac stood before her, hands in pockets, dressed in a starched white shirt and dark slacks.

"Aww, thank you, Mac." Noelle handed him a plate and fork. "And look at you! All dressed up. Did you enjoy the wedding?"

"Aye. 'Twas what any wedding should be. Short and sweet."

"Did you get to meet Adam yet?"

"Adam?"

"Yes." She gave the same old speech. "He's an old friend. And the architect who's working on the school renovations. Oh, here he comes. Let me introduce you."

Adam approached the table with that infectious smile of his. He had charmed the entire village already. It was Mac's turn. Noelle made the introductions, and they exchanged a firm handshake. Mac gave his best attempt at a smile, but Noelle thought she read a suspicious look in his eye as he met Adam's gaze. Maybe Mac was just being protective. In the short months she had known him, Noelle discovered that only part of his duties were of the gardening variety. Mac watched over not only the gardens but also the cottage, as well as the occupant inside, much as he had probably done with Aunt Joy. A sort of dedicated watchdog, prowling and protective. In a sense, he was sniffing out Adam while shaking his hand.

Mac gave a gentleman's nod to Noelle. "I'd better be off. Stayed too long as it is."

Noelle waved goodbye then lifted a plate and fork up to Adam. "You haven't had any cake."

"Neither have you, I'll bet."

"True." The coast finally clear and everyone served, Noelle selected a piece and joined him on the other side of the table near the fireside. "Mmm. So good. I've been smelling it for an hour," she said with her first bite. Dense white cake layered with rich cream cheese frosting. "Heaven."

They watched from their little isolated corner as the traditions began. Joe, bent on one knee, reached around his new wife's leg for the garter. A crowd had gathered, and the bachelors of the group stood in a huddle, prepared for Joe to fling the garter. Thankfully, Noelle had already missed the bride throwing her bouquet, always her least favorite part of a wedding.

"Oh, I think that's my cue." Noelle put down her plate and wiped her mouth with a napkin. "C'mere." She grabbed Adam's sleeve and led him to a table with two baskets, each piled high with tiny bundles. Noelle placed her hands around the rim of one basket and said proudly, "I made these." She picked up a bag and displayed it in the palm of her hand like Vanna White showing off her letters.

"Impressive. What the hell is it?"

Noelle faked offense and batted the bag at his chest. "Birdseed, dummy. To throw at the bride and groom as they leave. Not the whole bag—the seeds inside the bag."

"Ah. I knew that."

"Help me pass them out?"

"Sure."

She gave him one of the baskets, and they waited for the guests to start lining up to receive the bags. In a matter of minutes, the bags were handed out and opened, the birdseed sprinkled at the bride and groom as they ducked and ran past the wedding guests. When Noelle wasn't looking, Adam showered her with a palm-full of birdseed.

"Adam!" She feigned irritation and waited a beat before returning the favor.

"Ow!" He put a hand up to his eye.

Noelle's smile disappeared. "Oh, no. Did I really get your eye?" She reached her hand up to his face.

"Gotcha!" he said, grabbing her wrist.

"You wanker," she whispered, trying to wriggle out of his grasp. They had drawn unwanted attention. Mrs. Pickering had stopped to stare, which meant others would likely follow. Adam released her wrist, and Noelle cleared her throat and started to collect empty bags.

Once the happy couple had driven away, streamers and shoes attached to the trunk of their car, Noelle and Adam walked back inside to help with the cleanup, but Mrs. Forsythe stopped them.

"Oh, no, Noelle. You've helped enough today. And yesterday as well! My goodness, take the rest of the day off, you two. Go enjoy yourselves."

Noelle wished Mrs. Forsythe hadn't been so transparent, that little nudge-nudge, wink-wink as she included Adam in her command. Knowing that protesting would only egg her on more, Noelle said, "Thanks. We will." She grabbed her purse and coat, then she and Adam headed back outdoors, where the clouds had disbanded in at least one broad corner of the sky.

On their brief drive to the cottage, Adam spotted the gallery. "I had a chat with your curator at the reception. Fred?"

"Frank."

"He says you're painting again. Is that right?"

"Guilty as charged. I'm also taking an art class. In London. Are you impressed?"

"Terribly. And glad for you. I think it's important for a person to keep up with their talents."

"You think I have talent?"

"You know I do."

Back at the cottage, Mr. Darcy emerged from his usual sleeping spot and followed them upstairs. Noelle's updo was giving her a headache, so she unclasped her hair and combed it out with her fingers. The braid had created relaxed, airy waves in her usually straight hair.

"Is that the room? Where you found all those paintings?" Adam pointed across the hall.

"That's the one."

"Mind if I peek?"

"Sure. Not much in there at the moment." Of course, she meant in the way of Aunt Joy's things. But the minute Noelle said the words, she remembered something else in that room, one of her own paintings-in-progress, not ready for public viewing yet. Too late now, though.

She led him to the door and cracked it open. He walked in, skimming the entire room then moving closer to the canvas on the easel.

"That's Joy's. Her last piece," Noelle confirmed before Adam could ask.

"Rather haunting, isn't it?"

"It's probably worth something, but I couldn't bear to part with it. I always wonder if she knew... whether it might be her last."

Noelle's own half-finished canvas, a church with a cemetery beside it, lay propped against the wall. "This one's great." He inched closer to it. "Yours?"

She nodded, her nerves rising as he squinted.

"I see some of your aunt's techniques here. The little detail of the cross up top, the shadow beside it." He pointed to the church's steeple. "It's very good."

"Thanks." Relief. Empty flattery wasn't Adam's style. "Oh," she said, "I nearly forgot. I want to show you something else. I discovered it last night."

"Another find?"

He followed her to the master bedroom, where she opened the nightstand drawer to produce the ring box. As with the journal, she planned to tell only Adam about the ring, no one else. Noelle wasn't comfortable sharing either treasure with the world.

He reached for the box she offered and cracked it open.

"I found it in that same secret compartment, in the side of the desk." She pointed to it. "Deep inside, which is why I missed it the first time."

He inspected the ring, brought it closer. "The symbol. There it is. I wonder who gave this to her. Are you going to tell anyone, share the news?"

"You're the only one who knows about it. I'll keep it for myself as an heirloom."

"Really fascinating. Wish we could figure out that blasted symbol. The answer is probably right under our noses."

Adam returned the ring to the box then handed it back to her. He put his hands in his pockets and rocked on his heels, producing the first pause between them all afternoon. She didn't know what to do with it.

"Well," she said, closing the drawer. "My shoes are killing me. And I'm tired of being in this dress. I think I'll change."

"Yes. And I need to go dry out the rest of my car."

"Take anything you need—paper towels, cloth towels. And your other shirt is dry by now. I'll meet you downstairs in a bit."

He shut the door softly behind him, and she shook off her heels, one at a time, hoping that in trying to fill the awkward pause, she hadn't shooed him away too urgently.

Minutes later, changed into a sweater and jeans, Noelle walked downstairs to find Adam. She'd half-expected to see the wardrobe bag draped over his arm as he stood at the front door, ready to leave for London. But he stood in her kitchen, leaning against the counter and waiting for the kettle to boil. In no hurry at all, apparently.

"Better?" he asked.

"Much. How's your car?"

"Beyond help at the moment," he said with a grimace. "Still quite damp. I did all I could do then left the top down to air it out. Thank God the rain stopped. Oh, and I put the towels into the wash already."

She offered him a selection from the basket of tea bags on the table. He thumbed through them and chose Earl Grey as the kettle whistled sharply. Noelle found two matching floral-patterned mugs, and Adam poured the water. "Let's go in here," she suggested, and they carried their mugs into the sitting room.

As if reading her mind, Adam added two logs to the fireplace and lit a fire, then sat opposite her in a chair. Mr. Darcy sprung up into Adam's lap and startled him. He let Mr. Darcy turn and hunch down into a furry ball, then he reached for his tea, laying his other hand on the cat's back.

"Aww. I need my camera," Noelle said.

"Don't you dare." He smiled.

"So, you were quite popular at the reception. I kept watching you being pulled aside by different people."

"It's a friendly village."

"Too friendly, sometimes. Mrs. Pickering probably filled your head with all sorts of gossip. Most of it untrue."

"The vicar and I caught up. A sort of impromptu meeting. We needed it, especially after the long holiday." He took another sip.

"I'm sure he was glad to have you back. How's the project coming?"

"Good. I kept working on it from home sporadically, so we aren't really behind. But I had to catch up on the firm's work. It's my bread and butter. Speaking of, Michael mentioned that the school received a pledge for a large donation, thanks to an 'anonymous donor.'" He stared at her, one eyebrow raised. "Perhaps from a certain someone who will shortly be coming into some major cash at a Sotheby's art auction?"

"I have no idea what you're talking about," she said with a sly tone.

"Hey, between the two of us, we'll get this school back on its feet in no time."

All this time, Adam hadn't yet mentioned leaving for London. Noelle took a chance. "Are you hungry for some dinner? I only had a little cake at the wedding. I'm starved."

"Sure. I'll help."

Noelle had already planned to make a simple cottage pie tonight, alone. But the thought of having someone else to share the meal with filled her with instant joy. As much as she'd gotten used to being alone, eating alone, she sometimes missed the presence of another person in the house.

She retrieved the ingredients from the refrigerator and the cabinets then found the proper pans and bowls. She knew the recipe by heart. Adam stepped in beside her at the table, watching her arrange the items, waiting to be instructed.

"How about the mashed potato part?" she suggested.

"Okay. I'm good at that." Adam gathered the potatoes and began washing and peeling them while Noelle chopped the carrots and onions. For several minutes, they worked together in a quiet rhythm. Occasionally, their arms brushed against each other as he chopped a potato or she reached for another onion. Noelle wondered if he ever cooked with Laurel. Then she wondered what Laurel might think, knowing Adam had attended a wedding today with Noelle and had lingered at her cottage. She should feel guilty, but she was having too much fun. Besides, it wasn't as if they'd planned all this. And if his fiancée's reaction concerned him that much, he would have called her before now.

Adam dumped the quarter slices of potatoes into the saucepan then added water and set it on top of the burner. Noelle had already placed her chopped vegetables into her fry pan, along with the ground beef, some herbs, and tomato sauce. The spicy aroma of the sizzling mixture filled the kitchen.

"Mmm… if I wasn't hungry earlier, I am now," Adam said.

They worked together to create the pie. Noelle carefully poured out her mixture while Adam spooned out his mashed potatoes for the second layer. Noelle sprinkled some grated cheese on top, with salt and pepper, and placed the dish into the Aga.

"Do you cook a lot?" Adam asked.

"Not really. I go to the pub a couple days a week, I guess. And do take-out at least once a week. How about you?"

"Lots of take-away or restaurants, usually. I hardly ever eat a meal at home. Or sometimes I'll work till late in the evening and eat at the office."

"That was me, back in San Diego. Always working."

"Yeah. I can relate. If I let myself, I can work seven days a week without a break. I have to make myself stop, remind myself it's okay to sleep sometimes. But I love it."

"You loved it as a teenager. Architecture, I mean. When you took me on my first tour of Bath, we were what, fifteen? You knew the history of the buildings and all the architectural details. I can't look at a cathedral as 'just' a cathedral anymore. I see the arches and the spires and the lancet windows."

"Good memory!" He chomped on an uncooked carrot. "I always thought I was boring you."

"You could never bore me."

The corners of his mouth curled up as he chewed, and Noelle's pulse beat faster. That smile...

The timer on the Aga buzzed, and Noelle stooped over to look at their creation.

"Here, let me." Adam slid his hands into two oven mitts and pulled the golden pie from the oven.

Sitting at the kitchen table, savoring all the flavors in the meal, they continued chatting about the project, the gallery, and the quirky people that made up the village. "They'd make for some great characters in a TV show, wouldn't they?" Adam smirked.

"Definitely. Feels like I'm in *Ballykissangel* or something."

Halfway through the meal, the hall clock chimed, and Adam put his fork down with a clink. "Bollocks. It's six o'clock? I didn't realize. Sorry. I need to check my messages. I shut off my phone during the wedding and forgot to turn it back on." He reached in his pocket and checked the cell's screen. He winced. "Four messages."

"Go ahead, check 'em. The food can wait."

For privacy, he walked to the sitting room. Noelle imagined all four messages were from Laurel, each growing sterner, wondering where he might be.

A minute later, he spoke into the phone, just scattered phrases. His tone sounded almost too matter-of-fact, as if he was trying to make his excuse too ordinary. "Stopped off... see an old mate..."

When he returned, Noelle pretended to be absorbed in her meal. Adam's shoulders drooped slightly. She assumed he often looked that way after speaking to Laurel. Especially if she often chewed him out.

"I need to head out. Sorry to be so hasty. I wanted to help with the cleanup."

"It's fine. No worries." Noelle walked him to the door.

He gathered his bag, fished his keys out of his pocket, and gave an apologetic grin. "Thanks for dinner. And for a great afternoon. I hope you didn't mind my dropping in, crashing the wedding."

"Didn't mind at all. And looks like you'll have good driving weather now." She cracked the door open and confirmed the sunshine.

"Yeah. My interior should be dry by now, too."

He hesitated. The slight wince, almost regretful, told her this wasn't the way he wanted the visit to end, so abruptly. He gave a little wave with the flick of his hand, and walked down the stone path to his car.

Palpable, the immediate stillness in the house when she closed the door. For an entire afternoon, Adam had unexpectedly brought her companionship and laughter. And as suddenly as it came, it disappeared.

Chapter Seventeen

*Use the darkness inside you—take something you long for,
something out of reach, and look for it inside your painting,
knowing you might not ever find it. Because that quest, that
hunger, will translate into something raw and real.*

"WHEN WE GET INSIDE, YOU'LL see a floor of display, sort of like a museum. This is where pieces that go up for auction are usually located, so people have a chance to browse and make decisions. And then inside the auction room…"

Frank had talked nonstop ever since they first drove off in his car nearly an hour ago. He figured Noelle needed an education on every little facet of what she was about to experience during her first time at Sotheby's. She let him drone on, feeding him an occasional cursory, "Mm-hmm" or "That's interesting," happy she didn't have to do any of the talking. She needed to be inside her thoughts right now.

Earlier, getting ready for this Valentine's Auction, Noelle came close to backing out. To calling up Frank and making up some sort of excuse that would fall under "legitimate enough" to miss her aunt's auction. Perhaps she'd inherited a bit of her aunt's hermit gene and simply didn't want to surround herself with mobs of hungry bidders, competing and clamoring to make a purchase. She pictured piranhas in a river, fighting over the same piece of food. But calmer and slower, and with British accents.

Frank deftly maneuvered through London's West End, turning sharp corners, dodging fast-moving taxis and tour buses, until finally they reached their destination with only a few minutes to spare. He found a parking spot a block away, the closest he could get. They were supposed to meet the General Chairman outside the auction room twenty minutes before it began.

The Sotheby's building stood multiple stories high, with a clean white façade and the navy flag stamped with "Sotheby's" flying overhead. As Frank opened the front door, Noelle caught a quick glimpse of the poster in the window announcing Joy's art collection. She caught the words "Exclusive!" and "Never-Before-Seen!" before Frank rushed her through.

As they swept past marbled floors, cafes, and exhibit rooms, she made a mental note to slow down later and do some browsing. An elevator took them to the auction room where Mr. Felspar, the General Chairman, was waiting.

"I'm so sorry we're late," Frank gushed.

"No trouble at all. Glad you could make it." Mr. Felspar, nearly bald except for trimmed tufts of hair above both ears, extended a hand to Noelle. "Lovely to finally meet you."

"You as well," she replied.

The time for courtesy had expired. The auction was about to begin. As Mr. Felspar led them through the side doors to their special seating up front, Noelle tried to take it all in. Hundreds of people seated on the main floor, the wall of people to the side who chatted on phones and stared at computer screens, and the podium and display stage up front where the auction would take place.

Finally, the excitement had started to set in. Noelle took her seat beside Frank and listened to the steady thrum of people buzzing, talking on phones, talking to each other. She wondered how many spectators or reporters attended only to leer and satisfy their own curiosity.

A man appeared behind the podium, which hushed the crowd instantly. He adjusted his tie and spoke into the microphone then welcomed the attendees. The man's gaze rested deliberately on Noelle as he put a hand out, and the crowd's attention followed. "Seated in our front row this day at Sotheby's is Miss Noelle Cooke, great-niece of today's artist, Joy Valentine. We are pleased to have her here."

A smattering of applause followed, and Noelle nodded at the crowd, hoping they didn't expect her to stand.

Then the man got down to business. He talked about the collection, told about how the paintings were discovered in Ms. Valentine's cottage, how she had produced them in her "reclusive" years, how they each contained a secret symbol known only to the artist. That drew a few scattered "Ohs" from the audience.

He waved his hand like a magician calling for his assistant, and two women wearing gloves appeared, carrying the first painting. Noelle recognized it at once, from the "Water" series. The ladies set it down on the easel with the greatest of care, and the audience craned their necks to see.

"We shall start the bidding at one hundred thousand pounds. One hundred thousand." He scanned the crowd and nodded. "One hundred. One hundred twenty-five? One hundred twenty-five?"

Another bid, another nod. Person after person raised a polite, deliberate hand to make a bid. Not piranha-like in the slightest. The people lined against the walls, on phones, staring at computers, made bids as well, likely from international collectors who couldn't attend the auction in person.

"Three hundred thousand," the auctioneer said. Noelle did some quick math in her head. Three hundred thousand pounds, translated into U.S. dollars, times thirty-four paintings, if each sold close to that amount. Noelle's estimate lay around seventeen million dollars, minus Sotheby's commission. Staggering!

Frank clenched her wrist so tightly that her pulse thumped hard underneath his grasp. She knew he wanted to jump up and shout for joy, and the only thing preventing him from doing so was holding onto her.

"Sold!" said the auctioneer, tapping his wooden gavel onto the podium with a *crack*. "For three hundred twenty-five thousand, to Paddle number 437."

Frank gasped. She didn't dare look at him lest he squeal aloud. He finally removed his grip and clutched his auction program.

Noelle was too stunned to gasp. She couldn't possibly wrap her head around an amount like that. The money represented someone, many someones, interested in Aunt Joy's paintings. The ones she painted all alone in that upstairs room, probably thinking they would never see the light of day. And here they were. The acceptance, the approval from an international audience, made Noelle's eyes mist over. Joy's presence settled on that room as the auctioneer announced the next painting in the series and the gloved ladies placed it on the easel.

Noelle's phone buzzed deep inside her purse and she retrieved it, the screen still blurry from her tears. A text.

Hey Sunshine. 325—that's a lot of dough!

She took in a sharp breath as her Adam Radar switched on. She tried to be subtle while she peered around the room, but she couldn't see him anywhere. Her phone buzzed again.

To your left. Other end of the room.

He sat far enough away that she couldn't see the details, but she still recognized his frame immediately. He was probably tempted to wave but stopped himself, afraid the auctioneer would mistake it as a bid. *You're here! Didn't know you would come,* she texted back.

"Two seventy-five," the auctioneer said. "A new bidder for two hundred and seventy-five thousand pounds..."

She hadn't seen Adam since the wedding two weeks ago. He had come to Chilton Crosse to walk the site with the general contractor, but Noelle had been in Bath on gallery business and had missed him. They hadn't talked about the auction lately, and he never mentioned attending.

Wouldn't miss it. Joy would be proud, he texted.

She smiled, knowing he understood what she was feeling by being here, that it wasn't about paintings and pounds.

She faced the front again, trying to focus on the auction, but Adam had unexpectedly divided her attention. She couldn't stop thinking about how he had made a concerted effort to attend. *Had he assumed I would be here, too? Had he hoped I would be?*

The auctioneer fell into a natural rhythm with the bidders as the next several paintings glided by swiftly, all selling for near three hundred thousand pounds each time, and one even nudging close to the four-hundred-thousand mark. Maybe the secret symbol had made the difference. She never expected them to sell this high.

About halfway through, she received another text from Adam. *You look bored. Wanna blow this joint?*

Bored, no. But mentally exhausted, yes. She'd had her fill of what she wanted to see, of why she'd come. And really, the excitement level had plummeted by now. She knew the routine, knew the paintings were valuable to people, and that was all she really needed to know.

Sure, she texted back. But the moment she hit "Send," she worried how rude it would be to step out. Especially being in the very noticeable front row. She couldn't up and leave, abandon Frank. What would Mr. Felspar think?

But when she looked for Adam, he'd already gone, and her phone buzzed again. *Meet you at your side. In hall.*

She tapped Frank's arm and whispered her plans. His mouth gaped open. "Now?" he whispered. "You can't leave now!"

But she wanted to. She was antsy, and Adam was waiting. "Adam is here. I'll text you where we are, and you can meet us after. Is that okay?"

She hated the disapproving judgment in his eyes—*leaving your own aunt's auction?*—but he would have to understand. At least she came at all. She could have backed out completely this morning, leaving Frank on his own. Finally, he nodded, patting her arm as she gathered her purse and tried to sneak out the side door without drawing any attention.

Adam waited with an enormous smile beyond the door. His hair was longer than she remembered from the last time, wavier. And his coat was new, a leather jacket. Probably a Christmas present.

"You gazillionaire, you," he said, teasing her. "Will you remember us little people when you buy your big mansion and hire four butlers? Your own private Downton Abbey?"

"Quit it." She play-slapped his arm. They walked together toward the elevator.

"No, seriously," he said. "Aren't you thrilled about this? They love her work. It's a hit!"

"It's amazing," she admitted. "A good day. An emotional day."

"I can imagine."

When they reached the bottom floor and the elevator opened, Noelle asked where they were going.

"There's a little pub down the street. Just thought you might want to get out of there for a while."

"You thought right. Pub sounds perfect."

Only a half block away, the Red Lion stood between a bookstore and umbrella shop. They stepped inside the cozy, dark restaurant, with a center bar similar to Joe's. Wading through the clusters of tourists and business people, they found a table at the back corner and wriggled out of their coats. They ordered coffee and sandwiches from the server, who returned with their plates and cups almost immediately. Adam slit open three sugar packets and dumped insane amounts of sugar into his coffee.

"I remember that about you," Noelle said. "More sugar than coffee."

"Hey, it's better that way!" Sitting back, he loosened his royal blue tie. "So how are things? Other than, of course, your becoming a gazillionaire?"

"Would you quit that?" she said but couldn't stop grinning. "Let's change the subject. Please."

"Fair enough."

"Well, you'll be glad to know that I'm doing well with my art classes. They're giving me confidence. And I'm learning a lot. I've never really studied art before."

"Good for you. Here in London, the classes?"

"Yep." Noelle pinched off a bite of her sandwich crust and ate it.

"What sorts of things are you learning?"

"So far, we've studied special techniques and classic paintings. Last week, Mr. Evans told us about the golden mean. He's got us looking at photography, how still-life images can be translated to the canvas."

"Golden mean? You mean Golden Ratio?"

Noelle bowed her head. "Yes. Exactly. That's what I meant."

"Yeah, that's a concept in architecture, too. All about proportion and balance. And geometry."

"Exactly."

"The Egyptians used it for their pyramids. That's where the ratio originated. Then the Greeks and the Romans..."

Noelle loved to hear him talk that way. His whole demeanor changed when he spoke about his passion. His eyes grew brighter, and he gestured more. When he paused, she said, "I never realized photography and architecture had so much in common."

"Neither did I. You know, I remember you with that camera of yours." He wagged his index finger at her. "Didn't your aunt give it to you on a birthday or something? That one summer, it became another arm. You never went anywhere without it."

"I remember," she said, surprised he remembered, too.

Moving the napkin around with the tips of his fingers, Adam paused thoughtfully and let out a sigh. "Those summers. We were so bloody young then."

"I know."

"Feels like centuries ago."

"Sometimes it does. But, other times..." She stirred her coffee in slow circles.

"What?"

"Well, other times those days seem closer. I'm still the same person inside. And sometimes it's like fourteen years haven't passed at all, and I'm back to being that girl again." *Like now, when I get so flustered around you that I can't even remember the Golden Ratio.* Noelle shrugged. "Didn't mean to get all philosophical... I'm talking nonsense."

"Not nonsense. Nostalgia. It's nice." He smiled and reached for his coffee.

"Well, it's ultimately Jillian's fault. For bringing us all together again in the first place."

"Cheers to Jill, then." He lifted his mug. "That makes her the reason we're having a coffee together right now."

"I guess that's true." She lifted hers too, clinking it against his. "Oh! I forgot to text Frank. He doesn't know where we are. He's my ride." She tapped out her message and sent it, wondering for a moment how the rest of the auction was going. Frank would tell her every last detail on the way home.

A group of college-aged students in the far corner raised a collective shout, drawing Noelle's attention. They had finished a darts game with congratulatory pats for the winners and profanity from the losers. They soon cleared away, gathering jackets and books to walk out the door.

Noelle smiled. "To be that young again. I do envy them—so much to look forward to."

"Yeah, the drudgery of a job, a mortgage, a car payment..." He smirked.

She threw a crust of bread at his tie. "That's not what I meant. They're lucky not to know the future."

Adam ate the last bite of his sandwich, wiped his mouth with a napkin, and looked at Noelle with a glimmer in his eye. "I forgot to tell you something."

"What?"

"This"—he waved his hand in a look-around-you gesture—"is a magic pub."

"Like haunted or something? Like those shows on the Travel Channel. 'Haunted Pubs of London.'"

"Nope. This pub has the ability to take you back in time. If we go over there for a darts game, I guarantee all your adult worries will vanish completely. We'll be seventeen again."

"Magic darts, eh?"

"Give it a try?" Adam stood up and offered his hand.

"Why not." Noelle took his strong, gentle hand and scooted from the bench, following him to the dartboard.

Adam rolled up his sleeves and sorted out the darts, offering Noelle her choice of color. "Ladies first." He stepped out of her way. "Oh, we forgot to set the wager."

"What wager?"

"This is a darts game. There must be a wager."

Noelle smiled. "Fine. What do you suggest?"

"Something sweet. Their best dessert."

"You're on!" Noelle focused hard on the dartboard. She remembered a brief lesson Adam had once given her long ago at a pub in Bath. "Shoulders squared, dart firmly between index finger and thumb, focus on bull's-eye, and release!" Her first dart landed an inch from the center of the board, and she jumped up, letting out a squeal.

"A fluke," Adam said. "Nothing to worry about."

They exchanged places, and Adam poised himself, readying the dart between his fingers. With the release, the dart sailed toward the board and landed an inch to the other side of Noelle's, away from the target.

"*Not* a fluke," Noelle mimicked.

"I'm rusty, that's all." Adam rotated his wrist over and over, stretching it out.

"Yeah, that's what they all say."

Noelle kept her lead up until her last dart, which sank into the edge of the board, nowhere near the target. Adam stood tall, confident, rolling his final dart between his fingers, studying the board with full concentration. At the precise second he cocked his hand back to throw, Noelle took an impulsive step toward him and blew on his neck. His dart flew wide off the board entirely and bounced off the wall.

Noelle suppressed a laugh, her hands up in feigned innocence.

"Soooo not fair," he said, shaking his head in mock-irritation. "You're a cheat!"

"Am not. You had the advantage, having pubs and darts around you all your life. I haven't thrown a single dart since high school."

"Well. When you put it that way. I concede."

They smiled together in the afterglow of a carefree game. A new batch of tipsy businessmen had gathered behind them, waiting to play. "You finished, mate?" one of them asked.

"Oh. Yeah." Adam placed a hand on Noelle's lower back and guided her through the crowd toward their seat. By then, Noelle had received a text back from Frank.

"We'll have two of your best desserts," Adam told the server.

Noelle read the texts: *Last few paintings. All selling well. Be there in half an hour.*

"All good?" Adam asked.

"All very good. The auction's almost over. Selling well. Frank will stop by afterward."

"What's that guy's story? Frank?"

"What do you mean, 'story'?"

"I met him at Joe's reception, and we chatted for a bit. He's a friendly chap but... odd. Does he have a family? Or a girlfriend? Around the village, I never see him with anyone. Except you, of course."

"I think art is his girlfriend," she replied.

Adam smirked and nodded. "Gotcha."

When dessert came, they talked about the school renovations, Jill's pregnancy, Adam's new clients, and the assistant he had to fire due to incompetence and missing several important deadlines in a row.

"Hey, if the darts are magic, maybe this will be magic, too." Noelle held up her last bite of cheesecake. "No calories?"

"Absolutely none," said Adam.

When the server returned with the check, Adam paid for the meal and desserts before Noelle could even reach for her wallet. "My turn," he reminded her. "And besides, a bet's a bet."

Noelle started to put on her coat and remembered Frank. He should've been there by now.

"You know," Adam said, breaking her thoughts. "This was fun. Maybe we can do this again. In London, I mean."

"Sure. I'm here for my class every week. It runs through next month."

Adam looked past her, and Noelle craned her head to see Frank approaching the table.

"It was a-ma-zing." Frank stood between them, clasping his hands. "The last painting, called Joy, it sold for... brace yourselves." He leaned in and whispered, "Six hundred."

"Thousand?" Noelle verified.

Frank nodded until his glasses nearly fell off the end of his nose. He pushed them back.

Adam whistled. "Whoa."

"Over half a million pounds?" Noelle asked. "That's..."

"A million dollars," Frank confirmed. "For one painting. One!"

"See?" Adam said with a wave. "Gazillionaire."

"Are you okay?" Frank said, touching her shoulder.

"I'm in shock, I think." Noelle couldn't take it in, didn't even know what that amount of money looked like. Or what she would possibly do with it.

Frank tapped on the table. "We need to hurry back to Sotheby's. There's a meeting with the Manager and Head Curator. For paperwork, et cetera."

"I didn't know."

"I didn't either. Mr. Felspar met me afterward."

"Did you cover for me?"

"I told him you were 'overwhelmed with joy.'" He winked.

"In more ways than one." Noelle grabbed her purse and stood. "You didn't eat anything."

"It's fine," Frank said. "There's a delicious café inside Sotheby's. The corned beef is particularly good." To Adam he added a polite, "You're welcome to join us, of course."

"Thanks, but I can't. I have plans tonight."

Plans. Noelle had forgotten about Valentine's Day, in spite of the red and white decorations draped around every inch of the pub. His plans tonight included Laurel.

"Have fun with your paperwork." Adam gave Noelle a quick kiss on the cheek then whispered, "And congratulations. I'm glad the auction went so well." He squeezed her hand and walked away.

"We'd better scoot," Frank prodded. "They're waiting on us."

After a lengthy meeting with the Sotheby's people—tedious, boring paperwork and information about the process, the transfer of funds, the legalities of sales and such—Noelle endured an equally tedious drive back with Frank. Once again, she let him ramble on about every last detail she had missed while at the pub. She tuned him out, shifted to look out the window, and thought about Adam. Thought about what he would wear tonight, where he would take Laurel, what he had bought for her. What sort of champagne they would drink, what sweet nothings they might exchange.

And there she sat with Frank. Looking ahead to absolutely no plans of her own. Perhaps she would turn in early, block out Valentine's Day. *What makes it more special than any other day of the year, anyway?* Maddening.

A few hours later, after a simple supper of a ham sandwich and some canned potato soup, she wanted to read another journal entry. After today, with Joy on her mind, she sought her counsel. Wished she could be there now, in the flesh, keeping her company and telling her what to do with those incessant feelings for Adam. She had to face it, that being "just" Adam's friend wasn't enough anymore. Every time she saw him, she seemed to fall harder. And it hurt more.

Deep under her covers, trying to banish the cold that seeped through the cottage windows, Noelle flipped the journal to the bookmarked page. The series title read, "Freedom/Captivity." Mr. Darcy purred at her feet as she detached six Polaroids. She had seen those paintings in person that very afternoon. They ended up being the highest bid-upon series, collectively. A wealthy businessman from Japan bought all six.

She studied them up close. Three of "Freedom"—a seagull caught in flight over a jagged coastline, a collection of bright blue graduation caps poised in midair, and a modern painting of different shades of red fading into one another. And three of "Captivity"—a caged tiger looking forlorn, a man's hands shackled in handcuffs, and a modern painting with blacks and grays and dark blues. Eagerly, Noelle turned the page to the matching journal entry.

Love is a paradox that endlessly fascinates me. I'll never come to terms with all its vast complexities, even after all these years of living.

At its worst, love has frightened me, devastated me. I've become vulnerable and raw and exposed because of it. The idea of putting my trust, my fate, into someone else's hands is the greatest risk ever asked of me. Because I lose control, become dependent, become captive—my hands, my heart bound in chains. A truly frightening prospect. And, heaven forbid, if that trust I so generously place in someone else is ever betrayed, it seems to shatter my faith in everything. At its worst, love has the potential to leave us imprisoned, helpless, and broken.

But at its best, love has made me soar, made me believe that anything is possible. It's a drug, intoxicating and thrilling. It makes me do things, feel things I wouldn't otherwise do or feel. Love allows me to be my best self, secure in the knowledge that I'm truly worthy of its receipt. There have been a handful of people in my life I would gladly die for. Why? Because of the matchless love I have for them.

That kind of power, to give one's life away for another, is why people spend their days longing for love, seeking it out. Some find it, and some never do. And some are blessed enough to find it later on, when they least expect it!

*So when we're handed an opportunity, the gift of loving someone,
especially when we thought our time was through, we should grab it.
No questions asked. We should fling aside the doubts and worries of the
consequences. Abandon ourselves to it. Because love happens as often as a
rare eclipse. And we're never guaranteed another in our lifetime.*

"When they least expect it… when we thought our time was
through." Noelle pondered what that meant about Aunt Joy's life. Like
the symbol, she would probably never know.

She stared at the pictures again, the paradoxes of love. Freedom
and captivity. Exhilaration and devastation. Security and vulnerability.
But Aunt Joy had forgotten to include one type of love. Perhaps the
most painful one of all, unrequited love. The "what ifs" and "we'll never
knows" that ate away at the soul, stealing pieces away, little by little.
Surely, nothing was more devastating than that.

Out of all the photos, the caged tiger spoke to her the most. She
pictured the tiger, restless, anxious, and pacing back and forth inside
the cage, eager to break loose of the bars and escape to freedom but
knowing he never could. His fate had been sealed.

She paper-clipped the photos back to the pages and shut the journal,
antsier than before. She thrust back the covers, startling Mr. Darcy. He
jumped down from the bed and followed her to the art room. Two days
ago, she had started painting a landscape, but it never quite worked.
The hills rolled along fine, with sheep properly dotted across them and
trees appropriately standing full and lush. But something bothered her
about the sky. Too cheery, too perfect. Something wasn't right.

Noelle sat cross-legged on the floor and picked up the brush. She
created a storm in the puffy white clouds. She blended the blacks and
grays, making the storm imposing, imminent. Dangerous.

As she painted, she entered the picture in her mind, feeling the lush
grass on her bare feet, the fierce wind on her cheeks, hearing the rumble
of thunder, seeing the brilliant flash of lightning ahead. Tears created
her own rain as her brush moved without stopping. Wiping her eyes
with the back of her wrist, not wanting to quit, she shifted her focus to
the other side of the sky, where she had accidentally left a patch of blue,
some hope in the storm. She stared at the contrast and pierced the blue

with bright streaks of sunlight, forming a fan of light. She thought of those rare days when she could look at one end of the sky and see black clouds then find rays of sunlight filtering through the opposite end, refusing to darken.

Finished. Drained, Noelle tossed her brush into the can and wiped her hands on the formerly crisp white cloth, smudged with every color of the rainbow. She looked at her creation from the other side of the room and stretched her arms high over her head to ease the tension in her back muscles.

She needed rest. She needed… something.

Chapter Eighteen

Pay attention. Don't just see the world with your eyes—see it with your whole being. Note the exact shade of blue in that little patch of sky. Or the dimensions of the pencil-thin shadows on the green lawn. Be diligent. If you stop paying attention, you're going to miss something wonderful.

"NOELLE, WOULD YOU MIND STAYING behind?"

She paused in the classroom doorway and took a few steps back inside. Mr. Evans sat on the edge of the desk, his hands clasped together on his thigh. The other students had already filed out, eager to make the most of the remaining hour of sunshine before nightfall. Tonight had been the final art class.

"Mr. Evans?"

"Please. Call me Preston." His warm smile melted the teacher façade. He'd always been a kind teacher, but he held up a professional wall between himself and the students—no strong emotion shown, no information ever given about a personal life. Now, though, his body language seemed more relaxed, the wall easing down.

"I don't mean to pry, but..." He inched closer. She hadn't noticed his height until this minute. Or the deep blue of his eyes. "Well, I overheard you earlier, talking with a student. About your aunt. Joy Valentine?"

"Oh. Yes. Great aunt, actually."

"I had no idea you were related to her. And so the auction three weeks ago? You discovered those paintings?"

"I did."

A student bounded into the room, laughing with another student behind him. Followed by another, and another, coming in for their next class.

Preston stared at Noelle, pondering something. "Would you... be interested in grabbing a coffee? We can sit at the college cafe. It's just... I'd love to hear more about your aunt. And the auction. I wasn't able to attend. I was a fan of her work from years back. I even met her once."

Noelle thought about the rest of her evening, only some dirty dishes to deal with and some bills to pay. Coffee with Mr. Evans sounded much more appealing. "Sure. Coffee would be good."

"Brilliant." Preston grabbed his textbook and reading glasses from the desk then waved a polite hand for her to exit first.

On the brief walk over, Noelle swatted away any recurring thoughts of this being inappropriate—calling him "Preston," saying yes to a coffee. *The art class is over, anyway. What harm is there in a quick coffee? He's only interested in Aunt Joy.*

Inside the cozy cafe, nestled in the back of the Student Center, Mr. Evans—Preston—found a secluded corner table and pointed to it, his expression a question mark. "This one okay?" She nodded, and he said, "What can I get you?"

"Just a small black coffee, please."

Uncomfortable being alone in public, Noelle pretended to check her email on her phone while she waited. When Preston returned, he handed her the coffee, and she realized he'd paid.

"Oh, here. Let me get mine." She reached for her purse.

"It's already done," he reassured. "Besides, this was my idea." When he smiled, fine wrinkles appeared at the corners of his eyes. She tried to guess his age. No more than forty, if that. She uncapped the piping-hot coffee, careful not to spill it.

He poured a bit of cream into his own. "How was the auction? I read about the results the next day. You must have been thrilled."

"I was shocked," she admitted. "And yes, thrilled. On a personal level, it was harder than I thought, watching those paintings walk out the door forever. They were a piece of her, I suppose. And after losing her, well, it just felt like losing her all over again." She smiled. "That sounds crazy, doesn't it?"

"Not one bit. Art is very personal. It's a little piece of your soul, right there on the canvas. It makes perfect sense that you would feel that way." His reassurance warmed her up as much as the coffee did. She liked this friendly, easygoing new side of him.

"And finding them the way you did." He whistled. "I mean, locked up in a hidden room. And you were the first to see them. Amazing." He lifted his cup to drink, his sapphire eyes staring at her over the rim, disarming her.

"Yes. Like something out of a movie, cracking that door open, seeing stacks and stacks of paintings. I thought I was dreaming."

She told him about the unfinished one on the easel, abandoned by its owner and waiting for Joy's return. She told him about the paintings hauled off by Sotheby's in the middle of the night. "I also donated some of them to local galleries and kept a few for myself."

"I'll bet the village has been insane with tourists wanting to gawk at the place where Joy lived and painted."

"Yes! I've caught a few people walking up to the cottage, taking pictures. They're harmless, but it's a little weird, living this way. And business at the gallery has boomed."

"Where are they now? The ones you kept?"

"I've loaned them out to a Bath museum for a bit. They're safer there. Until the renovations are done."

"Renovations?"

"I don't want to hog the paintings, keep them hidden away in my cottage. I want the village to have the paintings and enjoy them. So I guess you could say I'm building them a home, a second story in the gallery. With their own state-of-the-art security system."

"Nice."

They spent the next half hour talking about Aunt Joy, a little about her life, but mostly about her art. But even as his teacher-wall and her student-wall started to creep down, she couldn't shake the idea that she was having coffee with her professor. Still, as he deftly switched the topic to a new book he'd been reading, she relaxed. A second cup of coffee warmed her entire body, and the hint of jazz coming through the speakers mellowed the last of her nerves.

Nearly two hours after they'd first sat down, Noelle realized the time, nearly nine o'clock, and how dark her drive home would be. When she finally waved good-bye after he'd walked her to her car, it dawned on her that tonight might have been a date. Starting the engine, she replayed in her mind their non-Joy-related topics of conversation. San Francisco (he had lived there for two years), college (he had attended Oxford), and music (neither of them liked the latest Travis album). She had done some sharing, too, ended up telling him much more than she'd ever intended to tell her professor. Her parents' divorce, her first job in college, the last novel she'd read.

But Preston had made it easy. He nodded in all the right places, nudging the conversation along. An unexpected breath of fresh air. Air she wanted to breathe again.

On the way home, she called Jill for some girl talk but received her voicemail. And she certainly couldn't call Adam. Especially with the way things stood at the moment. After painting the storm the night of the auction, Noelle had crawled into bed and done a harsh reality check. Adam was taken. Engaged. And until those facts changed, she had lost the right to hope for something more.

Now, three weeks since Valentine's, she hadn't seen him once. He traveled to the village the week after the auction to oversee the first day of renovations at the school, but she'd gone to London to visit Jill. Adam had texted Noelle a few pictures of the exciting event, and she responded with a simple "Congratulations" a few hours later, out of courtesy.

The following week, Adam had found out about Noelle's gallery renovations secondhand from Mrs. Pickering. He'd left Noelle a voicemail, teasing her that she was cheating on him with another architect. She'd used someone from Bath, knowing Adam had his hands too full to consider the job. And knowing that Adam renovating her gallery would only put him in closer proximity to her on a daily basis. That was the last thing she needed.

When she stopped responding so quickly to his texts and calls, Adam started to get the message. Especially when she stopped responding altogether.

Last week, he'd quit trying. *For the best*, she convinced herself. She was tired of pretending, of spending time with Adam, of accepting his mild flirtations and flirting with him a little, too, when it was all in vain. No room to hope for more. Valentine's Day had snapped her awake. Friendship wasn't enough anymore.

Noelle was shocked that the combination of incessant hammering, noisy drilling, thick dust, and ugly plastic sheets inside the gallery hadn't deterred the tourists. Not in the slightest.

Since Joy's auction, people came in droves from all over, asking to see the paintings. Frank only had three to show at the moment, the ones he'd originally chosen for the gallery. As for the rest, Noelle directed the tourists to the museum in Bath. Most went away disappointed but still determined to make the short pilgrimage. Noelle couldn't wait until the upper story was completed—next week, the contractor promised—so Joy's paintings could be properly hung and admired in their new home.

"I'll finish these tomorrow," she told Frank, handing him the stack of bills.

Frank tried to speak, but some banging from upstairs jolted him. He clutched his chest. "My nerves can't take much more of this."

"I'm sorry. Only a few more days." She found her purse and headed for the front door, eager to leave the noise behind. She had put in full workdays at the gallery, had even completed a handful of paintings in the back room whenever the workers upstairs took their breaks. Frank had talked her into displaying two of them yesterday in the window, convincing Noelle that if tourists couldn't have many of Joy's paintings at the moment, at least seeing her niece's might pacify them.

She walked into the pristine afternoon and took a deep breath of cool air. Sweet, clean springtime air. Dust-free. She reached for her cell phone and found a voicemail from Preston. After their coffee chat last week, they had exchanged numbers, and Noelle had toyed with being the first to call him to touch base. But four days ago, before she could gather the courage, his name popped up on her caller ID.

He had called her twice more after that. The calls were easy and chatty, but he still hadn't asked her officially for a date. Until last night. At the tail end of their phone call, he said he wanted to take her out. London seemed the most obvious choice, with so much to do and see, so she offered to drive there next week. He'd said he would think of something "memorable" they could do.

Hearing his voicemail now, her adrenaline surged. "Hey, so, this is Preston. I tried to text you a picture of something, but it didn't go through."

She snickered, remembering their talk during coffee when he admitted to being completely "tech-illiterate." He didn't participate in Facebook or Twitter and admitted that his students often mocked him for not being able to text. For being so "old school." But she found it charming, and she was rather "old school" herself. She rarely spent any time online except to check her email. She didn't see the point of it.

"So," his voicemail continued, "I guess I'll just have to tell you this way, by phone message. How about the London Eye for our date?"

Noelle loved the idea. Something she'd never done but always wanted to do, glide far above London in that famous, enormous Ferris wheel. What a way to see the city!

"So, anyway, just an idea. Let me know how you like it."

She was about to click the "call back" button when Lizzie, beaming with her newlywed glow, approached her and reached out for a warm hug. "Just the person I wanted to see!"

"You're back!" Noelle slipped her phone into her pocket. "How was Scotland?" Lizzie and Joe had taken an entire month for a honeymoon and had returned last week.

"Beyond words. Breathtaking. We stayed mostly in the Highlands. I've never been to any place more beautiful. You should go there someday. On your own honeymoon." Before Noelle could respond, Lizzie produced a thick, pocket-sized book from her bag. On the cover, a picture of Joe and Lizzie kissing. "My grandmother surprised us with this—wedding pictures!"

Lizzie opened the album, and Noelle forced herself to act excited about it. Wedding pictures weren't something she enjoyed, especially pictures of a wedding she'd already attended in person, but this was important to Lizzie, so she tried to be a good sport.

"A few duds, but most of them came out well." Lizzie turned the pages. "You know, I'm experiencing a whole different wedding, looking at these. See that—I didn't even remember Mr. Ackerman being there! I guess all I could concentrate on that day was Joe. Oh. Look at this one!" Lizzie held the album higher, catching the sun's morning rays, then moved it toward Noelle. A candid shot of Noelle glancing down at her plate, smiling at something Adam had said, while he stared right at her, his expression thoughtful, pensive. "Smitten, I'd say. That is a man in love."

Flustered, Noelle pushed back the album toward Lizzie. "We're just friends, I keep telling everyone. He has a fiancée."

"Well, where was she that day? From the look on his face, I'd say he only has eyes for you." Lizzie reached into the pocket of the page and slipped out the picture. She handed it to Noelle. "Keep it."

"Oh, no. I—"

"Really. Keep it." She squeezed Noelle's elbow as she closed the album. "Gotta go. I'll show you the Scotland pictures when they're ready."

"Okay," Noelle replied faintly.

Alone at the cottage, she looked at the picture again without the pressure of someone else's watchful eyes. She took in every detail—the way Adam poised his glass, about to drink it; the way his eyes focused on her with intensity. One millisecond of time, captured. Always hard to tell with pictures, whether the image contained a true representation or just an accident, a flash of a moment on its way to being something else. Maybe Adam's stare *hadn't* settled on her. Perhaps he'd started to look over at another person and the camera had caught the in-between.

She noticed the steady warmth in Adam's eyes... *What if Lizzie was right?* "Ridiculous," she mumbled. She tucked the photo inside a drawer and decided to get busy with some chores.

Two hours later, she sat at the table on the back porch, safe from the rain under the awning. The clouds had rolled in, and what had started as a bright sunny day turned into a gloomy, foggy one. Typical English unpredictability. Still, even a day like this one held its charms, and Noelle chose to have her tea on the porch while snuggled up inside a flannel blanket.

Sparked by Lizzie's photo album, Noelle had brought one of her own outside to keep her company. In the process of dusting the living room earlier, she'd rediscovered an album sitting on the bottom level of the coffee table. She had placed it there ages ago, after sifting through one of Joy's many boxes. But she couldn't recall ever looking through it, until now.

It contained mostly pictures of the old days. Some black-and-white, some color. Most were taken at Gram's estate. Gram and Joy as little girls, then later, Gram and Joy with their spouses. As Noelle turned the pages, the pictures sparked a renewed interest in the *W* symbol. Maybe this book held some sort of clue to the past.

But by the time she finished her cup of tea, she'd reached the end of the book, and nothing in particular had leaped out at her except a picture of Gram and Joy posing with a woman Noelle had never seen before. They weren't at Gram's estate but at some sort of cottage, possibly the same Cornwall cottage Noelle had visited a couple of times as a little girl. Noelle slid the picture from its sleeve and turned it over to find Joy's handwriting, verifying Noelle's memory. *Rachel, Joy, Helen. Cornwall Summer Cottage, 1963.* The year before her mother was born.

Startled by footsteps, Noelle looked up to see Mac approaching. She closed the photo album. "Hi there. Would you like some tea?"

"No thank ye, lass." He wore his cap and a wind jacket and clutched his toolbox. "Just repaired that hole in the shed."

"In the nick of time," she noted as the rain pelted down harder.

"Aye."

"Well, at least come in out of the rain."

He obeyed and stepped under the awning, removing his cap and setting down his toolbox. "How did the auction go?" he asked as Mr. Darcy darted out of the rain and circled his feet.

"That's right; I haven't seen you since then. Things have been so busy." Noelle had spent less and less time at the cottage these days. "It went even better than expected."

"I heard about the money. 'Tis staggering."

"I still can't believe it. And honestly..." She shifted her empty mug in its saucer. "I'm uncomfortable with it. I mean, what does a person do with all that money? I've thought of charities, of course. The school here, some worthy causes. I think Joy would've approved of that."

"Aye."

"This sort of thing happens to other people. Not to me. I mean, it's like winning the lottery. And I've heard nothing but horrid stories of people who win huge amounts of money getting depressed or being hounded by poor relatives. They're miserable. In many cases, they regret the money entirely. I don't want this—the money—to end up changing me. Who I am."

Mac put his cap on and held the back of the chair. "You won't let it. See this money as the blessing that it is. From your aunt. No guilt, no worries. She would want you to enjoy it, do good things with it. I have no doubt you will."

As he always did, Mac left her with more comfort than doubt, more peace than anxiety. "Thank you, Mac. You always know what to say."

He shrugged and headed back into the rain with his toolbox.

Chapter Nineteen

Each new painting should be a discovery—of something you always knew but never acknowledged, of something unexpected. As long as art continues to intrigue and surprise you, it will be worthwhile.

PRESTON GRASPED HER HAND AS the giant glass bubble crept forward. It looked like a space capsule, egg-shaped, covered in windows. Noelle's feet tingled from fear. For the past few minutes in line, she'd managed to avoid looking up at the gigantic structure—over four hundred feet tall!—afraid she would chicken out altogether. Noelle recalled the first time she had seen the majestic London Eye, on her TV during New Year's Eve, 1999. The network had shown fireworks and celebrations from around the world, including London, where the world got its first glimpse at the incredible wheel.

Knowing about Noelle's fear of heights, Preston had assured her the experience wasn't similar to the Ferris wheels that frightened her as a little girl. He explained that the capsules were completely enclosed, and the Eye rotated so slowly she would hardly notice.

A man in a white shirt waved them toward the barely-moving pod. Preston squeezed her hand tightly. "Ready?"

"Yes. I can do this."

They entered the capsule behind another couple, and six other people joined them before the doors closed. Preston led Noelle to one end, putting an arm around her waist in reassurance. Dark blue carpet, a short, broad bench in the middle for seating. Nothing like she had expected. Comfortable, cozy, not scary in the least.

Preston and Noelle stayed close to the windows on the north side of the pod and watched the ground begin to shrink as the pod lifted. "See? Not so bad."

"Okay, you were right. Very smooth—and slow. Like a snail." She peered out at the city as they rose steadily higher. A few well-placed clouds eclipsed the late afternoon sun, so she removed her sunglasses to enjoy the view.

During the ride, Preston played the part of tour guide, pointing out sights: Covent Garden, Harrods, St. Paul's, and the Globe Theater. At one point, when she spotted the other pods slowly drifting upward on the other side parallel to them, Noelle mused aloud, "Can you imagine the planning it took to design this wheel?" and without thinking added, "Adam would love it." The minute she said it, she regretted it. She still struggled not to think about him, even after all her disciplined weeks of avoiding him.

"Adam?" Preston asked.

"Oh, yeah. This friend of mine. Childhood friend. He lives here—London, here—but he also works in the village sometimes as an architect. Sort of. School renovations, a pro bono project." He didn't need all these disjointed explanations, so she stopped. Preston didn't press for more, just made an "Mmm" sound and returned to the view.

When the ride was over, they stepped out of the capsule and walked toward the exit. Even in early April, the hour before dusk brought a brisk chill, reminiscent of autumn. Noelle had come prepared and brought a sweater. During the lengthy trek back to Preston's car, he held her hand the entire way then opened her door.

"Are you sure you can't play hooky?" Preston asked with puppy-dog eyes as they buckled their seat belts.

Noelle had signed up last week for a personal finance course at the college, wanting to learn more about how to manage her newly acquired funds. Conveniently, she had driven to the college this afternoon, before their date, where Preston was finishing some grading at his office.

"Tempting," she said, "but it's the very first class, and I don't want to miss anything."

"I understand. I've got some work to catch up on at home, anyway." He drove out of the parking space. "I'm glad we did this."

"Me, too."

Light traffic on the way helped them arrive at the college parking lot with a couple of minutes to spare.

Noelle unfastened her seat belt as Preston touched her hair. He was leaning in for a kiss. She hoped it might happen—at lunch, in the pod. But finally, it did. When his lips touched hers, the same mix of fear and exhilaration entered her body as when she'd stepped onto the world's biggest Ferris wheel. But the warm confidence in his lips helped her relax and enjoy the kiss. He backed away sooner than she wanted, leaving her dizzy for more.

"I want to see you again," he whispered. And all she could do was nod.

Noelle should have known drinking tea in bed was a bad idea. "Bollocks!" she shrieked, mopping up the coppery, transparent liquid that had splattered onto her comforter and onto Aunt Joy's diary pages.

Swiftly, carefully, she moved the teacup back to the table and assessed the damage. Only a few drops had permeated the page. She retrieved a hand towel from the bathroom and did her best to dab at the text without smearing it. Unfortunately, a few words became casualties, their ink fanning out and distorting letters in every direction.

Blotting the comforter as dry as she could, she settled back under the covers and noted the title of the series, "Regret," then studied the photos. The first canvas contained small figures in black attire, gathered around a hole in the earth. The second showed an enormous black bird, perhaps a crow, flying past a muted gray sky. And the third held a glorious blur of whites, golds, and creams, with one small pathway leading from the bottom of the canvas to the middle, disappearing in a cloud.

My sister died six days ago. I heard the news from a servant of hers, some young woman who found my phone number by accident and left the message on my answerphone this morning. All she said was that my sister had a heart attack and died on the way to the hospital. Maybe if we'd been in touch all these years, maybe if we had been important in each other's lives, I would've found out sooner. And I would've been able to attend her funeral.

But it's too late for that now. Too late for so many things. Ridiculous me, I thought we had time. I thought one day, one of us would find the boldness, the courage to reach out to the other, make things right. That it would just happen all by itself. That destiny or fate would take care of it. But "one day" never happened, and here I sit, clutching tissues and sobbing until the back of my eyes throb. She's gone, and I can't have her back. And the pain of that regret is something that will gnaw away at me until the end of my days.

The one comfort, the only comfort, is that she's at peace. That whatever hurt and pain I caused is gone for her. She's in that better place, void of tears, void of suffering and betrayal and rifts. And I pray that whenever I meet her in that place, she will have already forgiven me.

Noelle used the tea-stained towel to wipe away her own tears before they dripped onto the pages, staining them again. She wasn't thinking of Aunt Joy or Gram but of her own mother. Reading the entry, Noelle recognized that kind of gnawing, agonizing regret after someone's passing. That sickening feeling of not being able to right the wrongs, smooth over the rough edges. All these years, Noelle hadn't let herself experience the true stab of regret, not until she saw it in print through another's eyes. Regret from erecting a wall between her and her mother, sticking stubbornly to expectations she knew her mother could never fulfill. Almost a game, a dare. "I dare you not to let me down."

Yes, her mother had always been flaky, flighty, and undependable. That never changed. But instead of looking down her nose, judging her mother's choices all those years, Noelle should have accepted they were her choices to make. Her mother certainly never intended harm, but she didn't have the best discernment sometimes. And Noelle couldn't really fault her for that.

In fact, she'd actually learned lessons from it. Having watched her mother's poor decisions all those years, Noelle had made a point, even as a little girl, to make only wise, meticulous decisions. To think things through—the ripple effects, the consequences on others. But this life philosophy came with a price. It had made Noelle overly cautious. Afraid to let down her guard. Undeniably, her mother had made a direct impact on whom Noelle had become. For better or worse.

The day of her mother's funeral, Noelle had lingered at the gravesite, let all the mourners walk away, and put her hand on the casket. She wanted to utter something but couldn't form the words, didn't know how to interpret the discomfort. And so, after a few minutes, she walked away.

But glancing at the Polaroids, Noelle knew exactly what she'd wanted to say that day. What she should have said years before. To tell her mother she was sorry for not accepting her, flaws and all. And how she regretted being too proud to show her mother exactly who she was—the traits her mother might not approve of, the insecurities, the tendency to step back from situations. One apology could've changed their entire relationship.

She thought she had turned it off. Noelle listened for her cell phone, across the hall in her bedroom.

Pressing on, she continued working on her rose-colored sky, capturing the tail end of a sunset she'd seen last night in the village. The casting off of winter and the ushering in of warm spring weather had rejuvenated her lately, filled her with a youthful hope and vigor. For the first time in a long time, she felt settled, grounded. Maybe because of the gallery being finished and Joy's paintings finally hanging in their rightful place. Or the daily calls from a handsome art teacher, calls that made her feel appreciated and admired.

Or yes, maybe it was the money from the auction, which she had started to accept, psychologically, as part of her life. She couldn't deny the incredible amount of security it had brought. Uncomfortable at first with her new fortune, she started shelling it out. She doubled the pledge she'd made to the school renovations, bought all sorts of gifts for people, paid for the gallery's second floor, gave Frank and Holly well-deserved raises, bought Mac a new set of tools. When she ran out of ideas, she finally slowed down, tried to be more cautious. She hoped that money would last her a lifetime. She wanted to be wise about the gift Joy had given her, so she researched the financial course at the cottage and sought investment opportunities.

Ten minutes later, as she finished the wisp of a cloud in her sunset, her cell rang again. And again a half an hour later. Ignoring the first two rings, Noelle huffed at the third one, unable to push away the nagging sensation that the calls might be important. No one ever rang her that many times in a row. Not even Preston.

Setting down the brush, she wiped her fingers on a rag and walked into the bedroom to retrieve her messages. All from Jillian. In the first, a casual tone, just checking in with a quick question for Noelle. In the second, she needed to hear from Noelle more urgently. In the final call, more impatient but still bubbly, she demanded to know where on earth Noelle was on this late Thursday morning.

Half-smiling, Noelle dialed Jill back. They hadn't spoken since a week after the auction, both busier than ever. "Three calls in a row!" Noelle said when Jill answered. "What's the big emergency?"

"It's about time! I thought you had moved back to America or something!"

"Things are crazy busy around here. This is my first morning off in ages. How are you? How's the pregnancy?"

"Perfect. Had a doctor's appointment yesterday. Everything looks good."

"That's wonderful. Wish we could get together sometime."

"That's why I'm calling. I have a proposition for you."

"Oh, no."

"What does that mean? 'Oh no.'"

Noelle pictured Jillian's hand-on-hip faux indignation. "Nothing. Go on…"

"All right. Before you say no, you have to pause—a significant pause where you actually consider what I'm saying. Promise."

"Okay, I promise." Noelle sat on the bed. This apparently wouldn't be a short conversation.

"There's this man—"

"Jill!"

"You promised. A significant pause."

Noelle sighed loudly into the phone. "Pausing..."

"He's single, stunningly gorgeous, and supremely wealthy. He's a dermatologist and a new racquetball partner of Gareth's. After meeting him a couple of days ago, I handpicked him for you. He's perfect! In fact, if I weren't happily married, I'd snatch him up myself! You two have to meet. I want us to have dinner together, the four of us."

Noelle waited a beat, guilt rising for not telling her best friend about Preston. Jill would surely be shocked. Noelle had thought many times about telling her but didn't know what to say about it or what to call their relationship. Plus, she liked the novelty of having Preston all to herself for a while, not letting anyone else know about him. "Actually, I'm... seeing someone."

An audible gasp through the phone. "What? How could you not tell me this? Spill! Who is he, where did you meet, are you in love, when's the wedding?"

Noelle chuckled, wishing they could have this conversation in person. She would love to see Jill's expression, aghast and melodramatic. "His name is Preston. He's an art teacher. My art teacher. Well, he was. Class is over now."

"A teacher? How very daring of you. Teacher's pet! Is he yummy? Describe him."

"Very yummy. Tall, lean, with longish hair and striking blue eyes. We've been out a few times, and I really like him. But I don't know how serious it is yet."

"Have you had 'the talk'? That will tell you everything."

"What talk?"

"You know, the 'exclusivity' talk? Is he dating other people?"

The same question Noelle had asked herself the last few days. Occasionally, Preston seemed distracted, not fully engaged, or cut phone conversations short or shifted their date schedule around for classes, grading, or meetings. All perfectly legitimate excuses, but it sometimes left Noelle wondering. "Nope, haven't had the talk yet. And until we do, I'm a little insecure. Maybe that's why it took this long for me to mention him."

"Completely understandable. Maybe this will help. You need another perspective. From me! Back to that dinner—why don't you bring Preston along? We can make it a foursome!"

Noelle almost gave an instant "no" for so many reasons. *But what will it hurt, having Jill meet him, getting her point of view?* Besides, it might be interesting to observe him in other company, watch him interact with Gareth. She and Preston had only ever been out together, the two of them. Perhaps a double date was what they needed. "Okay. I'll ask him."

"Wonderful! I didn't expect you to say 'yes' so quickly."

"Neither did I," Noelle admitted.

"So, how about Sketch on Tuesday? It's this fabulous London restaurant I know you'll love. Seven o'clock?"

"Sounds good. I'll see if Preston can make it."

They hung up, and she pictured Jill, a grinning Cheshire cat as she told Gareth the news. As she dialed Preston's number, the jitters crept in. *Is it too soon for a double date? Will he even agree to it?*

When he answered, she told him about Jill, about Sketch. When he didn't immediately respond, she said, "But we don't have to do it. I don't want you to feel pressured. Double dates can be awkward, especially if you don't know the other people."

"No, it's not that. I have a faculty meeting that night," he explained. "I was trying to think about how we could do this. You said seven?"

After some brainstorming, they agreed that Noelle could ride with Jill and Gareth, while Preston would meet them at the restaurant a few minutes late. Noelle was about to phone Jill with the good news when her cell rang again.

"It's Jill. You're going to hate me. There's a glitch in the plan."

"What glitch?"

"Well, Gareth and I got our signals crossed. I said we should invite a couple for dinner to Sketch, assuming he knew I meant you and the blind date. But he assumed I meant someone else instead, and he's already invited them. When we realized what happened, I didn't want to cancel anyone, so I just changed the reservation to make it six people. I hope that's all right."

"A triple date. So, there's no glitch anymore?"

"Well, there might be. The somebody elses he invited are Adam and Laurel. I understand if you want to back out."

Noelle rubbed her forehead, wondering how the situation could get any more complicated. Stressful enough, the thought of Jill meeting Preston. But now Adam. And Laurel.

"You're upset, aren't you?" prodded Jill.

"No, no. Not upset. Just… surprised." Too late to wriggle out of it gracefully. And she certainly couldn't tell Preston the truth, that she wanted to back out because she couldn't bear spending an awkward dinner with her first love and his fiancée. "It's fine," Noelle said, not yet believing it.

"Excellent. I'm so relieved. I thought I had buggered everything up. Guess I'll be seeing you Tuesday, then."

Noelle ended the call and stared at the wall. "How do I get myself into these things?" she asked Mr. Darcy as he sauntered by. He answered her with a flippant meow.

Chapter Twenty

Prepare for rejection. Not everyone will want to buy your work, or will even understand or appreciate it. That's their right, just as it's yours to ignore it. Develop that thick skin early. Because not getting what you want is one of life's little guarantees.

"BE HONEST. TOO MUCH?" NOELLE twisted down the tube of darker-than-usual lipstick and waited for Jill's reaction. "No, very va-va-voom!"

Noelle peeked in the mirror again. The brick-red dress brought more color to her face, more life to her cheeks. She wanted to ramp things up a bit tonight. Maybe boldness in her looks would translate into a bolder attitude.

"Oh!" Jillian sucked in a breath and placed a hand on her stomach.

"What is it?"

"A kick!" She took Noelle's hand and moved it to the right side of her stomach.

Noelle waited, holding her breath, until either a tiny elbow or a knee bumped against her palm. "That's amazing!"

"It really is. I never get tired of her little way of saying hello. Can you believe? Only a few more weeks before I get to meet this little troublemaker." She checked her watch. "We'd better get cracking. Your date should be here any minute! Preston?"

"Preston." Noelle followed her out of the ladies room of Sketch, shaking out the nerves, clenching and unclenching her hand. On any other occasion, Noelle would've been dazzled by the quirky Art Deco and gold and red colors throughout the restaurant. Or more especially the Gallery room, with impressive black-and-white video displays of art and photography wrapped around the walls. But she could only focus on the intense pressure of having to be dazzling, too. In front of Adam and Laurel.

Noelle and Jillian found Gareth standing beside an empty, circular table in the corner. And alongside him stood Preston. He looked particularly handsome in a camel-colored blazer and dark jeans. When Noelle approached him, Preston leaned in for a quick kiss. Then she made the introductions. "Preston Evans—my best friend, Jillian Holbrook."

Preston offered his hand. "Lovely to meet you."

As Preston leaned over to pull out Noelle's chair, Jill raised her eyebrows and mouthed at Noelle behind his back, "GOR-geous!" Noelle had to look away to keep from snickering.

As Gareth helped seat Jill, Noelle asked Preston about his meeting. "Meeting?"

"Faculty meeting. Didn't you have one tonight?"

"Oh. Yes." He nodded. "Same as always. Boring and unproductive."

A server placed cloth napkins in their laps and filled their tall glasses with sparkling water. Noelle reached for hers and spotted Adam across the room, dressed in a dark suit, headed toward the table. In front of him walked a wispy brunette wearing an emerald-colored dress, her hair pulled back in some sort of taut twist.

Pretty, Noelle hated to admit. Prettier than Jill had said. She watched Laurel trying to fashion an appropriately social smile as they approached. Noelle remembered Jill's description of Laurel's discomfort on New Year's Eve, with a crowd of people, even with Adam at her side. *Will she text tonight away, too? Struggle to cover her boredom?* In the split second before the introductions, Noelle and Adam locked eyes, and his smile grew wider. She wanted to know what he was thinking.

Jillian took charge of the introductions, and Preston stood to shake Adam's hand across the table. Noelle had told Preston a little more about Adam a couple of days ago, re-emphasized that they were old friends, that they'd spent a few summers together and then reconnected again last year when she came back to England. They all took their seats,

Adam choosing one directly across from Noelle. Two tall candlesticks framed his face.

The server caught their attention by clearing his throat then rambled off the specials. He placed heavy, leather-bound menus in front of them, and a hush settled as they each studied the pages. So much to choose from. Noelle decided almost instantly on the rosemary chicken but continued to look at her menu to avoid the awkwardness of being the only one not reading.

Whispers across the table caught her attention, and she stole a glance at Laurel, leaning in to point at Adam's menu. Noelle vaguely heard her say something about "diet" and "sharing." Adam balked quietly, and Laurel whispered something. Adam shrugged and nodded, defeated, then closed his menu.

During the salad course, the conversations began. Anecdotes about work, the safest topic for a large group who didn't know each other well. Preston and Adam found a common denominator in their mutual love of soccer, or "football," and Noelle kept busy with her chicken when the main course arrived. She looked up to see Laurel discreetly pushing the mushrooms out of the gravy with the tines of her fork.

At the other end, Jill had been talking to Gareth, telling some story about Adam and a fish. Since Adam and Preston's predictions for the upcoming World Cup had died down, Jill shifted to Noelle to include her. "Do you remember?"

"Remember what?"

"That night, years ago. When Adam was sick as a dog—he ate that bad piece of fish, and you ended up taking care of him because his parents were out of town."

"Oh. Yes! I thought we'd have to take him to the hospital. I'd never seen him so sick. He looked horrible, ghostly pale. Death warmed over."

"Gee. Thanks."

"Well, it's true. That was on our birthday, wasn't it?" Noelle squinted, trying to remember.

"'Our' birthday?" asked Gareth.

"Adam and I have our birthdays one day apart," Noelle explained. "That was usually the week I arrived in England for summers, so we used to celebrate together."

"I didn't know that," Laurel said quietly with a frown.

"Yes, it made things very convenient for me," Jill chuckled. "Two presents with one stone… isn't that how the saying goes?"

Adam directed the conversation back to the fish. "It was bloody awful, that weekend. I hardly recall a thing. Three days of my life, vanished from memory."

"True. Except that the last day, you were faking." Noelle smirked.

"What do you mean? I was violently ill!"

"Yes, but not that third day. I caught you walking around the library, bored out of your mind, looking for something to read. You looked healthy enough to me! When you saw me, you faked being woozy, asked me to make you some blueberry scones. You had me wrapped around your finger, waiting on you hand and foot."

"And a fine job you did, too." He raised his wine glass to her. "Should have been a nurse. Missed your calling."

Everyone, even Preston, chuckled over the fish story. Everyone except Laurel. Her face contained only the slightest hint of a disingenuous smile as she caught Noelle's gaze.

"Well," said Jill as the server appeared with the desserts they had ordered a few minutes before, "I think this gives us another excuse to all get together. A double birthday celebration, like the old days. And since we can't celebrate at your Gram's estate, why don't we come down to your village? Didn't you mention something about a festival in May? Might be great fun!"

Noelle nodded, unsure she wanted to commit to yet another of these evenings. Especially not in the village with prying eyes. She liked coming to London, liked playing here, eating here, having dates here. She thought of the village as a home base, safe and serene. But this birthday proposition would merge her two worlds, and she wasn't ready for that. Besides, Preston had declined the couple of invitations she'd already made for him to come and see her at the village. She had no reason to think he would say "yes" this time, even for her birthday.

"That sounds interesting," Preston said beside her. "Why not?"

Pressure from all sides. She caved. "Okay, sounds good to me."

"Adam?" Jill asked.

"I don't think we can make it," Laurel offered on his behalf.

Adam frowned. "Do we have other plans? I thought we were just going to dinner. We could still do that and go to the village the day before, on Noelle's birthday."

"We'll see," she told Adam and turned to the rest of the table. "We're busy people," she explained. "I'm often out of town, and Adam is inundated with work at the firm. Especially since taking on the Castle Cross project."

"Chilton Crosse," Adam corrected. He ignored his fiancée and looked at Jill. "We'll make it work somehow. I'd love to come." Case closed.

Laurel, appalled that he'd just spoken for her, opened her mouth slightly. She'd probably give Adam the cold shoulder the rest of the night. Or even a good chewing out after they'd gone.

"It's settled!" Jill said.

Noelle pushed down all her concerns, bringing her focus back to this night. The proposed birthday party was still a couple of weeks away. It might not even happen at all. Maybe everyone said "yes" to appease Jill, with no intention of following through. Relieved, Noelle took a bite of her own sumptuous cheesecake then asked Preston how his tiramisu tasted.

"See for yourself." He guided the fork toward her.

Noelle let him feed her a bite, a luscious mix of cream and coffee. "Mmm. Delicious."

He stared down at her mouth, smiled, and leaned in for a kiss. Laurel, who'd been relatively quiet all evening, chose that moment to become suddenly chatty. As Noelle's kiss ended prematurely, Laurel talked about weddings.

"Is there a date yet?" Gareth asked.

Laurel said, "Yes! September 4th. Decided just this morning, in fact."

Adam focused on his fork, twisting it between his fingers, his expression unreadable. Laurel threaded her hand through Adam's arm, soaking up the expected, "Oh, wonderful/great/fantastic news!" reactions from around the table. Adam gave a cursory smile then picked at his chocolate cake.

When he looked up, Noelle mouthed, "Congratulations."

He mouthed back, "Thanks."

A few minutes after dividing up the bill, they gathered coats and purses and walked toward the entrance. Preston touched Noelle's elbow and led her gently off to the side. They hadn't talked about this second leg of the evening yet. Noelle had hoped he'd invite her over to his place, just to see where he lived, what his apartment might be like. She'd never been there, in all this time.

"I enjoyed tonight. Your friends are great."

"Thanks."

"Will you be okay going home?" he said.

"Oh. Well. Jill had invited me to stay over tonight, if I wanted."

"That's good." So, clearly, no invitation to his flat tonight.

"Yeah. I guess that's what I'll do, then."

Preston kissed her cheek, squeezed her arm, and said, "I'd better take off. I'll ring you tomorrow."

Joining the others, Noelle caught Adam's stare but used all her will power to keep her focus on Jillian instead, who whispered, "See? That wasn't so bad, the three couples."

"No, not bad."

They confirmed plans for Noelle to spend the night at the townhouse, and then everyone exchanged goodnights. Outside, Adam walked with his fiancée into the night air, toward the parking lot.

On the way to Jillian's, Noelle had already prepared for the grilling she would receive about Preston. As expected, Jill wanted every minute detail of their entire relationship. How serious things were, where things were headed, how they felt about each other. "I'm not sure" became Noelle's standard answer, because of the truth inside it. She *wasn't sure* about him, about the relationship. About how he felt or if he saw a future for them. Until tonight, Noelle and Preston's dating life had been private, simple. But because they had become an official couple in other people's eyes, Jill's questions became important ones. They became the same questions Noelle asked herself.

After a nightcap, and a decaf coffee for Jill, Noelle followed her friend upstairs to the immaculate guest room. Jill had set out a new toothbrush, a small basket of toiletries, and a pair of silky pajamas on the bed.

"You didn't have to go to this much trouble."

"What trouble? These are pajamas from my own collection. I didn't pay a penny for them. They're yours to keep." Jill squeezed Noelle's shoulders and told her to sleep late. They would have a big breakfast together before she left.

As she slipped beneath the million-count Egyptian cotton sheets with the evening's newly minted memories fresh in her mind, Noelle shifted and sighed. She'd made it through the most awkward kind of dinner, had put on a good show for everyone.

But as she treaded back over the evening's conversations, the significance of the dinner started to crystallize. Up until then, Laurel had only been a ghost in the shadows, a misty illusion in the background of Adam's life. But that night, the apparition became real. There she was, flesh and blood, touching him and leaning on him and announcing a wedding date. Someone else staked a claim over Adam. Someone else was allowed to whisper in his ear or kiss him whenever she pleased. Someone else saw him over coffee in the mornings, left little meaningless messages on his cell phone.

Absurd, Noelle's sudden ownership toward Adam. Especially since she had Preston. But she couldn't help it. In a sense, she did hold a prior claim. She knew Adam well before Laurel even knew he existed. She had witnessed his early development, watched him make the awkward mistakes of youth and discover his passion for architecture. Strange, that years ago she had been allowed to feed him chicken broth, wipe his brow with a damp cloth, whisper soothing words into his ear when he had fever, but she wasn't allowed to do that anymore. No, that was Laurel's job.

Banishing the images, Noelle tried to shift her thoughts to other things. She made a mental list for tomorrow, after breakfast. A drive home, a late morning at the gallery, a break for lunch, some household chores, a bubble bath before bed.

At least she could control a few things in her life.

Chapter Twenty-one

Have fun with your art. Don't be so serious that you forget to find the joy in what you do. There are times to free yourself, forget the rigidity of perfect angles or deep perspectives or creative subtlety. Sometimes, it's good to simply let go.

FRESH, CITRUSY AROMAS WAFTED THROUGH the entire cottage as Noelle iced the cake, a lemon yogurt recipe she had seen last week on Nigella's food show. She wanted to make something other than the traditional birthday fare. Plus, she knew how much Adam liked lemon-flavored everything. Mr. Darcy meowed in the corner when Noelle finished, reminding her that the cake was a temptation for him. As she licked the tart icing off her finger, she placed it high atop the baker's rack for both their sakes.

Kneeling to give Mr. Darcy some much-needed attention, Noelle thought back to the string of phone calls yesterday and the good fortune they had brought. Only Jill and Adam were coming. No significant others could make it. Gareth was on call, Laurel would be on yet another business trip in Wales, and Preston—well, she'd never expected him to follow through. As predicted, he claimed to have all-day faculty meetings that prevented him from coming. So, today would be about three old friends celebrating together, just as it should be.

Surely, Laurel couldn't be too upset at missing tonight's occasion. Adam's birthday wasn't until tomorrow anyway, and his parents planned to meet him and Laurel in London for a fancy dinner that night. Laurel wouldn't miss a thing.

Recalling the load of laundry she wanted to finish before her guests arrived, Noelle headed upstairs to collect the clothes. But before she reached for the hamper in the corner of her room, her cell rang.

"Hey, it's Jill. You're going to kill me."

"Now, why would I want to do that?"

"Because I'm not coming to your party." She flew through the words in a rush, as though doing so would make them less potent.

"What?" Noelle plopped on the bed and waited.

"It's not my fault, honestly. Blame this attention-hungry little creature growing inside me. I just got back from my doctor's appointment. Apparently, I have something called pre-eclampsia. He says it's mild, but it sounds dreadful, doesn't it? Something to do with high blood pressure."

"Oh, Jill. That's awful... how are you feeling?"

"That's the silly part—completely fine. No symptoms at all. But the doctor has ordered bed rest to play it safe. Isn't that absurd?"

Noelle smiled at Jill's indignation and pictured her trying to rest. "It's not absurd. In fact, honestly, I wasn't sure how you'd do it, being so late in your pregnancy and making the long drive in the first place. Do you need me to come and stay with you? Isn't Gareth on call tonight?"

"He's on back-up call, which means there's a good chance he'll be at home with me, his beeper attached to him all night. But the tragedy is that I won't be able to come for your lovely party."

"Your health and that baby's health are the only important things. We'll celebrate another time." Secretly, Noelle's heart sank at the thought of being all alone tonight, sorry for herself and gorging on lemon cake. Maybe she could invite Mac over. Or meet Frank at the pub for a pint.

"Adam should be there soon." Jill said it as though Noelle should've already known.

"What do you mean? He's still coming? I just assumed—"

"I've already spoken to him. Said he wouldn't miss it."

"Oh, he doesn't need to do that. Really. I'm sure he's got other things to—"

"Nonsense. I won't have you sitting there all alone in that cottage for your birthday. If you even *think* about canceling Adam, I'll drive down there myself. To hell with doctor's orders."

"Okay, okay," Noelle said through a smile. Jill would have made good on her threat. "Point made. Well, take extra good care of yourself tonight. Make Gareth wait on you hand and foot."

"Oh, I already have done. He's making me toast and jam downstairs as I speak. I'm the luckiest girl."

"You are. I'll call you tomorrow, see how you are."

"All right. Good-bye, darling. And the happiest of birthdays."

She hung up and realized the day wouldn't be a complete wash after all. Adam was coming.

Ordinarily when a car pulled up at the cottage, Noelle heard the faint rubbery squeak of tires or the slam of a door from almost anywhere inside her house. But this afternoon, nothing signaled Adam's arrival except the first knock at her front door. Caught off guard, she paused at the hall mirror for inspection: hair in a casual ponytail with side-swept bangs, makeup thankfully not smudged everywhere.

When she opened the door, he stood in a white shirt and dark green tie, shaking out his umbrella. He tipped it against the doorframe and smiled. "Oh—hey. It's a ghastly humid mess out here."

"Hi! I know. It's been this way all morning." She glanced behind him at the road. "Where's your car?"

"The whole street's blocked off. Had to park pretty far away. That bloody festival. I forgot all about it." Adam brushed past her on his way in, patting his feet on the doormat. "So," he said, facing her squarely. "Happy birthday to you! I come bearing gifts. I swung by the townhouse and picked up Jill's present, too." He paused. "Actually, they're not with me. They're in my car. Guess we can get them later. Mmm... I smell lemon."

"That's for tonight. My present for you. Well, one of them."

She shut the door and stood with her hands in her jeans pockets. She had decided to dress down, since Jill wouldn't be coming. She could change before dinner later on. Plus, she didn't want Adam to think she'd dressed up just for his sake.

"I saw the vicar yesterday," she said. "He gushes about you. Especially since the renovations are going so well. Adam this and Adam that. I think he's your biggest fan."

"I'm just relieved the project is going according to schedule. I don't want to disappoint anyone."

She never tired of hearing him say British things like "shhedule." Mr. Darcy emerged from the kitchen, padding cautiously down the hall to investigate the ruckus. "Make that your *second* biggest fan," said Noelle.

"There's my big boy." Adam scooped Mr. Darcy up. "You're getting quite chunky. What's your mum been feeding you?" Mr. Darcy purred his response and scrunched his eyes tight as Adam tickled under his chin. When Adam bent down to let Mr. Darcy free, the unmistakable wail of a bagpipe filtered through the cracked-open window in the sitting room. "Have you been down to the festival yet?" he asked.

"I haven't had time."

"Seems fun, from what I saw on my way over here." He dusted the cat hair off his sleeves. "Do we have time to go before dinner?"

Yesterday, Noelle had made reservations for three at Chatsworth Manor, the restaurant and hotel on the edge of the village. "I thought it was a 'bloody' festival?"

"Well, that was only when it made parking a nightmare. But it might be fun. Shall we go?"

She started to agree but put her hands on her hips. "Aren't you a little overdressed for a festival?"

Adam looked down at his attire and frowned. He removed the tie and handed it to her, undid two buttons, rolled up his sleeves, and untucked his shirt all the way, leaving long tree branches of cotton wrinkles. "Better?"

"Perfect."

As if by design, the exact moment they reached the edge of the festival, the rain weakened into sprinkles then a gentle mist. Adam and Noelle folded up their umbrellas and took in the sights. Storey Road had been blocked off, a festive party in full swing with Scottish and Celtic music playing intermittently and decorations of colorful streamers dangling around the streetlights and booths. Local vendors had set up stalls along the sides of the street—Julia and Mr. Bentley, selling their baked goods and pastries; Mrs. Mulberry, peddling knickknacks and antique jewelry; Mrs. Wickham, displaying her flowers. None of them had allowed the rain to dampen the day. Makeshift coverings, just removed, had served as shelter until the rain cleared away.

Adam and Noelle made their way toward the bustle of activity, avoiding puddles as they walked. Hyperactive children played hide-and-seek, meandering between the festivalgoers who strolled from stall to stall. The farmer, Mr. Elton, had even brought his two Shetland ponies for the children to ride, setting up a miniature corral at the edge of the first vendor. The line of impatient children to ride grew long, and parents attempted to distract them with candy and balloons.

Noelle and Adam stopped to sample Julia's just-baked apple tart then filtered through a rack of vintage clothing at Mrs. Bennett's stall. Mrs. Pickering summoned them over to her booth, insisting on hugging Adam's neck. She stepped back and clasped her hands together, looking from Adam to Noelle and back to Adam again. Her peach lipstick matched her peach blouse, and her salt-and-pepper hair was twisted into a tight bun.

"Don't you two look well together? Such a lovely couple you are."

"Mrs. Pickering..." Noelle lowered her head in embarrassment, wishing she had listened to her better judgment and avoided the stall altogether. "We're good friends. I've told you." She glanced at Adam for help, but his snickering made it impossible to respond.

"Oh, don't mind me. I'm an old woman living vicariously through the lives of you young folks. Since Mr. Pickering passed five years ago..." Her voice cracked and faded away. Noelle placed a hand on top of hers, patting gently. Mrs. Pickering squeezed it and winked at her, whispering, "You *do* look well together, you know."

Noelle rolled her eyes and smiled then dragged Adam, nearly doubled over with laughter, in the opposite direction. "What's so funny?"

"You. The look on your face. I've never seen quite that shade of crimson before."

"You weren't very helpful." She slapped at his arm. "You left me hanging! Maybe you should've mentioned Laurel. That would have shut her up." She said Laurel's name almost to test his reaction.

He changed the subject instead. "Look what I see." Adam placed his arm firmly around her shoulders and marched her over to a booth across the street, where a group of children stood in line for popcorn and peanuts. "Okay, what'll it be?" Adam dug around for his wallet.

"Peanuts, I guess. But you're allergic, aren't you?"

"Yeah. You remembered that?"

"You'd be surprised what I remember."

Adam tried to pay for the snacks, but Noelle insisted on going Dutch treat for the entire evening. "If you don't want to think of it as Dutch," she reasoned, "think of it this way—I'm paying for yours, and you're paying for mine. Happy birthday to each other."

"Can't argue with that weird logic."

They munched on their buttery caramel popcorns while walking near the stalls. Adam pointed at the next booth, where a man sat surrounded by drawings of caricatures. "You have to do this."

"I have to? Why?"

"Because! Because it's your birthday. And because, just for tonight, we have nothing in the world to worry about but having a good time."

"If I pose for this, then you have to pose for one, too. Dutch treat, remember?"

Adam scoffed and said, "Okay, whatever," then plunked down some pound notes for the artist.

Noelle handed Adam her box of popcorn and umbrella then sat down in the folding chair. "How long will it take?" she asked the artist, an overweight man with a bristly moustache.

"Not but a few minutes, darlin'," he responded in an Irish brogue.

Noelle folded her hands in her lap and shifted in the chair, trying to find a comfortable and flattering position. "I can't believe you talked me into this," she muttered.

Adam stood behind the artist. "Shh. Can't you see the man is trying to work?"

Noelle stuck out her tongue at him. "Oops. Don't put that in the portrait, okay?"

The Irishman chuckled and nodded.

Noelle tried to ignore Adam and steadied her focus on the artist. Adam, in her peripheral view, glanced at the canvas then at her. Canvas, her. She hated being on display and wanted to get up and hide somewhere.

After several minutes of wondering when the artist would finally finish, Noelle became restless and looked straight at Adam. He had been staring more at her than at the canvas. Intently. The normal, polite thing to do would've been for one of them to look away. But all Noelle could do was stare back.

"All done," the artist said, sitting back in his chair to assess his work.

Relieved, Noelle stood up and stretched her stiff muscles. Stepping to Adam's side, she studied the finished product. Her cartoon eyes, enormous and exceptionally blue, gazed out at them through long, exaggerated lashes. She resembled a princess in a children's fairy tale.

"Beautiful." Adam handed the artist a hefty tip. The Irishman placed the portrait inside a paper bag and gave it to Noelle.

"Your turn," Noelle insisted.

"We don't have time. Besides, look at that line of little kids who want their portraits done." Indeed, a group of three children waited patiently. "I wouldn't want to go in front of them."

She scowled at him. "Fine. You do make a good case. I'll let you off the hook this time."

They discarded their popcorn and slowed their pace, taking small steps in the direction of the cottage. At the edge of the festival, where the crowds had worn thin, Noelle stopped without warning, and Adam nearly ran into her. "Wow," she said. "Look at that."

She pointed up toward the hill of her cottage. The sun had faded over the horizon, leaving the spectacular glow of burnt oranges and coral pinks filtering through leftover rain clouds. "I wish I had a canvas right now," she said.

Adam pressed his chest lightly against her back as he extended his arms out in front of her, his hands shaping into *L*'s as he framed the picture of the sunset for both of them. "The Golden Ratio?" he suggested in her ear.

"Mmm. Definitely."

He put his hands down but didn't move away. His chest grazed her back slightly whenever he breathed, putting her Adam Radar into overdrive.

Adam whispered, "On second thought, maybe it's best to see it this way, not try to capture it on canvas. Just see it for what it is. Beautiful and fleeting."

Noelle swiveled to face him. "You're awfully philosophical tonight."

"You bring it out in me, I guess."

If they were a couple, this might have been the kiss moment. The sunset, the romance of a carnival, the ease of flirty banter, all just a prelude. But they weren't a couple. He wasn't hers to kiss.

Oddly, she hadn't thought about Preston once tonight, not the entire time. She wondered if Laurel had entered Adam's thoughts. Or whether this village, like Adam's Magic Pub, was a time machine that lured them back to teenage days, and teenage feelings, so easily. Too easily.

The cheery twang of Celtic music rose up from a platform near the pub and interrupted Noelle's fantasy before it began. White lights twinkled above a wooden stage that Joe and some of the construction workers had erected. People gathered in groups, with a few brave souls stepping onto the stage in pairs. The Irish dancing had begun.

"Let's go!" Noelle grabbed Adam's hand and tried to lead him toward the music.

He stood firm. "Oh, no. Not me. Dancing is one thing I don't do."

"Adam Spencer, it's my birthday. Are you going to stand there and deny a birthday girl her one wish?"

"Your one birthday wish is to dance?"

"Yes." They stood, unmoving, wondering who would cave first. Still holding hands.

"Okay. Let's go." Adam took off, pulling her toward the stage. "You don't know what you've gotten yourself into. I have no idea how to do these country dances. I'm going to step all over your feet. It won't be pretty."

"You think *I* know how to Irish dance? I'm a California hippie! We can learn together."

They set down the portrait and umbrellas at the end of the stage, hoping they'd stay safe, then Adam helped her up the two steps to the stage. Instantly, they were pulled into a pulsating, rhythmical swell of people moving along in a sort of disorganized circle—skipping, clapping, turning, laughing. Even the postman and his wife, usually prim and proper, had been swept away by the music and danced alongside them. Three songs later, Noelle and Adam were finally able to mimic the other pairs' steps convincingly. Hop left twice, step right, hop right twice, step left.

The infectious jangles of the Irish whistle and fiddle moved the dancers along, and people watching clapped to the beat. Something magical and freeing happened, an energetic wave of people flowing and bouncing in the same direction at the same time. Noelle let go, forgot everything, and danced.

Chapter Twenty-two

Layer your paintings with texture, with contrasts and shadow and light.
More than straight colours on a canvas. Just as life isn't black or white,
isn't simple to figure out or easy to define, neither should your art be.

WHEN THE IRISH BAND FINALLY took a break, Noelle's smile lingered. She couldn't remove it if she tried.

"How about a pint?" Adam suggested, out of breath as they walked down the stage steps and retrieved their belongings.

"Yes, please."

They meandered their way over to the pub, where Joe had set up an outside booth serving appetizers and alcohol.

"See? You had fun dancing. Admit it," she said.

"Yeah, yeah," Adam confessed. "Okay. Wasn't as bad as a root canal or anything."

Lizzie greeted them from behind the stall, and Adam ordered two lagers.

"You two were having fun out there," she noted. "Quite a fine pair of dancers."

"She made my two left feet look good."

"Well, you'll likely be having the town gossips working overtime."

"What do you mean?" Noelle took the Styrofoam cup from Lizzie.

"Legend says that if a couple doesn't change partners after four Irish dances, they're going to get married. And you two danced six. Together."

"You counted?" She blushed at the thought of people watching them.

"Business was slow. Nothing better to do." Lizzie shrugged. "Lagers are on the house, by the way."

"Thanks. Tell Joe I said hello."

"I will. Have a good night, you two," she called out as Adam and Noelle turned away.

They maneuvered through the shuffling crowd, trying not to spill their drinks. When they reached the edge of the winding street leading back to the cottage, free of crowds, she stopped. "Oh, blast!"

"What?"

"The reservations. I booked a table for the three of us at Chatsworth tonight, before I knew Jill had to back out. I completely forgot."

"What time are they for?"

Noelle looked at her watch. "Eight-thirty. We can still make it. But honestly, the last thing I want to do is eat a heavy three-course meal. After all the snacking we've done."

Adam chuckled. "We've made quite the pigs of ourselves, haven't we?"

"And we'll make bigger pigs of ourselves at the cottage, I'm afraid. I made dessert for you."

"That lemon thing I smelled this afternoon?"

"Thing? You mean lemon yogurt birthday pound cake with iced sugar glazing?"

"Mmm. Yeah, that thing. I say cancel those reservations."

Noelle called the restaurant, apologizing for the last-minute cancellation. She and Adam took a couple more gulps of their lagers then ditched them into a nearby trash receptacle and left for the cottage. First, they made a quick detour half a block away to fetch the gifts. The faint sounds of tinny Celtic music floated from the dance again, and part of her wished she possessed the energy to go another round. She could only imagine what Lizzie would have to say about that.

Adam insisted on carrying the gifts while Noelle took the umbrellas and portrait up the hill to the cottage. Aside from the yellow glow of the porch lights and the hint of a full moon winking behind passing clouds, the sky was dark, the road difficult to see.

A few feet from the cottage gate, Noelle tripped on something, and she couldn't stop the fall. She lunged forward, and her palms hit the muddy ground with a hard slap, driving sharp pebbles into her skin.

Adam crouched by her side with his hand on her back. "Are you okay? What happened?"

She tried to push herself up, but the ache in her hands and knees wouldn't let her. "I'm not sure. Just klutzy, I guess. It's hard to see. I tripped over something." She hoped her palms weren't bleeding too badly. They stung as she raised one off the ground.

"Anything broken?"

"I don't think so."

"Here, let me help."

He lifted her gingerly under both arms. When she stood, he wrapped a hand around her waist to steady her. She grunted as a sharp pain shot up her leg. She had twisted something lower down.

"What is it?"

"My ankle, I think."

"Can you walk?" His grasp loosened to give her room to try.

She put her weight on it and winced. "I think it's just a bad sprain. Maybe I can try."

"No need." He lifted her up in one quick swoop to carry her in his arms. Caught off guard, she had grasped onto his shirt and still clung tightly to it. "Don't worry," he assured. "I've gotcha." He kicked open the gate gently with his foot and walked down the stone path as Noelle held on, one arm around his neck.

When they reached the front door, she remembered. "Oh, the portrait. And the presents."

"No worries. I'll go back for them. Let's get you inside first." He chuckled.

"What's so funny?"

"The irony. Twenty minutes ago, we were dancing all over the place."

"And then I trip over a stupid rock. It's like a sitcom. Call me 'Grace.'"

"Okay, Grace. Where's the key?"

Still hanging onto his neck, she dug out the key from her jeans pocket and sucked in a breath as her palm stung again.

"Can you reach it?" He leaned her forward toward the keyhole.

His breath warmed her cheek as she inserted the key with a click. Inside, a few steps away from the safety of the sofa, Adam started to trip. She gripped onto him so hard that her nails sank into his skin. But he righted himself and stood with a long pause, catching his breath. Their faces were inches apart.

"What happened?" she asked.

"Damned cat. He darted right in front of me. I nearly squashed him."

She feigned offense. "You just cussed at my cat."

"Not really at him. More like, *about* him. He nearly killed us." He knelt forward and tipped her carefully onto the sofa then placed a cushion under her ankle. Mr. Darcy leaped up and sniffed Adam's hand.

"Sorry I cussed about you, Big Guy." Mr. Darcy meowed his forgiveness. "Be right back with some ice."

She reached for some tissue on the nearby table and examined her hands. Not too bad. No bleeding, just scrapes. Mostly mud and grime, with only a couple of pricks from the pebbles. When Adam returned, he held a frozen bag of peas, which he carefully pressed to her ankle. Mr. Darcy jumped to the floor as though realizing he was in the way. She sucked in a breath.

"Sorry. Is it bad?"

"No, just cold. I think my hands hurt even more right now. They took the full impact."

"Hang on..." Adam said and disappeared again. A minute later, he pulled up a footstool and sat down beside her. "Here..." He took her wrist and tilted it palm-up to apply a cool, damp cloth.

Noelle winced.

"Sorry again."

"It's okay," she whispered. He moved to her other palm. She forgot her own hands for a minute and watched his at work. Beautiful. Distinctly masculine—the shape of them, the thick breadth and texture. So unlike her petite hands. And there they were, cradling hers. *More like a sappy Lifetime movie than a sitcom*, Noelle thought, chuckling.

"What?" Adam asked.

"Nothing. Just this. My making a mess of a perfectly good evening."

"I don't think anything's a mess. Well, unless you count the presents. Probably ruined by the mud. I'll go check on them." He handed her the cloth and disappeared a third time. When he returned, he sat again on the footstool, juggling everything in his lap.

"No mud?" She glanced at the shiny paper.

"Guess they got spared." He shrugged. "Just some flecks of dirt. Did you have one from Preston? I can get it for you."

"No, there isn't one. Since he couldn't come to the village tonight, I'm sure he'll bring something next time we see each other." Not that she had any clue when that would be. He'd been drifting away since their big double date at Sketch. She couldn't pinpoint why.

"Mmm," Adam said then handed her the first gift, obviously from Jill, wrapped in pink.

Inside lay a beautiful lavender scarf that matched one of Noelle's summer dresses perfectly. "Oh, gorgeous!" She held it up to the light, forgetting about her injured hands.

"And here's mine." Adam passed her a rectangular-shaped package, poorly wrapped with a whole corner peeking out at the edge. She unwrapped it to find a Nigella Lawson cookbook. "You mentioned her in one of your emails."

She carefully flipped through the pages with her fingertips. "I watch her show all the time. Thank you. Very sweet."

"That's not all. One more."

"Who from?"

"Me again." He produced a small round blob of tissue paper, tied haphazardly at the top with a purple ribbon.

"What's this?"

"For whenever you get homesick. A little reminder."

Curious, she started to untie the ribbon but struggled with the too-tight knot. Adam reached over to help. She opened the tissue paper to find a beautiful seashell, dark blue with white streaks, perfectly symmetrical. "Oh, Adam... thank you."

"C'mon. Only cost me two pounds or something."

"I don't care. I love it. This has been such a great birthday."

"Even with your fall? The rain? The cancelled dinner reservations?"

"Yes. Even with all that. Mostly because you're here." Hoping she hadn't crossed any lines, she looked down at the tissue paper. "Are we really this old? Thirty-one? I mean, is this what thirty-one is supposed to feel like?"

"Speak for yourself, old woman. I'm still thirty."

"Only for another day!" She threw the wadded-up paper at his head, but he caught it in one snatch. "No, I'm serious," she said. "Getting older is bizarre. I remember being eighteen and knowing exactly how my life would look in my thirties. I pictured my life in a very specific way. I'd be settled, comfortable. All the clichés—marriage, kids..."

"Yeah." Adam rolled the paper ball between his palms. "Things don't look the way I thought they would, either."

She studied his face, expecting him to toss the ball back at her with a flippant joke, but he didn't.

"I thought we'd be married." He rolled the ball up tighter in one hand, methodically smashing the life out of it.

"Yeah, well, you're about to be, so I guess one of us has been a success."

"No. I meant to each other." He unraveled the paper, revealing the thousand creases he'd made, and met her gaze. Before she had a chance to collect her thoughts or utter a word, he smirked and added, "Hell, what did I know? I was just a kid." Adam unfolded his legs and stood up with a stretch. "Let's have some cake!"

He left the room, and Noelle used the couple of minutes to compose herself. *He thought we'd be married.* Adam had never verbally acknowledged feelings for her, even decades-old feelings, beyond friendship. Not until this moment.

Adam returned, balancing two pieces of lemon cake and two glasses of cold milk. He fidgeted a bit with them, from either too many items to juggle or embarrassment after his big reveal minutes earlier. Noelle didn't know which.

After handing her the plate and fork, he made a fire in the cast-iron stove. Following his flippant lead, wanting him to know she hadn't been fazed in the slightest by his revelation, Noelle sank her fork into the cake and attempted a lighthearted tone. "Hey, I should injure myself more often. I'm enjoying all this pampering."

"Guess I owe you. For the pampering you gave me that summer during my food poisoning."

"Ha, true." She took a bite of cake then pointed to the table beside him. "Time for your present."

"Hang on. I've got to try the cake first." He returned to the footstool and took his first bite. "Mmm. Incredible. Best lemon cake ever."

"Actually, it's a Nigella recipe."

Adam finished off his cake in three more bites before setting down his plate and reaching for his present. He rubbed his hands together in anticipation. His eyes lit up as he unwrapped the architecture book she'd bought weeks ago.

"A first edition!" Adam leafed through it. "And signed. How did you—?"

"There's a little bookshop in London that sells out-of-print books. I saw this one and thought of you."

"Perfect. Thank you!" Adam closed the book. "Happy birthday."

"You, too." She started to set the plate on the table, but he did it for her. The soft chimes of the grandfather clock counted out the hour.

"Blimey, it's late." Adam suddenly busied himself gathering up all the discarded wrapping paper, plates, and cups. "I think I probably should go."

"Yeah, you need to get home. Big day tomorrow."

"Big day?"

"Your birthday. Aren't you going out with Laurel and your parents for a night on the town? Jill says you're going to an expensive restaurant."

"Oh. That. Yeah. Honestly, I'd rather have something more low-key."

"Some Irish dancing and caramel popcorn, maybe?"

"Yeah. Throw in a gorgeous sunset and some lemon cake, and you're spot on." Adam took the trash and plates into the other room. When he reappeared, he unfolded a blanket and spread it over her as he would a tablecloth at a picnic. "Need anything else before I go?"

"Nope. I've got Mr. Darcy for company."

Adam stood over her, running a hand through his hair, looking a little lost. "I hate to leave you injured this way—"

"Go. Really. I'm fine. Better already."

"Okay." He leaned down, and she closed her eyes, expecting the usual quick peck on the cheek. But this time, he hovered, moved slowly. And when his lips finally did make contact, they grazed the corner of her mouth. She held her breath until he pulled away, then opened her eyes.

"Night, Sunshine," he whispered then rubbed Mr. Darcy's ears before walking to the front door.

For the first time all evening, a thick silence hung in the air. Noelle gathered the blanket tighter, wincing as she forgot about her tender palms. She still held the seashell. She touched the crevices with the tip of her index finger and pictured Adam spying it in a shop somewhere, thinking of her.

She stared into the fire. The flames danced, hypnotic and mystical. She thought of another fireside she had shared years ago, at Gram's estate. Gram had retired for the evening, but Noelle and Aunt Joy remained wide awake, as they always seemed to, both night owls who fought the idea of sleep, despite Gram's disapproval. Noelle could still see Aunt Joy's nimble fingers working on a half-finished needlepoint, her eyes focused on the delicate fabric.

Noelle had come in that evening from yet another tennis match with Adam, and before she sat down beside the fire in the parlor, Joy had commanded her to "Go forth and shower." She hadn't even looked up from her needlepoint, and Noelle knew better than to try to convince her she wasn't sweaty and wouldn't leave a mark on the chair. After the quick shower, Noelle had returned and sat on the dense white carpet beside the warm fire, rubbing at her damp hair with a towel.

"Who won?" Joy asked, still not making eye contact.

"Me, of course. Adam still can't get his backhand straight."

She watched Joy's steady concentration and thought about how different she looked from her sister. Gram's skin was flawless ivory. But when Noelle looked at Joy's face, wrinkles betrayed the years of smoking that made her look a decade older. Even more than that, her face held a distant sadness behind the eyes that Noelle could never put her finger on. Though she'd had the same privileged upbringing as her sister, Joy's face reflected the life of someone who'd experienced inordinate disappointment and pain.

Her deep-set brown eyes turned to ice when angry and sparkled when content. People who didn't know her well assumed Joy was uncaring, distant. But Noelle knew better. The little errands she sometimes ran for her sister, unasked. The gentle way she talked to a mother bird in the tree when she thought no one was listening. The patience she showed while teaching a novice Noelle to paint. Underneath the unsmiling countenance lay a soft, genuine heart.

"Aunt Joy, may I ask you a question?" Noelle folded the damp towel at her feet.

"Certainly."

"What does love feel like?"

Joy's fingers paused as she looked in Noelle's direction but not actually at her. "Well, that's a question," she stated, even-toned, her fingers moving again. "You're only sixteen. You have plenty of time ahead to ponder the intricacies of love."

"I just… wanted to know." Noelle played with a loose string on the white towel, expecting Joy to dismiss her altogether.

After a moment, Joy sighed and abandoned her needlepoint. "Love. Well, there are many different sorts of love."

"What about romantic love? Like in the movies."

Joy's shoulders raised and lowered in a chuckle. "People dancing about, being silly and giddy and ridiculous? That kind of love?"

"Well…" She thought back to yesterday, Adam piggybacking her to the manor after she sketched his sneaker.

"Actually, being in love can feel that way." Joy finally made eye contact. "But it's temporary. You lose yourself and become an idiot. However, when you come to your senses—if it's real love, true love that lasts the length of your life—it settles into a kind of peace in the pit of your stomach. A security that compares with nothing else. A warm blanket on a winter's night. Now, *that* sort of love is worth everything."

"Is that what you had with Uncle John?"

"Yes. It was." She returned to her needlepoint.

Noelle had hung on her words, memorizing them and knowing they wouldn't come again. Aunt Joy always chose her words with a sort of exactness that made them weighty.

Hearing her aunt's voice again through memory, Noelle wondered if Joy had suspected the source of her questions. Likely, she knew precisely whom her grandniece had in mind.

Noelle nuzzled her chin into the blanket and wished so badly Joy could be sitting at this fire with her needlepoint, telling her what to do.

Chapter Twenty-three

People will let you down, mark my words. But the canvas will not. It will always be there for you, waiting to be filled—with your hopes, your anger, the thoughts you can't even form. It's your ally, your comfort, your place of refuge. Another world you can step into, when your own world has become too toxic to bear.

"NO MATTER HOW LONG I live in this country, I will still expect a wheel to be on this side," Noelle said, her hands out, clutching an invisible steering wheel.

Preston chuckled as he rotated his real one, taking them onto a London street Noelle didn't recognize.

"Okay, another guess," she said, the glass of wine from thirty minutes ago making her flirty. They had just come from dinner at an Italian restaurant. "The War Museum."

"Too boring," Preston scowled.

"Ooh! I know. Notting Hill. To visit the blue door."

"Blue door?"

"Where Hugh Grant lived."

"You're talking about that movie, aren't you? That chick flick."

"So, not Notting Hill, then?"

"Nope."

They had already passed London Bridge, the river still in sight. "Something on the water?" The traffic became snail-like, making Noelle all the more curious.

"Nope. Actually, we'll have to park far away, do some walking."

"Okay, I give up. I'm out of guesses."

"We're going to The Globe Theatre."

Noelle took in a breath. "Seriously?"

"You mentioned it once. I made a mental note."

"I did?"

"You said you took a course on Shakespeare at university, and this was the one touristy place you'd always wanted to visit. So, here we are."

Filled with excitement, Noelle kissed his clean-shaven cheek as he maneuvered through the sea of other cars. In the two weeks since her birthday dinner with Adam, Noelle had floated steadily back down to earth. The morning after he'd left, she'd lain in bed, looked at her bruised, scratched palms, and done another reality check. Yes, the birthday had been magical. She and Adam had flirted, bantered, danced, and hugged, all without reservation or consequence. But in the light of a new morning, she saw things differently. Nothing had changed. Adam was still very much engaged.

So, she would put all her efforts and energies into Preston, an un-engaged man, free and available to spend time with her. She wanted to make more of an effort, show him she was all in. "I didn't realize the Globe would be open for tours this late," she told him.

"We're not touring. We're going to see an actual play. *Othello*."

Noelle's smile widened. "Seriously? You're spoiling me, Preston."

Her cell rang. She stuffed her hand inside her purse and glanced at the lit-up screen. Adam again. He had called three times in a row this morning, but she'd been too busy at the gallery to call him back. Knowing his ability to taint her thinking, she ignored the call and placed the phone back in her purse. She didn't need the distraction.

"You deserve spoiling," Preston said, reaching for her hand. He brought it to his mouth and kissed it.

Her phone rang again. "What does he *want*?" she grumbled.

"Who?"

"It's just Adam." She checked the screen to make sure. "Again. I guess I'd better get it. Might be important." She tapped on the phone with a more-irritated-than-she'd-intended, "Hello?"

"Noelle! I'm glad you answered. The baby's coming."

"Baby?"

"Jill's baby! She went into labor an hour ago."

"But it's too early."

"Only by a week. That will make a big difference. Gareth's in with her now. They're prepping her for a C-section. Because of her blood pressure."

"Oh my gosh! Okay. Where are you?"

"St. Thomas's."

"Be there as fast as I can!" She had promised to be there for Jill, not to let her go through this experience without her. Noelle ended the call and told Preston, "It's Jill. She's having her baby. I'm sorry, but I—"

"Say no more. This is important. *Othello* will just have to take a rain check." He grinned, undaunted by the traffic as he wedged his way into a U-turn. "Which hospital?"

"St. Thomas."

He put a hand on her knee. "She'll be all right."

In a matter of seconds, Noelle had shifted from carefree and giddy to concerned and nervous, and it had given her a headache. All she could think about was Jill, in some clinical hospital room, scared and anxious. She squeezed the phone with one hand and placed the other on top of Preston's.

Thirty minutes later, they entered a hospital elevator. Most people disliked hospitals, but Noelle even more so. Flashbacks of her mother's death, no matter how hard she tried to bat them away, always forced themselves into her mind. The smells, the sounds, the fluorescent lights. But entering a hospital for a joyous occasion was an entirely different matter. This was about life. Not death.

She and Preston reached the third floor and found the maternity waiting room, where Adam sat in a corner, leaning on the arm of a chair, staring ahead. The room didn't favor a traditional hospital décor. Not with its burgundy carpet, cushioned seats, and soft lamplight. The room even had a mini-kitchen with a coffeemaker.

"Hey," she said as Adam stood up. "Any word?"

His gaze shifted to Preston and turned flat. Noelle waited for a cordial smile or greeting from Adam, but it never came. Very un-Adam-like, to be so cold. Finally, to break the awkward pause, Preston extended his hand. Adam shook it then told Noelle, "Not yet."

"How did you find out?"

"I was finishing up at the office. Gareth called, saying he'd brought Jill here. She'd been having contractions."

"I'm worried. Her blood pressure—and she's been on bed rest."

"She'll be all right." Adam squeezed her hand then released it.

"That's what Preston just said."

"She's a fighter. We're talking about Jill here."

Noelle smiled for the first time in half an hour. "True."

Preston flinched, searching his pocket for his buzzing cell. "Sorry. I have to take this," he whispered to Noelle. He kissed her cheek and walked into the hall to answer it.

"Here—let's sit down." Adam gestured toward the row of chairs.

Noelle took the seat next to him and said, "So," in her waiting-room whisper. "Where's Laurel?"

Adam rubbed the palms of his hands together as though trying to warm them. "Los Angeles. On business."

"That's far away."

"Yeah." He glanced at her sideways. "You look nice." He noticed the hint of a flowered dress peeking out from beneath her long raincoat. "On a date?"

"Yes."

"Things are getting serious?"

"You certainly are full of questions."

"Well, they're not difficult questions. Or are they?"

She ignored the curtness in his tone and said, "Things are progressing."

"Into what?"

She shifted to look at him. "Adam, is something bothering you?"

He tapped his knee against the chair and searched the floor. Before he could answer, Preston returned.

"Sorry—I'm afraid I have to leave."

Noelle wanted to ask him why, press him for details, but Adam's stare weighed on her. She could find out later.

"Oh, blast," Preston added. "You're stranded. We left your car at the restaurant."

"I can give her a ride," Adam said without hesitation.

Everything happened before she could protest, could insist on hailing a taxi. Noelle walked Preston to the elevators. "I hate to leave you," he told her after pushing the button then brushed his fingers lightly through her hair. "I'll explain later."

"It's okay. I have no idea how long I'll have to wait. Might be all night. You go on."

"I'll call you later. I hope everything goes well with your friend."

Noelle stood on her toes for a kiss, holding Preston's jacket lapels for balance. When the ding of the elevator interrupted them, she said good-bye and watched the doors close.

The stuffy room had Noelle struggling out of her coat on her way back to Adam, who had carved designs deep into an empty Styrofoam cup with his thumbnail. The mellow voice of a newscaster offered weather predictions as Noelle settled into her chair. Adam picked little chunks off the top of the cup, creating a symmetrical pattern on the rim.

"It's supposed to be 'unseasonably cool' tomorrow," Adam informed her.

"Yes, I noticed a chill tonight." Noelle re-crossed her legs, folding her coat in half.

"You want a coffee, something to eat?" Adam offered, finished with his art.

"No, I'm fine."

"I didn't know whether you'd already eaten…"

"We did. The restaurant was amazing." Noelle reached for a magazine and browsed a few pages. When she looked up, Gareth was rushing through a set of double doors at the end of the hall. He wore blue scrubs and a broad smile. Noelle and Adam met him halfway.

"It's a girl!" Gareth's voice trembled with excitement. His accent sounded more Welsh than usual. "You knew that already. Well, she's tiny, beautiful, and very pink. And healthy. She's perfectly healthy."

"Oh, congratulations!" Noelle leaned in to hug him. "I'm so, so happy for you. That was awfully fast—what happened? How is Jill?"

"She's all right. They had to do an emergency Cesarean. Her blood pressure spiked, so they had to deliver the baby immediately. Jill's in recovery. She wants to see you, but it'll be another couple of hours before she can have visitors. But you can see the baby now. They're taking her to the nursery. You can peek at her through the window, if you want."

"Absolutely!" Noelle and Adam said in unison.

"I need to return to Jill. Can you find your way there?"

"Sure," Noelle said. "You go on. Be with Jill. Give her our love." Gareth returned to the double doors, and Noelle's eyes welled up.

"You okay?"

"Yes." Noelle wiped her cheeks. "Tears of relief."

"C'mon. Let's go get our first glimpse of this little troublemaker."

Three long hallways and two sets of doors later, Noelle and Adam stood behind a glass wall, staring at a symmetrical row of empty beds. "Must've been a slow night," Adam cracked as Noelle elbowed him.

"I think that's her!" Noelle pointed to a nurse carrying in a shrieking newborn.

"Oh, that's definitely Jill's baby. What a set of lungs!" Adam said, receiving another elbow.

"Shh. Behave yourself."

The nurse placed the newborn into a clear plastic bed near the window, with a label that announced its newest resident proudly: *Eveline Bartleby-Holbrook*. Swaddling her into a pink blanket, the nurse remained calm as the baby continued her bloodcurdling protests, her bottom lip trembling with each new breath. "Oo-wah! Oo-wah!"

Miraculously, the very instant the nurse swaddled her, the baby stopped crying, settling into the blanket with a contented sigh.

"Look at that. Magic," Noelle whispered.

"I think I see some red in her hair," said Adam. "Welcome to the world, Eveline."

Noelle waited for the sarcastic comment to follow, but it never came. He made a sweet scrunched-up face at the baby and touched his fingers to the glass. The newborn lay peaceful, and Noelle wished life would be like that for her always.

After leaving the nursery, any leftover weirdness from the waiting room having evaporated, Adam and Noelle spent the next two hours biding their time. Getting coffee, viewing the art exhibit in the first floor atrium, and stopping off at the gift shop, two minutes before closing, for a vase of abundant roses that spilled over the sides. Finally, they tapped on Jill's door and heard an enthusiastic "Come in!"

Jill, her cheeks pale and her hair tucked behind both ears, cradled Eveline on one arm and motioned them into the room with her other.

Gareth passed them on the way out, excusing himself to make more phone calls to friends and family.

"Jill, how are you feeling?" Noelle kissed her cheek.

"Pretty awful. And exhausted. But the 'awful' was so worth it, don't you think? Look at this precious creature."

Noelle reached out to touch the baby's feather-soft cheek. "She's beautiful. We took a peek at her in the nursery earlier."

"Adam, come closer," Jill insisted. "Little Evie, you've just met your Auntie Noelle, and this is your Uncle Adam."

Adam set down the flowers and slipped his finger beneath Eveline's hand, and she grasped it tight. "Lovely to meet you." He beamed at her. "Hey, nice grip!"

"I'm so glad you're both here." Jill looked from one to the other, her eyes gleaming. "This means the world to me. Look at the three of us. Childhood friends, together for a big life event. Most people aren't this lucky, are they?"

"No, they're not." Noelle peered at Adam, suddenly nostalgic.

The baby squirmed and gurgled, raising her invisible eyebrows up then down into a frown, making cooing sounds.

"Look. I think she's having a dream," Noelle whispered.

"Well, either that, or an enormous amount of gas," Jill stated.

"Or both." Adam smirked.

"So, where are your other halves? Oh, Laurel is in the States, isn't she? And your Preston?" She looked up at Noelle. "You're all dressed up, in fact. Tell me I didn't disrupt one of your dates."

"Well, actually—"

"Ha! Leave it to me to pick the perfect time to have a baby."

"He'll make it up to me, don't worry," Noelle said with more innuendo than she intended.

A nurse walked in with an extra blanket, and Jill waved at her. "Would you be a darling and take our picture?" She shifted her focus to Noelle. "Do you have your phone with you?"

"Yes, great idea."

"Gareth took a million pictures already, but I want one with the two of you. To mark the moment."

The Jill that Noelle knew wouldn't dare be photographed without a stitch of makeup. But the Jill holding her newborn didn't seem to mind one bit.

The nurse obliged and took Noelle's phone while Adam and Noelle crouched at either side of Jill's bed. "Say cheese," said the nurse. After the photo, Jill winced as she shifted in the bed.

"You need your rest," Noelle said. "You've had a long night. Is there anything I can get you before we go?"

"No, Mum should be back in a moment. I'm sorry you missed her."

"Another time… I hope you sleep well tonight."

"Ha! I think I've seen the last of that for the next year."

"Probably so." Noelle smiled. "I'll call you tomorrow."

"Love you both," Jill said as they walked through the door.

Downstairs in the parking lot, Noelle followed Adam's lead, clasping her lapels together at the neck to keep out the cool breeze. At his car, he opened the door for her. "You know," he said, shutting his door and clicking his seatbelt, "I didn't think Jill would have the first baby."

"What do you mean, 'first' baby?"

"Out of the three of us. She's the last one I thought would settle down and have a family." He started the engine and backed out of the space.

"Yeah. I never really pictured her having kids at all. But she seems happy. I think she'll be a fantastic mother. You know, one of those 'cool' moms your friends are always jealous of."

"The ones who let you have a late curfew, host cool parties, allow you alcohol before you're supposed to have it?"

"Yep. That's the one." Noelle crossed her legs and adjusted her purse in her lap as Adam exited the parking lot. She told him to head south toward the restaurant where her car was still parked. "I don't know if I'll ever have kids," she confided.

"Really?" He frowned. "Why do you say that?"

Noelle shrugged. "I don't know. I guess I thought I would've had them already. There's this window that's closing, and… Well, maybe I've

222

already missed it or something. I mean, I want kids. I'm just not sure when it will happen."

"There's still plenty of time."

Noelle's cell jingled inside her purse. "I'd better get this."

"Hey," Preston said when she answered. "How's Jill?"

"She's fantastic. Everything went really well. She and the baby are resting."

"Glad to hear it. Sorry I had to leave. Something that couldn't wait."

"That's okay. I'm the one who cut our date short in the first place."

"Rain check?"

"Of course."

"I'll call you tomorrow. We'll set something up."

"Okay. Talk to you then." Noelle ended the call with a tap.

"So, what was the big emergency?" Adam said, not even trying to hide his sarcasm.

"He didn't say. But I'm sure it was important."

Adam grunted under his breath.

Noelle couldn't take it anymore. "Adam, what's going on? You've been weird about Preston all night."

"I have a bad feeling about him. About you with him."

"A bad feeling." Her frustration grew. "What does it matter to you who he is or what he means to me? Jill has someone. You have someone. Don't I have a right to have someone?"

"Nobody said you didn't. Just… be careful."

Their usually playful banter had evaporated into the night air. "What do you mean by that?"

"I don't want to see you get hurt, that's all." His eyes focused on the road, and Noelle mused whether, face to face, he would've still avoided eye contact.

"Why would he hurt me? Do you know something I don't?"

Adam sighed and scratched at his chin, as if sensing he might be in dangerous territory. "I found something on him."

"What do you mean, 'on him'?"

"I Googled him this morning. It's why I called you so many times, but you never picked up. I didn't want to leave a message."

"Why would you do that? Google my boyfriend?"

"Call it a gut feeling. The point is that I found something."

"What? You're making me nervous."

"I'm pretty sure he's married." They had stopped at a light, and the glow tinted his face a dull red. Noelle studied his profile in silence. His lips drew tight and thin, as though regretting his confession.

"Pretty sure?" She glowered at him, even knowing Adam couldn't see her. "Well, you're either sure or you aren't sure. What did you find?"

"So, you never researched him yourself, never Googled him? I thought that's what people did these days. Check each other out."

"He told me he doesn't go online, doesn't Facebook or Twitter or anything. So I assumed there wouldn't be anything to Google. And you're avoiding the question. How do you know that he's married?"

The light had changed, and he pressed the accelerator. "There was this article, some teacher banquet he attended, and the caption said 'Mr. and Mrs. Preston Evans.' She's a pharmacist or something."

Noelle's cheeks grew hot as she glared at the car in front of them. "Maybe that's an old picture. He's probably divorced."

"The picture was a few weeks old, I think. And wouldn't he tell you if he was divorced? Didn't you ever ask?"

Noelle didn't need to justify her relationship to Adam. She didn't feel like making an idiot of herself by confessing she never did ask. She just assumed that if Preston was married, divorced, separated, or anything else, he would've had the decency to tell her up front.

"Just be careful, okay?" he repeated. "I don't want to see you with the wrong guy."

Her voice became thick with frustration. "How do you know he *is* the wrong guy? And why should you even care if he's married or not? This situation is none of your business. You're making judgments about something you know nothing about."

"Cool down, okay? I'm just trying to protect you."

"All these months, and I've never said one thing about that fiancée of yours. You meet Preston for two minutes and think you know everything about him. And you're not even sure."

"Hey, wait a second. What *about* Laurel?" His expression shifted into a defensive frown.

"She's this cold, distant person. Like she's sitting back, judging people."

"That's not fair. You barely know her."

"I know she's not very friendly in public. And I know you're more comfortable flirting with me than you are with her." The conversation had headed to places she wasn't prepared to go. She took a deep breath then lowered her voice and looked out the window. She recognized the street, relieved the restaurant was only a few blocks away. "Look, let's drop it. This has been an emotional night for both of us."

"Fine. Consider it dropped." Adam switched on an eighties station, and they spent the rest of the drive listening to sugary pop music. Noelle stared out the window and tried to block out Duran Duran singing about new moons on Monday. The dynamic changed so quickly, it frazzled her, jarred her. One minute, she and Adam were rejoicing with Jill over her new baby, and the next... accusations, tension, anger.

And as he turned another corner, Noelle shoved down the equally jarring notion that Adam might be right.

Chapter Twenty-four

*Listen to your artistic instincts, that first impression. Go
with your gut every time. It always ends up being accurate.
Otherwise, we waste time following another path, another way,
when we knew all along the first idea was the right one.*

S HE KNEW WHAT SHE HAD to do the moment she entered the
cottage. All the way home from London, Noelle had fought it.
Made excuses, gone over every square inch of her dates and phone
calls with Preston since that first night they'd had coffee. Impossible,
that he would be married. *What about all our London dates? If he had a
wife, what lies did he give her? A "night out with the boys"? Late faculty
meetings that went overly long?*

With a quick pat of Mr. Darcy's neglected head, Noelle made her way
to the kitchen, wriggling off her coat as she went. Though she would've
loved some tea, maybe even a scone, they would have to wait. Google
beckoned. She typed in his name, along with the college name to specify,
and voila! Everything she needed to know. *Why didn't I do this weeks ago?*

After skimming past the first three useless links, she paused: "College
Banquet Honors Teacher Award Recipients." Noelle clicked the link and
scrolled down the article. Definitive proof. Preston, one arm wrapped
around the waist of a pretty blond woman. The caption confirmed it.
Mrs. Preston Evans.

Just to be sure, to be absolutely sure, she scrolled back to the top of
the article. Three weeks ago. Right around the time he had sat beside
her at Sketch.

Angry tears blurred the text. Sometime during her fight with Adam, Noelle had actually known. Something about his words made an odd sort of sense. Before now, she couldn't put her finger on it, but something had been "off" about Preston. A measured distance, an occasional bumbling or stutter. Times when he would cancel a date abruptly or end one early, without a solid explanation. He had a wife to get home to, apparently...

With closer analysis, she remembered other things. A resistance to let her see his apartment—they were always meeting at restaurants or the college instead. The pattern of taking her to big touristy London places, places a London-based wife probably wouldn't visit. The way he isolated their relationship—he never introduced her to his friends, rarely talked about his own family.

Noelle closed the laptop and stared ahead, waiting for the numbness to wear off so she could decide what to do. How to extract herself from the situation, from a person with no regard for her reputation, her character. Or apparently his own. Surely, he knew he'd be discovered one day. But maybe he loved the thrill of the game, enjoyed the possibility of being caught.

The thought of other female students he'd "asked for coffee" made Noelle groan. She envisioned her own relationship from Preston's point of view, knowing how easily she had fallen into his trap. Flirting with him, laughing at his jokes, listening intently to his stories about art.

More than anything, she felt sucker-punched for believing him. For giving him every benefit of every subconscious doubt. She'd invested time getting to know him, invested future time thinking the relationship might actually go somewhere. She'd started to care, started to count on his calls, on their weekly dates. On his kisses. When all along he wasn't hers to kiss in the first place.

Tears streaked down, and she wanted to call the one person she could talk to, count on. But Jill had much more important things to deal with tonight. Of course, Noelle's second choice normally would've been Adam, but she couldn't face him. Call it pride or embarrassment, even though he'd been right. No, she'd have to deal with it alone.

Mr. Darcy sprang up onto the chair beside her, his whiskers spreading in a melodramatic "meow."

"C'mon, my little man." She picked him up, glad for a diversion. Even if the diversion only entailed pouring cat food into a bowl.

It had been Jill's idea to arrive at the end of Preston's art class. Give no hint of anger, of having been enlightened. Then lure him in and drop the bomb. At first, Noelle didn't know if she would be capable of even seeing him again. But she wanted to do this with dignity. She wanted closure, to see his face drop when she told him she knew.

She also considered calling him out, phoning up the wife, telling her everything. *But why should I be that person?* The one who might instigate a breakup of a marriage. Besides, the wife might not even believe her, might not want to believe her.

Six days had passed since Jill had given birth and the bottom dropped out of Noelle's relationship with Preston. She'd called Jill yesterday to let her know the situation, and Jill had been every bit as infuriated as Noelle had predicted. "Bastard!" "Two-timing wanker!" "Total prat!" were only some of the choice words she'd spat into the phone.

Noelle conjured them up for strength now as she waited outside the classroom. The timbre of Preston's voice emanated through the door as he wrapped up his lecture.

Finally, when class finished and students gathered their books and bags and followed each other out the door, Noelle stepped inside, catching him off guard as he clicked off the projector.

"Hey, beautiful." He smiled and walked toward her, leaned down to kiss her. She tilted her face to dodge the kiss. "Are you okay?" He rubbed at the side of her arm. A gesture that used to melt her now made her cringe. "Do you want to eat? I can call for reservations at Luigi's."

"Don't you think your wife would mind?" His expression shifted to confusion as he dropped his hand and took a step back. She wanted to read all the frantic thoughts running through his mind.

"Wife?"

"Yes. Wife. I guess you have a special amnesia when you're with me." Noelle enjoyed the calm, methodical taste of the words. "Pretty blonde, works as a pharmacist, I believe."

Surprise darkened his face, a mixture of guilt and shock in his eyes. He'd been caught, foully, and had nowhere to go. No defense, no preparation.

Rather than drag this out, watch him squirm, or listen to a million excuses, Noelle was finished with the conversation. With him. Tired of the games, of trying to wrap her brain around "Why?" and "How could he?" "Good-bye, Preston. I'm not coming back."

"Noelle, I..." he said as she left the room. At least he might stay there awhile, dumbfounded, with worried questions of his own. "How did she find out?" "Did she tell my wife?" "Have I just screwed up my marriage?" Or perhaps he *could* live with himself, would soon move on and find another victim. Noelle didn't know him well enough to know which type he was. Thank goodness, she never would.

"How did things go?" Jill asked the moment Noelle stepped into the sitting room. Gareth had let her in, taken her coat, and offered her tea, which he'd just disappeared to retrieve. Home from the hospital a couple of days before, Jill lay on the sofa, covered in a silky crème blanket and looking healthy and content.

Noelle set down her gift on the coffee table and kissed her friend on the cheek, "You look radiant. How's that beautiful baby girl?"

"Beautiful but loud. I barely got a wink of sleep last night. Gareth put her down an hour ago, and so far, so good. Come sit." She patted the sofa. "Get to the good stuff. The bastard. How did you handle him?"

Noelle obeyed and sat, recounting their meeting an hour ago, the reserved, dignified tone Jill had coached her to use, the icy strength she'd gathered when she said good-bye, and finally, Preston's deer-in-headlights expression as Noelle walked away.

"Brilliant!" Jill exclaimed, smiling. "See? Didn't that feel good?"

"Well." Noelle winced. "I wouldn't say any of it really felt 'good.'"

"I'm sorry. I didn't mean it that way."

"It's okay. I'm just relieved it's over."

"You're much too good for him. Wanker."

"Thanks. I still feel a bit of a fool, though."

"How on earth are you the fool?" Jill snapped. "He never gave you reason to believe he was married. This is entirely on him. Don't you ever forget that."

"I agree. I really do. But I can't help wondering… that I should've known, somehow. Been more aware. I should've paid better attention to the signs."

"What signs? He didn't give you a single clue, did he?"

Noelle sighed. "No. He didn't. Well, at the hospital that night, he got a couple of calls then left suddenly. Probably had to get back to 'the wife.'"

"Men are absolute beasts. Except Gareth, of course."

Right on cue, Gareth entered the room with two cups of tea and placed them on the table.

"Thank you, darling," Jill called as he left the room again.

Noelle handed Jill her cup and said, "Adam knew."

"What?"

"That night at the hospital, we had this awful fight in his car. Adam told me to be careful. He actually Googled Preston, said he had a gut feeling about him. Adam's the one who told me Preston was married. I, of course, didn't want to believe it. I defended the jerk."

"Have you spoken to Adam since?"

"No."

"Don't worry. You'll make things right. You two always do."

"Okay, enough of all this," Noelle insisted. "I didn't come to vent all my troubles. I came to help out, to welcome you home! To shower you with gifts. Speaking of, are you ready for yours?" She set aside her tea.

"Ooh, I adore presents!"

Noelle reached for the cellophane-wrapped basket she'd put together this morning at the cottage. Homemade scones, fashion magazines, and a silk nightgown she'd bought at Mrs. Mulberry's shop, all wrapped in tissue paper and decorated with a sprig of lavender. "I know we had a shower for little Evie weeks ago, and all the presents were for her," Noelle explained. "But it's time to pamper the mother."

"You know me too well."

Noelle nudged three hefty shopping bags onto the kitchen table, rubbing her wrist at the place where the straps created an indentation. She'd spent the loveliest day in Bath, browsing shops, stopping for an ice cream, splurging on Irish lace and even a new Wedgwood vase, which would be perfect for the white roses blooming in the garden. Retail therapy, Jill had called it when she ordered Noelle to get out of the house this morning. Pleasantly refreshed, she poured a glass of water in the kitchen and sat down to check her email. Nothing important except for one from Mr. Lester, about the Cornwall cottage's lease expiring at the end of June. The current tenants didn't wish to renew, so he suggested renting it out during the summer to vacationers. She agreed and responded briefly back then closed her laptop.

She thought about her trip to Bath, wondering how she could busy herself next. It had taken two weeks since the Preston fiasco to navigate through the varying stages of shock, anger, and finally, indifference. The only temperature left for him was lukewarm, much like the tap water she sipped.

She realized, even through her anger, that her involvement with Preston all those weeks had ultimately been selfish. In a way, she had used him, too. She couldn't deny that she enjoyed having someone handsome on her arm to show off in restaurants or in hospital waiting rooms. For the first time in a long time, she hadn't been the only person without a relationship. Ultimately, the main reason for her anger was not that the relationship had ended, but that the truth had blindsided her.

As she petted Mr. Darcy, her cell rang on the table.

"Hey, Sunshine," Adam said when she accepted the call.

She hadn't spoken to him since the fight. Neither one of them had made any effort to reconcile. For a moment, she wished she hadn't answered. "Hey, yourself."

"How've you been?" he asked, his voice light, friendly.

"Fine. Busy, but fine. What about you?"

"The same." Another pause. Adam cleared his throat. "So. The reason I called..."

"Yes?" she prompted.

"This is hard. You're not making it easier."

"What did I do? All I said was 'yes.'"

He sighed and said, "Okay. Look. I'm sorry. I was wrong about the whole Preston thing. I shouldn't have judged him without knowing for sure. It's your life, your business. I'm a jerk. I stuck my foot in my mouth. It happens. Okay?"

"You weren't wrong."

"About what?"

"About Preston. You weren't wrong. He's definitely married." She sighed.

"What happened?"

"I don't want to get into the gory details. Let's just leave it at you were right."

"Wow, that sucks. Are you okay?"

"Yes, I'm okay. I think I'm okay. Just can't believe this happened again. Why do I attract all the cheaters?" Noelle drank her water, wishing she'd plopped in a couple of ice cubes. Mr. Darcy sniffed at his empty food bowl and skulked away.

"You're a nice girl. And the jerks can always sense that. Jerks take advantage of nice girls."

"Thanks. I think."

"It was a compliment. I'm just glad you left before you got in deeper."

"I'm sorry, too. About the fight. About getting all defensive and upset when you were only looking out for me. I'm just stubborn. And I didn't mean to drag Laurel into it. I shouldn't have mentioned her."

"It's okay. I know how she comes across. Her personality can be... intense. She's one of those people who has to work at being happy. It can get pretty draining sometimes."

For her, or for you? Noelle thought.

"So, we're friends again?" Adam asked.

"We never weren't friends. We only had a little fight."

"I tried to email you a dozen times but couldn't bring myself to hit 'send.'"

"I did the same thing. I wanted to text you about something funny the vicar said the other day but thought you weren't speaking to me."

"What are we, in high school or something?" Adam chuckled.

Noelle rolled her eyes. "Basically, yes." She balanced her feet on the rim of the opposite chair and twirled a strand of hair through her fingers.

They spent the next hour and a half talking about the project—the glitches and workarounds, the natural stops and starts involved with a renovation that size. Nothing Adam and his competent team couldn't handle. By the time they hung up, things were right with the world again. Still, she should have been the one to call Adam first. High school behavior, indeed.

Chapter Twenty-five

Don't be afraid to let darkness or loss into your paintings.
It's a part of life. Why shouldn't it be part of your art?

PURE BLISS. BLINDING WHITE CLOUDS shaped like dinosaurs and cauliflower, sheep grazing idly in nearby fields, a balmy June wind blowing through the half-cracked window. Noelle couldn't have asked for a more beautiful day to drive to London.

She'd volunteered to browse a small gallery in hopes of adding a piece or two to the collection. Holly, a caretaker to her three younger sisters, needed time with them today, and Frank often spouted arrogantly how he "despised" London for its congestion. So Noelle offered to go in his place.

The breeze whipping her golden hair as she drove, Noelle lifted her sunglasses to take in the colors of the countryside. Lush emerald greens of the pastures, ocean blue of the sky. She wanted to stop and snap some pictures, but she'd never get to London if she did.

Without warning, the steering wheel jerked and wobbled. She knew almost immediately what had happened, and the rhythmic bumping confirmed it. A flat tire.

She found a patch of empty grass and pulled off the country road with a grunt. This wasn't supposed to be happening. Not on such a beautiful day. Surely, the tire just needed some air. But when she checked, she found it as flat as the crepes she'd eaten earlier at Joe's.

"Damn." She fought the initial tendency to let the panic rise—by herself, stranded in the middle of nowhere. Even if "nowhere" involved a perfectly safe English country road. She searched the trunk and pulled back the plastic mat to reveal a full spare in good condition.

"How hard can it be?" She used every ounce of physical strength to lug the spare out. The tire felt like it weighed more than she did. Then she found the wrench and jack and paused. In theory, the steps seemed simple. She remembered, vaguely, being taught to change a tire in Driver's Ed class many years ago. Still, it might save her some time to have someone talk her through it.

She stepped a few feet off the road to lean against a stocky stone wall and dialed Mac's home number, but with each ring, hope diminished. Mac didn't own a cell phone or answering machine. He was sweetly old-fashioned that way. Ironically, he was likely at her cottage, tending to her garden.

Before she could put the phone in her pocket and accept the challenge of changing a tire on her own, a text jingled. Adam. *Headed to CC. Lunch maybe?*

Rather than tapping out her situation in lengthy text-ese, Noelle called him.

"Hey, you got my text?" he said.

"Yes. And just in the nick of time. You wouldn't want to do me a favor, would you?"

"Well, that depends."

She explained about the tire, and that was all she had to do.

"I'm on my way. Where exactly are you?"

She told him the details and gave him some landmarks.

"Be there in twenty minutes."

She pulled a notepad from the backseat and spent those minutes pencil sketching a nearby tree from the driver's seat. Knowing Adam was on his way removed all anxiety.

Soon, his car pulled up to park behind hers and she opened her door to greet him. He got out wearing his suit and tie. He looked like a male model in a car commercial—sporty sunglasses, thick McDreamy hair, and a million-dollar smile.

"What seems to be the problem, ma'am?" he said with a fake Southern drawl.

"That's the problem." She pointed at the sad-looking flat tire.

"Yeah, that's a goner. But the spare...?" He kneeled down to inspect the tire she'd propped up against the side of the car. "In good condition." He stood up, wriggled out of his jacket, removed his tie, and handed them over to Noelle. Then he rolled up his shirtsleeves and cracked his knuckles dramatically. "Here goes nothing."

Noelle leaned against the stone wall, watching Adam work. When he bent down to place the jack beneath the car, she couldn't help but check out Adam's "rear view" in those perfect-fit slacks. He loosened the lug nuts with several hard twists of the wrench, letting out only a couple of quiet grunts in the process. Because of her small size and lack of upper-body strength, it likely would've taken her an hour to do what he did in a few minutes.

His motions looked fluid, all knowing, as though he'd done it thousands of times before. No hesitation, no second-guessing. One movement led directly to the next. In no time, he'd removed the flat and had secured the spare onto the studs. She'd been staring too long, so she tapped on her cell phone and pretended to be fascinated with a news piece she hadn't been reading. When Adam looked up, he would find her distracted by something other than his glistening forearms.

"All done," he said.

"Oh. Wow, that was fast." She handed him back his coat and tie. "I really do appreciate this. I'm sure you had somewhere important to go."

"I'd call this fairly important." He pushed his sleeves back down. "Just glad I could help."

"If we weren't headed in opposite directions, I'd buy you some lunch for helping me."

"There's another village about ten miles back. We could try their pub." Adam buttoned up his cuff.

"Perfect."

From within the jacket draped over his sleeve, his cell rang. "Oh, bollocks. Let's hope this isn't work." He answered it. "Hello? Hey, Mum. Wait, I can't hear you..."

He covered his ear to hear. "When?" Adam's eyes clouded over with worry. "Okay. I'll be right there. You hang on." He tapped his phone and reached into his pants pocket, producing his keys.

"What's wrong?" Noelle asked, her hand on his sleeve.

"Dad's in hospital. In Bath. He's had another heart attack. This one's bad."

"Oh, Adam…"

In trying to juggle his phone and keys, he dropped them both to the pavement with a clack. "Shit!" he said, squatting.

"Listen. You're in no shape to drive all the way to Bath. Let me take you. Follow me about three miles to this B&B, and we'll leave my car there."

He nodded and rushed to his car. At the B&B, she hopped into Adam's driver's seat and tried to clear her mind and focus only on the road, on getting him to Bath as quickly as possible. Occasionally, she glanced over to see him staring out the window, rubbing his jaw, or tapping his knee with his phone. All he needed was silence, so she gave it to him.

They reached the edge of Bath in under an hour, and Adam gave fragmented directions to the hospital. After she parked, she followed him through the hospital's sliding doors, wondering what her role should be. Watching the numbers light up in the elevator, Noelle thought about the stark contrast between this hospital visit and the one a couple of weeks ago with the birth of Jill's baby.

The elevator doors dinged open to the ICU, revealing an ample waiting area. At the information desk, Adam asked about his father's location then grabbed Noelle's hand, guiding her down another hallway. She didn't know if she should be going so far. Perhaps she belonged in the waiting room with all the other friends and acquaintances.

"Mum," he said as he let go of Noelle and walked into his mother's arms. She buried her face in her son's shoulder as he comforted her. "How is he?" Adam asked, releasing his grasp.

"Stable. The doctor is in with him."

"What happened?"

"Your father had gone for a swim, and when he came inside the house, he complained of a pain in his chest." Her voice cracked, and she placed a handkerchief to her mouth to suppress a sob. "I didn't take him seriously. You know how he's always complaining about every little thing."

"Then what?"

"A few minutes later, he collapsed in the hall. The servant found him and did resuscitation. I called for the ambulance. They sent a helicopter…"

"Oh, Mum." Adam pulled her in for another hug. "At least he's here now. In good hands. Don't worry, don't worry."

Noelle stepped awkwardly back down the corridor toward the waiting area, but Adam called her name.

"Where are you going?" he asked, holding out his hand.

"I thought I'd give you some privacy."

"Mother, you remember Noelle Cooke. From the summers in Bath at Windermere. She drove me here today."

Noelle smiled shyly. "Mrs. Spencer," she said, "It's good to see you. I'm sorry about these circumstances."

The light dawned. "Ah, yes. Noelle. The American. I do remember you." Noelle couldn't tell from her tone if that was good or bad.

A doctor emerged from a room behind Mrs. Spencer. "You may see him, but only for a few moments."

"Will you wait for me?" Adam asked Noelle in a whisper.

"Of course."

He squeezed her hand then followed his mother inside. Machines whirred as he closed the door.

For the first time in what seemed like hours, Noelle took a full, deep breath. She wandered back down the hallway to an empty row of chairs. She imagined Adam in his father's room, a fidgety hand running through his hair and a supportive arm around his mother as they approached the bed, trying to ignore the tubes, the beeping monitors. Trying to look past all the equipment and recognize the father and husband lying there.

Then she imagined herself in a hospital room ten years ago, a frightened twenty-year-old squeezing her mother's hand but knowing she was already gone. The doctor had just told Noelle that "decisions" would have to be made. That the car accident three days before had caused extensive, irreparable brain damage. Two days later, she held her mother's limp hand again after the nurse removed the life support tubes. Her mother's life ebbed away in small gasps and erratic breaths as Noelle choked back tears.

Usually, Noelle forced the jarring memories out before the sounds and images took her back to that moment so vividly. But being in this place again, under these circumstances...

Adam rounded the corner looking wearied, older than his thirty-one years.

"How is he?" Noelle asked, banishing her memories and rising to meet him.

"He's... lying there, unconscious. I'm in a bad dream."

She reached for his hand, but he brought her close in a warm hug instead.

"I'm so glad you're here," he whispered, tightening his grasp.

"I'm always here," she whispered back. Out of the corner of her eye, Adam's mother watched them with an unblinking stare. Clumsily, Noelle backed out of the hug. "So," Noelle said. "You and your mother need food. I'm going to go pick up something. None of this hospital food. I'll find something edible."

While she spoke, she slung her purse over her shoulder before anyone had a chance to object. Getting food always seemed like a productive thing to do in difficult times. She remembered all the well-meaning people bringing casseroles and pies after her mother passed away, not knowing how else they could help. She found a crowded deli several blocks from the hospital and ordered sandwiches and soups, comforting but hearty.

Driving back in Adam's car, she considered how much longer she should stay. As long as Adam wanted her, she supposed. She arrived back at the ICU, surprised to see Laurel standing beside the main desk, wearing a crisp navy business suit and speaking with Adam's mother. Adam was nowhere in sight.

"Oh. Hello." Noelle hoped her smile was convincing enough.

"Noelle. Adam says you drove him here, to the hospital," Laurel said. "We're appreciative." Laurel's stony expression appeared more suspicious than grateful.

"No trouble. I wanted to help."

"And I see you brought food." Even now, in a tense, emotional situation, nothing could break through that frosty exterior of hers. Or maybe she intended that frostiness for Noelle alone.

She set the hefty bags down. "Yes. Enough for everyone—sandwiches, soups."

The awkward silence told her she needed to leave. She'd hoped to say good-bye to Adam but didn't want to disturb him. He was likely back in the room with his father. "Well, I need to get going. I'll keep Mr. Spencer in my prayers," she told Adam's mother. "Please let me know if there's anything else I can do."

"We certainly will," his mother responded.

"Oh. Adam's keys." Noelle pulled them out of her pocket. "I had to park pretty far—row L. Beside the street light."

"How will you get home?" Laurel asked.

"I have a friend I can call." She rushed toward the elevators, which had started to close. Noelle slipped through the doors and into the crowd, wanting to disappear altogether.

"Be there, be there, be there," Noelle chanted under her breath, holding the cell phone tightly to her ear.

She had found a deserted bench outside the hospital entrance and sat cross-legged, bouncing her leg on the pavement.

Noelle had never been more grateful to hear Mac's growling voice.

"Thank goodness you're home!"

"Lass, you sound out of breath."

"No, I'm just anxious. I have the biggest favor in the world to ask you." She winced.

"Name it."

She explained about the flat tire, about Adam's father, about her car still sitting at that B&B in the middle of nowhere. Before she could say "please," he had interrupted with, "Say no more. I'll be there."

Near tears, she hung up the phone. Rescued twice in one day.

While waiting, she tried to call Jill but got no answer, so she sent a text about Adam's father. Jill would want to know.

Storm clouds gathered a few miles away, and by the time Mac pulled up in his Subaru minutes later, Noelle was caught in the middle of a downpour. She covered her head with her purse and fled toward the passenger door. She nearly sat on a paper box in the seat before Mac scooped it up so she could plop down. "What's this?" she asked as he handed her the carton and turned the steering wheel.

"Figured you'd be hungry."

"You're too good to me." She opened it to find fish and chips from her favorite fast-food eatery. Greasy, crispy comfort food. Exactly what she needed. "Mmm. Thank you, Mac. For everything."

"Eh, can't work in the garden while it's raining, anyway." He let her eat in silence, taking the occasional chip when Noelle offered one.

Halfway to the B&B, Noelle wanted to talk. "Ever have one of those days that's the complete opposite of what you pictured when you woke up that morning?"

"Aye."

"I feel like I've spent the whole day in the car. I'm exhausted."

"You're concerned about him," Mac said.

"Mr. Spencer? Sure. I can't believe he came that close to dying today."

"No. I meant your young friend."

"Oh. Adam. Yeah. I am concerned. I've never seen him that way before, scared and vulnerable. I'm used to him being the strong one." Drowsy from a full stomach and the steady rain beating against the side of the window, Noelle let her eyes close. She fell into a light sleep for the rest of the journey, waking up at the B&B where her car waited for her. She thanked Mac again before getting out.

"I'll follow ye back. It's nasty weather," he insisted.

"Okay." She darted to her car, dodging the rain and cursing the flat tire that got her into this mess in the first place. She checked her rear view for Mac as she drove away. The glow of his lights in the mirror comforted her all the way home.

Within an hour of stepping foot in the cottage, she had made a quick call to Frank explaining about the botched London trip, taken a hot shower, bundled up in a soft robe, made a cup of tea and then a crackling fire. Mr. Darcy seemed to sense her exhaustion and curled up at her feet on the couch. As she reached for the TV remote, her cell rang. She let out a groan then tapped her phone. "Hello?"

"Noelle. Hey, it's Adam."

"Adam!" She set her tea aside. "How's your father?"

"Same." She pictured him standing in some corner trying not to disturb anyone, dark circles under his eyes from all the stress. "They're putting a stent in tomorrow. A couple of stents, actually."

"Is that good?"

"It's supposed to be. We'll see. I wanted to check on you. And to say thank you again."

"You don't have to—"

"No, really. You were a lifesaver today. I don't know what I would've done without you driving me to the hospital. I couldn't think straight."

"I was glad to help. You helped me out too, with that tire."

"Oh. Yeah. That was today, wasn't it? Seems like days since this morning happened. I didn't realize you'd left the hospital. Mum told me you brought food and then called a friend to help you home. I guess you got there all right?"

"Yeah. Mac came to get me."

"He's a good man."

"The best. Are you staying at the hospital tonight?"

"Yeah. Mother's going to stay in Father's room. I'll sleep in a chair in the lobby or something."

"That doesn't sound very comfortable."

"I don't mind. I need to be here. Especially in the morning, for the surgery."

"And what about Laurel?"

"She's already gone to London. It's work—prepping for meetings tomorrow. In fact, I apparently interrupted a meeting when I called her about my father."

"Well, I hope you can sleep. Let me know how the procedure goes."

"I will. Good-night."

"'Night." She hung up and reached for her tea again, remembering how he held his frightened mother today. Adam could be so tender, always available to help someone out, offer encouragement, be a light in a dark situation. Mrs. Spencer was lucky to have him.

Noelle didn't know Mrs. Spencer well. In fact, before today, she'd only seen her twice before. Once, years ago, when Gram invited Adam's family to Windermere for tea—and later, during that last fateful evening in England.

During Noelle's final summer at Windermere, a late August evening, the humid breeze blew in at dusk, and the birds sang their final symphonies before the winter migration. Adam had called Noelle that morning and ordered her to "dress in your finest." He was taking her out. She didn't know the occasion, but the romantic in her grew giddy over the possibility of a second chance at their almost-kiss in the river two weeks before. Finally, after four summers of playing games, they might move beyond friendship and explore the something deeper she'd been waiting for.

Noelle had spent the hours after Adam's phone call browsing boutiques in Bath until she found the perfect navy blue dress, his favorite color. Gram had seen the excitement in her eyes and decided to treat her— any dress, at any expense. Aunt Joy got the hint and told Noelle to choose a pair of earrings from the jewelry box in her bedroom. Noelle touched the expensive pieces with hesitant fingers, pretending she was getting ready for the prom. A monumental evening. After much deliberation, she chose two prospects, one of which slightly matched the purple paint drop pendant she wanted to wear tonight. Uncertain which would look better with the pendant, she clutched a pair in each hand and tiptoed down the grand hallway in her bare feet, ice cold on the marble floors, to seek out Gram and Joy for their opinions. Reaching for the doorknob of the elegant parlor where Gram was sitting and reading, Noelle paused. Through the cracked door, she had heard Adam's name spoken.

Noelle squinted through the opening. Gram sat on the settee, talking to someone, but Noelle couldn't see the someone. Against her better judgment, Noelle carefully moved her ear closer to the crack. If Gram caught her eavesdropping, she'd have grounded her from going out with Adam. Listening in on private conversations was one of Gram's greatest pet peeves, right up there with malicious gossiping.

With the second mention of his name, Noelle deduced this was Adam's mother. She'd always been a mystery—extremely refined and formal, a bit cold, standoffish. Nothing like the woman Noelle imagined had raised such a warmhearted person as Adam.

"Yes, we're so extremely proud of him," Mrs. Spencer said to Gram. "And I have some news. Well, it's not news, as yet."

Noelle waited impatiently through the dramatic pause, not caring that the news wasn't intended for her ears. If it regarded Adam, she wanted to hear.

"Adam has been dating an Oxford girl. She's bright and beautiful, and comes from the best of families." Her voice bubbled with pride. "I have every reason to believe he'll propose sometime this year. His father and I couldn't be more thrilled."

The diamond earrings dropped from Noelle's hands and clinked on the marble floor. Dazed, she bent over to collect them, an exaggerated version of the word "propose" echoing in her head. She scurried back down the hall to her bedroom, gulping tears. She shut and locked the door behind her, jarred by her own face in the mirror opposite. Mascara had run down her cheeks into a tear-stained, streaky mess.

The questions tumbled on top of each other faster than she could process them. *Who is this "Oxford girl?" Why hasn't Adam ever mentioned her? And how has he even made time to see her? He's spent all his time with* me *this summer.* None of it made any sense.

Then, suddenly, something did. That almost-kiss. After she and Adam had been interrupted, he'd turned so cold so quickly, not speaking to her the next few days. *Was it guilt? Over almost cheating on his mystery girl?*

Still clutching the earrings, she leaned her back against the cold door, allowing the sobs to have their way. Her chest heaved until it ached as she abandoned all the careful control she'd practiced for years. Like a broken dam, the tears spilled out in a rush. *How could I be so stupid? So wrong about everything?*

"Noelle?"

Gram tapped her cane on the other side of the door, and Noelle froze in the middle of her sob. She stepped toward the middle of the immense room, usually a warm, comforting place, but right now, no place could be comforting. She wiped her cheeks as fast as she could and cleared her throat. "Yes?"

"Adam just phoned. He'll be here in a few minutes. Noelle, there's something I must speak with you about first." Noelle knew by Gram's urgent tone that she wanted to convey the news. But she couldn't bear hearing it all over again.

"Gram, I'm not ready. In fact, I'm feeling ill."

"What's the matter, child? You don't sound yourself. Unlock the door and let me in."

"I'm sorry, Gram, I can't. I think I've... developed a sudden cold, and I don't want to give it to you. Or to him." She cleared her throat again. "Please, please phone him back and tell him I'm not well. I can't see him. I'm sorry..."

A beat of silence, then Gram's understanding reply. "I'll do as you wish. I'll have Esther come and look in on you, bring you some tomato soup."

"Thank you, Gram." As the taps faded away down the hall, Noelle sank down onto the dense Oriental carpet, her dress fanning out into a delicate, crumpled navy flower as she continued to weep.

The next day, Noelle bought a plane ticket back to the States. She'd written a brief good-bye note to Adam, making some excuse about school starting sooner than she'd thought, and wishing him a successful year at Oxford. He never wrote, never asked why she'd left in such a rush. And with his silence, he had given her the answer she had so achingly hoped against for the past four summers. He hadn't cared for her the way she had cared for him.

Mr. Darcy meowed Noelle back to reality, back to her tea and her cozy fire, and she rubbed his chin. Revisiting old memories came with a price. A person could get lost inside them, stuck. Noelle mused over the value of going back at all, of remembering. Memories were pictures, moments frozen forever, as is. Never allowed to be relived or altered. She wished she could take a memory and rip it down the middle as easily as a photograph.

Chapter Twenty-six

At its best, art is a mirror. It has the ability to reflect people's emotions, even challenge what they think they see in themselves. Art should hold more than colours on a wall. It should inspire people to become something bigger than they already are.

NOELLE SKIMMED THE PICTURES FOR a third time. She'd taken photos of Jill and the baby a couple of weeks ago at Jill's house and today wanted to fine-tune them and print them off on photo paper, then frame them as a gift for Jill. Close-up shots of perfectly formed hands and toes, black-and-whites of baby with mother.

Noelle did her best to ignore the constant scratching of Mr. Darcy at her bedroom door. "In a minute," she responded, but the mere sound of her voice would only make him scratch more frantically. A gray paw flashed from underneath the door in his desperate attempt to be included. Noelle had learned the hard way that Mr. Darcy's pouncing and jumping skills extended to nearly all surfaces in the house, especially dangerous when she attempted something important or delicate. Once, thinking her printed-off research of a new Bath artist remained safe high atop her bedroom dresser, she returned to find the documents scattered all over the floor and Mr. Darcy playing innocent, licking his paw in the corner. She'd learned to place a closed door between the surface and the cat—the only way to prevent a mishap or disaster. If she could only ignore the scratching...

"This one," she whispered. Eveline looked directly at the camera with wide, inquisitive eyes. Noelle needed a special photo to place inside an expensive frame she'd bought in Bath. Jill would love it. As she inserted the print and secured the mounting board on the back of the frame, her cell rang.

"Hey." That had been Adam's typical greeting every time he'd called to update her on his father. The stent surgery a week ago had been successful, and Adam's father was released from the hospital three days later. But a follow-up appointment yesterday revealed there might be long-term damage to his heart. How much damage, they weren't yet sure. With each day that passed, Adam's tone grew hollow. The weight of the week had taken its toll.

"Where are you?" Noelle clicked on the speaker to free up both hands and wrap Jill's present. "I hear birds."

"I'm at the river. You know that place behind your Gram's estate? At that bend we used to go to?"

"Yeah. I remember."

"Can you meet me?"

"Now? It's kinda late. To be at the river, I mean. It'll be dark soon."

"So what? Come sit with me. Hang out. I can use the company. We won't stay long."

She would've asked where Laurel was, but she already knew the answer. Working. Or out of town on a business trip. Always one or the other. In fact, Laurel had chosen some meeting over sitting with Adam during his father's surgery last week. And since then, Adam had only mentioned her visiting once.

"Please," he said with that irresistibly pathetic tone.

Noelle sighed. "Okay. I'll come."

"Brilliant."

Noelle approached the area where she thought Adam might be and spotted him sitting under a tree, facing the river. She had walked at least half a mile but hadn't minded. The sun beamed down on her arms while the breeze carried its fresh summer sweetness to her. She held a basket of scones she'd baked earlier, along with some fresh fruit and bottled water. Adam probably hadn't remembered to eat today.

"What'd you bring me?" he shouted from a distance, standing up and dusting off his jeans.

"A picnic." She handed him the basket. He hadn't shaved in a few days. She'd never seen him with heavy stubble before, and he looked devastatingly handsome. The shadow of a beard made his eyes darker, more intense. The stubble, a by-product of not caring about his appearance during a stressful time, had Noelle selfishly wishing he would wear it that way more often, on purpose.

He set down the basket and helped her spread out the white blanket she'd also brought. "So, how's your father today?" Noelle asked as she sat to his right, facing the river. She folded a scone and a couple of strawberries into a napkin and passed it over.

"Tired. But coherent. Actually made a joke this morning." He bit into the juicy strawberry.

"And how are *you*?"

He swallowed and looked straight ahead. "Fine. That's the standard response, right? The one everybody wants to hear."

"I'm not 'everybody.' I'll take the real answer, please."

"Numb. Terrified, exhausted. Guilty."

"Guilty?"

"I never saw enough of my father. Before his... attack. We only live two hours apart, but I was always 'too busy.' Even when we were together, we sat mostly in silence, maybe talked about cricket scores. Nothing substantive. Watching him lie there now, weak and out of energy, I wonder if we've run out of time. I don't know how to talk to him." As he spoke, his gaze had remained on the river, but now he glanced over at her as though hoping for some sort of reassurance.

"You're being too hard on yourself. Adult children lead busy lives. You've been there when you could be. And most importantly, you've been there when he needed you this past week. That's everything."

Adam pinched off part of a scone, his focus returning to the drifting water. "I love this place. I used to come here all during my twenties, right to this very spot. To decompress after a hard exam or shitty job interview."

"I didn't know that."

"Yeah. It's a place that makes you think. Take a long look at yourself."

She leaned back on her hands and crossed her ankles, glad to know this place had been there for Adam, too, all those years ago.

"You know, it's weird…"

"What?" She waited patiently, reminded of the long pauses he used to take during their talks under oak trees as teenagers.

"I should actually be happy. I mean, my dad didn't die, right? He's alive."

"Very good point."

"So why do I feel empty?" He found a small rock in the dirt beside him and pitched it toward the river.

"Well…" Noelle watched a squirrel bury a nut in the ground several feet away. "You've been through a lot in a few days—this shocking event you weren't prepared for. You're still processing everything."

"I think I'm going through an early mid-life crisis. I mean, my dad having a heart attack—this sounds really selfish—it's made me look at my own life. And to ask myself all the big questions. Where have I been? Where am I going? What the hell do I want to do with my life?"

"The big events can do that. One minute, you're sailing along then *wham*. It happened to me when my parents divorced. Then, especially, when different people in my life died. Each time, it makes me stop and think harder, see things through different eyes, value life in a new way. It's like I'm shocked out of my own life or something."

"Yes." He shifted to make stronger eye contact. "Yes, exactly. This unexpected thing happens, and it changes your perspective. You start to weigh things out—your past decisions, your current relationships, your future—and everything sort of… tilts."

Flicking an ant off the corner of the blanket, Noelle considered what that meant. Some sort of opportunity or window that might have just cracked open. "Are you weighing anything specifically?"

"My future, I guess. What I want it to look like."

The silence that followed told Noelle he wasn't willing to explain. So she leaned forward and brought out another strawberry in a napkin. "Here," she offered.

He wore a genuine, relaxed smile for the first time since she'd arrived. "I seek life's answers, and you offer me comfort food?"

"Yep. I can't guarantee it'll solve the mysteries of life, but it's all I've got at the moment."

He took the napkin, his finger grazing her palm.

"It's enough."

She stared at the Polaroid. Reading the entries over the months, Noelle had created a sort of game: study the photos first and try to figure out the theme before peeking at the journal entry's title. The first painting in this series displayed uncharacteristically modern, offbeat tones. Aunt Joy had scattered blurry words and phrases across the entire canvas, all different sizes, colors, and fonts, painted on a dark background. Most, impossible to interpret, but Noelle caught a few: "witch," "freak," "loner."

The second painting contained shadowy-looking people, wispy ghosts, speaking into each other's ears, their faces gaunt and vacant, soulless. The last painting showed a wooden door with vivid oranges and yellows running down it. She couldn't figure out the symbolism or the paintings' similarities, their connection to each other. Giving up, she turned to the entry to read the series title, "Whispers."

People are cruel. They seem to thrive off half-truths and rumours, accepting them blindly as gospel. Makes them feel self-important, I suppose—spreading lies about people, their eyes darting to and fro, making sure they're not caught. But they don't realise that their gossip and lies hold great power. To destroy and unravel and cause pain. Lies upon lies lead to a warping, a distortion of anything good in a person. I should know.

I spent the better part of my morning helping Mac scrub egg off my front door. Year after year, Halloween after Halloween, the children and teenagers make their pilgrimage up the hill to my cottage, to put into action what their parents do with their tongues. Gossip, belittle. The children think I'm a witch, living secluded in this house, hardly ever going outside. They make up stories about me, each one a little more gruesome and more untrue. Instead of leaving me to my peace, they mock me. And I'm left to scrub away the remains of it.

Whispers seem so harmless on the surface. To the ear, whispers sound as soft as a gentle wind. But it's the words inside the whispers that do irreparable damage. That leave the lasting impression. That don't ever, ever go away. I hear them. They don't think I do, but I hear them.

Certainly, not everyone is cruel. Some have reached out, tried to help, tried to know me. But I'm too far gone. I don't want their help. I only want to be left alone. Above all, it's none of their business who I am or who I'm not. And just as I do not go rummaging into their affairs, their business, their daily lives, I wish they would offer me the same courtesy. And leave me alone.

Noelle hated that Aunt Joy had faced cruelty, even from only a handful of villagers. She recalled Joe's question, months ago, asking if anyone had egged her door last Halloween. She couldn't imagine people in the village capable of it. Surely, Aunt Joy's isolation created in her a sort of hypersensitivity to things. A person could become quite paranoid, never leaving the house, always speculating about what other people were thinking. And the eggings at Halloween didn't help. But maybe they were only a coincidence, just an immature group of bored local boys killing time, not discriminating with their targets. Other houses might have been egged as well, but Aunt Joy would never have known.

Then again, the village wasn't a perfect one. She'd witnessed Mrs. Pickering's gossip firsthand. *Isn't it human nature to speculate, to gossip and wonder about other people?* Especially someone reclusive and misunderstood, like Aunt Joy. The temptation for the villagers to gossip about her probably grew stronger with each reclusive year she spent in the cottage. Perhaps the truth lay somewhere in between Aunt Joy's version and Noelle's own experience of the townspeople. She only wished her aunt had seen more of the good in them—the fund-raiser the village had tried to put together to save the gallery, the way people still beamed with pride at the mention of Aunt Joy's name, the excitement over the Sotheby's auction.

If anything, the series of Polaroids solidified Noelle's choice to keep the journal private. Though she understood the emotion behind them, the words might only serve to reinforce some people's stereotypes and presumptions of her aunt—quirky, eccentric, out of touch with the world, even bitter and lonely. Paranoid and unstable. Even if that presumption might not have been fully true.

Better to let them study the "Whisperings" paintings and wonder. Wonder if they might even see little glimpses of themselves in those shadowy, gossipy figures.

Chapter Twenty-seven

*Ignore the critics. In the end, their insight holds little water because
1) they don't have a clue what it feels like to sit at an easel all day,
and 2) their job is to find fault. Even if their ultimate goal is to
help you improve, you still know what's best for you in the end.*

"OKAY, LASS. FINISHED. WHAT'S NEXT?" Mac stood in the
back doorway of Primrose Cottage holding three burnt-
out light bulbs.

Noelle took the bulbs from him and placed them delicately into
the trash. "Let's see..." She recalled the list she'd made. "Leaky faucet,
impossible-to-reach bulbs, broken disposal. Yep, that's all I can think of."

"Ye need to come up with a real challenge next time."

"I'll work on that." Noelle smiled and started to describe the
dripping in her upstairs bathroom sink when a light tap on the front
door interrupted her. "Oh, let me get this."

"Aye, lass. I'll be in the back garden, taking care of the fountain."

As Mac closed the door, a pair of glowing orbs glared from a dark
shadow beneath the chair in the next room. Mr. Darcy had been to
the vet for his shots this morning and seemed to blame Noelle. She
had assumed his pouting would've ended already, but from the looks of
things, his pity party would continue for the rest of the day.

She snickered at him on her way to the front door. She opened it to
Adam, smiling a healthy, rested smile—no five o'clock shadow, no bags

under his eyes—wearing her favorite black leather jacket. The one that made him look particularly GQ.

His father's check-up yesterday had been the best possible news—the stents successful, the doctors optimistic about a full recovery.

"What are you doing here?" she asked, horrified she hadn't a single stitch of makeup on and that she had thrown her hair into one of those casual, messy knots. She hadn't planned to see anyone except Mac on this rare stay-home day.

"I brought you something." He produced a gorgeous bunch of white day lilies in a purple glass vase.

"Oh! They're beautiful." She brought them closer for a whiff. "Mmm. My absolute favorite."

"I know."

"What's the occasion?"

"It's for a lot of things. For taking me to the hospital. For letting me gripe and whine about my life every day thereafter. For being such a perfect friend."

Noelle waved him inside. "Well, thank you. I accept. Come in. Anyone who brings me flowers deserves at least a cup of tea." She ushered him in to the living room at the exact moment Mr. Darcy darted out from beneath his hiding place and into the little nook beside the iron cast stove. He watched Adam's every move with increasing suspicion.

"What's up with him?" Adam pointed, chuckling as he moved to the couch.

"The evil vet." Noelle gave the lilies center stage on the table by the window. "Mr. Darcy had his round of shots, and he's still mad at me."

"Aw. Poor thing."

"Yes, the poor thing who nearly got me sued—he actually bit the vet's assistant."

Mr. Darcy hissed from his shadowy corner.

"Hmm. I think I'll give him some space today," Adam said.

"Good idea. I'll go get our tea." Noelle soon returned with two cups and saucers. She handed him one and sat beside him, sipping hers before it spilled over. The back door closed behind her, and Noelle twisted around to see Mac in the doorframe.

"Getting some water. Don't mind me." He nodded at Adam before walking into the kitchen.

"I'm so happy about your dad," she told Adam.

"It's a huge relief. I went to visit him this morning. He still gets tired easily. But he looks better than I've seen him in weeks. Mom's been doting over him—he begged me to distract her for a while so he could get some peace." Adam set down his tea and reached for his ringing cell phone. "I feel like I'm on call these days. Every call could be important. Sorry." He glanced at the screen, grimaced, and put the phone back into his pocket.

"A client you're trying to avoid?"

"A fiancée I'm trying to avoid." He propped his head on the pillow behind him and clasped his fingers together on his chest. "I don't get why she has to make a big deal out of everything."

"Did you guys have a fight or something?"

"*A* fight? I wish it were only one." He extended his arm on the couch, his hand nearly touching her sleeve. "I can't seem to do anything right. Yesterday, I didn't tie the trash bags in a very specific way. This morning, I forgot to call the shop about my tux. Maybe it's all the stuff with my dad, you know, my being away for long periods of time, but Laurel and I haven't been... connecting. We're out of synch or something."

She couldn't stop her heart from lifting at the thought of a significant crack in Adam's relationship. And the way he spoke so candidly about it. *Was this what he meant the other day, weighing his future?*

The back door closed again. She had forgotten Mac was in the kitchen all that time.

"Adam, can I ask you something?" She felt like taking a chance, putting him on the spot about Laurel. She had nothing to lose. And she would have done the same for any other friend, like Jill or Desha.

"Sure."

"Are you happy? I mean, I'm no expert on marriage, and I know that no relationship is perfect. But Laurel hasn't been around much when you needed her. Is that what you want? In a marriage?"

"Well, she really did have all these meetings. She's trying to get a promotion. And work is just super important to her."

You should be important to her, Noelle wanted to say. Even though he was more honest than usual about his disappointments with Laurel, they clearly hadn't pushed him to do something drastic. Like call off a wedding. Noelle wanted to shake him, wake him up, and make him see. But like an addict, he had to come to those conclusions on his own. She couldn't force them.

"And anyway," he added, "weddings create a lot of pressure. Ours is almost ten weeks away. It's a fast-moving train that I can't get off of."

Maybe the disappointments *were* becoming enough. "What do you mean? Get off of?"

"Nothing. I'm rambling. Pre-wedding jitters, maybe." Adam checked his watch and stood up with a wince. "I'd better run. Thought I'd surprise the workers with lunch today."

"That's a nice gesture. Glad you stopped by here first." She walked him to the front door.

"Yeah, me too. Thanks for the tea."

"Thanks for the flowers."

He gave her a quick peck on the cheek and vanished as quickly as he'd arrived. She walked back to the living room, to the beautiful lilies that enveloped the entire room with their scent. She dipped her head down to smell them again—light and fragrant, almost sensual—as Mac knocked on the windowpane. She waved him inside.

"I repaired the leak in the fountain. 'Twas a small one," he assured, removing his gloves. "Did your friend leave?"

"Yes, Adam's gone."

"He brought you those." He pointed to the vase matter-of-factly.

"Yes."

Mac nodded.

"You don't like him very much, do you?" Noelle surprised herself with her own bluntness.

"I'm sure he's a nice enough fellow," Mac said in a voice more gravelly than usual. "I have no ill will 'gainst him. As long as he's good to you."

"I'm fine, Mac."

He nodded again. She couldn't read his expression—disappointed, concerned. "I'll be off, then."

She closed the door behind him, wishing the awkward walls between her and the men in her life—even Mr. Darcy!—would soon crumble.

Later that night, before heading for bed, Noelle checked her email. Two pieces of spam, and one email from Adam.

Had fun this afternoon. Thanks for listening to my issues. I know Laurel's not your favorite subject. And I know I've said this a million times, but I appreciate your support during those dark days with my dad. I don't know what I would've done without you there.

You're the best,
Adam

Oh—and before this email gets too disgustingly sappy—tag, you're it:

*P.S.—I Still Haven't **Found** What I'm Looking For—U2*

Noelle smiled and hit "Reply."

The lilies were beautiful. I can smell them all over the house, a little piece of heaven. And you don't have to keep thanking me. It's a two-way street. You've listened to me ramble about my aunt and let me confide about the diary and the ring. I think we're even by now.

Noelle

*P.S.—**Looking** for a New Love—Jody Watley*

Tapping her sock feet on the mat at the kitchen sink, Noelle shook her hips to the rhythm of a Pink song. She wiped out the last remnants of murky water and rinsed out Adam's purple vase. The lilies had begun wilting yesterday, and today they stank. She intended to place white roses in the vase and return it to the living room table. Sorting through the roses she'd laid out a few minutes before, on the verge of belting out the lyrics, she jumped at the sight of Mac standing a few feet away inside the back door.

"Mac! Goodness. You scared me to death!" Out of breath, she muted the laptop.

"Sorry, lass. I knocked, but you didn't hear."

Noelle smiled, her heart still pounding fast. "You need your paycheck." She found the envelope with his name on it. "Here you go."

He turned the envelope in his hands, over and over, his lips pursed into a thin line.

"Is something on your mind? You seem distracted."

"Aye."

Noelle pulled out a chair for him and reached for the teapot.

"No, thank ye. I'll stand. No tea, either."

"Oh. Okay." She placed her hands on the back of the chair and waited patiently.

"I'm not the type of man to beat 'round bushes. So I'll just say what I came to say."

With every pause, Noelle grew more concerned. Mac wasn't one to be melodramatic.

"Over the past several months, you've become a sort of daughter to me." He removed his cap and slicked back stray gray hairs.

"I'm honored. But Mac, you're making me nervous. What's this about?"

He cleared his throat. "That friend of yours... Adam. To be frank, I'm not sure your relationship with him is... healthy."

Noelle shook her head in confusion. "This is about Adam?"

"Aye."

"What are you talking about, 'healthy'?"

"Lass, I've held my tongue. I don't go interfering in things that aren't my business. That's not my way. But after seeing you two together a few days back—"

"What, when he brought me flowers? Oh, that was nothing. A small gesture of friendship."

"'Twas more than that. Take it from a man who knows. That lad feels more than friendship. 'Tis in his eyes, in his mannerisms."

"That's ridiculous." She gripped the chair harder. Though deep down, she wanted to believe his instincts were right, Mac's concerns came out more like accusations. Like judgment. Her defenses rose.

"Then why are you both the talk of the village? Ye have been for months. People think you're a couple. It's gossip I've ignored. Until now."

"I can't believe you're so concerned. Gossip is nothing. People talk. Especially in this town. Doesn't mean it's true."

"Appearances matter, lass. May not be fair. But they count for something."

"Mac, he's getting married in, like, two months."

"Aye. That's the point."

Noelle flushed with heat as her annoyance grew. "Mac, you have no right—"

"I didn't mean to upset ye. I thought 'twas my duty—as your friend—to tell you to be careful."

"Well. I appreciate your concern." She freed her hands up to gesture as she spoke. To make this clear. "But you are not my father. You are my gardener. You have no business coming in here and flinging accusations around. Adam and I are only *friends*. That's all we've ever been. I'm so tired of repeating this to people over and over again. No lines have been crossed. And even if they had been—that is none of your concern. I have nothing to explain to you. Or anyone else in this gossipy, spiteful village."

"'Twas not my intent to hurt ye..." Mac bowed his head and placed on his cap, shuffling backward steps toward the door.

Noelle glared down at her hands as he shut the door softly behind him. Flustered, she pivoted toward the sink, staring out the window at the dark green leaves of a tree rustling in the wind. *Where is this coming from?* Mac had never warmed to Adam, but his sudden confrontation confused her, made her feel guilty for something.

She placed a cold palm to her forehead and closed her eyes to steady her breathing. A perfect afternoon perfectly ruined.

After a few minutes of stewing, she knew the best way to face it was to ignore the visit entirely, sweep it from her mind, and get back to her day. She had the power to set the day right, place it back on its rails and move on. She pushed away from the counter, reached for her laptop again, and clicked on the music defiantly. Cranking up the volume, she returned to her previous task. She picked up the vase once more and dried the inside with a rag. When she reached deeper into the bottom, the vase slipped from her wet fingers and onto the floor, where it splintered into a hundred pieces at her feet, sending Mr. Darcy into the next room.

"Shit!" She suppressed the desire to sit down and bawl. Or to scream with frustration. Instead, she collected the shards of purple glass, which started to form a tiny mosaic in the palm of her hand. A representation of how something so beautiful could shatter so unexpectedly.

The next morning, Noelle decided to make a day trip to see Jill. After her argument with Mac, and after fighting insomnia most of the night, Noelle needed a break, from Mac, from the entire village. From the whispers. She called Jill and offered to bring breakfast.

She arrived bearing an assortment of delicious breakfast treats. Jill opened the door, holding Eveline over her shoulder. "She won't burp," Jill said with a frustrated sigh, her hair unusually disheveled. She wore no makeup, and Noelle could see all her freckles.

"Want me to try?" Noelle offered.

"Oh, please do. I'd love an extra pair of hands. Gareth is always working, and right now, it seems Evie and I are the only ones in the world. I didn't know motherhood would be so isolating."

Noelle took the baby from Jill and placed her over her shoulder, bouncing lightly as she followed Jill into the sitting room. Evie smelled sweet, like baby powder. "She's getting heavier, isn't she?"

"I'm using muscles I never knew I had with her. That kid will only go to sleep if she's held. It's exhausting." Jill peeked inside the bags Noelle had set down. "Mmm. Delish. Let me get plates and napkins." She disappeared into the kitchen.

Noelle patted Eveline's back as she puffed out little breaths on her neck. Just what she needed. An infant clasped to her, not wanting anything but to be held and comforted.

Jill returned and placed the croissants, bagels, and Danishes onto plates. "Pick your poison."

"Danish," Noelle responded. "Oh!" Small contractions on Evie's back startled her. "I think she has the hiccups!"

Jill walked behind Noelle to see Evie's face. "Believe it or not, that's usually a signal she's about to fall asleep. Finally. Let's put her down. You can have some breakfast." She carefully lifted her daughter out of Noelle's arms and placed her into the bassinet then joined Noelle on the couch. "Well, this is certainly a treat. I hadn't expected to see you today." Jill picked a croissant.

"I just needed to get away."

"From?"

"I had a little... disagreement with Mac."

"The gardener?"

"And my friend. Though you wouldn't know it from yesterday. I was quite rude to him, actually. He was only looking out for me, only telling the truth." When she'd calmed down last night, given herself time to roll everything over in her mind, she knew how immature she'd been. Mac hadn't said anything Noelle hadn't thought of at one time or another.

"Truth about?" Jill coaxed.

"Adam. Mac thinks we're becoming too close."

"Are you?" She set her food aside and focused on her friend.

"We haven't done anything, if that's what you're asking. We're—"

"Just friends. It's what you keep saying. Wasn't it Shakespeare— methinks thou protest too much?"

First Mac, now Jill. Noelle could take only so much truth at this point.

"You know I just want the best for you," Jill reassured. "And for Adam."

"But that's the thing. What *is* best for Adam? Is it Laurel?"

Jill looked down at her lap for the first time in the conversation.

"What is it?"

"I didn't want to say anything, but we've been talking lately. Laurel and me. I think she's trying to make friends. I don't know that she even has any friends."

"You like her."

"'Like' is a strong word. Feel a bit sorry for her, maybe? Like she's misunderstood, like we've been too hard on her?"

To Noelle it felt like a stab of betrayal. Irrational, yes, because Jill could befriend whomever she wished. But Noelle couldn't help it. Jill was crossing to the other side, even a little bit, and it stung.

"We're even scheduled to go shopping for her bridesmaids' presents," Jill continued. "She can't decide and wants my opinion."

At that point, nothing Noelle said would make a difference. If she showed disapproval, Jill would consider her rude or unfeeling. Jill was trying to reach out to someone who needed a friend. *How can I possibly fault her for that?*

Chapter Twenty-eight

*When the world falls apart, paint. Escape life for a while to
save your sanity. This is when being an artist is the ultimate
gift. Something no one else can understand. Like that wardrobe
closet in the Narnia books, step into another universe. Separate
yourself from unspeakable loss or pain; suspend it in time
until you're stronger, braver, and better able to handle it.*

NOELLE WALKED UNTIL SHE FOUND the familiar knotty tree
then sat down under its shade. The *shush* of the river drowned
out a squirrel's rapid digging nearby, perhaps the same squirrel
that had begged for food during her picnic with Adam weeks before.
This place had brought him solace in the past, and perhaps it would
do the same for her. She couldn't believe nine months had passed since
she'd torn open the letter that had brought her to England, the letter
that had ended up changing everything.

On her trek through the woods to the riverbank, she'd snapped some
lovely pictures of Gram's estate from afar. Standing there, seeing the
manor, she ached inside, missing its occupants. Gram and Aunt Joy,
even Jill and Adam, the way they used to be.

She'd packed a bag full of snacks and some light reading, the latest
British Vogue and other assorted magazines. She wanted to be alone,
have a rare day to herself. To regain something she'd lost in the past
several days. She popped open a bag of crisps and flipped half-heartedly
through the magazine's pages but found her mind unable to focus,

drifting like the river. Her cell's ring surprised her. She could've sworn she'd turned it off. Seeing Jill's name, she answered it.

"Hey, you." She reached for another chip.

"You're there! I'm glad you picked up."

"I'm in Bath, actually. Having a picnic of sorts. It's a gorgeous afternoon, and—"

"I need to tell you something."

"What's wrong? You sound upset." Noelle instantly thought of the baby or Gareth.

"I just got off the phone with Laurel."

"Is Adam all right?"

"Adam's fine. Laurel was calling about you."

"About me? Why?"

"Well, how I do put this?"

Noelle sat up straighter, waiting to hear.

"Laurel found a series of emails you and Adam have been exchanging over the last several months."

"Emails? It's no secret we sometimes talk by email."

"Apparently, it was a secret to Laurel. She called me, sobbing, saying she thinks you two are having an affair."

Noelle choked on a chip she'd eaten and had to reach for her bottled water. She found her voice again. "An affair? She gets this from a few innocent emails?" Noelle's heart thumped harder.

"Laurel said she found lots and lots of them. Dozens. One of them talked about Adam giving you flowers? And confiding in you during the stuff with his dad? And then him keeping your secret about some diary and a ring?"

"It's not what it looks like. Trust me. This is nothing. Why can't anybody seem to understand? We're only friends. That's all!" Noelle crushed the half-empty bag of crisps in her fist. "I feel caught over something I haven't even done."

"Noelle, listen to me. It's not just the emails. She also checked Adam's phone records—apparently, tons of calls and texts to you and from you."

"Mostly about the school project at Chilton Crosse."

"I tried to tell her that, but she didn't buy it. She became hysterical. Plus, she asked me about your birthday."

"What about it?"

"All this time, Laurel assumed you had a party of three that night. That I had gone to your village with Adam back in May, and the three of us had celebrated together. She didn't know until today that I'd had to cancel. She brought up the birthday party to me, and I didn't think it was a secret that Adam went to see you without me, that he'd spent the entire day there with you. But I guess Adam never made that clear to her."

"Jill, it's insane. *Nothing* is going on. She's got this all wrong."

"Look, I'm on your side. I stuck up for you. But she didn't seem to believe me. Her mind was set. She probably thought I covered for you because we're friends. I don't think she's too happy with any of us at the moment."

"Unbelievable. Has she talked to Adam yet?"

"I'm not sure. Noelle, no matter what the truth is, the situation doesn't look good. I only wanted to call and warn you, let you know."

Noelle pressed her fingertips to her forehead. "I appreciate that. I know it's awkward for you, being stuck in the middle. Jill, you do believe me, don't you?"

"That you and Adam aren't having an affair? Yes. Though I do believe there are deeper feelings there, on both sides. But I know neither of you would ever cheat."

"No. We wouldn't. We haven't. Maybe some harmless flirting. But nothing else."

"Well, I'm sorry this is happening. I hope you can sort it all out. My advice? Hunker down and steer clear of Adam for a while. That's the best thing. Maybe it'll just blow over on its own."

"Thank you for warning me. I still can't believe this."

"Call me tomorrow, okay?"

"Okay. Bye." Noelle clicked the phone off, fascinated by the power of a single call. One minute, she had been relaxing, enjoying nature. The next, a tornado had struck, sending debris flying. And she didn't know how long it would take to assess the damage.

One thing was certain. She couldn't possibly continue to sit at a place so peaceful when the tornado inside her kept spinning. She gathered up her bag and started the long walk to her car.

Still wide-eyed at 4 a.m., Noelle couldn't push Jill's phone call from her mind. Or her heated conversation with Mac from the other day. The accusations, the insinuations, all untrue. Threatening to jeopardize lives, futures. Threatening to destroy whatever relationship remained between her and Adam.

Rising to a sitting position in her pitch-dark bedroom, she decided not to let it happen *to* her, the swirling, unfounded rumors running rampant all over the place. She had to squelch them. Immediately.

Her first thought—call Laurel, face her head-on. But somehow, she knew that would backfire. Laurel might choose to see defiance as a veil for hidden guilt. Or Noelle's words might get twisted while trying to explain, making things even worse. Her next option—speak with Adam, talk things through, find a way to redeem themselves and put the rumors to rest. Together.

Mildly satisfied, she sank back down and slept three more hours. Instead of waking up in a fog as she'd expected, she woke up restless, seeking a distraction until a decent hour to call Adam.

But while down on her hands and knees, scrubbing the cold, hard bathroom tile, she thought again about Mac. About everything he'd said—village gossip and the importance of appearances. Flashes of recent Adam memories popped up like slides clicking on a screen. Pub lunches, contractors meetings, Joe's wedding, the festival and all that dancing. All innocent, but if she had been a villager observing those moments between her and Adam, she might not have passed them off as nothing, either.

Noelle paused, removed her soapy gloves, and sobbed for the first time since the silly ordeal had started. The acoustics in the bathroom made her sobs echo and bounce off the walls. After a moment, she struggled through aching knees to get up.

Downstairs, she clicked on her laptop to skim all the old emails. Hers to Adam, Adam's to her. This time, she read them slowly, through a fiancée's eyes. It didn't matter that the messages were innocent. They seemed like more to Laurel, and that was the point. By the time she finished reading two hours later, Noelle knew what she had to do. Yes, she did have to call Adam. But not with her original intent to brainstorm a solution, wiggle their way out of this mess together. She needed to issue something stronger. An actual, purposeful good-bye. Before she lost her nerve, she called his cell and got his voicemail. "Blast," she whispered.

Instead of hanging up to try again later, she left a message, afraid she wouldn't be able to say any of it to him in person. So, when the beep sounded, she took a breath and said, "Adam. It's me. Noelle. Jill told me about Laurel's suspicions... about us. And I just... I feel bad. *Not* that we've done anything wrong. But I've done a lot of thinking, and maybe it's best if we just, well, cool things for a while. Say good-bye. My friendship with you is causing trouble, maybe even costing your relationship, and that's not what I want. So it's maybe... better this way. If we just... if we stop. I'm sorry. And I hope you understand."

She hung up and turned off her cell, leaving him no chance to talk her out of it. Not today. She was too weak.

Something occurred to Noelle as the screen turned black. Something she'd shoved deep down with all her will since Jill's phone call at the river. Underneath the embarrassment at appearing to be the "other woman," and underneath her newfound sympathy for Laurel's end of things, also came a bit of relief. This was what she wanted, at her core—Laurel and Adam broken up, Adam finally free. But not this way. Not at someone else's expense. Noelle didn't want Adam by default. If he was ever going to be with her, it must only be because he chose her. Deliberately, wholly, without a single doubt in his heart, without any baggage or reservations.

Two hours after her voicemail to Adam, Noelle took two aspirin and tried to return to bed. As she rounded the corner of the staircase, a car door slammed outside, and she stopped, mid-step. *Please, please, please let it be a delivery. Or a stranger, asking for directions. Anyone other than him...*

She couldn't ignore the front-door knocks that followed, as much as she wanted to. If Adam stood on the other side of the door, it meant he'd traveled a long way, from London, for an explanation to her voicemail. And she owed him at least that much.

She opened the door to find Adam as haggard as she felt. He wore jeans and a faded T-shirt, and his eyes held deep, dark circles. He'd had a rough night of his own.

"Come in." She opened the door wider than she needed. She had to create space between them somehow.

He walked in then whirled back around as she shut the door. "You turned off your phone. I couldn't get you. That voicemail of yours? I don't understand. You're making a big deal out of nothing."

"Like Laurel is doing?"

"Yes. Exactly like Laurel is doing." She'd never seen him so upset. Over anything. His tone clipped, his eyes sharp. "I think I'm in the Twilight Zone sometimes. People jumping to conclusions, making decisions for me. You can't just end a best friendship on a voicemail. It shouldn't work like that."

Noelle didn't have the energy to do what she needed to, but Adam's frustrated tone gave her no choice. He craved answers, and she would offer them the best she could. "You're right. It shouldn't work like that," she agreed. "But can we do this outside? I really need some fresh air."

"Sure. Whatever you want." His tone fell flatter, weary.

Noelle grabbed a light coat from the nearby rack and led him down the hall, out the back door to the garden. They bypassed Mac's bubbling fountain and kept going toward the vast countryside. Dark clouds threatened rain, but Noelle didn't care. She didn't want the future memory of their conversation to take place anywhere near her cottage. Adam followed her all the way out past the back gate and into the emerald-green field. A stately oak stood fifty feet away, leaves shimmering. She finally stopped at the edge of a pathway she liked to travel when she wanted to do some thinking.

"Here?" he asked.

"Yeah. Here's good."

He propped himself against the stone wall lining the pathway and folded his arms.

Even with her coat, the sharp wind still left her shivering. The wind, or something else. "So," she said. "I guess we should start with Laurel. You've obviously talked to her."

"Not really talked. She yelled at me for twenty minutes and made me sleep on the couch last night. I tried to explain, but she wouldn't listen. She kept waving printed emails in my face, saying something about 'broken trust' and 'lies.'"

Laurel's accusations only verified Noelle's decision. She had to do it. She paced as she talked, unable to look at him. "I need to explain my voicemail. But I need you to not interrupt, or I'll never get this out. Okay?"

"Fine."

"You and I haven't crossed any lines. But Laurel doesn't believe that, and yesterday, I didn't think it mattered. But today, it matters. This morning, I put myself in Laurel's shoes, and I didn't like how they felt. Our emails and texts and calls—it doesn't matter if they're harmless to us. They're not harmless to her. The bottom line is I wouldn't want my fiancé confiding in a female friend the way you've been confiding in me. It would seem inappropriate. Laurel thinks we're having an affair. Which leaves us with one choice."

"Saying good-bye," he said, mocking her voicemail.

She stopped her pacing. "Yes."

"But *why*?" He unfolded his arms and gestured with open hands, pleading. "Why does it have to be that drastic? All or nothing? I don't get it."

"You're about to be a married man. It's not appropriate for you to be emailing and calling and visiting me, even if we're strictly friends. Especially since we've known each other half our lives. There's a connection we have. A history we share."

"Isn't that the point? That it's something we shouldn't just throw away?" He pushed himself away from the stone wall, frustrated.

But she clutched the edge of his shirt to make him listen. "We have no choice," she said, steadily, evenly. "Your relationship with Laurel is in danger. We need to back away from our friendship. I'm not saying we can't talk from time to time, send Christmas cards, but we can't keep going the way we have been. No more flowers. No more meeting at the river, calling up for late-night chats, or emailing on a whim." Even as she said the words, the very thought of their intimate conversations stopping forever created a pit in her stomach.

"Noelle…" Adam held her stare and shook his head. "I don't know if I can do that."

"Why not?"

"Because I want you in my life. We found each other after fourteen years. Do you know what the odds are? Why should I be asked to give you up?"

"You can't have us both, Adam! Don't you see?" She'd been shouting, her voice competing with the growing volume of the wind. She couldn't think of a different way to explain things, to make him understand. This was painful for her, too. And if he kept looking at her that way, lost and hurt, she might falter and weaken, not be able to do the right thing after all.

Something wet brushed Noelle's cheek, and she looked up to see coin-sized rain pellets dropping from the sky. They both looked for shelter. The cottage was too far away. Adam pulled her elbow—"Over here!"—guiding her to the tree.

By the time they reached the trunk, the rain had soaked them almost clean through. Out of breath, Noelle slicked back her wet hair and rubbed at her eyes. Drops of rain still sprinkled where she stood, but the lush leaves above shielded them from most of the drops. And with no dangerous thunder or lightning, they could talk safely there.

"Great timing, Mother Nature!" Adam yelled at the sky.

Noelle folded her arms and tucked her hands deep inside her armpits, the pressure creating instant warmth.

"Cold?" Adam wiped his face.

"I'm okay," she lied.

He stooped over, hands on knees, slightly out of breath. He glanced sideways at Noelle. "Can I ask you something?"

"What?"

He squinted at her through the sprinkling of rain. "Why didn't we ever try?"

She knew exactly what he meant but said, "What do you mean?"

"I mean, all those years ago, all those opportunities when we were kids. Why didn't we ever cross that line?"

Noelle had no business engaging in this particular conversation. But she also knew she'd waited to engage in it for well over a decade. This was their chance. Probably their only chance. "I don't know." Her defenses began to dissolve. "I guess... I guess I thought you didn't want me that way."

He stood up straight. The rain had made his dark hair darker, curlier. The intensity in his eyes pierced straight through her. He pointed to himself, and his tone softened. "I thought you didn't want *me*." His total lack of hesitation caught her off guard. "Did you?" he asked. "Want me?"

She wanted to lie, wriggle out of it, save her heart, run for the hills. But instead, she said, "Yes. I did."

Adam tossed up his hands, more frustrated than before. "Then why in hell didn't we do something about it?"

Noelle shrugged. "Just scared, I guess. And I think we got close. Something almost did happen. That day, in the river."

"When we nearly kissed."

Noelle nodded, unable to hold steady eye contact. "Yes."

"And then I asked you out on that date, but you backed out. Got sick or something. And you left the next day for the States. I never understood why."

All those years, Adam had been holding questions, too. He'd experienced the same lack of closure she did. Noelle tightened her grip on the edges of her jacket, not knowing where to start. The rain had let up enough so that shouting became unnecessary.

"When you asked me out that night, I thought it might be a real date. I had big expectations, even dressed up in your favorite color, let myself get all hopeful. But a few minutes before you came to pick me up, I overheard someone in the parlor talking to Gram. It was your mother."

"My mother?"

"Yes. And I got curious, so I eavesdropped. I heard her telling Gram all about this girl at Oxford you'd been seeing. How she was perfect for you, and you'd likely end up marrying her."

"What?" He took a step closer as though he literally hadn't understood her.

"And it killed me. I thought you had been hiding this girl from me all summer. I felt like an idiot. And it confirmed that you only ever saw me as a friend, nothing more. I couldn't stay there. Things were too confusing, too hard."

"So you cancelled our date. And left the next day on a plane."

Noelle watched Adam connect the dots. "And when you never wrote me, I just assumed—"

"What are you talking about?" Adam frowned. "I did write you. Multiple times. Letters asking what happened, why you had gone. If you were okay."

"I never got them," Nicole said, searching her memories. "Not a single letter. And for me, it confirmed what your mother said. You had someone else."

"None of this makes any sense." Adam wiped a hand through his damp hair and said, "I'm confused about this other girl. I wasn't dating anyone."

"Then why would your mother say it to Gram? Why would she lie?"

Adam's turn to pace. He took a couple of steps, still underneath the shelter of the branches. "I remember there *was* a girl, Miranda, from some wealthy family that Mother kept pushing on me—inviting her to dinner, encouraging us to go places together. But that was all Mother's doing. I didn't want this girl. In fact, I remember being quite rude to her, knowing what my mother was up to. Nothing happened. There's no reason she should've told your grandmother any of that."

"Unless I wasn't good enough for you."

"What do you mean?"

"That's why your mother came to the estate that day. It makes sense now. She wanted *me* to get the message, through Gram, that you were with someone else. So that I would back off. And it worked. She knew you and I were spending too much time together. I'm sure she even knew about our date that night. The timing was too coincidental. She saw me as a threat. I wasn't rich, my father was American—I wasn't good enough."

"That's just bollocks."

"Maybe, but I think it's true. It all fits."

"This is insane. So there you were, thinking I was practically engaged, and there I was, thinking you'd rather run back to America than go on a date with me."

"And when I didn't hear from you again, I assumed you'd forgotten me. Moved on with your life, married the girl."

"Mother," Adam said. "She probably blocked my letters. We always put the outgoing mail on this tray in the hall that James took care of every day. She must've seen them there, done something with them. She had to know I would write you."

Noelle pictured his mother snatching the letters from the tray, hiding them somewhere. Or more likely, thrusting them into the fire before anyone could take notice. *How can that woman live with herself, even now? Ending her son's relationship without giving him any choice?*

Adam rubbed his forehead and looked out at the rain-soaked meadow. His gaze found her again, filled with frustration. "I can't believe this," he said, his voice steady. "A stupid lie, some missing letters. *That's* what kept us from trying? For all these years?"

But in seconds, the frustration lifted, replaced by compassion, softness, something she couldn't read. Almost like he saw everything at once and was crossing the wasted years to meet her in this moment. He drew closer, shaking his head.

"I'm so sorry." He cradled her face and looked down, unblinking, saying a thousand things with his eyes. His lips grazed hers in a tender, lingering kiss. This couldn't be rushed. She parted her lips to accept his kiss, accept everything about him. All the built-up years of hurt, repression, misunderstanding, found their center in that kiss as hot tears washed down Noelle's cheeks. He reached one hand down to her waist, drawing her in even closer. She couldn't get close enough.

Sooner than she wanted him to, Adam backed away gently, still breathless, tracing her lips with his thumb. The softness in his eyes said everything she needed to know. She wanted to memorize the moment, stay inside it the rest of her life.

But something wouldn't let her. The rain had stopped. A ray of sunlight pierced through the clouds behind Adam, bringing a stark realization. They weren't seventeen anymore. And they were no longer free to act as if they were

Adam clasped her shoulders. "What is it?"

Noelle stepped out of his grasp and put her fingertips to her lips, still feeling the kiss. "You're still engaged," she said, backing away, shaking her head. "I can't do this." Her voice grew stronger. "I can't!" She darted out from under the tree, mud sucking at the soles of her shoes. As she ran, a woman's familiar figure standing on a nearby hill caught her eye.

"Laurel," Noelle whispered and ran even faster toward the safety of her cottage. Laurel had followed Adam to the village. She'd caught them.

Entering the house through the back door and locking it, Noelle hastened up the stairs, leaving muddy tracks behind. She paused long enough to throw off her shoes and peel off her socks before rushing to her bedroom, slamming the door behind.

She couldn't control the sobs. The image of Adam's kiss blended with his fiancée's silhouette, leaving her dazed with humiliation and guilt. She imagined Laurel spouting angry obscenities at Adam in the middle of an open field, with Noelle as the cause. With one kiss, she'd managed to fulfill and validate every rumor, every suspicion Laurel believed.

Stripping off her wet jacket, her pants, her shirt, she searched for the largest, softest plush towel she could find. She wrapped the towel all around her, enveloping her body inside the cocoon, aching to disappear. She sank into the chair beside the window and brought her knees up to her chest, unable to stop the shivering.

The sobs subsided, but the tears kept coming. She rested her forehead on top of her knees, her hair falling in damp, clumpy strands around her face. Even with her eyes closed so tightly they burned white, she couldn't erase those images. They played in a loop—the argument, the rain, the tree, the kiss. And Laurel.

She wondered how something so beautiful, something she'd waited for so long, could make her feel so sick inside.

Chapter Twenty-nine

Try painting the "afters"—the fresh new covering of white after the first snowfall. The calm of the morning after a raging storm. A fresh perspective is always gained in the "afters." A sort of calm in hindsight. Something healing, restorative.

A HANGOVER WITHOUT THE ALCOHOL, NOELLE thought, sitting at the breakfast table, blowing on the surface of her second cup of black coffee. She held little memory of anything after the "tree talk." She had taken a sleeping pill to calm her nerves and slept the rest of the day away. Then she awoke around midnight, watched two hours of news, and returned to bed, her forehead pounding with a migraine. Several hours later, Mr. Darcy had sprung up on her bed to lick her cheek with his sandpaper tongue. She poured herself out of bed and sneezed eight times in a row, furious that she hadn't had the good sense to dry her rain-soaked hair before sleeping.

At the table, mid-afternoon, Mr. Darcy's fur rubbed against her ankle as she finished off her coffee. "Hey, boy," she whispered. "I forgot to feed you this morning, didn't I? Give me a few minutes to feel human again."

She rinsed out her cup, but even the small things took great effort. Anticipating another sneeze coming on, she held her head in advance to cushion the blow and prayed away a potential cold. Just her luck.

Reaching for another tissue, she noticed the screen of her cell phone blinking. She blew her nose and picked up the phone to retrieve a voicemail.

Jill, touching base. She had the best of intentions, but the last thing Noelle wanted was to explain anything that happened yesterday. She had embarrassed herself enough already.

Noelle reached for Mr. Darcy's bag of food but paused. Normally, she didn't make a habit of checking her caller ID history, but today, she filtered through the callers, one by one—Jill's name and number, a couple of wrong numbers and sales calls. Then Adam's number. Three times. He had called her once last night and twice this morning but hadn't left her a message. So little to go on. He wanted to see how she was doing but couldn't commit to leaving a message. Maybe he didn't know what to say. Maybe he didn't know what to feel. At this moment, neither did Noelle.

Mr. Darcy yowled his hungry meow, disrupting her Adam analysis. Noelle abandoned the caller ID. "Okay, okay." She scooped out the tiny x's of food and dropped them into his nearby bowl. "At least there's somebody in my life whose mind I can read perfectly."

She flipped the meat patty with her spatula, and a stream of smoke billowed upward from the sizzling pan. She followed suit with the other two patties, enough for leftovers, and breathed in the strong, smoky flavors. The garlic and seasonings she'd sprinkled on them earlier had infused the entire kitchen.

The headache and sneezing had finally taken their leave after a hot, soothing shower and another round of aspirin. The hall clock chimed six, reminding her that she hadn't eaten anything in over twenty-four hours. So she decided on burgers. Hearty and substantive.

As she was plating the patties, someone knocked faintly on the back door, and Noelle paused, unprepared for visitors. Making sure she turned off all her appliances, she took a few seconds to cover the meat with paper towels then walked toward the door, bracing for the worst.

She recognized Mac's profile immediately through the window and opened up the door. She let him pass through, wondering if the conversation would end like their last one and praying it wouldn't. She didn't have the energy.

Mac glanced into the kitchen at the steaming plate of food. "I've interrupted your supper. I can come again." He started to leave.

"No." She touched his sleeve. "Stay. This can wait. It's only food." She led him to the sofa, and they sat together.

Mac stared at the floor, shy and nervous, as though about to confess to a neighbor that he'd accidentally let their dog out of the yard. "That argument the other day. I was... wrong. 'Twasn't right of me to say the things I did. 'Tis your life. None o' my business. I had no right to accuse you of things I know aren't true."

"Mac..." Noelle touched his rough, weathered hand, fielding the wave of guilt as Adam's kiss flashed through her mind. "Don't apologize. I was horrible to you. I should never have spoken to you that way. I'm ashamed of myself. I don't know what came over me." She continued, her voice hushed, "You were being my friend. I know you only want the best for me."

"Aye, lass. True. I wanted to protect you."

"And I appreciate it."

"Well," he cleared his throat and she put her hand back in her lap, "There's something I haven't told you. Which should explain my reaction about your male friend."

"What do you mean?"

"I was your Aunt Joy's only friend, during those years."

"I know. I'm so glad she had you."

"You don't understand. We had more than that." Tears formed in the corners of his eyes. "We loved each other."

Noelle stared, mouth agape.

"I even asked her to marry me. Four times, I asked her. She said no every time."

She kept rigidly still, no idea how to respond.

"Mind you," he continued. "She loved me, too. 'Twas not a one-sided affair. But she was set in her ways. Told me she was too old to get re-married, and that walking down an aisle at her age would be barmy.

So, things stayed as they were, on her terms. For nigh eight years. 'Twas well after I was widowed. And after your aunt had shut herself away. We became friends. And then we became more."

"Mac. I had no idea." Her mind raced to fit together the pieces—Mac's melancholy at her passing, even his lonely intoxication during Christmas.

He continued, finally able to look at her as he spoke, "During all those years when she isolated herself, I had to endure the villagers' cruel remarks, their speculation and gossip. I had to defend her carefully without giving away our secret. So many times, I just bit my tongue. I know firsthand the sort of damage rumors can do. That's why, when people started talking about you and your male friend—"

"You got so protective."

"Aye."

"Oh, Mac. I wish you'd told me sooner. About you and my aunt."

"There's something else." He bounced his cap in his hand.

"What?" She could barely stand the suspense. Surely, it couldn't top what he'd just told her.

"I know what the symbol is. In your aunt's paintings. You thought it was a *W*. 'Tis my crest, the MacDonald family Scottish crest. A castle with three turrets, the middle one the tallest turret. She'd asked me one day about the crest, and I drew it for her on a napkin. With the motto underneath, 'My Hope is Constant in Thee.' That became our theme, I guess you might say."

"The ring!" Noelle said. "I found a ring upstairs, in her desk. With that symbol on it."

"Aye, I gave her that ring many years ago. 'Twas as close to a wedding ring as she ever had."

"Oh, Mac..." Tears welled up again as her head throbbed with another emotional headache. "That's beautiful. She must've loved you so much. She put the symbol inside all of her paintings. A little piece of you."

"Aye." She couldn't see his eyes anymore. He'd bowed his head low, looking at the floor.

"Just a minute." She patted his knee and stood to go upstairs. Two minutes later, she joined him again, the ring in her palm. "This belongs to you."

Mac wiped his cheek with the back of his hand and reached for the ring. He brought it closer, saw the familiar symbol, and nodded. "Are ye certain?"

"Absolutely. It's yours. Please take it."

"Thank ye, lass."

Noelle saw her aunt, truly, for the first time. How sad to live a secret life, to hide away your greatest love. But then again, how incredible to *have* a greatest love, someone to mourn your loss the way Mac still grieved now.

"I'm so grateful she had you in her life," she said. "My aunt was lucky."

"I was the lucky one, lass."

He might balk at what she had in mind, but she didn't care. She wrapped her arms tightly around his shoulders, smelling the musty wool of his jacket. With his free hand, he squeezed her arm in return. Even in all her guilt and confusion over Adam, Mac's confession about Aunt Joy gave her unexpected peace.

"He means a lot to you, doesn't he?" Mac said. "Your young man. Adam."

"Yes, he does. He means everything."

Mac nodded as though he'd already known all along.

"Look at us." She chuckled through her tears. "We're quite a pair, aren't we?"

"Indeed."

"I really don't want to eat this meal alone. Would you join me? Please?"

"I'd be honored, lass." He rose from the sofa, clutching his cap in one hand and his ring in the other.

Chapter Thirty

*When you're overwhelmed, step down, and take a break. Leave the
canvas. Because if you don't—if you keep seeking the Muse when
you know she's vanished—your work will only suffer. The Muse will
eventually return. But you must give her a bit of space once in a while.*

SOMETHING ABOUT BEING AT THE gallery always set Noelle at
ease, even while her insides churned. Tonight, she was visiting
Joy's paintings after hours in the newly renovated upper room.
The layout echoed the downstairs gallery—long, dark wall, benches in
the center to sit and analyze the paintings as long as people wished.
Polaroids weren't good enough tonight. She wanted to see the paintings
in person.

Two days had passed since the kiss, and Noelle remained as frustrated
as ever. She hadn't heard from Adam, and the more time that passed,
the less she expected to hear anything at all. Moving from painting to
painting, she breathed in the rich quiet of the space, a hush similar to a
library, tranquil and restorative.

Noelle reached the end of the wall and checked her messages out of
habit. Nothing. She replaced her phone and sat on the bench across from
the painting of the ship lost in a storm. Noelle had no idea what had
transpired since that day on Adam's end of things, and part of her didn't
want to know. Since their talk, that kiss, she'd hidden away in her little
cottage, her little gallery, her little life. Oblivious to the repercussions
of the kiss or its effects on certain relationships. Occasionally, she let

herself presume, pictured a furious Laurel calling off the wedding and a distraught Adam wondering what to do next. Mostly, she wondered whether he had let the kiss alter his thinking, done something as drastic as broken up with Laurel and "chosen" Noelle. If so, he would already be at her door.

Sure, he had called her a few times afterward, and part of her wished she'd had the courage to answer the phone. But committing enough to leave an actual message? Coming to see her at the cottage? Pounding on her door to be let in? Refusing to leave until they'd talked? That hadn't happened. And Noelle wasn't about to do anything to coax that into happening. The ball was not in her court. She didn't have a fiancée to consider. She wasn't even sure what her reaction would be if she did see Adam at her door.

She had to extract him from her mind. But the ghost of his memory lived in every single nook of the village. He'd been in every room of her cottage, including the art room, talked to Mr. Darcy a dozen times. He'd been in the pub, the gallery, the bakery, even the church. So it became a challenge, selectively dislodging him from familiar places. But she had no other choice. He'd already made his.

Back at the cottage, Noelle stepped in front of the Cornwall seascape Joy had painted and wished herself into it. The picture drew her in again like a magnet, as it had the day she opened the letter in San Diego. She craved the ocean more than ever. She remembered some children's book she had read when she was about ten, where the main character actually walked into a painting, made friends with the wildlife, explored a beautiful new world.

Peering more closely at the brush strokes in the painting, Noelle almost heard Joy's voice again, instructing her on technique. "Watch the brush transform the colors, blending them to make new ones. And if I'm not satisfied with that color, or if I make a mistake, I wipe it away with my rag and try again. And in the end, no one will ever know."

Why can't life be as simple as hopping into paintings or blotting out mistakes with a stroke of a rag? Noelle thought as tears blurred her vision, turning Joy's oil painting into a watercolor.

As she stood at the sink peeling carrots for supper, an idea germinated. She couldn't get the Cornwall coastline out of her mind. An escape to the sea. She abandoned her carrots and found Mr. Lester's cell number. She hated to bother him on a weeknight, but it couldn't wait. She wanted to inquire about the cottage in Cornwall. Last she recalled, the tenants were moving, but she couldn't remember the details.

"It's available," he confirmed when she asked. "I haven't found someone to lease it yet but have had some inquiries about renting for the summer. Nothing concrete. As of now, it's unoccupied. Why?"

Thrilled at the prospect, she told Mr. Lester her desire to visit the cottage, perhaps stay for a week or two, a brief vacation. He gave her the cottage address and directions.

She hung up and smiled at her temporary solution. She couldn't sit in this cottage day after day and wait for life to happen. She had to move, get out, get away.

She started packing and making arrangements, including courtesy phone calls to Mac then to Frank, so neither would worry about her. For the first time in days, she controlled her own destiny. She decided not to bring Mr. Darcy along. Too cruel, placing him inside a tiny cage, inside a noisy train. He would be much happier at home, with Mac checking in on him.

A mere two hours after first considering such an insane idea, Noelle stared out the window of the train, watching the shadows of trees pass by. She didn't want to drive. She wanted someone else to take her to the coast. Plus, she, Gram, and Joy had traveled by train those couple of times they'd visited Cornwall. The glow of a stunning full moon came into view when the train veered slightly southward, illuminating the patchwork English countryside.

As Noelle peered up at the moon, a vivid image appeared of two innocent fifteen-year-olds, lying on a blanket at midnight and staring up at the sky. Noelle had spent all of that particular day with Adam, at the river with a picnic and later, walking the grounds of the estate to soak up the glorious sun. They'd said goodnight hours before, but what sounded like hail on her bedroom window had awakened Noelle in the middle of the night. Confused, she slipped out from under her covers and tiptoed over the lacy pattern of moonlight on the floor.

Peering down cautiously, she spotted Adam waving at her. She unlocked the window. "Are you crazy?" she shout-whispered down to him.

"Come down!" he shout-whispered back, releasing the remaining pebbles he'd planned to throw.

She clicked the window shut and slipped on the silk robe lying on the back of a chair then stepped into the fuzzy slippers Joy had given to her for her birthday. Careful to avoid creaking steps and creaky doors, Noelle snuck out of the house, tiptoeing carefully past Joy's room then Gram's room, and found Adam sprawled out on a blanket, wearing jeans and a jacket, staring skyward.

"Are you drunk or something?" Noelle asked, standing in front of him.

"Not drunk. Couldn't sleep. Have you seen this moon tonight? Stunning." He munched on something as he spoke and patted the empty side of the blanket. "Wait." He sat up, wriggled out of his jacket, and handed it to her. "You look cold."

"I am." She put on the jacket, and his leftover warmth radiated through to her skin.

He lay back down and patted the blanket again. "C'mon."

Excited, Noelle lay down beside him. She inched as close as she could to him, shoulder to shoulder, and looked up. Probably the roundest, most angel-white moon she'd ever seen. So bright it almost hurt her eyes.

Adam passed her a crisp. "Okay, I've always wanted to know," she said as she munched. "Where is this 'man' everyone keeps talking about?"

"Are you telling me you've never seen the Man in the Moon?"

"Don't laugh at me. I've tried. I've looked and looked, but I don't see anything. No eyes, no nose, no mouth. Only a bunch of dark shadows and craters. This must be some kind of idiot test or something."

"Try looking for a cartoon man, not an actual man."

Noelle squinted and explored the vast circle with her eyes. "Nope. Can't see it."

Adam sighed and rolled toward her at an angle then pointed in her eye line toward the sky. His face was inches from hers. "There. Big eyes. Nose sort of in the center. Lopsided mouth."

Suddenly, like magic, the features came into view. "Two big eyes at the top—they're not the same size, and they're sort of off-center, but I think they're eyes. And a sort of nose."

Adam snickered and reached for another crisp. "Cool, huh?"

"Very cool." Proud of herself, she pointed upward. "But to me, it's not really a cartoon face. It looks like it's been painted. A dab up there, a splotch over there." She lowered her hand and smiled at the moon, glad Adam had tapped on her window. "Thank you," she said.

"You're welcome."

Either the gentle clicking of the wheels on the train tracks or the memory of a drowsy summer evening made Noelle's eyelids grow heavy. She leaned her forehead against the cool window, wishing to stay on that blanket in that moonlit moment just a little bit longer.

Noelle hooked the last of her hanging clothes onto the rod inside the narrow closet then padded over to the kitchen for a cup of tea. She needed some comfort after the long journey. Her bare feet slapped across the linoleum floor as she made her way from the back bedroom through the compact living room then took a quick left for the tiny kitchen. It stood nearly as small as Noelle's first college apartment kitchen, she mused. This one only had a half-sized fridge and no dishwasher, with faded yellow and white wallpaper. Surprising, that people as wealthy as Gram and Aunt Joy had owned a modest, two-bedroom cottage. Perhaps, though, the simple, unpretentious cottage life had charmed them. No servants, no elaborate meals to plan, no fancy entertaining. Just the salty sea breezes and crisp fresh air.

Even at nearly midnight, she wanted to sit on her porch and linger in her coastal surroundings. Noelle slipped on her shoes and a light jacket then carried her tea out to the porch and sat on the swinging wooden bench. Because of the luminous moon, the craggy coastline's jagged cliffs became eerily visible. And further, the twinkling movement of the sea, which she heard in shushing waves. She imagined Aunt Joy setting up an easel on the porch, or maybe further down, on the hill above the ocean. All those years ago.

Still, a hundred miles away from anything recognizable, she thought of Adam, where he was, what he might be doing. She couldn't help it. She pictured him struggling with sleep, punching at his pillow and shifting positions every two minutes. Or perhaps he was somewhere outside, contemplative, looking up at the same bright moon. Or maybe he was snugly comfortable in his familiar position next to Laurel. Sound asleep, pretending nothing had ever happened at all.

"Stop!" Her lip quivered. These questions without answers were precisely what she'd been fighting against. The entire reason she'd boarded that train in the first place. She splashed the remains of her tea into the nearby grass and walked back inside, wondering how many hours of sleep she wouldn't be getting tonight.

Noelle had no idea the sea breezes would be so strong. Or so piercing. A far cry from the balmy California weather, even in July. Fighting to gather her whipping hair and maneuver it into a tight ponytail proved an interesting challenge.

After a restless night's sleep, a heightened sense of energy filled her, and she made a decision to take control, to banish all thoughts of Adam or Laurel. She wouldn't allow them even in the fringes of her mind today. To that end, she had stuffed some items into a tote bag and headed for the cliffs a few hundred feet from the cottage then walked along the edge to divert her mind with the glories of the sea.

Maybe tomorrow she could venture down to the actual beach where Aunt Joy had painted Noelle as a little girl. She'd spotted a steep-looking pathway that cut into the rocks of the cliff, but it looked rather dangerous. Today, though, she found an ideal spot, a fourth-mile west of the cottage. Several rocks jutted up around her at random, adding character to the landscape. Through the brilliant sunlight, she viewed the colors of the sea, the pale greens and navy blues crested in white foam.

With her phone, she snapped picture after picture. She remembered the Scottish novelist Rosamunde Pilcher had set many of her novels in Cornwall. Gram had owned an entire collection of those books, and Noelle often passed the rain-soaked summer days in the library, reading about the romance of the sea. Seeing the coast in person, Noelle knew that even an author's brilliant descriptions couldn't do this place justice.

After snacking on a ham sandwich she'd tucked away in her bag, she snapped more pictures. Before long, Noelle's eyes had dried out from the relentless wind. Needing a break, and a hot shower, she gathered her things and trudged back to the cottage. Rather than walk along the cliffs, she took a different path that led to a neighboring property, a detour.

At the cottage next to hers, an elderly woman hunched over in her yard, picking weeds. The woman paused and waved with her free hand, and Noelle waved back. Though she'd hoped not to speak to another soul the rest of today, Noelle wanted to be friendly. They were neighbors, after all.

"Good morning," Noelle yelled over the wind, drawing closer to the woman. Mercifully, the wind died down as she reached the cottage.

"Hello." The woman smiled and offered Noelle a withered hand. "Lovely to meet you," she said, her voice raspy but warm.

"You, as well. I'm Noelle Cooke."

She pointed to herself. "My name is Helen Michaels."

Helen. Something rang familiar for Noelle. The woman in that picture, inside the album. The woman standing with Joy and Gram at this same cottage, all those years ago.

"Are you next door?" the woman asked.

"Yes, that's me. I came last night."

"First time in Cornwall?"

"Yes. Well, no. I was about five years old when I first came with my grandmother. And my aunt. She painted me at the seaside, but I don't really remember it. I think you might actually have known her. Joy Valentine?"

The woman's mouth parted in surprise, and she smiled. "Oh, how lovely. Yes, I knew her. Not very well, mind you. She sometimes came to the cottage alone, liked to keep to herself and paint. Well, except when her husband came with her, on occasion."

"Husband? You mean John?"

"I think that was his name. It's been so long ago." Her face turned wistful, as though revisiting past images in her mind. "Such a pity." Helen tsk-ed.

"Pardon?"

"About her husband. Killed in such a horrible accident. And leaving her with that baby to tend."

Noelle crinkled her forehead. "I'm sorry? Baby?"

"Oh, yes. I have the image in my head, clear as day, your aunt waddling around the property with a beach ball for a belly. I always felt so sorry for her, poor dear. Being a single mother."

"Single mother?" Noelle kept repeating everything the woman said, but she couldn't help it. Surely, she had mixed Aunt Joy up with someone else. Maybe even Gram? But she seemed so sure.

"But Aunt Joy never *had* any children," Noelle said emphatically. "Are you sure? Could it have been my grandmother? Her name was Rachel."

"No, I'm sure. It was the artist. Months after her husband passed away. In fact, I brought her tea once, came to her cottage for a little chat. And there she sat on the porch, in front of her easel, the palette perched on top of her large belly. I was bold enough to give her a warning not to sniff too much of that paint. It wouldn't have been good for the baby."

Noelle's heart raced at the implications. *Where is the baby now?*

"I was sorry to hear of your aunt's passing last year," Helen said. "I read it in the papers."

"Thank you." Noelle stepped away. "I'm afraid I need to go. Very nice meeting you."

Noelle entered the cottage, stripped down, and stood in a steaming-hot shower, still stunned by this new information. She went through all the possible scenarios: Helen was a raving lunatic; Helen had mixed up Aunt Joy with another woman... another artist. Or Aunt Joy had gained a great deal of weight, leading Helen to assume a pregnancy. Noelle couldn't think of another option except Helen was right, and Aunt Joy had indeed been pregnant but hidden it from the world. *But why?*

Still, Noelle went there. Just for a minute. She stepped out of the steamy shower and combed through her wet hair, playing with the possibility that everything could be true.

Perhaps the baby died. Or maybe Joy had to give the child away. She'd been a widow, after all. Maybe raising a baby on her own had been too much to bear. Especially with its features constantly reminding her of John.

Noelle tried to push away the resentment, finding out such a personal secret from a stranger named Helen. *Why didn't Aunt Joy trust me with this?*

Surely, Aunt Joy would have referenced the pregnancy more directly in her journal entries. Those sacred pages where she revealed all her other secrets. Maybe Mac would know. Then again, perhaps not. He apparently hadn't known what was locked behind that bedroom door all those years. Some secrets Joy had kept only to herself. A baby was likely one of them.

Late the next morning, Noelle remembered to bite the bullet and call Jill, a welcome distraction from yesterday's bizarre talk with Helen. Noelle had waited much too long to call, especially with Jill's daily voicemails. Her Adam issues weren't with Jill. And she couldn't afford to push away her closest friend.

After lunch, she thought and walked out the door to find the local market. At the nearby village, about a half mile away, she purchased ingredients for a nice meal—chicken, snow peas, French bread, and homemade chocolate cake for dessert.

Back at the cottage, after putting in the chicken to bake and getting the vegetables ready, she decided to start on the cake. A giant feast for one. She could save the leftovers for tomorrow. But while she snipped open the plastic bag of cake batter, her cell rang from inside her purse.

"You're there!" said Jill. "I was all prepared to leave my hundredth message. I've had more of a relationship with your voicemail than with you lately!"

"I'm so sorry I haven't called you back." Noelle moved to the living room and plopped on the sofa, running her fingers along the floral pattern. "I've... been busy."

"Bollocks. You've been avoiding me. At least be honest. We're close enough friends for that, aren't we?"

"Yes. We are." She sighed and said again, "I'm sorry."

"I don't want an apology. I want to know you're okay. I've been worried sick about you."

"I am. I'm okay," she said, half-believing it.

"I'll bet you haven't left your cottage in days."

Noelle hesitated. "Well, I'm not actually in Chilton Crosse. I'm in Cornwall."

"Good heavens! Whatever are you doing all the way out there?"

"I don't know. I came on a whim." She suppressed the tremble in her voice. "I felt a little lost. I needed to get away…"

"Well. The fresh sea air is probably good for you."

"Have you heard from Adam?"

"Not a word. Or from Laurel. Or from you. Why did everyone suddenly go radio silent?" Noelle sighed. "You'll be sorry you asked. It's bad."

"I can handle bad. What I can't handle is silence. Start from the beginning."

And so she did. From her noble intentions about breaking things off with Adam, to their revelations under the tree, to the kiss. In all its beautiful, gut-wrenching detail. And finally, about who had seen them together.

"Laurel? Are you positive?" Jill gasped. "Couldn't it have been somebody else?"

"No. I'm sure. I'm surprised she didn't call you."

"She knows you and I are friends. I'm sure she knew my loyalties were with you. Now, back to that day. What in hell was she doing there? Following him?"

"I guess so, or she probably came looking for him on her own at the village, found my cottage, saw Adam's car in front then started investigating. After all her suspicions, she probably wanted to see for herself. And boy, did we give her something to see." The shame stuck in her throat as she said the words. "I never thought I'd hear myself say this. Jill, I'm the 'other woman.'"

"You are not the other woman. *He* kissed *you*."

"But I kissed him back. And it was—"

"Great?"

"Incredible." Before Jill could relish in that image, Noelle added, "But wrong!"

"Well, maybe, but you stopped. And you removed yourself from the situation. You had a conviction, and you followed it."

"This is all my fault." Noelle rubbed her temples, watching tears splash into her lap.

"No. It isn't. It's the universe's fault for having such shitty timing. You two should be together. You were made for each other."

"I think so, too," she whispered. "Have you heard anything? About the wedding being on or off?"

"Not yet."

"I love him, Jill."

"Oh, darling," she said, her voice full of compassion. "This is bloody awful. I don't know what to tell you."

"That's the stupid part. There's nothing I can do. It's too late for us." She sniffed away the tears. Hearing everything aloud only made it real.

"I'm curious," Jill said. "What's the answer to Adam's question? In hindsight, why didn't you try? You both had all these emotions, spent all those summers together. I mean, you can't tell me that one stupid misunderstanding was the only reason. You had four long summers together to try."

"I think we were both too scared, maybe? Or too young? Or it was never the right timing? It's a mystery." The timer buzzed. "I've gotta get that. I made chicken. Not that I feel like eating it anymore." She pushed herself off the couch and headed for the kitchen.

"I'm sorry for making you talk about it."

"It's okay. I needed to. Maybe I can start to move on." She turned off the buzzer and clicked on the oven light. "Thank you, Jill. For not judging me... about Adam. The kiss."

"Sweetie, I've done too many regretful things in my life to judge anyone. Besides, you went with your heart. There's nothing ever the matter with that."

Chapter Thirty-one

Always make room in your life for art, yes. But also leave plenty of room for what's real—even more real than an easel or brushes or turpentine. Something that can't be created with a brushstroke. Make room for love.

THE FINAL ENTRY. NOELLE WASN'T ready yet to stop discovering all her aunt's secrets. To stop hearing her aunt's voice through the journal. Maybe that was why she had taken her time. She didn't want to reach the end. But after struggling to piece together the shocking new information Helen had given yesterday about a pregnancy, Noelle had to know whether the last entry might hold the final piece of the puzzle.

She changed into flannel pajamas and lay back on the bed, propping two pillows behind her and cracking open the journal. Only one Polaroid remained. An incomplete series. The painting she'd found months ago in that locked room, half-finished on the easel, could have been Number Two. That fresh, pretty landscape, colorful and happy.

The Polaroid she held contained a beautiful lush garden—Gram's estate. Noelle recognized the placement of sculpted shrubs and the cherubic fountain. Even the bench to the side, where she'd spent hours reading books and watching blue jays taunt the squirrels.

Noelle turned to the diary entry dated three weeks before her aunt passed away, entitled, "JOY." She cheated, skimming ahead for news of a baby, a pregnancy, anything. But she found nothing. So she read from the beginning.

I've spent the last week looking at old photos, revisiting old memories in my mind. And I realise with all the valleys and dark shadows I've allowed my life to contain, there is also one other constant. Joy. I have been utterly blessed by good health, a rich family heritage, the passion of painting, and finding love again. What more could a person ask for? I also realise how selfish I've been, hiding away in this place all these years. Shoving people away, ignoring a kind hand reaching out. How ridiculous, in retrospect, the fears that I fought all this time. Fears that kept me isolated from the rest of humanity.

Revisiting those memories, I've found my perfect day. In all those years, there was one particular afternoon I wouldn't mind living over and over again. The sky was a brilliant blue, with enormous clouds rolling past. Summer in the garden. My sister had just told me a dirty joke about a vicar's knickers, and we were laughing until our sides ached. When Noelle, just eleven, asked why we laughed, we only laughed harder, knowing she was too innocent to understand, knowing it wouldn't be appropriate to tell her anyway. She started laughing, too, and the three of us roared for several minutes, tears streaming, muscles aching, until we hardly remembered why we were laughing in the first place.

We had dinner in the garden that evening, under the moon with the fireflies blinking all around us. We ate succulent strawberries with rich cream and listened to the music of Benny Goodman floating from my sister's old gramophone. I remember wishing I could have captured us on canvas that way, caught our moment in time. But we were the painting. We lived it and breathed it and enjoyed it as it happened, and it's captured in my memory forever.

Perfection. And so, with my life's clock ticking, when I become fearful of what lies before me, the Great Unknown, I will meditate on that perfect day. I will remember, and laugh, and I will feel joy.

Clutching the pages to her chest, Noelle closed her eyes and remembered, too. A summer before she'd even met Adam. That particular evening, Noelle had walked up to the edge of the garden, led by the sound of cackling laughter in the air. Gram and Aunt Joy on a blanket, doubled over, mouths open, smiling. They tried to talk to her between contagious giggles but couldn't catch their breath long enough. By then, Noelle was laughing, too.

She also remembered the sweet goodness of the strawberries, the mellow clarinet of Benny Goodman, the dancing fireflies. How wonderful, how amazing, that her aunt remembered it, too, just the way she had. A single shared memory connected Noelle to Joy stronger than anything else did since her death, more than the paintings, the diary, the gallery, the cottage.

Noelle needed to remember this today. To be drawn into a place of bliss and joy during her own time of shadows and isolation.

But the bliss only lasted a moment as she shut the book on the final entry and looked around at the bedroom, jarred out of the memory. Isolated in a cabin, miles away from anyone, alone with her own thoughts. She listened. Being so alone produced an eerie quiet, nearly suffocating.

She wanted to go home. She was tired of running. Escape had *always* been her answer. In fact, escape had become a pattern she didn't even know she had formed. She could trace her habitual need to run away back to that last summer in Bath as a teenager. When she thought Adam was seeing a girl at Oxford. When she disapproved of her mother's string of new boyfriends. When she kissed an engaged man under a tree. She ran away. Every time.

Physically, literally, ran away.

But that hadn't changed anything. Coming to Cornwall certainly hadn't made her feelings for Adam disappear. They had only grown stronger, especially after talking to Jill. And escaping hadn't erased that incredible kiss.

Time to stop running. She leaped up from the bed and marched toward the closet, laying the empty suitcase onto the bed with a bounce. It wouldn't take long to pack—some hanging clothes, a bundle of sweaters and jeans from the drawers, a few toiletries. She could be on the train within an hour.

She had no idea exactly what she'd be returning to. She hadn't thought that far ahead. One thing she did know, as she folded a sweater's long sleeves. She wanted Adam. Wanted to relax into his arms, hear his laughter in rhythm with hers, and be his companion for the rest of her life. She'd wasted so much time looking back that she'd failed to look forward. To picture her life in days to come. And she couldn't imagine those future days without Adam there.

In order to have even a chance that he'd be in her life, she needed to fight for him. At least to know that she'd tried. That she hadn't run away.

Rushed and anxious, packing the last of her toiletries, Noelle stopped cold. A strong *thud* against one of the cottage's walls made her gasp. She clutched the toothbrush in her hand and listened. Another smaller thud followed by a muffled voice. Noelle tiptoed into the living room. A blur of a shadow passed by the window. Petrified, she dropped the toothbrush and searched the room for some kind of makeshift weapon. An umbrella on the dresser three feet away caught her eye, and she snatched it tight, held it like a bat, both arms quivering.

Adrenaline raced to the top of her head, and her pulse thumped faster. In the middle of nowhere, in the middle of the night, isolated, vulnerable, on her own. She couldn't even remember where she'd put her cell phone—in the bathroom, on the bed. Too late to call for help, anyway.

Steady footsteps thumped on the porch outside. The screen door pulled out with a squeak. Then a three-tap knock.

Still leery, Noelle loosened her grip on the umbrella. An intruder wouldn't knock.

Another knock, "shave-and-a-haircut." She inched closer, a few feet from the door, wondering how on earth to respond. A muffled male voice spoke through the door. "Noelle?"

Still shaken, she reached for the knob and cracked the door hesitantly. There stood Adam, hunched shoulders, wearing at least a three-day beard, his right eye swollen and bruised. Her body went limp at the sight of him, the mixture of fear and relief rendering her weak. Seeing the umbrella clutched in her hand, and the ashen look on her face, Adam stepped forward and wrapped her up tight in his arms. She melted into him.

"I scared you. I'm sorry." He cradled her head.

The umbrella slipped down, and she gripped the sides of his suede jacket, burying her head in his chest. After a moment, he nudged her forward into the living room, shutting the door on the cool night air with his foot, still holding her tight.

"Shh. Hey, it's okay," he whispered. She had started to cry.

He stroked her hair, and she was safe again. She wished she could stay this way forever, but knew they had some talking to do first. She backed away slightly, wiping tears with her hand. "Sorry. I thought you were an intruder. I'm a little emotional tonight."

"I tried to call, but your cell was off." He wiped her other cheek.

She thought he would release her, but he stayed close, his hands still around her waist. She winced when she saw a black eye again. "What happened?"

"Oh, this?" He touched his fingertips just below the crimson half-moon. "That's nothing. You should've seen it this morning—swollen shut."

"Who did that?"

Adam raised an eyebrow. "Laurel's father. Long story."

"Does it hurt?"

"Not too bad."

"How did you know I was in Cornwall? I bet Jill told you."

"Nope. Mac told me. I went looking for you tonight, at your cottage. Mac was there and told me how to find you."

"Adam, about Laurel—"

"I didn't come here to talk about Laurel. I came to talk about something else." His eyes held a solemnity. She saw it that day his father went into the hospital, and she recognized it again tonight. A desperation, an urgency, a concern that he was about to lose something precious to him. He reached into his jacket pocket and produced a crinkled piece of paper, unfolding it with his fingers. "Do you recognize this?" He held the paper between them.

Noelle touched the corner, the faded pencil sketch of a sneaker. "Yes. You read me a story under the tree, and I ignored you and sketched your shoe." She looked up at him, puzzled.

"I found it inside one of my architecture books when I moved in with Laurel. Way before I even knew you were back in England. I must've carried it around with me all these years, from dorm rooms to apartments, tucked away in that book. That morning of your birthday, and the festival, I got sort of nostalgic and rummaged around and found it again."

Adam folded the paper and returned it to his pocket. "But I didn't put it back inside the book. I sort of… hid it away. In this drawer in my study. I thought I put it in a safe place, but—"

"Laurel found it. That's what first made her suspicious. She saw my name in the corner of the sketch."

Adam nodded. He placed his hands back on her arms and looked squarely at her, the earnest gaze returning. "I don't want to talk about a sketch, or a festival, or Laurel. I want to talk about us. I've had feelings for you all the way back to when we were teenagers. And they've only grown stronger this year. I should've raced to that airport all those years ago when you left England. I should've fought for you, no matter what hurdles my mother had put in our way. It wasn't up to her. It was up to me. I was too bloody young and too bloody stupid to do anything about it. But I'm older now. And when I kissed you under that tree, I knew everything had changed. I'm going to tell you something I was too scared to say back then. I love you. We belong together. You know we do. This can be our second chance."

Noelle opened her mouth to respond, but she could tell he wasn't finished.

"I'm a free man. It's a long story, but Laurel took off before I could speak to her that day under the tree. I had to track her down at her parents' house, all the way to Scotland. Call me old-fashioned, but I had to settle things, end them with her before I could come to you again. I wanted to do this right. Clean slate."

"She didn't take it very well, did she?"

"Neither did her father. Hell, I deserved it. I've been an idiot, fighting the truth for months, leading Laurel on, giving you mixed signals. But something about that kiss told me you felt the same way. Look, we can't go back and change things, but we can start from right here. If that's what you want."

She watched his eyes, unblinking, waiting for her response. "I need to hear it again," she said.

"Which part?"

"The part about you loving me."

"Oh, that." He grinned. He touched her face with both hands and said purposely, deliberately, "I love you, Noelle Cooke."

"I love you right back."

Their lips met in a deep, exuberant kiss. Urgent at first, then softer, slower. He shifted his arms to her waist, his grasp firm and confident as he lifted her inches off the ground. Noelle savored his lips, caressed his hair, his neck. No hesitation or guilt. No running away or stings of regret. Only certainty and tenderness as he set her back down.

She outlined his mouth with her fingers, sensing the last piece of the wall crumble. *He's mine.* "I can't believe you came all this way to find me. I'm glad you did."

"So am I."

"And you were just in time. I had started packing when you showed up."

"Why?"

"I was coming to find you."

Adam tilted his head and whispered, "Here I am." Then he kissed her again.

Chapter Thirty-two

Pause to enjoy the process—the bristles on the canvas, the glorious scent of newly squeezed-out paint, the very first stroke that won't come again. Savour it, always.

"Evie, I've told you before—don't pull on Mr. Darcy's tail! Leave that poor creature alone!" Jill blew on her fingertips. She and Noelle sat at the breakfast table of the cottage, painting their nails, an act that took longer than it should have, considering all the stops and starts Jill had to make with Evie. "I'm sorry. You don't need a rambunctious one-year-old frazzling you on this day, of all days."

"Hush, you know how much I love her. Having you two here is like family."

"Speaking of, was your dad able to come?"

Noelle sighed. "No. Said he had an interview for some coveted new job in Texas that he couldn't reschedule. He sent some really-expensive crystal bowl yesterday as his guilt-gift."

"I'm sorry," Jill said, her voice softening.

"Thanks. Really, the only ones I'm missing today are Joy, Gram, and Mom."

"I realize this isn't a replacement for any of them, but you'll have more friends there than you'll know what to do with. They're family, too. The whole village is turning out."

Noelle nodded.

"Evie!" Jill shouted again, putting down the polish with a huff. "Sorry, I need to scurry after her and try to put her down for a nap. You'll be lucky if she hasn't already broken something of tremendous value. I had no idea what little terrors they can be when they finally learn to walk!"

Noelle chuckled, watching Jill stomp away after her daughter into the sitting room. The cottage hadn't seen so much activity in ages. Noelle loved it and hoped for more of the same in the near future. She finished her pinkie nail, painted "rosebud pink," and smiled. She hardly believed today had come. Finally.

A knock at the back door startled her. Mac nodded through the window, and she waved him in then blew on her nails as he walked into the kitchen.

"How are ye, lass? Nervous?"

"Not in the least, thanks for asking. How about you? Nervous?"

He grinned and answered, "Not in the least."

"Join me." She pointed to a chair. Jill struggled with Evie in the hallway then tapped upstairs to the guest bedroom for a nap. Mac placed a manila envelope on the table and slid it toward her.

"What's this?" Noelle asked.

"Something old, as the tradition goes."

"Would you mind?" she said, waving her still-wet nails.

"Oh. Aye." He opened the envelope and produced a document, multiple pages.

Confused and curious, Noelle took it delicately, using the pads of her fingers. She drew the letter closer, recognizing the handwriting immediately. She looked up at Mac. "This is from Aunt Joy."

"Aye. A wedding present of sorts."

Recognizing that familiar rising excitement that she'd experienced months and months ago when she'd discovered the key to the locked room, all those paintings, then the journal inside the desk and the ring, she turned to the letter. She hadn't expected any more surprises.

Dearest Noelle,

If you're reading this, it means that Mac has followed my instruction. He will give you this letter when he feels you're ready to receive it. I want it to be on a happy day, a day you'll remember. If you're reading this, it also means that you're about to learn a secret that only three people in the world know. Mac, your Gram, and myself.

It's important that you know a bit of history first. A confession that will change everything. By now, you've probably already found my journals, where I hinted at a betrayal against your grandmother. It's true—I had a brief affair with your grandfather, George. We were intimate. I never meant for it to happen. Really. But John had just died, and I found myself sobbing, and suddenly an arm was around my shoulder, holding me. His strength made me fall into him, and for a moment, the pain was gone. He absorbed it like a sponge. And I wanted that feeling again. And again.

George and I did love each other, but not in a romantic sense. He comforted me during a time of unbearable grief. Our affair was brief but impactful.

Three months later, I realized I was pregnant. Everyone assumed it was John's child, conceived just before his accident. But I knew that was impossible. Still, I let everyone believe otherwise—yes, even your Gram. Most especially her. With every new kick of the baby inside, I felt the guilt with new intensity. Along with the guilt came the agony of being a young widow, and I knew I couldn't raise my child on my own. I wouldn't make a good mother, but I knew someone else would. Someone who desperately wanted children but couldn't have any.

So, a few nights before the baby was born, I made the torturous decision. I would give this child—your mother—to Gram and George to raise as their own. It was the right thing to do. The only thing I could do. My penance, my punishment. After I gave up the baby, I found Primrose Cottage in Chilton Crosse and made a new life there, to focus on my art. And to leave behind the pain of not being a new mother.

Decades later, only two short months after your precious mother died, Gram discovered something in the attic, in an old box—a letter I thought had been destroyed. A letter George had kept (written by me), confirming his suspicions about the baby. I thought he'd burned the letter, as I'd begged him to. But when Gram found it, that was all the proof she needed of the affair and your mother's paternity. That revelation, coupled with the grief of losing your mother, drove her to my art show that night. She stormed in, and we fought. I'd never seen her so livid, so devastated and betrayed. And the fact that I was responsible crushed me, sent me into an emotional spiral I couldn't recover from. That night was the last time we ever spoke.

So, why am I telling you this, years later? And why did I wait until after my own death to do it? I suppose I'm a coward. I couldn't bear to see the look of disappointment and shame or perhaps confusion and pain that might flash across your face when I told you the truth. But you needed to know that I'm your grandmother. It's the reason I've always had a special connection to you, especially during those summers, that superseded the way an aunt might feel about a niece. I saw parts of me in you—your passion, your single-mindedness, your creativity. It took everything in me not to let you know back then. But I couldn't bear breaking my sister's heart. It was a risk I couldn't afford to take.

I wish I'd been closer to my daughter. I was never allowed to call her "daughter." Even in her death. The secret was still intact at her funeral. But that was as it should be. Your Gram was truly her mother, in every sense of the word.

I pray you'll finish my letter with more compassion than anger, more love than hate. "Aunt" and "Grandmother" are only labels. Always know that I loved you as my own flesh and blood. That you and your mother were special to me in ways I was unable to express. In fact, I'm free to say this now, so I shall. Perhaps because you reminded me so much of myself, I always felt that you, Noelle, were my daughter.

Whatever your emotions, please understand that I love you. And that, in revealing this news, I wanted to show you how very precious you were to me. I'm only sorry I wasn't a braver person, to let you know sooner, while I was alive.

All my love,
Grandmother Joy

Noelle looked up to an empty kitchen. Mac must've known she needed privacy, space to comprehend the incredible news. It would take days, weeks, to digest everything. But it all made sense. The final piece had snapped into place. The old woman in Cornwall, Helen, was right after all.

Noelle couldn't be angry or disappointed in Joy for the secret or even for the affair, because out of that situation came her mother and her. She didn't even regret seeing Gram all those years as a grandmother. Because she *was* her grandmother. She fit that role well.

Joy was right. It was about love, not labels. In the end, Noelle felt blessed to have both those women in her life, whatever their titles.

Clutching the letter, Noelle thought about the upcoming day and reflected on something else. When she came to Chilton Crosse last year, she'd arrived a virtual stranger, empty-handed. An alien in a foreign land, alone and out of sorts. But not today. She would spend the afternoon with new friends as dear to her as family, old friends she'd never truly let go of, and a man who would become her family in a matter of hours.

Grandmother Joy hadn't only given Noelle a cottage and a gallery. She'd given her a new beginning.

"Ready, lass?"

"Ready." Noelle squeezed Mac's arm, entwined with her own, and stared ahead. Mozart floated up from the string quartet as Mac took the first step, guiding her down the stairs toward the lush garden at Windermere. Noelle had booked the estate months ago for her wedding.

She breathed in the sweet honeysuckle while a warm June breeze caressed her bare arms.

For years, she'd pictured her own wedding, imagined the details. She'd seen the same moment played out in movies dozens of times, had watched it happen in real life to her closest friends. But she wasn't prepared for the surreality of it all. As though she stood high above, watching another version of herself glide slowly down a rose-petaled aisle toward the grand fountain, smiling at all the beloved people in her life rising to their feet to watch her pass by. Holly and Frank, Lizzie and Joe, Mrs. Pickering, even old Mr. Bentley and his daughter Julia— practically the entire village had turned out. In the front row sat Jill and Gareth, bouncing Evie on his knee. All the people closest to her.

Noelle shifted her gaze forward. There he stood in a crisp black suit, hands clasped in front, and his face radiant with a wide smile. *Too good to be true*, she thought, passing her bouquet to Jill, who nodded tearfully. Noelle raised her free hand to touch the purple paint drop around her neck.

"Who presents this woman to be married to this man?" the vicar asked.

"I do." With a kiss on the cheek, Mac returned to his seat.

Adam caught Noelle's hands in his, warm and reassuring. "Hey, Sunshine," he whispered.

She smiled and took in all of him, freezing the image in a mental snapshot. The warm brown eyes, the dark, wavy hair, and the tender expression on his face that told her he would love her for the rest of his days.

"Ready?"

"More than ready." She squeezed his hands, eager for her new life to begin on this, her most perfect day.

Acknowledgements

To my precious mom, Pat Borum. My best friend, my confidante, my editor, and my biggest fan. You taught me how to read, one of the best gifts you could ever give. You supported my writing, from those silly detective stories I wrote as a twelve-year-old to my most recent novels. You attended conferences with me and bolstered me up whenever I got discouraged (not an easy task sometimes!). You never gave up on me, which gave me the courage to try one more time.

To my beloved grandparents, Della Sandifer and Lillian and Val Borum. Maw, you were the inspiration for the art references in this book. I enjoy all our many talks about art and writing and their great similarities. Thank you for reading my books! I always love the call I get after you've finished one of them. Grammy, I adore our common bond over books and reading. It's always been strong. I appreciate your endless support and constant encouragement. You've read all of my books—often more than once!—and never failed to show how much you believed in me, even on my long and challenging journey to get published. Pappy, you're the smartest man I know. You're the backbone of our family. The importance you've always placed on education very likely influenced me to become a teacher and writer.

To my sister, Karen Ratekin. Your input and enthusiasm for my writing has been such a joy to me. Thank you for reading my books! And for adding humor to a daunting process. You always know how to make me laugh until I snort. And that's a very good thing.

To Augusta Malvagno and Sandy Graham, my dear friends. All these years, your genuine, supportive interest in my writing has kept me going.

I always felt like I could share my joys and frustrations equally with you. I knew you would listen, understand, and offer words of comfort and compassion. I'm so grateful that you've read all my novels all these years, but more than that, I'm grateful for your consistent friendship.

To Mary Lou Robinson, Becky Bray, Karen Peterson, Linda Bratcher, Desha Stewart, Charles Johnson, Stephen and Laurie Stine, Paul and Karen Reinhard, Hazel Mendez, my extended family members, and my fellow Pitizens. What a strong support system you've been for me all these years, cheering me on, consoling me when things got tough, and being proud when "it" finally happened. Thank you!

To my beloved Commandos. You know who you are. I am blessed to know you and call you dear friends. I love your snarky humor, your strong friendship, and your constant encouragement. There's no doubt that we're kindred spirits, sisters through thick and thin. I'm so glad God brought us together all those years ago.

To the entire Red Adept team, but particularly Lynn McNamee, Alyssa Hall, Michelle Rever, Jenn Loring, the acquisitions editors, and the proofreaders. I'm so grateful for your faith in my book. Lynn, your strong work ethic and desire to turn out the highest-quality book at every step in the process has made the company what it is today. Alyssa, I can't tell you how lucky I am that you "got" my book. You respected the tone and intention of it, and your suggestions only made it better. Jenn, you have an eagle eye, an amazing ability to see details so clearly. Your notes were impressive and incredibly helpful. Michelle, I so appreciate your wise insight and guidance with the book cover. You totally nailed it!

To the team at Streetlight Graphics, particularly Glendon Haddix. You outdid yourself with such a beautiful cover. It looks like a painting I want to walk into, live inside. You've made all my first-cover dreams come true!

To all the teachers who have lit the spark of creativity in me over the years: Mr. D. from Crockett, Donna Walker-Nixon, and Fred Damiano. You were placed in my life at all different stages to inspire me, teach me, and help me become a better writer.

To author Mary Fan for putting together my beautiful book trailer (found on YouTube), and to composer John Hobart of Scorpio Music

Productions for providing the gorgeous composition. His music needs to be heard!

To Chuck Sambuchino and Victoria Strauss. You are always so kind, so easy to approach. You never made me feel like I was bothering you, even when I had a mountain of questions. I admire you both for being such strong advocates for writers. We need you!

To Elaine English. Your wise guidance and input along the way helped to make tricky waters *much* easier to navigate.

To the entire TJC English Department. Your keen interest in my writing all these years has been a blessing. This is the *best* department I could ever hope to work with, and I'm honored to call you my colleagues and friends.

To my Creative Writing students (both former and current), and all my Facebook friends who have been so supportive. Thank you for letting me ramble on about my publication journey and my writing.

To Mandy Barrow at ProjectBritain for providing incredibly helpful information about specific aspects of English life.

To Renina Baker and Danielle Roper at Motophoto for your professionalism and quality picture taking. Thanks for making me feel so at ease!

Finally, all thanks to God, whose guidance and inspiration made this book entirely possible. He's the Source.

About the Author

TRACI BORUM IS A WRITING teacher and native Texan. She's also an avid reader of women's fiction, most especially Elin Hilderbrand and Rosamunde Pilcher novels. Since the age of 12, she's written poetry, short stories, magazine articles, and novels.

Traci also adores all things British. She even owns a British dog (Corgi) and is completely addicted to Masterpiece Theater–must be all those dreamy accents! Aside from having big dreams of getting a book published, it's the little things that make her the happiest: deep talks with friends, a strong cup of hot chocolate, a hearty game of fetch with her Corgi, and puffy white Texas clouds always reminding her to "look up, slow down, enjoy your life."

Made in the USA
Lexington, KY
03 June 2015